# FREECURRENT III
## DYNASTY

*To Alex,*
*Thanks for reading my tale!*

*Deanna J Compton*

*2014*

## DEANNA J. COMPTON

# ACKNOWLEDGEMENTS

This novel is dedicated to the victims of drug addiction. It is a sad reality that has impacted the lives of too many individuals. Before taking that first pill or doing that first hit, research online what ten years down the road looks like. The shackles of drug addiction are not easy to live with or to remove once in place. Choices such as these should not be taken lightly. If pain or stress is too much to deal with, please seek help. There are better alternatives available. Hope is a powerful thing, but is sometimes elusive and must be pursued bravely, like a hero on a quest seeks out a talisman or treasure. Pursue hope. Enjoy my story. Reviews are greatly appreciated.

Dare to dream.

e-mail Deanna Compton at: freecurrent@comcast.net
Check out my website: freecurrent.net

# PRELUDE

C andaz seethed with anger as he walked. He had been chased out of his own land by the children of those who had stolen everything from him. The son of Theo and the son of Serek were mere puppets of their fathers, used as tools to further the older men's ambitions and lust for power. They were not even worthy to lick his boots and yet they had pursued him until he was forced to make his escape. He kicked at the dirt instantly raising up dust. The landscape around him was stark and terrible as were his thoughts.

The girl Jesse would have to be stopped. She could be the one named in the prophecy, the one who was destined to end his life. He would get rid of her one way or another. The girl was a thorn in his side. He would pluck it out and grind it into the ground with the heel of his dusty boot. A plan was forming in his mind. She was obviously the type that would go out of her way to protect a loved one. He would use that against her. Her soft heart would be her downfall.

He wasn't sure what Zeth was up to. Perhaps his plan was to infiltrate the enemy's camp or perhaps he was dead. The look on his son's face was one of anguish. Understanding the boy was impossible. Regardless of Zeth's intentions, the boy had defied him and Candaz boiled with anger because of it. Zeth would pay for his insolence if Candaz found him alive when he returned.

He paused in his march and found a little bit of shade to rest in for a moment. From one of his pockets he withdrew the small bottle of elixir and took a shallow sip. The liquid burned as it went down. He returned the bottle to his pocket and reached into another one. His fingertips traced the delicate silk wrappings that held the withered and mummified hand of his beloved Molly. In his dark and twisted mind he justified his actions as retribution for their love that was long lost. He let his obsessive grief motivate him in his hate for all others. It was beyond his ability to comprehend that Molly never would have approved of the man he had become. His insanity rationalized that the love they shared for such a short time in his youth was enduring and that what he did was in essence for her. Although the present ruling families had nothing to do with the death of Molly, the transference of blame and the resulting drive for revenge made sense in his strained mental state. He hated them all and he would make them pay.

# Chapter 1
## GALAXY EARTH

A sense of urgency motivated Jesse forward as she quickly exited the cave into the surrounding desert. Beside her were her two best friends, Felcore and Tempest. The odd thing about both of them was that they donned a disguise. Felcore was a golden retriever, a companion of Jesse's for many of her seventeen years. However, at this moment Felcore was a yellow striped cat, changed by freecurrent magic before their trip through the gate in order to keep him safe from the authorities who may or may not have targeted him for extermination. Her other friend, Tempest, was disguised as a small white dog, a mix between a West Highland Terrier and a Yorkie. Tempest was in truth a large white dragon, bigger than the biggest elephant, but more petite than her peers back on Risen. She and Jesse communicated telepathically and although it was the dragon who suggested being changed into a dog, she was not happy at the moment about being one.

# FREECURRENT III

*"My legs are too short. Why didn't you make me a big dog? I am the size of an appetizer,"* Tempest complained.

*"Little dogs have big attitudes and that suits you, Tempest,"* Jesse replied while she tried to get her bearings as she looked around. Immediately she started hiking to the southeast and after about a half an hour spotted the road off in the distance. Mostly it was deserted but every now and then a car would speed by.

Suddenly she felt a sharp pain in the back of her head. Defensively she turned and came face to face with Candaz. The corrupt sorcerer seemed to tower over her as he moved quickly to subdue her. He took out her feet and was on top of her before she knew what was happening. She struggled against him, but he was extremely strong for an old man and she was unable to push him away. Planting his knee on her chest, his long black robe blanketed them both as he sneered down at her with penetrating black eyes. His dark hair had a dusting of gray as the long locks fell into his face. Jesse felt fear assault her like it never had before.

Tempest was biting ineffectively at his ankles and Felcore was spitting and growling and clawing at his arms. He swiftly flung both animals aside and reached for the gold medallion that hung around Jesse's neck. Although she tried to fight him off, he wrenched it from her, breaking open the clasp in the process and brought his prize up before his eyes. It glimmered brilliantly in the sunlight. "Well, sweetheart . . . " he began.

Managing to spin underneath him, Jesse succeeded in getting out from under him and quickly back on her feet. She kicked him and swung with her left arm to land a punch but missed. He had side-stepped out of the way. Aiming for his legs, she tackled him and he went down hard on his back with an audible grunt. He watched as the medallion sailed from his hand and landed in the sand a short distance away. Without slowing, he rolled and was quickly back on his feet again. They both dove for the now dusty piece of gold at the same time. Jesse had her fingers on the chain, but Candaz ripped it from between her fingers. She landed a backhand across his face and followed with a well-aimed kick. As she reached into her boot for Kali's knife, he turned his back to her and began to run toward the road.

She gave chase, accompanied by Felcore and Tempest, but Candaz was fast and timing was on his side. Just as he reached the road, a car came by and in less than a minute he was in the passenger seat and gone.

"Stop!" she screamed, but the driver either didn't hear or didn't comply.

Her hands rested on her knees as she sucked in air to catch her breath. Automatically she reached for the medallion that was no longer there. "Damn! He has grandmother's pendant," she said to no one in particular. "*Tempest, can you still hear me?*" she asked tentatively.

"*I told you that you should have made me a bigger dog. I could have inflicted damage on that tiny human,*" Tempest commented dryly.

To her side the yellow cat added her own two cents, "Mmowrl."

"*Okay, maybe you have a point. I should have made you a Rottweiler. Maybe I still can,*" Jesse said. After she recovered her breath, she put her hands softly on Tempest's head and closed her eyes. Picturing in her mind a very big Rottweiler, she opened her eyes and before her stood a little white dog. "*Why didn't it work?*" she asked.

"*You didn't focus,*" Tempest said.

"*I focused. Let me try again,*" Jesse said and she did just that, but the results were the same; Tempest remained a little white dog. A couple more attempts resulted in the same outcome--no change.

"*You have got to focus the freecurrent, Jesse. You no longer have the medallion to do it for you,*" the dragon who was disguised as a dog said. Tempest was trying to be helpful, but was instead becoming aggravating.

*"I have been trying. It's not working,"* she said in frustration. Jesse was getting tired and discouraged. She sat down on the desert floor and rubbed the bump on the back of her head. It still hurt. Felcore climbed into her lap, curled up and began to purr. She took comfort in the gesture and began scratching the cat's ears affectionately.

When Jesse looked up, she spotted two men walking down the road in the distance. They were glaringly out of place. Strolling with brazen attitudes of warriors, their swords strapped to the sheaths on their backs, they made their way down the road oblivious to their unusual appearances. Jesse couldn't have been more thrilled. She jumped to her feet and began to run toward them as quickly as she could. They were still about a quarter mile away when her feet met the black top.

As soon as they spotted her, one of the men started toward her at a dead run. "Jesse," he called as he threw his arms around her and swung her up and around. Holding on to her, he found her lips and kissed her happily. When he finally put her down, he reached out and hugged her to him again. "Jesse, you're here," he said.

"Nicholas, I didn't know how I was going to find you and Stephan. Candaz just left in a car. We've got to go after him," Jesse said as she reached out and grabbed his hand. When Stephan walked up, she turned to him and said, "Stephan, thank God I've found you two." She let go of Nick's hand to give his cousin a brief hug. "Where have you been anyway? I thought you were on his trail."

Stephan smiled, "We got lost. Nicky's sword led us in the wrong direction."

"I told you we needed to go south instead of north," Nicholas said.

"I did go south," Stephan said.

"Apparently not," Nick retorted.

She went back to Nick's side and talked quickly. "Well, you are found now. We have to hurry or we'll lose Candaz. Let's try to get a ride," she said as she looked at them both critically. "Try to look *normal.*"

"Don't you have horses or a dragon or two you could summon?" Stephan asked in all seriousness.

"They don't have horses here, Stephan. Don't you know anything?" Nick said to his cousin in a superior tone.

"Well, if you, as a kendrite, could transform yourself into something more practical like a dragon or a horse we wouldn't need an alternative," Stephan said.

Jesse knew that having these two in her world would be a challenge, but she really had no idea just how much of a challenge it was going to be. "Actually," she said, "we do have horses, but we don't have dragons. But, what we usually use for transportation is what is called a 'car'." She looked down the street and saw one coming toward them. "Okay, here we go. Let me do the talking," she said to her confused companions.

As they stood by the side of the road and awaited the approaching SUV, she realized that *normal* was something beyond possible. Quickly she thought up a story. She waived down the car and hoped the driver wouldn't be too frightened to stop. There was a man in the driver's seat; a young man, probably around thirty years old, dressed nicely in a blue dress shirt with a jacket draped over the back of the passenger seat. He rolled down his window while his eyes took in the group of them and asked, "Can I help you?"

She approached him with a winning smile and rested her hands on the edge of the door. "Thank you for stopping. You wouldn't happen to have seen a film crew wandering around?" she asked. He shook his head no. "I'm afraid we," she indicated Stephan and Nicholas with the wave of her hand, "were up here filming and got lost from our crew. My cell phone is back in my car and we seem to be stuck. Do you have a cell I can borrow?"

The man hesitated for a moment, watching the strangely dressed men as they walked around his SUV as if they had never seen one before. After a second he slowly handed Jesse his phone. She smiled and said, "Thanks. I'll just make a quick call." She punched in a random number and hit send. "Oh, man. Nobody's answering. They must be in the middle of the shoot. Say, if you wouldn't mind, could you take us as far as the Santa Fe? We can meet up with the rest of the crew there." Handing him back his phone she implored him with her beautiful copper colored eyes.

Tempest spoke in Jesse's head, *"I'm not getting on that thing."*

*"Tempest, don't be difficult. Besides you get in it, not on it,"* Jesse answered back mentally while she smiled at the man.

It was clear when he made his decision by the look of resignation on his face, as if saying *"Oh, what the hell."* Instead he said, "I'll take you and your friends as far as the Santa Fe. Serial killers don't usually walk around with long swords, so I guess you're safe. Hop in."

"Thanks. I'm Jesse. This is Nick and Stephan. We are grateful. Maybe you would like to be an extra in the film? You would look great on the big screen," she said as she opened the back door and indicated for Nicholas and Stephan to slide in. They unbuckled their swords and climbed in as the driver watched closely. She bent over and picked up Felcore and placed him on Stephan's lap. When she went to pick up Tempest, the little dog backed away out of reach.

"*Tempest, let's go,*" she said.

"*No way,*" Tempest declared.

"*Sweetie, it's okay. I promise. I've ridden in cars hundreds of times. I've even driven one. Come on. We have to go after Candaz. Let's go,*" Jesse insisted.

"*No way,*" Tempest repeated adamantly.

Jesse decided to appeal to the dragon's stomach, "*I promise you a nice juicy steak.*"

"*I'll do it for a cow,*" Tempest renegotiated.

"Okay," she said. *Anything,* Jesse thought.

Tempest let Jesse pick her up and she got in next to Stephan in the back seat. As soon as she had the door closed the car took off down the road. Stephan's whole body tensed and Jesse put her hand on his leg, turned to him and mouthed the words "*it's okay*". He relaxed a little.

"What are you filming?" the man asked.

Jesse thought fast before answering, "It's a film called 'Warrior'. Have you heard of it?"

"No. You are what they call 'on location'?" he asked.

"Yes, right. We're on location," Jesse answered.

"Have you been in the acting business long?" This question was obviously directed to the men.

Jesse elbowed Stephan in the side. "Um. Yes. A long time," he said. He gave Jesse a questioning look and rubbed his side.

"*This is fun,*" Tempest said in her head. "*I like riding in this thing. You can keep the cow. I like this.*"

"*Glad to hear it, sweetie. See. You have to trust me,*" Jesse replied.

"*I do trust you. You are my Jesse,*" Tempest said.

"Are the animals in the movie?" the driver asked.

"Oh, no. The cat is Stephan's and the dog is mine. Oh, look. There's the Santa Fe. We really appreciated the ride," she said as they pulled up to the front of the hotel. "I would give you my card, but I left them with my cell phone. If you're interested in being an extra, give me a call. Just tell the people at the desk that Jesse asked you to call and they'll put you through. Thanks again. You really saved our lives and maybe my job too," she said.

Jesse got out of the car, followed by Stephan and last of all Nick. "Yes. Thank you," Nicholas said and he strapped his sword back on. The three of them noted quickly that it was glowing blue.

"That's an interesting sword. Is that that glow stick stuff?" he asked.

"Something like that," Jesse said. "Thanks again. Bye."

"Good luck with the movie. I look forward to seeing it," the man said to them and immediately drove away, leaving them in front of the large hotel.

At that exact moment a taxi drove by. It was just leaving the valet parking area and out of the back window appeared the face of the man they hunted. Candaz actually waved at them as the cab took off down the road.

"Look! There he is! We need to follow that cab," she said. Jesse removed the small backpack from her back, opened it up and rummaged through it. She withdrew from it three dollar bills. "This won't get us far. Let's get a taxi," she said. Stephan and Nicholas were watching her with lost expressions on their faces. "Come on," she said as she grabbed Nick's hand and led them over to a cab that had just dropped a passenger off. She handed the driver the three bills and said, "Take us as far as you can on this. Follow that cab!"

The driver looked at them suspiciously for a moment and Jesse thought he might kick them out of his cab, but instead he said, "Okay." They got on the road well behind Candaz and followed for several blocks before the taxi driver pulled into a parking lot. "That's it," he said. "That's as far as I can take you on three dollars."

"Really?" Jesse asked.

"Sorry," he said, not really sorry at all.

They all got out and Jesse looked around. There was a pawn shop on the far corner. "We need money. What have we got to pawn?"

"Jesse, we don't know what you are talking about," Nick said to her quietly.

She looked up into his beautiful gold eyes and sighed in exasperation. "We need money to function in this place--in my land. That shop over there will give us money in exchange for something of value. I have my MP3 player. But, that won't get us very far," she said.

Stephan said, "How about my sword? It has a gold and silver hilt. I'm sure it's worth quite a bit."

Jesse hesitated only long enough to evaluate Stephan's offer. "Yes. Give me your sword. A driver's license is required to pawn and I'm the only one here who has one. I'll be right back. Try to look *normal*. Nicky, you might want to put your vest on over the top of that sword."

Once Jesse had obtained a good amount of cash by pawning her MP3 player and Stephan's sword, they immediately went shopping. She bought jeans and t-shirts for the men and a light hoody for Nicholas to wear that covered his sword and sheath. She also picked up three pre-paid cell phones and time cards.

They took a cab to the Las Vegas strip. Jesse spent the car ride getting the cell phones activated. She programmed each other's numbers into each of the phones. When she had them working, she gave one to Nick and one to Stephan and explained the basics quickly to each of them. Nothing too complicated--just dial, send and end. As a trial she dialed Nicholas's number and listened to it ring. She instructed him to pick it up and hit the send button and put it up to his ear. Jesse said into her phone, "Say hello."

Nick repeated, "Hello."

"Can you hear me?" she asked, pointing to the phone.

"Of course I can hear you," he said, "you're right here," putting the phone aside. "I don't really see the point in this thing, Jesse."

This was going to be harder than she thought.

Nick's sword was important to finding Candaz, so they kept it with them as they walked the streets looking for a lead. Although it was hidden beneath his sweatshirt, he would still feel the free-current against his back should it be triggered.

By that evening, Jesse was exhausted so they checked into a hotel. She went up to their room to sleep along with Tempest and Felcore. The men were going to continue looking for Candaz for a little while longer.

Later in the night Jesse was awakened by Nicholas, who came into the room excited with news, "Jess, you won't believe what happened."

She sat up in bed and rubbed her tired eyes. Nick sat on the edge of the bed as he talked. "Stephan played one of those machines and won a car!" he said excitedly.

"What?" Jesse asked.

Nick said, "Yes. He won a shiny red car. And then he won a bunch of money on another machine. There was some guy that sold him some type of paperwork that he needed to get the car and the money. The paperwork was only five hundred dollars and Stephan won ten thousand dollars plus that fancy car. It seems like a good deal, don't you think?"

"Where is he now?" Jesse asked when she was awake enough to get the story straight in her head.

"He's with a girl who offered to teach him how to drive his new car," Nicholas said as he suppressed a yawn.

"What?" Jesse's voice was getting higher as more information was disclosed.

Nicholas laughed, which Jesse found extremely aggravating considering the seriousness of their situation. He had no idea what kind of trouble this could cause. Stephan was with a stranger in Las Vegas with a pocket full of money. He could be in grave danger. "You know. People of your land are *very* friendly," he said.

"Yeah," she said. *Oh boy,* she thought.

"Could you call him and ask him to come back to the hotel? I want to talk to him immediately," Jesse said. When Nicholas gave her a blank look, she reached for her own cell phone and selected Stephan's number. It went to a message that indicated that the mail box for that recipient had not yet been set up. "Shoot." She tried again, "Stephan, answer the phone," she said into her own phone. "Shoot!" she said again when he didn't answer.

She lay back onto her pillow and sighed. *What were they going to do? How were they going to find Stephan?* Nicholas lay down next to her and wrapped her in his arms. She lay there and pondered their situation but had a difficult time focusing with Nick so close. The scent of him was inspiring a physical reaction in her that both scared and thrilled her. Before she knew it they were kissing each other greedily and their bodies responding forcefully. "Jesse," Nick whispered, his voice husky against her neck.

"Nick, give me a minute," she said as she swallowed her passion and extricated herself from his arms, climbed off the bed and escaped to the bathroom. The hotel had provided her a new toothbrush and toothpaste and she used them now to brush her teeth. Using cold water, she grabbed a washcloth and wiped her face and washed her hands before she gazed at the face that looked back at her in the mirror. Excitement and fear churned in her stomach. It was exhilarating the way she felt about Nicholas. How she could feel so in love in such a short time, she couldn't begin to understand. It was all wonderful, even magical. Her fear came from the fact that her body seemed to respond so strongly to Nick that she didn't know if she could control herself. She didn't want to compromise her values in the heat of the moment. It was important to her to save sexual intimacy for marriage, for her husband. Holding true to that conviction was more difficult than she expected. She brushed her hair, regained her composure, and returned to Nicholas where he waited on the bed.

Sitting next to him, Jesse took his hands in hers and looked into his eyes, which encouraged another kiss. Instead she said, "When we first decided to get together I said I wanted to take it slow." He nodded and she continued, "I'm saving myself for marriage. As much as I believe that you are the one for me, Nick, I want to wait to share my body with you. I just want to be clear . . . I mean we're here alone and I don't want you to think . . . well, that I don't want you, because I do . . . it's just that . . . ."

Smiling, Nicholas reached up with his hand and brushed Jesse's hair away from her face before giving her a gentle kiss and saying, "You are precious to me. I am more than willing to wait for you to give yourself to me freely. I love you, Jesse. Someday I am going to marry you." His gold eyes sparkled with light and passion.

"So it's okay that we wait?" she asked.

"If that is what you want, I will respect your wishes. But, if I ever lose control and push you further than we've agreed to take this, feel free to slap some sense into me." The crooked grin on Nick's face made Jesse's heart race and shook her resolve.

"That goes for me too," she smiled and leaned in to kiss him again, long and lovely.

When he pulled away he said, "Right, this is going to be *easy*."

"Yeah, easy," she agreed sarcastically.

Tempest said in Jesse's head, "*Dragons do not make relationships so complicated.*"

"Really?" she asked.

"*Humans make everything more complicated than it has to be,*" Tempest said.

"*I suppose you're right,*" she replied, quickly kissing Nick before picking up her cell phone again.

"Right now we have a serious problem. Stephan isn't answering his phone. We're going to have to find him. He could be in a lot of trouble. I shouldn't have left you two alone, obviously," Jesse said.

"*Obviously,*" Tempest agreed.

Jesse's phone bleeped. Both of them jumped and Felcore meowed. She hit "send" and said, "Stephan?"

A woman's voice said, "No. This is Tawny. Are you a friend of Stephan's?"

"Yes, let me talk to him," Jesse demanded politely.

"Sorry. He's indisposed at the moment," she said. She laughed and Jesse could hear more laughter in the background. *This is not good.*

"Listen, *Tawny*, I really need to talk to Stephan now. It's important," she said. Jesse's eyes were serious as they glanced at Nick where he sat on the bed.

"I told you he isn't available right now. He's such a party animal. I'll tell him you called, honey." The call ended.

Jesse's face portrayed clearly the panic that she felt as she tried Stephan's number and got the annoying mail box message again. *Damn.* She should've set up his voice mail. Good ole' twenty-twenty hind sight rears its ugly head. Felcore came to her and rubbed against her leg and meowed insistently. She paused to pick him up and cradled him while she paced. "This is really bad, Nick. Stephan's in some kind of danger. I can feel it. Do you have any idea where he might have gone? What did this girl look like?" she asked as she let Felcore leap to the floor.

"I tried to stop him from going with her, but he wouldn't listen to me. After the casino paid him his money and gave him the car keys, they said they wanted 'pitchers' and this woman came along side Stephan and started hanging all over him. She was beautiful, long blond hair, long legs, wore a short black dress. She and Stephan seemed to really like each other. When she said she was going to take him for a ride, I asked him not to go, but he wouldn't listen. He'd lost his senses. They took off in that little red sports car. I don't know where they went. I shouldn't have let him go. I should have stopped him. I should have followed him. 'Should haves' don't help, I know," he said. Nicholas had his head in his hands. He looked exhausted. Jesse came to him and put her arms around him. She rested her head against his shoulder and closed her eyes.

Felcore rubbed against her leg and meowed and then jumped up on the bed and pushed against Jesse's arm and meowed. "What is it, boy?" she asked.

Felcore sprang over to the table where Nicholas's sword lay and meowed again. The blade was glowing bright blue at the very tip.

"Nick, the sword," Jesse said as she got up.

He walked over and picked up the weapon. "Do you think it could be Candaz?" he asked.

"Maybe," Jesse replied as she put on her moccasins and grabbed her backpack. "Let's check it out."

Nick had the sword sheathed on his back. Through his shirt he could feel the freecurrent exceedingly well. Over the sheathed sword he wore an over-sized hoody that concealed it well enough. They headed down the hallway to the elevator, followed by a cat and a small white dog. When they entered the elevator Jesse hit the button to go down to the lobby of the hotel. As they descended, Nick became anxious. Jesse looked at him questioningly.

"The freecurrent is fading from the sword," he said.

"Okay, let's try up," Jesse said.

When they reached the lobby, the doors opened and a young couple entered. The woman pressed the button for the third floor before she turned to the man and said, "I can't believe you lost all of your money already."

"That machine is ready to pay off. I know it is. What do you have left?" he asked her.

Unexpectedly she laughed and said, "You had yours and I have mine. We both had a limit, remember?" She turned to him and wrapped her arms around his neck. "Let's just call it a night." They were still kissing when the elevator doors opened on the third floor.

After they were gone, Jesse pressed the highest floor, twenty-five, the elevator doors closed and they started going up. She wrapped her arms around Nick's waist and rested her hands on the sword. Freecurrent surged through her and she could feel the sword's intensity increase as they ascended. When they passed the nineteenth floor, the freecurrent in the sword began to wane. "Nineteen," Jesse said to Nick. The elevator again came to a halt and Jesse pressed "nineteen".

"Nineteen it is. But, what are we going to find?" Nick asked. He was completely on edge. Felcore and Tempest seemed to echo Nick's tension as they clung next to Jesse's legs. Tempest was quiet, which made Jesse more nervous as the elevator doors opened and the four of them stepped into an empty hotel hallway.

Nicholas led the way past Room 1922, 1924, 1926. He caught Jesse's hand and turned around and stopped in front of Room 1924. "This is it," he whispered.

Jesse squeezed Nick's hand and knocked on the door. There was no answer at first, and then they heard, "hang on."

# Chapter 2
## LEAVING LAS VEGAS

Stephan groaned as Tawny left him to answer the door. They had ordered room service and were expecting a late night snack and a bottle of champagne. He was already spinning with whatever she had given him, actually more like soaring. It felt good. He wanted more of the same. At first he'd been hesitant, but Tawny had assured him that it was just a little bit of fun, something to help relax and enliven the celebration. When the door opened and Jesse and Nick stood there, he felt a little ashamed and more than a little irritated at their intrusion. Tawny's friends had just left and he wanted to be alone with her. She barred them from entering until Stephan said, "Let them in."

"What are you two doing here?" he asked.

Jesse gave Tawny a look that said *back off* as she approached Stephan where he lay sprawled on the bed. "We've been looking for you. Why didn't you answer your phone?" she asked.

"I've been busy," he said defensively.

"We've got to get going, Stephan," Nicholas said, looking uncomfortably at Tawny, who was watching them closely.

"No Nicky, I'm staying here," Stephan replied.

"Look, Stephan, we need to find that man that we came here to get. We don't have time to delay longer," Jesse said.

Although Stephan loved his cousin and Jesse, too, he wasn't ready to go just yet. He wanted some more of whatever it was that Tawny had given him that made him feel so good. Already it was starting to wear off and he wanted another dose. It hadn't cost him too much and he knew she had more. Nick and Jesse could find Candaz without him. They really didn't need his help he figured. He was just a third wheel anyway he rationalized. "I'm going to stay here with Tawny. You two go ahead. I'll catch up with you later," he said amiably.

Jesse didn't seem to be convinced and she said, "Stephan, can we talk to you alone?"

"Whatever you have to say to me you can say in front of Tawny," Stephan replied.

"Really, Stephan, I think you should come with us now. You don't look very good," Jesse said as she looked into his eyes. "Are you high?"

Tawny stepped in, "He's fine. Why don't you leave us alone?" She grabbed Jesse's arm.

Felcore growled and hissed while Tempest started barking.

Jesse pulled away from Tawny's grasp. "What have you done to him? What have you given him?" she asked.

Tawny's smile showed her irreverence.

Nicholas reached out to grab Stephan by the hand to pull him up off the bed. "Come on, Stephan. Let's go," he said.

Stephan resisted. "I think you two need to leave now," Stephan said. "You've overstayed your welcome."

Nick said pleadingly, "Stephan, don't do this. Come with us. Let us help you."

He laughed and said, "I don't need or want your help. Can't you see I'm busy here, cous? Please leave now."

Jesse wasn't going to give up that easily. She said, "Stephan, come with us and we'll talk about it."

"No. You go on. I'm fine," Stephan said.

"You are not fine! She has given you some type of drug. You are not yourself," Jesse said adamantly.

"Come with us," Nicholas insisted.

"No, Nick!" he said. Anger propelled Stephan off the bed and he hurled a punch at Nick's face. His fist landed alongside his cousin's cheek bone, cutting through the skin. He recoiled with an expression of remorse touching the anger. "Get out!" he yelled.

Although Nicholas reached for his sword, he did not follow through with drawing it. "Stephan, come with us! You don't know what you are getting involved with," he said instead.

Stephan backed up, but didn't back down, "I'm staying here. Good night, cousin."

"Stephan," Jesse began.

"Jesse, let's go," Nicholas said as he headed for the door. "He has made his choice."

"Nick, no," Jesse said, grabbing his arm to try to stop him from leaving.

"Come on, Jesse. Let's go," he said and she finally followed after beseeching Stephan with her eyes to change his mind. He turned her down by averting his gaze. Her two little animals followed her out the door.

Stephan watched them go with mixed feelings. He felt deep inside that he had just shut the door on something very important in exchange for something very self-serving. All of his life he had been responsible and had always fulfilled his position gladly. He rationalized that this was just a little break from all of that, a much deserved break.

He turned his attention back to Tawny and let her draw him further down the path he had chosen, a path that was plagued by monsters that devoured young men and threw them back up without regard for feelings or responsibility.

## *Pushed Away*

Jesse left Stephan's room reluctantly. She wanted to drag his brawny hide out of there with or without his permission. She was enraged by what had just occurred. The man was being used and she was sure Tawny would chew him up and spit him out. She would kick him to the curb as soon as the money ran out. It was obvious there were drugs involved. Stephan's eyes were glassy and weird. He was high on something. She wanted to go back in there and demand he listen to her. How could he be so irresponsible? This wasn't the Stephan she had come to know. Her Stephan was sweet and charming and funny. He had been corrupted. Of course that's why the sword had led them to Room 1924. She turned around spontaneously and ran smack into Nicholas's chest. She took a step back and said, "Nick, we have to go get him. We can't let this happen."

"What are we going to do, Jesse? Drag him out of there?" Nicholas asked.

"Yes! If necessary," she replied adamantly.

"Jesse, we can't. He is a grown man. I cannot *make* him do anything. We'll try to get him to see reason again in the morning. Right now I need to sleep or I'm going to collapse," Nick said.

She considered what he said and came to the same conclusion quickly. He was swaying dangerously. "Okay. I guess we have no better choice," she said. She gave in and started for the elevator.

Tempest broke into her thoughts, *"I'm hungry."*

*"Of course you are, Tempest,"* she returned with sarcasm that was lost on the dragon. *"What would you like to eat?"*

*"A ripgar would be very tasty. But, maybe a cat would do,"* the dragon said.

*"No. You are not eating Felcore. I'll get you a hotdog from the snack bar,"* Jesse said tiredly.

*"A hot dog? What kind of a dog is that?"* Tempest asked.

*"It's made of ripgar I think,"* Jesse told her.

After she left Nicholas and the hungry dragon and Felcore in their room, she went down to the snack bar to get a hotdog for her dog-dragon and some tuna for her cat-dog. When she got back to the room Nicholas was fast asleep. She fed the animals and lay down next to him and was soon asleep herself. Her dreams were of monsters devouring her friends.

The next morning when she and Nicholas went back up to Room 1924, the maids were there cleaning. There was no sign of Stephan or Tawny. He was gone.

Nicholas was overcome with worry. Jesse didn't know what to do, she was so upset. Finally, they gathered their meager belongings and their pets and went down to the parking lot to see if Stephan's car was anywhere to be seen. She really didn't expect it to be and it wasn't. She checked with the registration desk, but they did not offer her any useful information. Trying Stephan's cell phone just made her angrier when she got the annoying mail box message again. They were at a dead end.

Jesse went to the lounge area and sat on the cushy couch to calm down. Nicholas had gone to use the restroom. On the large television that hung on the wall the news anchor was talking about the latest headlines, one tragic event right after the other. They cut away to a broadcast coming out of Flagstaff. The reporter was standing in front of a burning building that was identified as

"Yes, I think we need to go there. How about a lift, Jim?" Jesse asked.

"That is why I am here. Nicholas?" Jim said.

"Yes, sir?" Nick responded.

"Grab your stuff. Let's go," Jim said.

Nicholas looked around at their lack of luggage, grabbing nothing. He held out his hand to Jesse and hand in hand they followed Jim out the door.

They all climbed into Jim's old gray Ford pickup and they left Las Vegas going through Boulder City and over Hoover Dam into Arizona. The desert landscape that surrounded them was beautiful in its sparseness. Vegetation grew in congregations where rain water ran in washes and pooled in low lying areas when down pours occasionally hit the desert floor. The rocky terrain provided a textural myriad of subtle desert hues, ever-changing with the differences in lighting from dusk to dark and then afterward in the moonlight. The highway wound through the mountains as they made their way southeast. They climbed in elevation as they approached Flagstaff and the landscape reflected the increased average rainfall becoming increasingly green and lush.

Jesse told Jim about her brief visit to Risen and the reason for the necessity of her return. She filled him in on Candaz's recent activities, including the acquisition of the instruction manual to the gate. "Candaz and his son Zeth stole the book from the Tower of Ornate. It belongs to the wisps of Elysia and I intend to get it back from him," Jesse said.

"How is Gabriel?" Jim asked.

"Grandmother is well. It was so wonderful meeting her. She is very much like my mother, and yet stronger, tougher in many respects. I'm looking forward to getting to know her better when we get back to Risen," she said.

Nicholas added, "I've known Mistress Gabriel most of my life. She is indeed tough. As a child she never let me get away with anything, unless of course, she was distracted by her studies. I remember once when I was about twelve, I was at the tower, Gabriel was watching me, but she was up in the library all day and I was left to fend for myself. I had a great time taking out ingredients and baking cakes in the kitchen, which I devoured and was subsequently sick all night because of all of the sugar I had consumed. After Mistress Gabriel nursed me back to health, she spent all of the next day giving me cooking lessons after she made me thoroughly clean up the mess I had made the previous day."

"I'm jealous," Jesse said. "That's the kind of 'grandmother' moments I didn't have with her growing up."

"I guess she was more like a grandmother to me. I'm sorry you didn't have that with her," Nick said, grabbed her hand and gave it a gentle squeeze.

Jesse smiled and said, "It is what it is. Now I have a chance to get to know her and I'm good with that."

"Nicholas," Jim said, "I noticed that your eyes are gold. Are you a shape-changer?"

"I am half kendrite. Yes, I can transform into a wolf, an eagle and a dolphin," he replied.

"There is a story handed down in my family from generation to generation. Long ago a young maiden named Yellow Eyes was not of the people, so it is said. She was born of a different world, altogether. She had come through the gate located in the mountains north of the valley known as Las Vegas Valley. The gate was inside of a cave marked distinctly with the sign of the lightning bolt, so it is said. Yellow Eyes said to the people, 'The lightning gate can take a warrior to many different worlds if he has courage and bravery.' She shimmered before their eyes and became a glorious golden eagle, soaring into the sky and coming to land at the feet of the warrior who was to become her husband. The other warriors coveted Yellow Eyes' magic. They went in search of the lightning gate and were never seen again, so it is told. Yellow Eyes remained with the people and gave her husband many beautiful children. The story has been in my family for many generations. The maiden Yellow Eyes was my great great grandmother."

"You are part kendrite?" Nicholas asked, amazed by Jim's story.

"I do not know that name 'kendrite', but it is my ancestry," Jim said.

"Are you able to change?" Nick asked.

Jim laughed and said, "I wish I could, Nicholas. What is it like?"

"It's hard to explain. It is natural to me, like breathing. The sense of freedom in each of the different forms is powerful," Nicholas said.

"I would imagine it is remarkable. Although there are stories about some of my people having the ability to shape-change, they have mostly been written off as fantasy. I would very much like to see you do the change some time," Jim said. His eyes were sparkling with the delight of discovery.

Jesse drew their attention to the sword that lay at their feet on the floor board. "The freecurrent is glowing brightly. Where are we, Jim?" she asked.

"Just coming into Flagstaff," he said.

"Do you know where the bank is that Candaz torched?" Jesse asked.

"Yes. It's at the next exit," Jim said as he passed a car, pulled into the right lane and prepared to exit the highway.

"Wait! Stay on the road," Nick said after wrapping his hand around the hilt of his sword. "Can you go faster?"

Jim pushed on the accelerator and the old truck rattled in protest, but responded by giving up more speed. He passed car after car quickly on the left and the right. "What are we . . ." he started to ask. They came up behind a silver Volvo that was darting in and out of traffic.

"There he is," Jesse said. "Keep up with him, Jim."

They darted around a slow moving minivan and almost ran into the back of a semi-truck, which Jim quickly swerved around on the left. The silver Volvo sped up, having spotted that it was being tailed. Jim kept up in his old pick-up truck, handling it like it was a sleek sports car. Around one car, and then another, a blur of gray and a blur of black flashed by. The truck sped after the fast silver Volvo. They descended out of the Flagstaff area back into the desert as they gave chase. When Jesse caught a quick glimpse at the speedometer, it read over one hundred miles per hour.

"Oh my God!" Jim exclaimed as he eased off the gas.

When Jesse looked up, the car in front of them was fish-tailing as the driver lost control. The Volvo left the road and spun out in the dust, coming dangerously close to an embankment before it came to rest facing in the opposite direction from which it had been going.

Jim hit the brakes and slowed down quickly. He drove the truck toward the stationery car and parked right in front of it.

Nicholas grabbed his sword and jumped out of the passenger side door. Jesse and the two animals followed closely behind him. Jim joined them with casual vigilance. The driver of the silver Volvo exited the car and confronted them. Anger exploded from Candaz's face as his eyes locked on the approaching party.

Nicholas raised his blazing sword and commanded, "Come on, Candaz. Let's be done with this. Draw your weapon!"

He retorted, "You are as arrogant as your father, young pup. Do you really think I wish to fight you? I have much bigger plans." Candaz's eyes focused on Jesse. "You cannot stop me, little girl. Your family will bow before me."

Felcore approached the sorcerer slowly, in a cat stalking crouch, growling low and ominously. Candaz's attention turned to the cat and with a quick flick of his finger, he sent the animal sprawling in a haze of blue light. Felcore lay on the desert floor panting and crying in pain.

Without hesitating, even before Jesse could react, Tempest launched herself at the man and sunk her teeth into the calf of his leg. Fortunately for Candaz his leather boots protected him from most of the little dog's bite. He kicked his leg out and sent the dog flying, to land in a heap at Jesse's feet.

At the same time that Jesse ran forward, Nicholas swung his sword aggressively. "Draw your weapon!" he ordered.

Candaz sneered and brought both of his hands up and threw balls of brilliant blue fire at Jesse and Nicholas at the same time. Although Nicholas was able to use his sword to absorb the energy, Jesse was hit direct in the gut. She felt it enter her body and burn through to her bones. Down she went.

Jim was instantly beside Jesse, trying to revive her. He called her name and gently rubbed her hands and her face, but she was unresponsive.

Nicholas rushed at Candaz but overshot his target and slammed into the side of the car.

Diving back into his Volvo, Candaz started the engine and flung the transmission into reverse. He peeled away spitting gravel and dust behind him as he went, leaving Nicholas without gratification.

When Nick turned around he found Jesse on the ground with Jim hovering over her. Immediately he was beside her. "Is she okay?" he asked.

Jim replied as Jesse opened her eyes, "She's coming around."

"Jesse?" Nicholas put his hand alongside her face and looked into her eyes. "Are you okay?" he asked.

"Don't know," she replied groggily.

"*Jesse?*" Tempest voice came in her head.

"*Tempest?*"

"*The gold wolf cat is injured,*" she said.

"Nick, help me up," Jesse said as she let Nicholas lift her up off the ground. She felt queasy and her head was spinning horribly out of control. Her legs felt like noodles and were useless in supporting her. Without Nick's strong arms around her she would have collapsed. "Where's Felcore?"

Jim had the cat cradled in his arms. The yellow striped tabby was out cold. Jim brought him over to Jesse and let her examine him. She put her hand on the animal's forehead and focused the freecurrent energy to draw the corruption from the cat and into her own body. Her focus was off, limited, so the effects were limited as well. With a surge of disgust, she felt the corruption enter her body, but she was unable to expel it. The sickness overwhelmed her and she bent over the vomited.

Felcore recovered enough to open his eyes and say weakly, "Mroowrl."

"Let's get her to the truck," Jim said.

Nicholas easily scooped Jesse up in his arms and carried her to the passenger door. He placed her gently on the seat.

"I don't feel good," Jesse said right before she leaned out and vomited again. Nick held her hair out of her face while he kept a firm arm around her so she didn't fall off the seat.

"Sorry," she said miserably as he kissed her on the forehead.

Jim got in and started the truck. Nick got in next to Jesse and she lay down on his lap and groaned while he stroked her hair. The animals curled next to Nicholas's sword at his feet, with Tempest lying protectively around Felcore.

"I know of a place where we can take them, a woman I know," Jim said as he started in the opposite direction down the highway back toward Flagstaff. After a short time he turned off the highway and headed south toward Sedona.

# Chapter 3
## RELATIVELY CLOSE

Gabriel removed her fingertips from the sight water more abruptly than she intended. The contact she had through the water had been with the cat-dog Felcore and something happened when Candaz attacked him that severed the connection.

It was good to see that Jim McCaw was with Jesse and Nick. He was a very insightful and resourceful man. Gabriel knew Jim from way back. They had met over thirty years ago when Gabriel was on her way home from Risen to her family. Jim had a kind heart. He had been compassionate and at that time in her life she very much needed a friend. They had stayed in touch throughout the years periodically. Even though Gabriel hadn't seen Jim in many years, she trusted him completely.

The situation with Stephan concerned her deeply. She had been able to access his mind through the sight water for a short pe-

riod of time before she lost the connection and could not reestablish it. She had seen enough to know he was using heroine. Opiate
addiction wasn't something she had a lot of experience with, but
she knew from her studies that it could be very difficult for the
individual and the family of that individual. Once one went down
that path, it was a long arduous journey back from dependency.

On Risen, this form of addiction no longer existed. Alcohol was
widely used in the form of wine or ale, and in its hardest form, nectar, which was not hard liquor, but something more like a cordial.
However, alcohol abuse was rare among the population. Tobacco
was never used or even heard of. She felt a sense of urgency to rescue Stephan from whatever it was he was involved in. Obviously,
he was not making choices that were beneficial to his future. The
mother in her was screaming adamantly to intervene.

She descended the stairs to her bedroom to refresh herself.
The voices of Zeth, her thirty-year old son, and Terese, a kendrite
woman could be heard conversing in the kitchen. An aroma of
fresh tog, a banderg coffee, wafted up to her.

"Good morning," she said as she entered the kitchen.

Zeth stood up and greeted her with a hug and then offered her
his chair. "Good *afternoon*, mother."

She looked out the window and noted that the position of
the sun indicated that it was indeed late afternoon. It had been
just past noon on Earth when she had lost contact with Felcore.
No matter.

"Gabriel, what did you discover?" Terese asked her as she
picked up her tog mug and drank a sip of the rich brew.

She answered as she wrapped her hands around the warm
mug of tog, "Nicholas and Jesse continue to pursue Candaz.
Stephan has been waylaid in Las Vegas. I'm afraid he's in some
type of trouble."

"What do you intend to do?" Zeth's eyes were bright with anticipation.

Gabriel appraised her son's face for a long moment before answering, "I think it would be prudent to make a trip to Las Vegas and find Stephan."

"Yes?" A smile spread across Zeth's face and he raised his eyes with a silent appeal.

"Yes, you can go," Gabriel said and returned his smile briefly before standing up and walking to the sink.

"Gabriel," Terese was reserved in her manner, but her own excitement was evident in her voice, "I can accompany you?'"

"Yes, you may go as well. The sooner we get going the better. Pack light, one change of clothes and essentials only. The dragons should be here shortly to convey us to the gate. Hopefully, the constellation cycle will be in our favor," she said.

When Gabriel was back in her bedroom she packed a small bag with clothes that would be acceptable in tourist-rich Las Vegas, along with her toothbrush, hair brush and Shareen's spell book. She kissed the picture of her long-dead husband, John, lovingly touched a picture of her also dead daughter, Marguerite, Jesse's mom, before turning to go. On a whim she contacted Stephan's dragon, Zlato. "*Zlato, are you at all able to talk to Stephan?*" she asked him.

The gold dragon responded immediately in her head, "*He is gone.*"

"*Yes, I know he is not on Risen,*" she said.

Zlato continued, "*I do not think he can hear me. My feelings are that he is unable to be mindful. I am not sure how to explain it. Although I can 'feel' that he exists, it is not possible to 'be' with him at the moment.*"

Dragons could be so elusive sometimes. "*So, you cannot talk with Stephan, but you know he is alive?*" she asked.

"*Yes. I want him home. I miss my Stephan,*" he whined.

"*Of course, Zlato. I will see if I can find him,*" Gabriel told the dragon.

"*Thank you, Mistress. Tell him to come home,*" Zlato said.

She quickly ran down the stairs and joined Terese and Zeth who were already heading out the door. Zeth looked back at her and offered his hand to assist her like a gentleman. Taking it, she smiled. She was so happy to have him back in her life.

The last time Zeth had been to the Tower of Ornate was with his father, Candaz. He had been willing if the need arose to kill Gabriel should she be present when they broke into her home. Although at the time he was conflicted emotionally about his mother, he would have carried out the murder with a sick sense of pleasure. Whatever had been twisted in him had been cured by Jesse when she had healed him. The old Zeth was gone. He would now lay down his life to protect his mother.

The three dragons waited for them on the grass in front of Ornate. Their images reflected in the shiny black stone of the tower. Grace and Gold Stone were now almost fully grown dragons with luminous green and gold scales on their massive bodies, respectively. They stood tall and proud with heads that were about the size of minivans and bodies behind which could hide large RVs. In back of the two huge baby dragons was a shimmering silver dragon with swirling red eyes who watched Gabriel intensely as she approached him.

"*Hello, Mistress Gabriel. You are looking lovely as always, sweet lady,*" Skymaster crooned.

"*Thank you for coming, Skymaster. We need to go north to the gate,*" she said. Gabriel climbed the ladder Zeth had placed beside the dragon and began tying the straps of the soft leather saddle onto his ridges after which she secured her backpack and climbed into position. She brought up the ladder and secured it with another set of straps. Zeth and Terese were already in place and awaiting her lead.

*"Are we stopping at Castle Xandia?"* Skymaster asked.

She thought for a moment before answering. Stephan was Kristina and Serek's son and he was in trouble. Her eyes fell on Zeth, her own son, and decided that if it were her child that was in trouble she would want to know about it. She needed to have a face to face discussion with them. *"Yes Skymaster. Stop at Castle Xandia, please,"* she said.

The three dragons launched themselves into the colorful sunset that was painted with orange, pink and purple. Mirror images bounced in a muted fashion off the surface of the water that edged the grassy plain. The reflections of the dragons glittered beautifully as they skimmed over the lake, beginning their journey north.

As night claimed what was left of the day, a chill touched the air that deepened as they rose in elevation. The first moon made its appearance and was a full lantern in the sky. Gabriel dug into her pack and pulled out a hooded wool coat that would help protect her against the cold. The stars were bright and the constellation of the Condor was clearly visible to the north. They flew well into the night before making camp.

A late start the next day brought them into Saberville early the following evening. Soon Castle Xandia came into view with the towers illuminated brightly and invitingly. Skymaster descended in a leisurely circle and landed in the courtyard. The two baby dragons came in softly next to Skymaster moments later.

Breezerunner, Serek's dragon, who was silver but tinted with a glimmer of blue, trumpeted a greeting from the darkness overhead and came in quick, but landed gently beside Skymaster. On the dragon's back was a dark haired man who wore a stern expression on his bearded face. His dark gray eyes flashed at the sight of Gabriel. *"Greetings, Mistress Gabriel!"* Breezerunner offered amiably.

*"Greetings, Breezerunner!"* she returned.

"Hello, Serek," Gabriel said after the dragon had folded his wings and the dust had settled.

Serek was a strikingly handsome figure, tall and lean, with long dark hair that was pulled back in a ponytail. He wore tall leather boots and a long black cloak over a white tunic that was belted at the waist. A weapon was not visible on his ensemble. He did not smile. "Gabriel. Is there something wrong? Tell me," he said.

*Good ole' Serek--always straight to business.* She admired that in him. He helped Gabriel down off from Skymaster's back. "Serek, I'm afraid there is a problem. Where's Kristina?" she asked.

"She's at Castle Brightening visiting Theo and Jessabelle. Breezerunner just got back from there this morning. Does this involve Stephan?" he asked.

"Yes. Stephan has chosen to leave Jesse and Nicholas in order to pursue his own interests in a place that could be dangerous. I am especially concerned for him at the moment and am going to do my best to find him," Gabriel told him.

Zeth and Terese, walking hand-in-hand, joined them. Terese said, "Help from us Stephan needs. To Earth we will go."

He asked, "Why am I just learning of this? What kind of trouble is Stephan in?" Serek's face was camouflaged in danger masking a strong paternal love.

Gabriel was direct, "I asked Skymaster to keep it to himself. I wanted to talk to you personally. He's taking drugs and is messed up with a girl who is questionable in her intentions."

"What are these 'drugs'?" he asked.

Gabriel was watching him closely as she answered; as if he was made of delicate glass and she expected him to shatter. "It is a substance that alters the mind. The danger in it is that once the receptors in the brain are changed, they are altered for good. Once a person experiences the false euphoria the drug induces in the brain that person craves that feeling again, but only the drug in ever-increasing amounts can duplicate that feeling. Over time the brain itself is changed so that simple joys no longer produce enough of that feel-good juice called dopamine, only more of the drug will suffice. A person becomes addicted to the drug and will set aside their values and virtues in order to obtain it. It is sad but recovery is possible. I'm not sure what Stephan is involved with. Although I fear the worst, I hope for the best. Regardless, the sooner we get to him the better."

Serek did not move for a moment, but stared at Gabriel in shock. He turned toward the castle and started walking, stopped, turned and said, "I'll be right back. I'm going with you."

"Serek, it isn't necessary that you go. I can handle it," she said.

He fixed her with an intent look and said, "I am going."

"Serek," Gabriel said, "don't bring your sword. You won't need it this time."

He just kept walking without a response.

A short time later Serek returned and they all mounted the dragons and headed north.

It was a brief journey on dragon-back from Castle Xandia to the lightning cave. They unburdened their dragons from the saddles and ladders and left the items, including Serek's sword which he had brought anyway at the edge of the cave in which the lightning gate was located.

Gabriel, who had spent much time studying the instruction manual to the lightning gate, had a rough idea on how it worked. Constellations through the lightning bolt shaped opening rotated at a rate of approximately one every five minutes. The constellation indicated the galaxy that one would be transported to when traversing through the gate. They desired to go to Earth, which was identified by the constellation The Big Dipper. Appearing only on a schedule of about once per week, the constellation they sought, according to Gabriel's observations and calculations would be appearing at about this time in two days.

Even though the word "galaxy" was used to identify the various places, they were actually "worlds", located in various universes throughout various galaxies. The gate had more magical properties than scientific, although some natural laws still applied like gravity and time. Time itself depended upon the world and its rotational values around its axis and its sun. Of course, it was much more complicated and would take someone a lifetime to fully study and understand all of the aspects of the gate. That was the wisps job.

They built a fire and spent the evening waiting anxiously around it. It was going to be a long two days.

## *Brightening*

Theo was in the conference room with his wife, Jessabelle; his sister, Kristina; the torg delegate, Kaltog; the banderg delegate, Kali; and the newest member of their group, Jacoby, the kendrite delegate from Colordale, who was also Jessabelle's brother. They had spent the afternoon, in actuality most of the week, going over plans for establishing trade routes between the nations. After months of negotiations, they were close to concluding their talks by ironing out the remaining details.

"Timing is crucial," Kaltog was saying, "when it comes to shipping fresh fish from the west coast to Brightening and Skyview. Over the winter months the ice harvest in Saberville could be shipped and stored in a facility built under Farreach to be accessible throughout the summer months and be easily managed during the fishing season. It makes sense to ship the ice during the colder months and have it on hand in the store houses at Skyview. The dragons can make the trip from Farreach to Skyview in less than a day's time. With the amount they can carry, we could do deliveries of fresh fish once a week or more if needed. The facilities at Skyview are well suited to be able to handle the storage once the shipments start arriving. Brightening, however, needs to upgrade storage capacity before we can even begin supplying the kitchens here."

Jacoby addressed them in his usual aloof fashion, "With the torg nation, Colordale intends to work during the fishing season to help bring in the catch. Coordination it will take by both parties."

"*Theo,*" B.F. spoke to the king telepathically, "*what are you doing? I'm hungry.*"

"*Working,*" he replied.

"*Gabriel told me to tell you that she, Zeth, Terese and Serek are going through the gate to a place called Las Vegas to find Stephan. Can we go hunting?*" he asked.

"*No, I can't go hunting. When did she tell you this?*" Theo asked.

"*Just now. They are delayed temporarily while they wait for the gate to cycle. Why can't you go hunting?*" B.F. responded.

"*How long before they go. . .and why? What's wrong with Stephan? Where are Nicholas and Jesse? Why am I the last to know anything? What exactly is going on?*" he asked in frustration. Theo's eyes rested on Kristina as he waited for answers from the dragon. She noticed his countenance and her expression became troubled.

"*Just a minute I'll ask,*" B.F. said. There was a momentary pause in their mental conversation. "*Mistress Gabriel says that Stephan is in trouble and that Nicholas and Jesse are still chasing Candaz. Apparently Stephan is making some poor choices and she is afraid for him. She says that they should be able to go through the gate in two nights' time. Why can't you go hunting with me?*" he asked again.

"*Because I'm working B.F. I am the king. I do that,*" he said.

"*If you are the king why can't you get somebody else to work for you so you can go hunting with me?*" B.F. persisted.

"*It doesn't work that way, B.F.*" Theo said with amusement.

*"I don't see what could be more important than hunting,"* B.F. said.

*"I'm sorry, B.F. Another time?"* Theo asked.

*"You are always busy working these days,"* B.F. complained.

*"I promise we'll go hunting together soon,"* Theo vowed.

*"Don't break your promise or I'll burn down your castle and kidnap your wench,"* B.F. threatened.

Theo laughed out loud making all eyes at the conference table turn to him. *"Good luck catching Jessabelle,"* he said.

To those gathered at the table he said, "We have a problem. Gabriel, Zeth, Terese and Serek are going through the gate to find Stephan, who seems to be in some kind of trouble. They leave in two nights."

Kristina stood up and said, "I must go with them. Theo, can you take me up to the gate tonight?"

"Kris, I don't think that would be the best course of action. Let Gabriel and Serek handle this. We still have a lot to go over while we are all here and I don't see what good it will do to have you go there," he gave his opinion.

"I am his mother. Do you expect me to stand by and do nothing? If something is wrong with my son, I want to help him," Kristina lamented.

"Of course. I understand." Theo stood up and said, "I'll take you. It is a long flight though and we may not arrive in time for you to join them."

Jessabelle stood up as well and said, "Go with you I will."

"Wait," Theo said as he listened to B.F.

*"Mistress Gabriel says that she needs you to do some research for her while they go to find Stephan. Hang on. Let me get the details from her,"* B.F. again paused to listen to Gabriel and then continued to relay her message to Theo. *"She needs you to go to New Chance. The library there may have records on of how to deal with what she calls 'drug addiction'. She believes that the first settlers of New Chance*

*had problems with drug abuse and she thinks that it would be beneficial to learn about what they encountered and how they overcame it. Most of what is left in the library has turned to dust, but she is hoping that something of value remains intact."*

"Tell her we will do what we can," Theo said to B.F. through their mental link.

He addressed Kristina and Jessabelle, "It looks like we need to go to the library in New Chance to find out all we can on dealing with drug addiction."

"Drug addiction? What is that?" Kristina asked.

"Find out I guess we will," Jessabelle said. "Let us get packed. Road rations will be necessary. Time research takes."

"I'm going with you," Kali said.

Kaltog nodded his head, "As am I."

"Jacoby," Jessabelle addressed her brother, "You can come as well. Good with researching texts you are."

His face turned a bit red and he looked down at his hands before saying, "I do not know."

"Yes. You can come," Jessabelle insisted.

He looked up at her and slowly acquiesced, "Okay. Go I will."

Theo clapped his hands together and said, "Good. Gather your things. We'll meet downstairs in one-half a turn. Jessabelle have the kitchen pack us some supplies. Kaltog and Kali, call your dragons to meet us down at the stables in one-half a turn."

As they all left to get ready for their expedition, Theo wrapped his arm around his sister's waist and whispered, "It will be all right, Kris. We'll make sure Stephan is okay. Try not to worry."

"I'll quit worrying when he's home safe. Let's do what we have to do," she said.

"Right," Theo said. "Let's go."

# Chapter 4
## THE ITSY BITSY SPIDER

Sunlight filtered through the shades with bright rays blasting through the broken edges onto the floor and bed. Rolling over, Stephan groaned and looked at the clock on the bedside table. It read twelve ten and he groaned again. The woman next to him was sleeping soundly. He nudged her awake and she opened her eyes but didn't move. "Tawny, get up," he said. "You need to go meet Dodge."

"Why? What time is it?" she asked sleepily.

"Past noon. Get up," he said again while he lay back on his pillow and closed his eyes.

She rolled off the bed and walked to the bathroom. He heard her brushing her teeth and soon the shower was running. Feeling very anxious and a little nauseous, he tried to go back to sleep but couldn't manage it. When he heard the woman at the table light a candle and begin cooking what little they had left of the white powder in a spoon he crawled out of bed and joined her. There would be enough for both of them this time and maybe a little for later too.

The substance he put into his veins with the needle brought instant relief to the anxiety and brought with it a wonderful sense of euphoria. Stephan lay back down on the bed and relaxed. Tawny was going to meet her dealer and buy more of the white powder she called heroine. It was strange how he was afraid to be without it now. Tawny seemed used to living with it, as casual about it as he used to be about having dinner. Now he didn't care much about food. In fact he didn't care much about anything except making sure they didn't run out of the drug.

Briefly he remembered why he had come to Las Vegas. Nicky and Jesse were still after Candaz. He probably should have gone with them. But, if he had he couldn't have the drug too. Stephan couldn't let go of *it*, not yet. He could catch up with Nick and Jesse later. The sword that he pawned he had gotten back after winning money on that machine. He had his sword now, but after paying for it and the powder, most of the money was gone. The red sports car was parked outside. Probably he could trade that in and get some more money. If he got more money he could also get more of the drug. He would have to think about it. Right now he just wanted to crawl back in bed.

Tawny slipped away, taking his car keys and the rest of his money with her. He didn't hear her go. She would not be coming back.

## *www.evilsorcerer.com*

With his heart racing from the recent encounter, Candaz sped down the highway toward Albuquerque, New Mexico. He withdrew a small vial from the pocket of his cloak, pulled the stopper out with his teeth and took a small sip. The elixir went straight through him like lightning, warming everything, making him feel young and vibrant again. He quickly restopped the crystal decanter and put it back in his pocket. The effects were wearing off more quickly with each dosage he consumed. He would need to obtain more. The small stash he had was tucked carefully away back on Risen.

A moment of brilliance flashed through his mind. If he could discover the contents of the elixir, he could duplicate it. If he could duplicate it, he could use it on Risen to control the masses. The elixir could be distributed as a youth serum. Once people became hooked on it, he would have control over them. They would bow down to him once again. He could regain the power he had lost so many years ago. The more he considered the possibility, the more he liked it.

He had spent last night at a hotel that had a computer on which a person could pretty much get any information one desired. The woman who had assisted him with the computer and the internet was easily fooled by the cover story he had given her and once he had used his charms on her she was more than willing to help him out. The key to any story was to keep it simple. He had convinced her that he had lived most of his life without a computer, which of course was true. What she didn't know was that he was not from her world at all. Even though it was incredulous to her, she took him for his word and gave him lessons on how to use the mouse and search the internet.

It was an amazing machine. He spent most of the night exploring this foreign land in the comfort of the hotel lobby. Analysis of the elixir could be accomplished at a laboratory. There was one in the area he was headed to near Socorro that would meet his needs. Like on Risen, money would motivate the proper person to get the job done. With a couple of clicks of the mouse he found a place to get the elixir analyzed. That would be his first destination.

A small obscure mining museum was his second destination. He wanted to discover all that he could about explosives and he had an idea that it would be a good place to start his education. After gaining the knowledge he needed, he would obtain the materials necessary to destroy the lightning gate.

The third thing he accomplished was to find out the location of Jesse's family. Jesse's brother Jacob was a star soccer player and newspaper articles mentioned the school he attended. Although he didn't have a home address, he could find the boy at his school. It would be fairly easy to grab him and afterward elicit cooperation from the father. Jesse and Gabriel would have no choice but to concede victory to him. It would be a pleasure to watch Gabriel grovel at his feet.

With these three goals in mind, Candaz headed south when he got to Albuquerque. He had obtained the Volvo from a man who would not be needing it anymore. He had put an enchantment on the machine so it would be less visible and easily overlooked. It did not take him long to learn how the machine worked. Driving a car was easy but he didn't understand the speed limit signs. What was the point of limiting one's speed? He didn't really know, but was just a little curious about this strange world.

As he drove he thought about the numerous people he wished to take revenge upon, something he enjoyed contemplating often. Of course, Gabriel was at the top of his list. She had defied him numerous times and had ultimately been responsible for his downfall after the destruction of Castle Xandia thirty years ago. King Theo Wingmaster would pay with the loss of his kingdom at some point in the near future. He and his kendrite wife would be overthrown when Candaz gained control over Brightening. The usurpers presently in charge of Castle Xandia, Serek and Kristina Landtamer, would bow down to him after he introduced them to the 'youth serum'. When he had Jesse's brother, Jacob, and her father, William, he would be able to get that girl to do whatever he wished. Her boyfriends, Nicholas and Stephan would lay down their arms if she told them to. After he was back on Risen, he would blow up the gate leaving Jesse and her friends back on Earth; three less meddlesome individuals to deal with. With all of his plans in place, he would have the ultimate authority. He would have to find his son, Zeth, and put him in charge of distribution of the elixir. It would not take long at all to seize all power for himself.

It didn't take long for him to reach Socorro, a small college town right off the highway. After much searching, he figured out how to find the address he was looking for. The laboratory was a small plain white building with a red tile roof. One car was parked out in front of the place. When he entered through the door, a small counter was directly in front of him. Upon it was a computer, a bin for outgoing mail and another flat stacked bin that was neatly piled with multi-colored folders. A small bell sat on the counter with directions for it to be rung for service. Candaz tapped it experimentally the first time and then struck it again to make it ring louder.

After a few minutes a large woman in a white lab coat entered from a door on the other side of the counter. She didn't smile, but greeted him with a nod and annoyance in her eyes. "Hello. What can I help you with?" she asked.

Candaz smiled his most charming smile and said, "I have a substance I need analyzed for content. Can you do that?"

She reached under the counter and brought out a piece of paper which she handed to him along with a pen and instructed, "Fill this out. A basic analysis will cost two hundred dollars. With a basic we include identification of components with an automated analytical process. You should have your results in a week to ten days."

Candaz looked at the paper without touching it. With his right hand he sat two pieces of gold on the counter. "This is extremely important. I need the results immediately," he said as he pushed the gold toward her.

The woman looked at the coins and then her eyes locked onto Candaz's face. "It doesn't work that way," she said.

Without hesitation, Candaz sat another piece of gold next to the first two and said, "I would really appreciate it if you could help me."

The woman in the lab coat swept one gold piece into her hand and said, "I'll just go check this for authenticity. I'll be right back." She disappeared through the door and returned a few minutes later. "I could get fired for this," she said as she took the remaining gold pieces and stuck them in her pocket. "Do you have the sample?"

He smiled and brought his small crystal decanter out of his pocket and set it on the counter. "How much of this do you need?" he asked.

She grabbed a little vial from under the counter and slowly poured a small portion into it. After handing his bottle back to him, she said, "Check back in an hour."

He took back his decanter and placed another gold piece on the counter. "For your trouble madam. I will be back soon."

After checking into a nearby hotel, he returned to the laboratory and received an envelope that contained a piece of paper that thoroughly broke down the contents of the elixir. He thanked the woman and left. Sitting in his car, he read the piece of paper that he had paid quite a bit for. It listed the first two ingredients, which were known to him. The third ingredient listed was an "opiate". He was unfamiliar with the term, but was sure that the plant it was from was grown on Risen. The next three items listed were identified as organic materials with names he did not know. He would look them up tonight on the internet and see if they were recognizable to him under a different name on Risen. The measurements were also unfamiliar to him, but he could easily figure out the proper ratios for mixing the concoction once he located all of the ingredients.

He had a small stash of elixir hidden away in an underground cavern outside of Saberville. The origin of the elixir was New Chance from a past that was forgotten. It was produced a long time ago by a people who no longer existed.

Neatly he folded the paper and put it in his pocket before leaving the parking spot and heading out to find the mining museum. It was on the outskirts of town and difficult to find, but eventually he located the poorly marked building. A washed-out sign just to the side of the door indicated that the museum was open.

When he opened the door and walked into the poorly lit space, a young man removed his ear buds and greeted him remotely, "Five bucks, dude."

Candaz's cold dark eyes froze the teen in place as he pulled a fresh twenty dollar bill out of his cloak and set it on the counter. The fifteen in change that was returned to him was left on the counter as the boy went back to his oblivion and the old man entered the museum and began to look around.

A display in the corner caught his attention right away. It was a diorama of men working in an underground mine. They were using dynamite to blast away the rock to find the elusive treasure they sought. A display case contained the many tools and equipment used in the acquisition of the precious metal. He read the captions on the objects in the case, quickly taking note of the items and assessing their condition and viability in his plan. There was a whole section on the progression of explosive materials throughout the years, complete with components from dynamite sticks, C-4 blocks, detonators and blasting caps used in mining.

He glanced back at the boy and noted that he was absorbed in some type of hand-held device. Candaz placed a hand on the cold glass and drew an intricate rune which immediately began to glow a brilliant blue. The solid covering wavered as he reached through it and removed the items he desired. He took all of the explosives, detonators and blasting caps and stuffed them into the pockets of his cloak. With a gentle wave of his hand he wiped the rune off the glass surface and it resumed its solid form. Another glance at the teenager assured him that he had not been seen. Without further delay, he left the museum without even the slightest acknowledgement from the boy.

Back at the hotel, Candaz spent more time on the internet researching explosives and how they worked. With what he believed was adequate knowledge, he stored the items he had obtained in the trunk of his car. It was late so he decided to get a good night's sleep before taking the next step in his plan. The following day was Monday and the child Jacob would be in school. That is where he would abduct him.

Far into the depths of sleep his mind remembered with exquisite clarity the face of his beloved Molly. She was so beautiful and fair, innocent and young; bright with the vibrancy of life. They ran from the oppression of Candaz's father, fleeing to a future together. An arrow pierced her back as they rode and she fell dead upon the ground. Molly! His Molly was dead. She would never smile at him again. He would never again feel her warm skin against his. Molly! He gathered her into his arms and walked with tears in his eyes to the nearby cliff. After placing a kiss on her cold dead lips, he tossed her body off the side. He watched as she fell slowly with the skirts of her silk dress billowing around her. Before she hit the surf below she opened her eyes wide with terror and screamed his name. "Candaz!"

He awoke with a scream on his own lips. Was what he saw real? Could she have been alive when he threw her over the cliff? No! Molly!

# Chapter 5

## BORN TO BE WILD

The old gray pick-up truck rattled down the dirt road with dust billowing in its wake. Jesse groaned again and made every effort to not let the motion of the truck upset the composure she had worked so hard to obtain. Taking deep breaths helped a little. She closed her eyes and wished the ride to be over. Nicky rubbed her back and neck with his warm, dry hands. Taking hold of one hand she brought it to her face, kissed it, and held on tightly.

Lying in Nicholas's lap, Jesse was missing the beauty of the landscape that they were racing through. Monolithic rock formations in bright rusty red ascended from the desert floor. Some were accented with white at the top and highlighted with vivid green foliage. Blue sky contrasted well with the colors in the red rock that stood stoically in interesting shapes and forms all around them. Jim turned down a smaller road that descended to a shallow river that ran right over their path. Along the river grew lush plants as they took advantage of the available water. After crossing the river, Jim took the left fork in the road and then turned right into a gravel driveway.

"We're almost there, Jesse. Hold on," Jim said with a calm tone.

"You'll be okay, Jess," Nick said quietly.

At his feet, Tempest whined and licked the top of Felcore's head. The cat was curled into a ball and had his eyes closed tight. *"Jesse?"* Tempest's voice sounded loud in Jesse's head.

*"Tempest?"*

*"The gold wolf cat is not very happy,"* Tempest informed her.

*"We'll be there soon, sweetie. Jim knows a lady who can help us,"* she replied hopefully.

They pulled up to a house that was so perfectly designed that it melted almost undetectably into its surroundings. A large pot of purple and red flowers stood just to the side of a short cobblestone walkway that led to an arched wooden door. The stucco house was painted the exact color of the natural rock that surrounded it. Jim put the truck in park and pulled out his cell phone. After finding her number, he left a message on her voicemail when she didn't answer. "It's Jim. I'm at your house and need your help. Call me."

"How do you know this woman?" Nicholas asked Jim.

"She is a woman I have known for a relatively short time in the course of a long life. As old as I am, she is much older. Although her years in this time are stretched thin, like the skin over knuckles, her spirit remains vibrant. You will meet her in a minute. Listen," Jim said, putting his index finger in the air that brought with it silence.

In the distance a low rumbling increased in volume as the source drew closer to their location in the driveway. Jim and Nick opened their doors at the same time and they all stepped out into the warm desert breeze. The scent on the air was sweet and dry and earthy at the same time. Jesse breathed in deeply, enjoying the fragrance and the feel of the hot afternoon sun on her face.

Into the driveway roared a motorcycle. A low rumble, signature of a Harley Davidson, purred to a stop behind the old truck. Completely covered in black leather, the small figure riding the cycle dismounted the shiny purple bike and removed her helmet slowly. Silver hair fell down around her shoulders in wispy strands. Wrinkles graced her face around her mouth and gray eyes, which went to each individual in turn until they rested finally on Jim.

"Jesse, it's her," Tempest said quietly.

"Her who?" Jesse asked.

"Jim," the old woman began, "tell me what has happened." The authority in her voice demanded complete obedience.

"First," Jim turned to Jesse, "this is Jessica Gates, granddaughter of Gabriel." He put his hand on Nick's shoulder. "This is Nicholas Wingmaster, son of Theo and Jessabelle. Kids, let me introduce you to Mistress Shareen Wingmaster."

Jesse leaned against Nick, who had his arm wrapped supportively around her waist. "It's Shareen," Tempest said inside her head.

"But, you're dead," Jesse protested.

"Well, that's what you were supposed to think. My cover is officially blown, Jim. Now, tell me what has happened," she demanded again.

"Your nemesis, Candaz, is what happened. Jesse and Felcore need your help," Jim replied.

Shareen went to the truck and reached in to pick up Felcore. "Bring her inside," she said to Nicholas, "great grandson! Imagine that!" she said as she laid a hand on the side of his face.

They entered the arched doorway into a wide expansive living room. Two chairs and a couch beckoned comfortably in the center of the room. Art work of all types surrounded them. Statues of animals, dragons and abstracts sat upon pedestals in every corner available. Paintings in a variety of genres covered the walls. Books were piled on the table surfaces. Propped on a pile of books on the coffee table in front of the couch was an open lap top computer.

"Please, make yourselves comfortable. I'm going to change and be right back," Shareen left the room quickly while Nicholas helped Jesse to one of the chairs.

"I can't believe she's alive," Nick said as he examined one of the abstract sculptures.

"Has she been here the whole time?" Jesse asked.

Jim, who was holding Felcore, sank down on the couch and took a moment to pat Tempest reassuringly on the head before answering, "Her health on Risen was critically impaired. The desert, especially in the Sedona area, offers benefits like nowhere else. It was necessary for Gabriel to take over for her so she faked her death to push that end and retired here."

Shareen entered the room wearing a comfortable cotton dress. She continued Jim's narrative, "Yes. Although it was difficult to leave, it was necessary for the good of Risen and for me as well. My arthritis has become tolerable living here. If I had stayed on Risen, I would have long ago given up on life. This place keeps me young."

Sitting on the arm of the chair next to Jesse, she placed her crooked hands on the sides of Jesse's face and examined her closely. "Hmmm. Nicholas, bring me the sword," she ordered.

Nick fetched the weapon from where it sat propped against the wall and brought it over to Shareen.

"Just hold it for me, will you, Nicholas?" Shareen said.

He let the sword lay on his hands as he held it out to Shareen. The blade had freecurrent electricity running up and down it in blue and green sparks. It was heavy, but Nick handled the weapon easily without burden.

Jesse groaned and said under her breath, "I think I'm going to be sick again."

"It's okay, honey. Just hold on another minute," Shareen said as she placed one hand on the sword and another hand on Jesse's forehead. Immediately freecurrent energy could be seen transferring between the two with Shareen as the conduit. Nick could feel pain in his hands where they made contact with the sword, but it didn't last long. Jesse sighed and sat up. Setting the sword aside, Nick embraced her.

"Thank you," Jesse said to Shareen. "I feel so much better."

"I'm glad," Shareen said.

"Can you help Felcore, too?" Jesse asked.

"Yes. Nick?" Shareen turned her attention to the little yellow cat. As she placed her hand on the cat and the sword simultaneously the freecurrent energy began to flow. Oddly, Felcore phased back and forth from his true form as a golden retriever and his disguise as a cat, finally returning to his authentic shape, a dog. The big golden retriever remained on Jim's lap for only a moment before jumping down. He stretched completely, first one leg and then the other before happily wagging his tail and going to Jesse for a proper scratching.

"Rrowff!" he said.

"Rrowff!" Tempest agreed as she joined them for her own scratching. "*You are better, Jesse,*" she stated.

"*I am better, sweetie,*" Jesse said.

"*Good. I am hungry, Jesse,*" Tempest said as she wagged her doggy tail.

"*Even though you are a dog, you have the appetite of a dragon,*" Jesse said.

"Mistress Shareen, you wouldn't happen to have something I could feed the dogs, would you?" she asked.

"Yes, honey. In fact, I think we could all use a bite to eat," Shareen said. "Nicholas, could you give your old granny a hand?"

His crooked grin flashed momentarily at Jesse, as he followed his great-grandmother from the room.

Jesse and Jim relaxed and quietly waited. Soon wonderful smells came enticingly from the direction of the kitchen. Within moments Nick returned with a large tray that was filled with bowls and spoons, a basket of bread, butter and a huge bowl of stew. Jesse cleared a spot on the coffee table so he had a place to deposit his burden. Shareen had two bowls in her hands which she placed on the floor for the dogs. "Nicholas, help me get something to drink for our guests," Shareen said.

They returned to the kitchen once more and reappeared with a large pitcher and four goblets and two more bowls. Nick poured water from the pitcher in the bowls for the dogs and divided the rest in the glasses.

After they had eaten their fill, Jesse and Nicholas cleaned up the dishes and joined Shareen and Jim in the living room. Jim was talking about their recent encounter with Candaz. "He mentioned Jesse's family. I'm not sure what his intentions are, but we need to find him quickly," he said.

Shareen almost muttered her words, "I can't believe he has reappeared after all of these years. I thought he was dead."

"It seems that he isn't the only one to make an appearance after being thought dead," Jesse said. "I don't understand how you could be here. Gabriel wrote in her diary that you went up in flames during a confrontation with Candaz, but here you are alive and well."

"Child, that was a long time ago," Shareen responded with an air of regret. She sighed. "Gabriel needed to take the reins to be the sorceress of Brightening. With me in the way, she would not be so willing to do what needed to be done. I was an old woman, even back then, and in a lot of pain from the arthritis that was slowly crippling my body. I had the opportunity to make a quick exit from my situation and I took it. When Candaz attacked me on that stage, I used it as a diversion to escape. Like a magician, 'poof' I was gone. Gabriel would take over and become a powerful sorceress and my family would grieve for me for a time, but life would go on. This place has brought me an enormous amount of healing, both physically and spiritually. Use of the freecurrent throughout the years has extended my life quite nicely. You would not believe my age if I told you. I am happy and content to live out my days here. I am sorry if I have caused pain to those I love by my actions, however. Now it seems that I should have finished the job that I started so many years ago. Candaz cannot be allowed to spread any more of his poison. He must be stopped for good."

Nicholas stood up and stretched out his lean muscular form before he turned to them and said, "He's a slippery devil. The next time I come across him, I won't be such a gentleman. I have given him too many opportunities to defend himself like a man. He has had his last chance with me."

Jesse got up, wrapped her arms around Nick's neck and rested her head on his chest. "Without the medallion, I feel weakened. It's like I am unable to focus the freecurrent energy properly. Now he has it and can use it against us."

"I can help you with that, Jesse," Shareen said. "It is a relatively natural skill to learn. It just takes practice. There are exercises you can do to develop your skill. I can start giving you lessons tomorrow."

"I'm afraid we don't have time for that, Mistress Shareen. I need to find my father and brother. I've tried them on my cell, but only get their voicemail. We need to go to Socorro as soon as possible, maybe even tonight."

"It is late," Jim said. "Let's get some rest and leave first thing in the morning. If your father and brother are in danger, we need to be in a position to help them. We will be no match for Candaz if we're exhausted by the time we find him and we *will* find him, Jesse."

Tempest and Felcore were already curled on the floor sleeping soundly.

"Yes, I suppose you're right," Jesse agreed reluctantly, "I guess that is wise. I'll keep trying. I can't understand why they aren't answering."

"Are you familiar with sight water?" Shareen asked Jesse.

"I've read about it in Gabriel's diary," she said.

"Come with me," Shareen said. "Let's see if we can find some answers about your family." The old woman held out a warped hand to Jesse who took it gently after only a moment's hesitation.

The two women, one very old, one very young walked to a room in the back of the house. In the center of the room sat a basin of water upon a pedestal. Next to the pedestal was an overstuffed chair that looked as comfortable as it did worn. It was big enough for the two small women to sit in side by side. Shareen explained what to do, "When I tell you to, gently place your fingertips on the surface of the water. Picture your father or your brother in your mind and let your mind seek one of them out. Which of them are you going to try?"

"I guess dad," Jesse said.

"Okay, Jesse, don't try to communicate with him, just watch through his eyes. Take your time and relax. Remember, it is important that you not speak to him through your mind like you would with a dragon, only observe. Are you ready?"

"I guess. Yes," she answered.

"It's okay, honey," Shareen comforted. "It will be okay. Relax."

Shareen took Jesse's left hand in her right and reached out to the basin. Gently she let go of Jesse's hand after giving it a reassuring squeeze. With her index finger Shareen drew a simple symbol in the water, which immediately began to glow green.

The younger girl felt the water caress her fingertips as she made contact. She pictured her father as she had last seen him in her mind. His gray eyes had been circled darkly with fatigue. The speckled gray hair on his head had needed trimming. Her heart ached as she felt the full force of missing him.

# No network

Bill looked at the error message on his cell phone with frustration and pushed it back in his pocket. The damn thing was worthless! Jacob was supposed to call him when he got back from the soccer tournament so he could pick him up. His service had always been reliable in the past. He didn't know if his battery was dying or what the issue was, but it was unacceptable. It was funny how easily he had gotten used to having a cell phone and relying upon it. After his teenage children nagged him incessantly, he finally caved in and purchased one. Only a short time ago his daily life did not rely on such technology, but now it was hard to live without.

Jacob had been gone all weekend at a soccer tournament with his team. Bill was unable to go because of work obligations. He hated not knowing where his son was. It was hard enough having Jesse gone, missing since last summer. Dealing with that on an everyday basis was horrific. He had to fight his tendency to want to control all of Jacob's life. Taking out his cell phone again, he hit "send" and received the same "no network" message. "Damn!" he swore.

He slammed the car door shut behind him and walked into the house. When he picked up the house phone silence met his ears instead of a dial tone. "What the heck?" Walking over to the computer, he quickly clicked on the internet icon and received an error message instead of the normal home screen. "What the hell is going on?" Grabbing the remote control to the television, he clicked it on, but there was no picture. The cable was out. "Was there a war that I didn't know about?" Bill asked himself.

He quickly changed his clothes and went back down to the car in the garage. His plan was to head to Jacob's friend's house to see if anyone was home. He would figure out his media issues after he found his son.

The house of Jacob's friend, Tony, was a couple of blocks away. The driveway was empty and nobody answered the door when he rang the doorbell. It was getting late in the evening. They should be home by now.

Perhaps the boys were at the school. The bus always returned there after a tournament to let the boys get cleaned up in the locker room and catch rides home. He headed directly there, driving faster than he should. There were a few cars in the parking lot, but none that he recognized. It was way past the time they should have gotten back, in fact, it was quite late. Where were they?

A flash of light immediately drew his attention to the parking lot entrance. His hope that it was the bus with the boys was short lived. He noticed a silver Volvo pull in and park in front of the school. The hairs on the back of his neck prickled instantly. His sense of foreboding heightened. He watched as a man got out of the car, strangely dressed in a long black cloak, and walked to the broad expanse of glass doors that served as the main entrance. It was locked and denied him entrance. He walked around to the other side of the building and out of sight.

Bill took out his cell phone to check and see if he could make a call. It still displayed the same error message "no network available" and he put it away with a few choice words. That man was up to no good. He had no evidence to go on, but he did have a feeling to go on, and that feeling was strong. Slowly and quietly he got out of his car and followed the stranger.

# A Wing And A Prayer

Jesse removed her fingers from the sight water and touched them to her face, feeling the cool wetness against her skin before she reached over and grasped Shareen's arm. Gray eyes penetrated her own intense gaze. "Candaz is in Socorro. He's at my high school. We've got to go now. Jacob . . . and Dad are in trouble. We must leave now," Jesse said as she rose from the chair.

Shareen grabbed her hand to stop her and said, "Jesse, we are a six hour drive from there. Even if we leave immediately, we may not get there in time. Let's try calling the police and give them a heads up. We might not be able to stop Candaz in time."

"We've got to try," she insisted.

"*Would it help if you changed me back into a dragon?*" Tempest asked in her head.

"*I wish, Tempest, but I can't have a dragon flying in the skies over New Mexico. It would surely end up on YouTube,*" she replied telepathically.

"*I am a very beautiful dragon, not at all tube-like,*" Tempest said.

"*Yes, you are very beautiful, Tempest. YouTube is a web . . . well, don't worry about it,*" Jesse said. She was already out the door and heading to the living room.

The two dogs greeted her with wagging tails and nudges to her hand. Nicholas was asleep on the couch and Jim was likewise asleep in one of the chairs. It had to be well past midnight. She hated to wake them, but had no choice. "Jim, Nick," she said quietly, "you need to get up."

Shareen was right on her heals and was not hesitant to waken them at all. "Let's go boys! Time to wake up," she said loudly. She clapped her hands and got two groans in response.

Nicholas automatically reached for his sword before he was fully awake and found it not there. It was lying on the table in front of him. His gold eyes reflected back the light as he opened them and spotted Jesse. "What's happened? What's wrong?" he asked.

"We've located Candaz. He's in Socorro, New Mexico. I think he's after my brother, Jacob. My dad is following him right now. They are in trouble. We need to leave now. We'll be lucky to make it in time," she told them.

Nicholas got up and immediately started looking for his boots.

"That's about six hours from here, Jesse. Let's get packed up and go," Jim said as he stood up and stretched. "Are you coming, Shareen?"

"I think that is what I must do. I've been hiding out far too long," Shareen replied.

Nicholas sheathed his sword on his back and grabbed his hoody. He gave Jim a long look. "I'm going to transform into my eagle form. I can make much better time in the air. You have kendrite in your bloodline. Do you want to give it a try?"

Jim's jaw dropped, but his eyes lit up with excitement. He asked, "Do you think it is possible?"

"I don't know. Are you willing to try?" Nicholas asked.

"I don't know how," Jim replied.

"I will guide you." Nick gave Jesse a quick kiss and said, "We'll meet you there, Jess. I can get there much much faster by flying. Do you have a map I can get a glimpse of?"

"It'll just take a second," Shareen said and went to her laptop and clicked a couple of times on the mouse. She showed Nicholas where they were and where they needed to go. He studied it closely, checking both the traffic view and the terrain image before setting it aside.

"Got it. Okay, Jim, ready?" Nicholas asked.

Jim handed Jesse his keys. "Be careful with her. She's old," he said, referring to his truck.

"I'll handle her with TLC. I promise," Jesse replied with a forced smile.

"Let's go outside," Nick suggested. They all followed Nicholas out of the door. The night was crisp, refreshing and welcoming. A canopy of stars studded the blackness with their brilliance. As they walked to the end of the driveway, Jim's casual stride contrasted with the anticipation in his eyes.

Nick turned to Jim and put his hand on the older man's shoulder and instructed, "You have to feel this in your soul. Reach inside yourself and find the ancestry that is in your core. Breathe and let go of what binds you to the earth. The stars beckon to you. Reach for them."

Jim sighed and gave Jesse and Shareen a significant look. His eyes caught the light from the house and reflected back to them as liquid gold. "What happens to your clothes?" he asked.

Nick laughed. "Really? *That's* your question." He laughed again before saying, "I don't really know. They just go and come back. I guess it's magic."

"I hope they come back if they go," Jim said wryly.

Jim gazed up at the stars. A coyote howled and then another answered back from a long distance away. A breeze blew gently in their faces with a scent that is distinct to the desert, a pure and dry scent like clean towels fresh out of the dryer. Breathing deeply, Jim closed his eyes and stood unmoving for several minutes. He shuffled his feet and said, "I don't know if this is possible for me."

"You have it within you. It is in your blood, Jim," Nicholas said.

He inhaled another deep breath and started to chant. It was soft and lyrical with a gentle rhythm in utterances that were not words but sounds. Before their eyes, the old man who stood before them began to shrink. His arms became wings and his torso became streamline. Feathers covered him and glistened golden brown in the moonlight. This all took place in a matter of seconds. When the transformation was complete, the golden eagle turned and captured them with his sharp gaze. He trilled as he spread his long wings and leapt into the air for the first time. Flying seemed to come naturally and he swooped down skimming the space just above the on-lookers heads before ascending once more.

Nicholas transformed and joined Jim as they watched with awe. Tempest jumped and leaped, trying to join them where she belonged soaring through the sky, but gravity held the little dog captive. As the eagles flew away, Jesse turned to Shareen and said, "Do you want to ride in the truck?"

"No. I'm going to take my bike. Give me a minute to change," she said and quickly went into the house and returned in her leather gear.

"We'll follow you," Jesse said as she, Tempest and Felcore climbed into Jim's truck.

"Let's go." Shareen mounted her Harley and put on her helmet. She gave Jesse a thumb's up before firing up the rumbling engine and heading out onto the road.

# Chapter 6

## INTERCESSION

The fire had burned down to glowing hot coals as the four people gathered around it slept uncomfortably wrapped in their cloaks. Out of the back of the cave a lone figure emerged from the lightning gate and approached them with stealth, the only audible sound being the hum of his wings. Much smaller than a man, about the size of a five year old child, and nude save for a discreet use of material around his genitals, he approached Serek and looked down into the sleeping man's face with a smile upon his own. The gold fur on the tips of his pointed ears twitched slightly as he hovered close enough to tickle the man's mustache.

Serek instinctively reached for his sword as he woke, but being without it came up swinging with his fists. The mustache tickler flew quickly to the opposite side of the cave. When Serek spotted his antagonist he stood and demanded, "Rew, get over here. What do you think you are doing? If I had my sword on me you would be a shish kabob."

Gabriel greeted her old friend warmly, "Rew, so good to see you. Where have you been?"

Rew gave Gabriel an excessively exuberant hug. "I've been on Elysia with my family. Why are you camped out in the cave?"

Serek answered him, "We need to go to Earth. Stephan is in a place called Las Vegas and we must find him and bring him back home."

"I will take you," Rew volunteered.

"Hello, Rew," Terese said as she opened her eyes. Zeth sat up at the same time and helped Terese to her feet.

"Hello, Terese. Zeth has been healed? This must be Jesse's doing," Rew commented with a light smile.

"Yes, Jesse enabled my healing," Zeth shared with Rew. "I no longer simmer with corruption inside of me. Forgiveness has been given to me by the people and dragons I have wronged. I am eternally grateful to them all. I heard you were hurt by my father. I am sorry that you suffered at his hand and for anything I may have done to harm you."

"That is for him to atone for. If the dragons hold you exonerated, I have nothing against you, Zeth. Are you and Terese . . . ?" Rew's finger went back and forth between them.

Terese blushed, but Zeth took her hand and said, "We are exploring that possibility," as he gazed into her eyes and smiled. She continued to blush.

"Rew, you said you could take us to Earth?" Serek asked, losing patience with the chit chat.

"Sure. When do you want to go?" Rew asked.

"Now," Serek snapped.

"Okay. Does anyone have some clothes I can borrow? I can't go to Earth like this," Rew said.

"I think I have something that will do," Terese said as she rummaged through her pack and pulled out a few items and handed them to Rew, who immediately put them on. The shirt fit loosely but tucked into the pants that he rolled up.

"I need a hat to cover my ears."

"Here. Try this." Gabriel took a square cloth, folded it diagonally and tied the cloth around Rew's head, covering his furry ears.

"Are you ready now?" Serek asked, his tone thick with sarcasm.

"Let's go, old man," Rew responded brightly.

"You are much older than me, *old* man," Serek returned as he followed Rew to the back of the cave.

The wisp, now looking very much like a young child, put his hand on the edge of the lightning gate speeding up the rotation of the constellations visible within. As soon as the Big Dipper appeared Rew removed his hand and led them through to the other side.

Gabriel and Rew had been to this cave before. Rew had been through the gate to Earth several times to keep an eye on Jesse as she grew up. Gabriel was from there, but she hadn't been back in a long time. She visited there rarely. Her home was now on Risen.

It was still night when they exited the cave. The desert was cool under an umbrella of stars. In the distance, the lights of the city illuminated the sky unnaturally. Serek's long stride set a rapid pace through the desert until they reached the pavement. "We're heading toward the lights?" Serek asked.

"We go that way," Gabriel said and pointed down the road.

They walked and walked and walked.

"I sure miss Breezerunner and my horse, Talon. I haven't walked this far since Breezerunner was a baby," Serek complained.

"Walking is for the birds. Well, not really *for the birds*. You know what I mean," Rew added his complaint. His beautiful wisp wings were trapped inside of his shirt, hidden from view.

"For Stephan we do this. Keep our spirits up we must," Terese chimed eagerly earning her scathing looks from the others.

"How are we going to find Stephan when we get to Las Vegas, mother?" Zeth asked.

"It's interesting how the freecurrent energy works. Everything exudes a distinctive 'vibration' which identifies it specifically. Although it can be very difficult weeding through each individual signature, it is possible. Because I know Stephan, with a little time I'm hoping to be able to locate him. Zeth, you can help me with the process. Although, you don't know Stephan as well as I do, you might be able to pick out his being through the multitudes of others just because of your shared origin. Let's get into the general area and get a hotel room where we can work in seclusion. I brought three hundred dollars with me. I hope that's enough," she said.

They had made it to the main drag into Las Vegas from the north, Highway 95. The sun was just peaking over the mountain on the other side of the city from them. Pausing, they drank water from Serek's water pouch. Once the sun was up, the heat would increase with the advancing of the day.

"Let's get moving. We have a long way to go, yet," Gabriel said as she started walking again. They all followed quietly, lost in their own thoughts.

As they continued on, the expanse of the city greeted them with its chaos. Cars zoomed by at an ever-increasing rate. Housing complexes were plentiful with their stucco exteriors painted one after another a variant of desert hues, all with red or blue tile roofs, fortressed by tall concrete walls, with names like "Desert Oasis Villas" or "Casa Linda". Tucked into the corners of major intersections were shopping centers, offering grocery stores, nail salons and bars along with various other shops. People went about their business of getting ready for their day by running last minute errands before heading to work or, in this twenty-four hour culture, heading home after an all-night shift.

Eventually, the weary travelers came upon a true oasis in the desert, a hotel and casino named the Santa Fe. Gabriel paid for a room which they thankfully retired to. They took turns showering while Gabriel ordered room service. After eating, Serek, Terese and Rew got comfortable and were soon sleeping soundly.

## Trail Of Tendrils

After taking a couple of hours to get some sleep, Gabriel roused herself and Zeth so they could get started. It was much like looking for a needle in a haystack by removing one piece of hay at a time. They sat cross-legged on the floor of their hotel room with their eyes closed in concentration. The tendrils of freecurrent energy wove through the air around them unseen by the human eye. Slowly and methodically they weeded through the intricacies that identified the sources of the energy.

"Mother," Zeth said in a hushed tone, "take my hand. I'm getting an indication of Jesse and the rest of them from close by, but from the past, like an echo. Stephan was with them. If we can get a hold of that tendril, we might be able to trace where he went from there."

Together they isolated Stephan's signature vibration in the energy patterns. They followed it into the heart of Las Vegas, deviating in intensity, but palpable. Gabriel felt confident that they could find him in the general vicinity that they had pinpointed.

"Zeth, we've located him. Let's go," Gabriel said.

She woke the others and they went down to the lobby and ordered a taxi. They watched from the back of the minivan as their taxi sped along the major arteries of Las Vegas along with hundreds of other commuters. They exited the highway and passed large impressive hotels and landscapes designed with elaborate themes to draw in crowds of willing gamblers. These expensive properties were left behind as they went to the other side of Vegas, the area where tourists seldom treaded.

Gabriel asked the taxi driver to stop at the nearest motel. It was an old property that looked like it was built in the fifties and remodeled in the eighties. It was long overdue for another remodel. She paid the driver and they rented a room. It was a far cry from the quality of the room they still had at the Santa Fe and it smelled of week-old socks and cigarette smoke. Gabriel was reluctant to stand on the carpet let alone sit on it. She grabbed a couple of towels from bathroom and covered a spot on the floor for her and Zeth to convene on. Serek and Terese sat on the bed and waited. Rew took off his clothes and flew around the room, stretching out his wings.

"Rew, I can't focus with you circling overhead. Could you settle down, please?" Gabriel asked politely even though she was teetering on the edge of her nerves.

"Sorry," Rew said as he stretched out on the bed on his belly so he could still flutter his wings.

Freecurrent energy swirled around the mother and son coming from every aspect of life around them. With their eyes closed they could see it, but it was not visible to Serek or Terese from where they looked on. It was a complicated task to sort through the myriad of distinctions. Having picked out Stephan's tone before, they knew what to look for, but even so, there was so much to separate out that the task took a long time.

Finally, Gabriel knew where to find Stephan. He was close by. She woke Serek and Terese, who had both fallen asleep on the bed. "I know where he is, Serek. Let's go get him," she said.

Rew threw back on his clothes and they left the motel and walked down the street toward downtown. They passed a law office, a pawn shop and a couple of more small motels before reaching their destination. It was another older motel, its days of glory long ago a faded memory.

Gabriel walked right up to room 34 and knocked on the door. A few minutes later Stephan opened it. The look of shock on his face was followed by one of confusion and finally displeasure.

"What are you doing here?" he asked, without opening the door to let them in. He looked like he had just crawled out of bed and, in fact, had. Stephan had always been well-groomed, meticulous about his looks and his hygiene. Now it appeared that he hadn't showered in days. Stubble of a beard darkened his face. His eyes had blackened shadows under them. The sparkle that had once emanated from his bright blue eyes was gone.

Serek positioned himself in front of Gabriel and in a controlled voice said, "We've come to bring you back home, Stephan. Get your things. Let's go."

"No. I can't. You don't understand," Stephan responded.

"Yes. You can," Serek said simply.

"I can't go, dad. I have to meet a guy. It's important. I owe him money."

"What's this about, Stephan? Tell me," Serek demanded.

Gabriel put her hand on Serek's arm and addressed Stephan, "Can we come inside and discuss this? I don't want to draw undue attention."

Stephan shrugged and stepped aside to let them in. The room was dark. Only one light in the bathroom was on. The bed covers were in disarray. On a small table was the necessary paraphernalia for cooking and injecting heroine, including a small baggy containing a whitish substance. "What is this?" Serek asked, holding his hand out to the trappings.

"That's why I can't go. I need it," Stephan said.

"How can you need it? What is it, Stephan? I don't understand any of this. What are you thinking?" Serek's voice rose as he got angry.

Gabriel stepped forward and took Stephan's hand. "Stephan, I understand . . ." she began.

He pulled away from her touch as if it hurt and said, "No you don't understand."

"Stephan, listen to me. We can figure this out. Come back home with us," Gabriel implored him.

"I can't," he said.

Zeth had been waiting in the background with Terese and Rew. He said from behind Gabriel, "You can take it with you. Let's get back to Risen and then figure out what you're involved in."

"Once I get back to Risen, I cannot get any more of what I need. I cannot go home again. Not now," Stephan was ringing his hands together with anxiety. He was not acting rationally.

Terese asked the obvious question, "Why can you not quit?"

Stephan looked down at his feet and mumbled, "I tried that already. I felt horrible."

"What can we do to help, Stephan?" Terese asked.

"I don't know. Nothing. I never should have let this happen," he said. Stephan's eyes went to the drugs on the little table.

Zeth sat down on the bed before he started talking, "There was a time not too long ago when I was plunged into corruption. I was lost to it, Stephan, with no way out. My greatest goal in life was to feed my compulsion to inflict pain on others. So tortured was my own soul that life was sour, bitter to endure on a daily basis. My spirit was broken. Corruption had claimed me for its own. I could not see that there was any hope. Nothing could have convinced me back then that there was something different for me. But, I have been healed. The weight of the oppression has been lifted from me. I have hope for the future now. Not only that, but I have fallen in love. I never could have expected that I could change nor did I want to, but I am healed. You can overcome this too."

Terese sat down next to Zeth and took his hand. She said, "Let us help you, Stephan. To this despair do not give in."

"You don't understand. It has me. I am trapped by this heroine. Even now it is all I want," Stephan said again.

Serek was starting to pace. Gabriel could see that he was about to lose all patience with his son. She said, "Stephan, why don't you gather your things. We'll get back to Risen and figure this out. Zlato desperately misses you. You cannot abandon your dragon. I already have your mother and uncle doing some research into this. I'm sure there is something we can do to help you through this. We will find a way."

*Zlato.* Stephan flinched upon hearing his dragon's name. They were right he could not abandon Zlato. The thought of that made his stomach feel sick, not as sick as being without the drug, but just *maybe* something could be done to end this. He wanted his life back. "Let me meet the guy I owe money to. Then I'll go with you," Stephan decided finally.

"When is your meeting?" Serek asked.

"He should be here soon. I'll give him the money I owe him, get some more stuff, and then I'll go with you back to Risen," Stephan said.

"You have made the right decision. Do not give up hope," Rew said.

"My sword is gone. I have no money left. What choice do I have," Stephan replied bitterly.

"What happened to your sword?" Serek asked.

"I sold it. I needed the money," he said. "The cell phone Jesse gave me is gone too."

"For more of this?" Serek pointed at the drugs. "That sword was your great-grandfather's. It was priceless." He was working hard to once again keep his anger in check, but much of it showed through the edges of his finely crafted mask.

"I'm sorry, dad. I couldn't help it," Stephan said defensively.

"You couldn't help it?" Serek roared.

"Maybe we can get it back," Gabriel offered. "I will return for it. I have plenty of cash at Ornate. Where did you sell it, Stephan?"

"At the pawn shop just down the street."

"Okay," Gabriel said to calm Serek, "I'll see what I can do. I'll be right back. I'm going to go talk to them, see how much they want for it." She left and the rest of them waited for the dealer to come and meet with Stephan.

# Chapter 7

## DISTRESSED

Three dragons, a golden eagle and a majestic bald eagle left from Castle Gentlebreeze and flew north. It was just prior to dawn and the sky was deep blue in color. The passengers of the dragons were Theo and Kristina on B.F.; Kaltog on Grand Oro; and Kali, who shared her dragon, Sweet Vang, with her dog Tica. The early morning was cool and promised of the rain to come.

It took them a few hours before they came to Anna's cabin in the woods. They landed for a short rest and to have lunch with their old friend. Link and Berry were at Anna's place visiting. The bandergs hadn't seemed to have aged much over the years. Link's beard was a little bit longer and had tinges of gray, but other than that they all seemed unchanged. Anna, as always, provided a lovely spread for lunch, which included spiced apples, soft cheeses, fresh blueberries, roasted chicken, crisp salad, and angel cake with whipped cream for dessert. Cold ale and hot tog were available also. Bandcrgs were notorious for their good hospitality and always set a good table.

Kali, who lived with Anna, spent some time catching up on some of her chores while the others relaxed and conversed. "How is the construction going on the north gate?" Theo asked Link.

"They are by all accounts finished. There is an official opening ceremony next week. My kitchen is in full prep mode now. I have a list a mile long," Link said as he pulled on his beard in his stress.

"Link, stop it," Berry said. "You have got to remember that your staff is very capable of handling things on their own without your constant input. Supervise. Do not micro-manage. You must reduce your stress."

"If only it were that easy," Link fussed.

"You know, Link, without delegating to my people, I would never get anything done. You have to rely on those staff members who have earned your trust in the past and let them do their job," Theo commented.

"Yes, I know, and I do, it's just . . . it's just . . .well, it's just that . . ."

Berry finished Link's sentence, but not with what *he* was going to say, "it's just that you can't help yourself from controlling everything all of the time."

Link made a noise that sounded something like a leaky tire, "Pkstchhoo."

Berry gave him a look only a wife can get away with. She loved her husband dearly, but he could certainly be a handful.

Kali returned and roused her companions from their leisure, "I'm all done. Tica is settled into the kennel. She'll be staying with Anna this time. Let's get going before the rain starts."

"Certainly, we are ready. Done the dishes are. Thanks to you, Anna, once again," Jessabelle said as she gave their hostess a warm hug.

"You are always welcome around my table, Jessabelle. Thank you for stopping by. I hope everything turns out well for Stephan. Let me know if there is anything I can do. Good luck with your quest," Anna said as she hugged them all goodbye.

After they all thanked and hugged and kissed and said their goodbyes, those who were riding dragon-back mounted, Jessabelle and Jacoby transformed their kendrite human forms into eagles, one bald, one gold.

The day warmed as late afternoon approached with the humidity building considerably. Thunder could be heard in the distance, a low rumble beyond the visible horizon. Down below they could see the beginnings of the forest on one side of the path and the swamp on the other. Kristina shivered as she thought of the swamp thing that had almost drowned her and Serek so many years ago. The return to New Chance now without Serek made her ache for her husband. He was where he needed to be though and she desperately hoped they would find Stephan. She still thought that she should be going with them, but she was stuck running this fool's errand for Gabriel. Okay, maybe *that* wasn't fair. They sought a solution to Stephan's drug addiction, whatever that was. But, she wanted to find her son, not be going to New Chance. Another low rumble of thunder made her feel an ominous foreboding and she shivered.

Kaltog was also remembering their trek years ago. He was glad to be high in the sky on Grand Oro and not down on path that led between the forest and the swamp. The last time they were there, the crazy monkey-bat things attacked them after tormenting them half the night and Serek and Kristina almost got eaten by the glowing swamp creature. It was not a pleasant place to be, especially at night. It was probably not too appealing during the day either. Gabriel had sent them to New Chance to find information, but he had little confidence that they would find anything except for dust that is. The place was a disintegrated tomb. But, he would do what he could for Serek, Kristina and Stephan; whatever it took to help them out in their time of need.

Theo, unlike his companions, was actually enjoying this ride on B.F. It had been too long since he had been out on an adventure. The job of being king and maintaining the kingdom was nothing but responsibility after responsibility. Sure, he was worried about his son and nephew, but it was better to worry about them on dragon-back with the wind in his face than sitting restlessly in a stuffy conference room.

Suddenly Jacoby plummeted. Jessabelle followed close behind him, trilling her eagle cry all the way down to the ground below. They landed hard on the path, first Jacoby and then Jessabelle right behind him.

Jacoby instantly transformed into his human form and lay curled up on the ground, panting harshly. His sister became human also and was quickly by his side. "Jacoby, what's happened? What is wrong?" she asked.

"I can't . . ." he sucked in air. "I can't fly."

"What? I don't understand," Jessabelle had her hand on his back as he leaned over and gasped for breath.

The dragons landed on the path close by. Around them, the air was thick and heavy as thunder broke like a crescendo of percussion, starting with the booming, rolling, crash of a large kettle drum. Lightning sliced through the air as the rain started to fall. Theo lowered the ladder and descended quickly to join his wife at his brother-in-law's side. "Is there something wrong?" he asked.

"Know I don't," Jessabelle replied in desperation.

Jacoby was starting to wheeze as he started to hyperventilate. Kali took out a leather bag from her pack and emptied it of its contents. She put the open end over Jacoby's mouth and held it there until his breathing became slower and manageable. "Jacoby, breathe. Calm down. That's it. Are you okay?" she asked.

"I," he gulped, "My shape, I couldn't maintain. Before changing back, it was everything I could do to make it back to the ground."

"Why?" Theo asked. Thunder started low and grew in strength and intensity before lightning ripped the sky around them. The darkness of the storm brought on a false night. Rain started to come down in earnest. "Can you change back now?" he asked as he looked around anxiously. Kaltog and Kristina had joined them. They also looked around them uncomfortably. There was screeching coming from the forest, loud and disturbing. From the swamp side of them, the water suddenly took on a sick green glow.

"Jacoby!" Jessabelle became animated. "Jacoby, change back! Let's get out of here, now!"

"Squawreeeeech!" A crashing, snapping, ripping sound came toward them through the forest at a furious pace. The trees rattled down to their roots as limbs were broken by the onslaught.

"Jessabelle, go! Get out of here! Everybody mount up. Jacoby, you ride with Kali," Theo ordered. "Let's go!"

Before any one of them could act, out of the forest came a flock of snarling, screaming creatures, hundreds of them. They were in a frenzy and attacked with brutal savagery. The beast was about the size of a large bird of prey, but had wings like a bat with long talons extending out from the point. Their bodies were clad in dark brown fur and had faces that were monkey-like with vicious fangs protruding from their pulled back lips. Little horns protruded from just behind their ears. Despite their wings, the creatures used their hands to traverse through the canopy of the trees.

The attack was not only coming from the forest side of them, but also from the swamp. Long tentacles extended toward them, searching for somebody to grab hold of. There was a gurgling, plunging sound coming from the swamp as a multitude of creatures started at a slow crawl toward them. Inch by inch they came. The skin on their bulbous bodies was luminescent and competed with the electric storm the raged around them.

"Good Creator! Let's get out of here!" Kristina yelled over the noise as she pulled her dagger free of its sheath. She brought it up in a flash and defended herself against one of the probing tentacles, slicing it off with a spray of black goo. Another quickly followed and she severed that one as well. With graceful movements she hacked tentacles and stabbed creatures as she defended herself.

Theo's sword was already in action, slicing and stabbing at the hoard that surrounded them. His weapon was soon dripping with blood from the persistent attack. He fought in a circle around Jacoby, protecting him from the onslaught. Speed and skill dominated Theo's motions into a well-choreographed dance of survival. His movements were fluid and beautiful, but more importantly, effective as his sword damaged any enemy unlucky enough to come within reach. Mud mixed with blood at his feet, covering his boots and splashing everywhere. "Jacoby! Get up!" he shouted.

Jessabelle also shouted at her brother, "Get up, Jacoby. Transform!" She had her knife in her hand and was using it to slice at the attackers at a rate faster than the human eye could see. Her actions were like a whirlwind as she spun and lunged, cutting with precision to do the most damage with the least amount of effort.

Kaltog yelled through the pouring rain, "We've got to move! Theo!"

The king tried to find Kaltog through the chaos, but was unable to spot him. He swung his sword as four creatures attacked from above. The head of one went flying off its body and a moment

later his blade pierced another's heart. Without pausing Theo
wrenched the sword loose and brought it down diagonally across
another attacker.

A single winged creature somehow managed to get through
Theo's defense and rake Jacoby superficially on the arm with its
talons. The frightened kendrite took out his knife and plunged
it at the creature while Jessabelle came to his aid, changing instantly into a wolf and attacking with ferocity of her own until the
monster was dead. She transformed back into a human and yelled,
"Kali, on Sweet Vang get Jacoby out of here!"

The bow in Kali's hand was projecting arrows effectively into
their attackers with awe-inspiring speed. She whipped dripping
hair out of her eyes and glanced in Jessabelle's direction only briefly
while she continued firing. "Kaltog get Jacoby," she urgently passed
on the task.

With his battle-axe Kaltog thrashed left and right flying beasts
and pursuing tentacles alike. Blood was flying everywhere in front
of the giant torg in sprays of red and black as he made his way over
to them through the ever increasing quagmire. He grabbed Jacoby
and threw him over his shoulder with an audible grunt. Jacoby
protested this treatment with a volley of loud complaints, which
were completely ignored by all.

The saturated air was filled with smoke from B.F. firing an in-
ferno at their attackers while at the same time keeping the fire
safely away from his companions. Although it was pouring rain,
the dragon fire was hot enough to burn with lethal results. The
baby dragons, although full grown, had not yet achieved the maturity necessary to make dragon fire. They watched their older peer
in wonder as they snapped at anything hostile that was foolish
enough to come within easy reach of their very sharp fangs. The
acid stench of burnt hair weaved through the smoke and blood
and rain sickeningly.

A tentacle wrapped itself around Kristina's ankle and began to pull her off her feet. She sliced at it aggressively with her dagger. "Not this time, slime-bag!" she yelled as she managed to loosen its grip enough to get free. She fell face first in the mud as the opposing force desisted, but quickly got back to her feet, wiped her eyes, and continued to fight.

Kaltog deposited Jacoby on Grand Oro's back and swiftly jumped on behind him. "Theo, mount up. Let's go!" he shouted.

"Jessabelle, transform! Get out of here!" Theo yelled at his wife again. Acquiescing this time, she instantly melted into an eagle and took to the air, quickly out-distancing the bat-winged creatures as she disappeared into the heavy down pour.

Theo grabbed his sister's arm and pulled her after him toward B.F. "Kali, get on your dragon. Let's go!"

Kali mounted easily as she continued to fire a volley of arrows at their attackers who were closing in fast. "Go, Theo, go!" she screamed over the tumult.

Sweet Vang reached down and grabbed one of the beasts in her massive jaws and crunched twice before swallowing it while it still thrashed. Three more she devoured before Kali had her launch into the sky and hover while they lay cover fire for Theo and Kristina.

Theo helped Kristina up before him while he fought off the beasts behind him. His sword was slick in his hand, but he maintained a firm grip in spite of it. As he reached up to mount B.F. behind his sister, he felt a hot pain in the back of his leg as one of the creatures tore through his flesh with its talons. As he screamed out in pain, B.F. bit off the offender's head and then quickly finished off the rest of it whole. The dragon flung himself skyward as Theo found his seat behind Kristina.

"*Thanks, B.F.,*" Theo said as he tore off a sleeve and wrapped it around his gushing leg.

The dragon responded, "*You are welcome. The taste of that thing was hideous. I hope you appreciate the sacrifices I make for you.*"

"Always, B.F. *That encounter left a bad taste in my mouth as well,*" he said as he sheathed his bloodied sword and wrapped his cloak more tightly around his body, trying to stave off the rain and the chill that was settling into his core. The back of his leg throbbed with his heartbeat. He was afraid the damage was profound. They were flying east along with the storm, so the rain and thunder and lightning continued to rage around them. "*B.F., we need to find a place to land and let this storm pass. Tell the other dragons as soon as you find a place to shelter,*" he said.

"*We need to get by this forest first, Theo.*" B.F. said. "*I am sure you do not wish to land again in that terrifying place. Hang in there for now.*"

"Do you see Jessabelle?" Theo asked with concern.

"*There is no sign of her, but even my vision is limited because of the lightning and the rain,*" he answered.

"Check with the other dragons. Have they seen her?" he persisted.

"*They say 'no'.*"

"How long before we can land and regroup?" he asked, feeling very anxious, not only about his wife, but about the weather, which seemed to be worsening.

"*Soon, Theo. The last of the forest is beneath us. I will look for a place as soon as it is behind us.*" It wasn't too long before B.F. started his descent. They were on the ground quicker than Theo anticipated and he had to steady himself by grabbing Kristina's waist for support as B.F. touched the ground. The blood loss from his injury was causing a slight light-headedness in the seasoned warrior and he fought against fainting and sudden nausea.

The other two dragons landed within sight shortly thereafter. Heavy winds swirled around them. Rain and hail pelted them before the tempest moved to the east. Lightning brightened the night sky moving further from them and closer to the far horizon long after the rain and the wind ceased. They watched and waited anxiously, but there was no sign of Jessabelle.

# Chapter 8

## HIGH SCHOOL TYRANNICAL

Calmly, but with determined purpose, Candaz walked to the back side of the school. It was late into the night and there was nobody around. He drew a symbol on the bricks, which glowed brightly and allowed him to walk straight through the solid wall. The hallway he entered was dark with the exception of the tiny lights glowing on items like the smoke detector and the security cameras. With a simple wave of his hand, he threw enough freecurrent energy at the cameras to disable the system. He had learned quite a bit about this culture in the few days he'd been here. They were, if nothing else, focused on always being able to know what was occurring at any time at any place. The cameras that were everywhere enabled them to see everything. It was a minor inconvenience to him at the most. He could easily disable them with a wave of his hand, which he did to every piece of equipment he came across as he stalked the hall.

Candaz had to find a good place to wait for the students to arrive without being seen. But first he wanted to find the chemistry lab. There were a couple of items on his list that he should be able to acquire in a basic high school laboratory, he assumed. After checking three standard classrooms, he found what promised to be the chemistry lab. He drew a symbol on the door and walked through it. Breaking into a locked cabinet in the front of the classroom was as easy as breathing. Inside he found more than he expected of what he needed. The basic components of the elixir were all available here. Spotting a backpack that had been left behind by a forgetful student; he crossed the classroom, quickly emptied the contents, and proceeded to fill it with the items he had carefully selected.

Leaving the chemistry lab behind, he found a room labeled "maintenance" and went inside. He used the time to get a little sleep, waking only when the first students came down the hallway. The chaos common with the start of a new school day bombarded his ears and echoed in his head as the students came and went. A tidbit of conversation caught his interest. He listened intently as one boy said to another, "The soccer team just got back. The bus broke down and they were in the desert all night without air."

Another boy commented, "Whew! No air in the desert with a bunch of sweaty jocks. That's rough."

"Yeah. The coach said they have to go to class today, too. They've hit the showers and should be in first hour. You'd think they would let them skip today."

"Whatever. They can sleep in class."

"Yeah, right. Mrs. Thomas catches Jacob snoozin' in class and she'll have his ass in detention again."

"Yeah, Gates is trying to learn Spanish subliminally in his sleep. What a douche."

The boys moved on still talking about the soccer team's misadventure. Candaz exulted in his luck. Jacob Gates is the boy he was looking for. Now he knew where to find him. He waited for everything to grow quiet and then slipped out of his hiding place and into the abandoned hall.

## ¿Hablas español?

Jacob listened to Mrs. Thomas without really hearing her. She was going over this week's vocabulary as she always did first thing in the morning before getting into her lesson. He repeated the words after her, as did the rest of the class, but he did so mechanically. His mind was elsewhere.

It had been a long hot night waiting for another bus to come and get them. He had slept a little, but it was an uncomfortable sporadic sleep at best. Concern about his dad was overwhelming after he was unable to reach him at home, or work, or on his cell phone. As soon as the bus reached the school that morning, he was going to head home whether the coach allowed it or not. Disobeying the coach this early in his high school career might get him kicked off the team, even if he was the "star freshman," but he knew his dad would be over the top with worry. The control he was wielding over Jacob lately was stifling. His over-bearing manner was somewhat understandable, but annoying none-the-less. As he was heading out the front door, he spotted his dad out of the corner of his eye pacing in the office. The relief on Bill's face was dramatic as Jacob let his father greet him in an embrace. Bill agreed to let him go back to class in accordance with the coach's wishes and to pick him up after school.

Jacob shook off his fatigue with difficulty as he willed his heavy eyelids not to close. He was losing the battle with his sleep deprived body and it didn't help that Mrs. Thomas's voice had a soothing cadence to it, like she was singing him a Spanish lullaby. His body shook as his head came back up after his chin almost touched his chest. He readjusted in his seat and tried to focus, but in a moment he had to shift again and refocus. After what seemed like a lifetime, the bell rang to end his torture. He stuffed his homework into his binder and quickly left the classroom.

Normally, it would only take a minute to grab the book for his next hour at his locker between classes, but he wanted to drink down the Dew he had stashed in his backpack, so he lingered there. They weren't supposed to snack between classes. He had only taken two swallows when he felt a heavy hand come down on his shoulder. *Busted.*

"Jacob Gates?" a voice that sounded like black velvet asked.

A shiver ran down Jacob's spine and he resisted the urge to shake the oppressive hand off his shoulder. He turned and found a tall dark man close behind him staring back with the darkest eyes he had ever seen. "Who wants to know?" Jacob demanded as he shouldered his backpack.

A slight grin touched the older man's face, but the look in his eyes was deadly. "Are you Jesse's brother?" he asked.

Jacob pulled back away from the man, slamming his locker shut behind him in the process. "Jesse's my sister," he said. "What do you want?"

The man's hand went to the gold medallion that hung around his neck and with a subtle stroke of his fingers brought Jacob's attention to it.

"Hey, that's Jesse's," Jacob said. "Where did you get that?"

"I know where she is," Candaz said quietly. "I can take you to her."

Jacob hesitated, not knowing immediately if this man was to be trusted. He casually checked his pocket for his cell phone and found it safely in place. If the man knew where Jesse was, he was going to have to take a chance. "You will take me to her?" he asked.

"Yes. Come with me and you will see your sister," Candaz confirmed. He again put his hand on Jacob's shoulder and after one more moment of hesitation, Jacob followed the man down the hallway toward the back of the school.

## Security?

From far above two large eagles dove at a break-neck speed, reaching over one hundred miles per hour as they descended to land inconspicuously behind a neatly trimmed hedge that landscaped the school entrance. Moments later two men, one young, one old strode boldly in through the front doors. Immediately an alarm sounded in the office alerting the staff that the metal detector detected something larger than just some loose change. The second set of doors locked automatically and Jim and Nicholas were forced to go through the office.

They were met by the vice-principal, dressed neatly in a suit and tie. "Can I help you?" he asked as he tried to evaluate what threat the two men posed.

Jim answered calmly, "We need to speak with Jacob Gates immediately."

"And you are . . .?" he asked.

"I'm his uncle. His father is hurt. We need to see him," Jim said.

The vice-principal looked from Jim to Nicholas with a stern expression. It was clear he was trying to determine the best way to deal with these dangerous-looking men. He answered, "That's interesting considering Mr. Gates was just here less than an hour ago." He turned to the secretary and instructed her to call the police.

Jim shot Nicholas a look of resignation and said, "This is getting us nowhere."

"I agree," Nick said and he drew his sword leaving a ringing vibration in the air. The tip was glowing with bright blue fire. He raised the weapon to the vice-principal's throat and said, "Unlock the door."

"No. I won't. You'll have to kill me first," the shaking man said bravely.

Jim had been watching the secretary and noticed her finger twitch away from a button on her desk. He leaned over and pressed it and the door latch clicked. He smiled at her reassuringly, "Don't worry. We just need Jacob. We're here to help him, not hurt him."

The two men were quickly through the door and down the hallway. Nicholas followed where the sword led him, the blue electricity inching up the length of the blade as they strode toward the back of the school with determination.

Any stray student they encountered gave them wide berth. Although the younger man with the messy blonde hair was exceedingly handsome, he was foreign and exotic with bright gold eyes and had a wild predator look about him. Grasped firmly in his hand was a very real looking sword. Obviously, he was not someone to be trifled with. The older man was less dangerous looking, but his eyes sparkled with the light of endless wisdom that demanded instant respect.

They came to the end of the corridor and turned right. Midway down the empty hall Candaz was drawing a symbol on the back wall while Jacob stood by and watched in fascination. The old sorcerer looked in their direction and turned to greet them with his usual arrogance, "Little Nicky Wingmaster, crown prince of Brightening, an honor, I'm sure. Who is your friend?" Candaz's eyes rested on Jim.

"Jim McCaw," Jim said, lifting his hat slightly. "Let Jacob come with us now."

"No," Candaz replied amiably. "Jacob needs to stay with me for now. He and I have plans, don't we boy?"

Jacob didn't look scared, or intimidated, or oppressed as he let his eyes fall first on Jim and then on Nicholas and last on Candaz. He answered with a calm, controlled voice, "He's going to take me to my sister."

Nicholas was slowly approaching them with his sword burning brightly. Although his form was relaxed, he remained poised to strike. "No, Jacob. He's lying to you. Jesse is with us," he said.

Candaz was playing with the medallion that hung around his neck, Jesse's medallion. He did not say a word, but watched Jacob closely. Although Jacob seemed to hesitate to consider Nicholas's words, the dancing medallion caught his eye and seemed to hold him hypnotized as he watched it flip over and over in between Candaz's fingers.

Jim spoke quietly to the boy, "Jacob, Jesse is my friend. She sent us to keep you safe. This man is lying to you. Look within yourself. You will find the truth is what I speak."

Jacob looked back at Jim, "Why isn't she here then? If she cares so much about me, why isn't she here?"

"She's on her way," Nicholas said. "I promise you, Jacob. She'll be here soon."

"Enough of this," Candaz spat. "I ask you, who has the weapon drawn? Have I threatened you at all, Jacob? No. I only promised that you would see your sister again. Now, these men here approach us with threats of violence, making promises that mean nothing. You are a bright boy, Jacob. Make your own choice who to believe."

Jacob seemed undecided and didn't move as Candaz finished drawing the symbol on the wall.

Nicholas made his move. With a flash of refracted light the sword arched up and down, the cutting edge coming within a hair of Candaz's hand as he reacted in defense by putting his palm up to deflect the blade. Instead of the sharp edge slicing through the soft flesh of the sorcerer's hand, the metal rang out loud and sparked as if hitting a solid surface. With the blade deflected, Candaz grabbed Jacob by the arm and propelled him through the magically trans-formed wall. They were gone in an instant.

Nicholas and Jim followed immediately after them, but ran into a sturdy wall. "Unbelievable," Nick said. "Let's go. Maybe we can still catch up to them." He turned and started back down the hallway to the closest exit. Shouts coming from the direction of the office did not stop them. They ran out the side door, split up and began a perimeter search of the school with Nicholas going one way and Jim the other.

They both stopped when they rounded the corner on opposite ends of the school and spotted the three squad cars parked out front. There was no sign of Candaz or Jacob.

Nick and Jim transformed into their eagle forms and met high above the school. They circled around and around, but could not get a fix on Candaz. Nick indicated to Jim to follow him and they went west in search of Jesse. He dreaded telling her that he had lost her brother and once again let that slippery sorcerer escape. "*What could I have done differently?*" he asked himself. Failing Jesse did not sit well with him.

The two eagles began to dive the moment they spotted the old pick-up truck rolling east down the highway following closely a woman on a Harley. Pulling over when Jesse spotted them, she and Shareen waited while the eagles changed back into men.

# Reunion

Jesse was immediately in Nicholas's arms. She looked up into his face, noting his grim expression with concern. "What happened, Nick?" she asked.

"We found them at the school, but we lost them again. Candaz got away with Jacob. I'm sorry, Jesse. I failed you," he said.

"We'll catch up with them. Check your sword. See if you can get a direction," Jesse suggested as she stepped back from him.

He unsheathed the weapon and pointed it in various directions. The freecurrent energy indicated a faint reading to the north. "That way," Nick pointed north.

"North then," Shareen said.

"Okay, but I'm going to go pick up my dad first. I'll meet you down the road in a bit. You still have your cell phone, Nick?" she asked.

"Sure," he answered as he patted his pocket.

"Let's make sure we all have each other's numbers," Shareen said as she took out her own cell phone. They all exchanged phone numbers quickly.

"I'm going to head north on 169. Maybe I can cut him off. Nicky, you and Jim head north along the interstate and see if you can spot him from above. Update me if you get a location on him. Jesse, go get your dad and follow us. I have a suspicion Candaz is heading back to the cave," she said. "We have got to stop him." Shareen put on her helmet, straddled her bike and was gone in a cloud of dust.

"Don't worry, Jesse. We'll find him," Jim said as he scratched Felcore's head. Tempest was at his feet and he bent down and picked her up, giving her a good scratching as well.

Nicholas sheathed his sword and wrapped his arms around Jesse once again. They clung to each other for a moment before she asked, "Is Jacob okay? He wasn't hurt, was he?"

"No, he looked healthy and strong, but I think maybe under some type of enchantment. He believed that Candaz would take him to you. We couldn't convince him that we were the good guys," Nicholas said.

Jesse laughed and gazed into Nick's eyes. She brushed the stubble on his unshaven face with her fingers and said, "You do have a sinister look about you, Nick."

"Maybe I am a wolf in sheep's clothing," he said, smiling his charming crooked grin that Jesse couldn't resist.

"Oh, you are a wolf all right," she said. Jesse kissed him, letting her passion for him take control before pulling away from the intensity of the emotions the kiss invoked. Feeling slightly dizzy, she was glad Nick's arms were holding her up right. "Um. We'd better get going. I'll see you later."

Nick regretfully let her go. "Be careful, Jess. Jim, you ready to go?"

Jim reacted by setting down Tempest. He answered, "Ready when you are."

Jesse watched as the men transformed back into eagle form and launched smoothly into the sky. They were quickly gone. Getting back into the truck with her two dogs, Jesse headed to Socorro to find her dad.

Bill Gates worked in a small office complex on the west side of town near the campus. He had been there for many years, and Jesse had been there more times than she could count throughout her life. She swung open the glass door and walked through the threshold, followed by her two dogs and immediately was greeted by her dad's secretary, Rosie.

"Jesse, oh my goodness!" Rosie exclaimed as she got up from behind her desk and gave her a big hug. "Your dad is going to be so happy to see you."

Jesse smiled and replied in a low voice, "I'll just let myself in."

She crossed the room and placed her hand on the door knob that led to her dad's office. Taking a deep breath, she opened it and walked in. Bill looked up from his desk and the phone that was in his hand fell to the desktop with a clatter. "Jesse? Oh, my God! Jesse!" He pushed his chair back and enveloped her in a bear-like hug before she could say anything. "Thank God. Jesse, you're here." He wiped away tears as he held her at arms-length and looked his daughter over. "Look at you. You've changed."

"Dad, I'm sorry I put you through this," she said as she wiped her own tears away.

"You have no idea how worried I have been. Where were you?" he asked, working to keep his voice under control.

"You wouldn't believe me if I told you. Dad, I need you to trust me," she said.

Rosie poked her head in the office and said, "Sorry to interrupt, Bill, but Jacob's school is on the line."

"Thanks," he said as he turned and retrieved the phone off his desk. Jesse waited while she listened to one side of the conversation. She could imagine what the phone call was about. "Yep," Bill said. "Two men, you say? Jacob's not in class? Mmm. How could this have happened? Mhmm. Did you try his cell phone? Okay. No, I don't think that's necessary yet. I'll let you know if he calls. Thanks." He hung up the phone and held Jesse captive in his gaze.

"Dad, that's why I've come, I know what has happened to Jacob. He's been taken by a very bad man. We have been following him since we came back to Earth. I want you to come with me now and we'll go get him together, but we must go now," she said.

The expression on Bill's face was one of confusion with anger at the edges. "What is going on, Jesse? Tell me now," he demanded.

"It's complicated . . . and unbelievable. There's a gate that goes to different worlds. I've been to a place called Risen. The man who has Jacob is a sorcerer from there. He is an old enemy of Grandmother Gabriel. She lives there now. I've met her," Jesse said. "Dad, this man is very dangerous. We can talk about this later. We should go now."

"You are right about one thing, Jesse. It is unbelievable. This is crazy! Are you doing drugs?" he asked as he came toward her, took her hands and looked deeply into her eyes.

"No, dad." She thought for a moment, walked over and shut the door. "Stand back. I'll show you."

"*Tempest, I'm going to attempt to show my dad your true self. Stay calm. I'm not sure I can do this,*" Jesse said in Tempest's head.

"*Surely this is the lowest of the low. First you turn me into a morsel of a mutt and now you are using me as a sideshow,*" Tempest groaned mentally.

"*I'm sorry, sweetie. I promise I will make it up to you someday.*" Jesse put her hands on Tempest's head and used all of her mental ability to focus the freecurrent energy to project the true image of Tempest.

The fur on Tempest's small dog body crackled with blue and green electricity and the room began to fill with all of her girth. The image of Tempest as a dragon became more distinct. Her shiny iridescent scales shimmered in the light. Ridges on her back and her mighty wings touched the ceiling as her tail wrapped around Bill's desk. Her image filled the room although it was not quite to full dragon size yet. Jesse removed her hands and the image disappeared. She picked up the little white dog and appraised her father's startled expression. "*Thanks Tempest.*"

"*I miss being a dragon. Can we go home now?*" she asked.

"*I miss you being a dragon, too. We'll go home soon,*" Jesse replied. "This is Tempest, Dad. She is a dragon from Risen and she is my friend."

Bill came forward and touched Tempest on the head. She growled low in her throat and he took his hand quickly away. Felcore pushed his face against Bill's leg, letting him know that he was available for petting. He reached down and patted the golden retriever's head. "This is impossible," he said to Jesse.

"Trust me, dad. I will take you there, you and Jacob. But, first we need to rescue him from Candaz. Do you want to go with me?" she asked. "You probably will not be returning here any time soon." She waited for his response.

"But, I have a meeting scheduled at four to go over a proposal with an important client. I have to finish putting together the Hansen project and get it to the printers before tomorrow morning." He looked around at his life's work and sighed. Picking up the picture frame on his desk, he removed the portrait of his late wife, Marguerite, and put it in his pocket and said, "Okay, Jesse, let's go. You and Jacob are my priority. Everything else will just have to wait."

She smiled, went to him and kissed him on the cheek. At that moment her cell phone rang. "Nick?"

"Jesse, we've spotted the car. It's heading into Albuquerque. I'll update you soon. Is everything okay?" Nicholas asked.

"Yes. Dad's coming with me. We're heading out now," she said.

"Okay. I love you. See you soon," Nick said.

"Love you too, Nick," Jesse replied, not unconscious of her dad's rapt attention to her conversation. She hit "*end*" and stuffed the cell phone into her pocket. "Let's go," she said to her dad.

"Who's Nick?" he asked, raising an eyebrow.

"I'll explain on the road," she said. "Let's go, dad."

As they were leaving he gave Rosie a warm hug and explained quickly that he wouldn't be coming back any time soon and assured her that she could run the office without him. He gave her a couple of last minutes instructions, wished her luck and left with her gaping after him.

They climbed into Jim's old pick-up truck with Jesse driving and headed north. "Now tell me about Nick," Bill commanded.

# Chapter 9
## THE BEST LAID PLANS

By the time Gabriel returned to the motel room, the meeting with Stephan's dealer had taken place. Serek looked ready to disembowel somebody as he paced the floor of the small room. On the other hand, Stephan looked placated. The pawn shop wanted two thousand dollars for Stephan's sword. She would have to come back for it some other time. She asked them to hold it for her, but whether or not they would was questionable. The cell phone that Stephan had pawned *was* something she retrieved. They hadn't wiped the memory yet so Jesse's number was still on it. Although Gabriel was unfamiliar with cell phones, it wasn't too difficult to figure out how to make a call. When Jesse answered, it *did* surprise her however. "Stephan? Thank God. I've been so worried," Jesse's voice said into her ear.

"No, Jesse. It's Gabriel," she said.

"Grandmother! What are you doing here?" Jesse asked with excitement.

"We came to find Stephan. He's going to go back to Risen with us. Do you need help with anything?" she asked.

Jesse replied with hesitation in her voice, "You take care of Stephan. That's one less thing to worry about. Candaz has Jacob and we're after him now. Nicholas and Jim are tracking him in the air and Shareen is cutting him off at the pass, so to speak. Dad and I are bringing up the rear. Shareen thinks that he might be heading back to the gate so you might set up an ambush on the other side in case we miss him over here."

Gabriel nearly dropped the phone. "Did you say Shareen?"

"Oh. Yes I did. She's alive, Grandmother. I'm sorry. I wasn't thinking. Are you okay? I didn't mean to drop a bomb shell on you," Jesse said.

"Wow. That's amazing news. Shareen is alive. I have to let that sink in. And you said Jim is with Nicholas? Jim McCaw?" Gabriel asked.

"Yes, Grandmother. *The* Jim McCaw. He has kendrite ancestry from way back. He can transform. Isn't that something?" Jesse's voice was animated.

"Wow. That is amazing," she said.

"I'm afraid Candaz has our medallion. He stole it from me," Jesse told her.

"That's not good. In his hands that medallion could be a very powerful weapon. I hope he doesn't realize it's potential. You must get it back if you can, Jesse. Be careful. I'll put something in place in the cave on Risen. If he gets through, we'll be waiting. I love you, Jesse. Be careful. I don't want to lose you," Gabriel said.

"I will be careful, Grandmother. Take care of Stephan. I love you, too. Bye," Jesse said.

The call ended and Gabriel put the phone in her pocket. *Shareen is alive and Jim is a kendrite. Wow.*

"Are you all ready to go? Stephan?" Gabriel asked the somber faces that looked back at her.

"Yeah. Let's go," Stephan answered unenthusiastically, looking back only once before slamming the door shut behind him.

The cab ride back was extremely silent. When Gabriel paid the driver to leave them in the middle of the desert, he did so without comment but regarded her with a questioning look. "We're going hiking," she told him with a smile. He didn't smile back, but accepted his meager tip and left.

Stephan was beginning to have second thoughts and was feeling extremely anxious. As they walked he started talking to himself, "I don't know if I can do this. I should go back."

Rew encouraged him, "Hang in there, Stephan. It will all work out. We'll help you through this."

"I'll try," Stephan said through clenched teeth.

The march through the desert took longer than usual because of Stephan's reluctance to go. Serek's long stride kept a brisk pace, but he had to constantly turn around and wait. Gabriel filled them in on what Jesse had told her as they walked.

The sun was beginning to sink low over the mountain. Night would soon be upon them and with it the air would cool and become more comfortable. The cave wasn't too far now. Gabriel remembered the first time she had gone through to Risen over thirty years ago now. Theo had been with her and she had no idea at that time how her life was about to change. She loved her home on Risen like a mother loves her child. It had become an important part of her and her of it. Earth still held a soft place in her heart, but it was different; a fondness of a memory rather than the warming comfort of belonging.

She spotted the entrance to the cave and climbed up to it with the others following close behind. Sweeping aside the brush that camouflaged the opening; she entered the darkness and experienced an uncanny sense of urgency. The conflict that had been brewing inside of Stephan erupted as he faced the inevitable consequences of his decision to leave Earth behind. "I can't go," he said and began to retreat in his panic.

Serek stopped his son with a strong grip on the other man's arm and said, "You are coming back to Risen with us."

"Let me go!" Stephan tried to pull away from his father's grip unsuccessfully. "Let. Me. Go!" he said.

"Stephan, listen to me. You have got to get help with this. I will *not* let you go. You are my son and I love you. I won't let you go. Not now, not ever," Serek was almost shouting and his eyes were filled with tears and terror.

Stephan stopped fighting and looked into his father's eyes with tears filling his own. "I'm afraid," he said. "My whole body rebels against my will."

"You have been trained as a warrior, Stephan. Face your fear. Defy it! Don't let this drug rule you." He released his grip on his son's arm and brought his hand up to the back of Stephan's neck. "You are stronger than this," Serek said.

"I'm not sure that I am, Dad, but I will try. I want to be done with this." He propelled himself to the back of the cave and waited by the lightning gate.

Rew was quickly by his side. He placed his small hand on the rock face and accelerated the rotation of the constellations within the lightning gate until the Condor appeared. With his bright blue eyes, Rew appraised Stephan's tense face and then took him by the hand and led him through to the other side where Risen awaited them.

Terese and Zeth followed closely behind, walking hand in hand. Serek took one glance back at Gabriel and then disappeared through the gate. Gabriel hesitated only a moment longer, thinking of Jesse and suppressing a desire to turn around and go after her granddaughter. Candaz had once again set in motion plans to harm her family. Jacob was in danger. Her old nemesis would stop at nothing to seize power for himself. She wanted to stop him. Her need for revenge was strong. But, she was needed on Risen and would have to leave the pursuit of Candaz in the hands of Jesse and Nicholas. They were so young for such a burden. She wanted to turn around and help them but her instincts led her back to Risen. Without further internal debate, she followed Serek.

Immediately B.F. was addressing her with his booming mental voice, *"Gabriel? Gabriel? Are you there?"*

*"What is it B.F.? We've just returned. Where are you?"* Gabriel asked.

*"We are just outside of New Chance. Jessabelle is missing,"* he said with his tone reflecting the seriousness of their situation.

*"What can I do to help?"* Gabriel asked as she watched Serek strap on his sword and throw his pack over his shoulder. His eyes had a vacant look that meant he was presently in communication with Breezerunner. Turning, he caught the distress on her face and stopped in his tracks.

*"I don't know what to do. We spent all day searching for her. Theo is beside himself with worry,"* B.F. told her.

*"All right, B.F. Tell Theo I'll meet you in New Chance,"* she said. *"I'll talk to Serek and see if he can send out a search party from Castle Xandia. Where was the last place you saw her?"* Gabriel asked.

*"We were on the forest path during a viscous thunderstorm. The rain was drenching. She took off and disappeared into the night. When the storm passed, we could not find her,"* B.F. said.

*"Okay, B.F. Let me make some arrangements. I'll let you know as soon as I can what the plan is,"* she said. Gabriel found Rew and motioned to him with a wiggle of her finger.

He left Stephan's side and was instantly before her asking, "What's wrong Mistress Gabriel?"

"Jessabelle is missing," she said. "She was in her eagle form and flying through a bad storm by the forest path. The rest of the party is almost to New Chance." She didn't need to tell Rew what she needed him to do.

"I'm going to go get some help on Elysia," he said. In a flash he was gone and back again. Accompanying him was a rather plump wisp and a female. He introduced them to Gabriel as Wes and Lodi. "She will be found, Gabriel," Rew assured her. Before the three wisps left, Rew flew over to Stephan and spoke to him for a moment privately.

The wind from their wings brushed Gabriel's face as they left and she called to Skymaster to come and get her.

Obviously the others had done the same because as Gabriel exited the cave there were five dragons putting down just outside. They landed one at a time. The first one on the ground was Stephan's gold Zlato followed closely by Zeth and Terese's dragons, Grace and Gold Stone. All of their green and golden scales sparkled brilliantly as they descended and a strong musky scent blew at the awaiting humans from the wind produced by the dragons' mighty wings. Breezerunner was next with his silver scales glimmering with hints of blue as he alighted calmly before a restless Serek. Being the senior and superior in the dragon pecking order, Skymaster was the last to descend in traditional dragon custom. The mighty dragon mage roared a greeting, letting the dust settle on his pure silver armor without concern.

The humans all greeted their respective dragons warmly and then got down to the business of saddling them and loading gear.

Stephan and Zlato's reunion was sweet to behold. It was the first time Gabriel had seen Stephan act like his old self since travelling to Earth. The man hugged the big dragon's nose and scratched his eye ridges, bringing happy growling noises from Zlato's throat. Stephan smiled happily for a time and laughed out loud as he communicated with Zlato. The sight gave Gabriel a measure of hope and strengthened her determination to help him get his life back.

They arrived at Castle Xandia late in the night. There was a cold wind blowing off the ocean and the waves were hitting the shore in a rushing rhythm, soft and ferocious in an oblique cadence. Lights illuminated the outside of the castle, but the interior was mostly dark. Although Serek and Kristina maintained a reasonably large staff, only a few select personnel actually lived in the castle and most would be asleep. Katia, Stephan's little sister was home, but at this late hour she would be sleeping soundly as well.

Serek was reluctant to let Stephan be on his own, but Gabriel convinced him to let his son go up to his room alone. Nobody really wanted to watch him inject more of that poison into his veins, anyway, so they let him go. Gabriel wanted to discuss things with Serek, Zeth and Terese urgently and make a plan. They settled quietly into the living room and Serek poured them all glasses of nectar from his favorite vintage and chose a comfortable chair to sink into. "Well? What now?" he asked.

Gabriel rubbed her tired eyes before she answered, "I told Theo I would meet them in New Chance, but I'm not sure that I should leave Stephan at this point. What do you think, Serek?"

"I don't know what to expect. Do you any idea what we face?" he asked.

"As far as I know, the withdrawal can be extremely difficult with vomiting, diarrhea, sweats, and muscle spasms. There is a high risk of dehydration. Once Stephan runs out of his supply, his body will revolt and he will suffer. The timing is questionable, but

I believe the harshest symptoms will begin within a couple of days after his last dosage," Gabriel told him as much as she knew.

"Is there anything we can do for him to alleviate his suffering?" Serek asked.

"That's the information we seek in New Chance. I think it best that I join them there. Skymaster can have me back here quickly enough should you need me. I do think that would be best." Gabriel shook her head affirming her own decision.

Terese looked meaningfully at Zeth and then said, "Stay here with Stephan, Zeth and I will and help where we can. Some herbs I can give him I know of that may at least help a little. Zeth?"

"We will do what we can. A doctor should be on call should we need one. How long will it be until this becomes an issue?" Zeth asked as he set his small glass down on the table and stretched out on the couch, laying his head in Terese's lap and yawning.

"I don't really know . . .a week maybe. Less? I don't know how long what he has will last him. I'm afraid I don't have all the answers," Gabriel replied without being definitive.

Serek stood up and refilled his glass, offering the bottle to the others with a silent gesture, which they all declined. "I can't believe this has happened to Stephan. He's always been so sensible."

"Yes, well, I guess addiction can happen to anyone, Serek. Where I come from people even get addicted to alcohol," Gabriel responded tiredly.

Serek looked at the drink in his hand. "Really?"

"Sure. Actually, it's more common than you would think," she said.

"Hmm. Well, I don't see how," he said as he drank down the nectar in one gulp and sat back down. "I think I'll lead the ground search for Jessabelle. We'll cover the area north of the forest. I'll go stir crazy sitting around here waiting for my son to become sick.

Breezerunner can always come fetch me at a moment's notice if I am needed here."

From out of the dark at the base of the stairs came Stephan's voice, "Got my baby sitters all worked out? Dad, sounds like you are getting out before all the fun starts?"

"Stephan, I . . ." Serek began.

The younger man walked into the room and fell into one of the cushy chairs and said bitterly, "No, no. It's all right. This must be difficult for you."

"I'm sorry, Stephan. If you want me to stay, I will. Just say the word," Serek told his son with sincerity.

"I should go with you to look for Aunt Jessabelle," Stephen said.

"Do you think you will be feeling good enough to go?" Serek asked innocently.

"No. Probably not. I hate this," Stephan fumed.

"I do too. We'll get through this, Stephan," Serek said quietly. "I promise."

"Right. Good to know you have my back, Dad," he said.

The sarcasm in Stephan's voice wasn't lost on Gabriel like it was on Serek. She didn't like it. Serek meant well in spite of his innocence and truly loved Stephan, but he had a hard time facing the pain of a loved one. He could easily send out a search party without leading it and stay home to help Stephan face what he needed to face, but the truth was that Serek couldn't face it himself. He didn't want to watch his son suffer so he found an excuse to escape the situation. She hoped this wouldn't drive a wedge between them. Time would tell. She stood up and said, "I'm going to get some sleep before I get going tomorrow morning. Goodnight."

"Goodnight, Gabriel," Terese said.

# New Chance

The dust flew all around them as the dragons landed on the street in front of the library in the ancient city of New Chance. White powder covered them all in a thin layer making them look like bedraggled bread bakers. B.F. sneezed and sent more of the fine soot swirling in the air.

"*Does it ever rain here?*" Theo asked his dusty white dragon.

"*Of course it rains, but it dries out again, and voila 'dust',*" B.F. said.

"*This place needs a good cleaning,*" Theo said.

"*This place needs to be torched,*" B.F. let fire escape his mouth to demonstrate his judgment.

"*Easy there, big boy. Why don't you take the other dragons and go fishing?*" Theo recommended as he dismounted and freed B.F. of his saddle and other equipment.

"*We'll go fishing and then take another sweep north of the forest and see if we can find Jessabelle,*" B.F. suggested sensibly.

"*Let me know if you see any sign of her,*" Theo said. He winced as he tried to use his injured leg. The red blood seeping out of his wound was a sharp contrast to the white powder that coated him.

"*Of course,*" B.F. replied with a compassionate tone to his mental voice. "*Have that leg looked after immediately.*"

"*Sure, B.F. Sometimes you can be very motherly,*" Theo said.

"*I'll take that as a compliment. Happy studying,*" B.F. said.

"*I'd rather be fishing,*" Theo complained.

"*Who wouldn't?*" B.F. replied before launching into the air, creating a whole new whirlwind of dust in his wake. The other two dragons followed their elder close behind. They were soon gone from sight.

"Find her," Theo whispered after his dragon. "Kris!" he yelled.

"I'm right here, brother," she said from behind him with a quiet and calm voice.

"Oh. Sorry. Kris, I need you to get the first aid kit for me," he said.

She quickly retrieved the box from one of the packs and Kali joined her. Theo sat on the steps of the library while the two women cleaned and stitched the laceration on his calf the best that they could and then bound the leg with clean cloth. They worked quickly and efficiently.

Jacoby was clearly uncomfortable with the whole procedure and excused himself to examine the architecture outside of the library far enough away from the trio on the steps that he couldn't accidentally see something he didn't want to.

The patient was quiet, letting his pain show only through his gritted teeth, letting a moan escape his lips just once.

Kali did not look satisfied with the finished task. She wore a frown as she repacked the first aid kit. Theo was quick to ask, "What is it? What's wrong?"

"I'm concerned about infection. The wound is quite deep and caused by one of those creature's claws. Wait," she said. "I have something in my bag," Kali started rummaging through her pack and withdrew a small pouch. "It's called yarrow and it will help with the bleeding and swelling. We can make it into a tea. I also have some garlic that we can mince up and you can swallow that down to reduce the chances of infection." She wasted no time getting to work preparing the yarrow and garlic for Theo's treatment. Kaltog built a small fire to make tea and prepared a small meal for them all while Kali administered the medicine.

"Eat something, Theo," Kaltog insisted. "You have to keep your body strong so your wound will heal."

"I'm not hungry," he growled.

"That's not the point, Theo. Eat," Kristina said as she put a cup in his hand and pushed an apple into the other.

He shut up and forced down the food they gave him. His thoughts were on Jessabelle. Although his leg was screaming with pain, the torture of having his wife missing was paramount. "Kaltog, do you think we could leave Kris, Kali and Jacoby here to do research while we go back and look for Jessabelle?" he asked.

The large torg looked at Theo for a long time before providing the king with an answer, "The wisps are searching right now as we speak. They have the best chance of finding her. Consider also the possibility that she is on her way here right now. She knows that we were heading to New Chance. Unless she is injured, I think she would head straight to the planned destination. My opinion is that we should wait for her here."

Theo's head sunk to his chest and he rubbed his forehead with his hand. "You are right, my friend. I can't stand it though. Where could she be? What if she *is* injured?" he asked as he stood up and started to pace, stopping with the first step on his injured leg. He quickly sat back down. "Oh Jessabelle, my Jessabelle, where are you?"

"Theo," Kristina said, "we're going to head into the library and see what we can find. Why don't you stay here and rest for a while."

"No. No," he said. "I'm coming with you. If I can't go after Jessabelle, I might as well do what we came here to do." He stood back up and wrapped an arm around Kris's shoulders for support. Together they climbed the steps and joined the rest of their party at the entrance. The large double wooden doors swung open easily.

The massive space within the structure was dark and forbidding. Kali brought out a lantern and lit it. As their eyes adjusted, they walked slowly through the dust covered foyer. A set of footsteps from over thirty years ago were visible crossing the room. Those foot prints belonged to Kaltog, Serek, Kristina, Link and Jessabelle. Rew had been there as well, but there were no prints to record his passing. The Table of Alliance was one floor up from where they presently were. Theo was curious to see it, but he didn't feel motivated enough to make the climb with his injured leg.

Bookshelves lined the main part of the library. Most of the former occupants had long ago turned to dust. Sporadically in the midst of the decaying text would be a single book left intact, standing stoically like a lonely soldier left to defend its territory unaided.

Without hesitating, Kaltog grabbed every remaining book he could find and deposited them on a nearby table. Each of them followed suit and after they had made a pass of the entire library, they met back at the table and surveyed their plunder. Eleven out of 'how many thousands' remained viable. Three were immediately eliminated because they were children's books. Two of the books were about architecture, which they could also eliminate. One book was a cookbook, which was interesting to Kali, but not what they were looking for. Jacoby picked up a large book that had a thick binding, but when he opened it the pages crumbled to nothing in his hands despite his careful touch.

There was another large book that when opened revealed a register of ships built, what they carried, who they carried and when they departed. Even though it was a large book, there were only a handful of entries. After each record the word "departed" was written. Seven ships had gone, none had returned. Ninety percent of the pages were blank.

Of the three books that remained, one had a complete history of the first settlers of New Chance. Kristina established herself into a comfortable position and began to read. The second of the three books was a ledger of properties bought and sold over a period of a century. Jacoby for some reason took an interest in it and examined it closely. The third out of three turned out what appeared to be the rantings of a mad man. Kaltog took on the task of combing through it. Theo put his head down on the table top and closed his eyes. Kali began to wander.

The king must have fallen asleep because when he opened his eyes again Kali was in the chair across from him reading a small leather-bound book. Her eyes flickered up and met his. "This is an amazing story," she said. "I found this in a desk drawer. It is the diary of a woman who apparently worked here for years. She talks about a secret that motivated the act of sending the ships out to sea. The secret involves an underground society that revolved around an elixir and the consumption of said elixir. This potion was made from a highly addictive poppy flower and was seriously undermining the civilization in New Chance. Its effects caused euphoria, but also had properties that caused physical aging to stop or even reverse itself over time. As it grew in popularity so did the problems associated with it. The decline of society in New Chance occurred over the course of decades as the elixir strangled the community. The acquisition of the elixir was the cause of chaos in that the laws of the people were pushed aside in order to facilitate its possession. Family values were being heavily damaged by those addicted to the elixir."

"What did they do?" Theo asked.

"She says that it was decided that they needed to eradicate the plague for good. A choice was given to the people who were addicted to the elixir. They could either remain in New Chance without the drug or they could take their elixir and leave. Ships were made available and many *did* decide to leave. Those who chose to stay in New Chance went through terrible withdrawals. Many could not handle living without the elixir and reluctantly decided to leave on the last ship available. Seven ships went out to sea and none returned. They were never heard from again. The remaining elixir was rounded up and disposed of."

"Does it say anything about how they treated those going through withdrawals?" Kristina asked.

"There is nothing mentioned here. If they had so many people suffering so desperately from the withdrawals, you would think that they would have found ways to treat them, but it says nothing about it. They obviously had no idea how to ease their suffering," Kali commented wryly.

"Neither do *we*," Kristina said ironically.

"You aren't going to believe this," Kaltog said. "This guy is all over the place in his writing, but some of what he says is decipherable. He mentions the ships in a way that indicates his disdain for shunning the people who were asked to leave. It goes on and on about the loss of freedom and the over-reaching arm of the government. It is not clear if he was one of those addicted to the elixir or not, but he clearly thought the situation was highly mismanaged. What is most interesting about what he says has to do with the disposal of the remaining elixir. Apparently, it was dumped in the swamp opposite the forest, the forest where the poppy flowers grow in the clearing."

"Poppy flowers in the forest? The elixir in the swamp? You've got to be kidding me," Theo stood up, but sat right back down again with a pained expression on his face. He brushed his hair out of his eyes with his hand. "What are the odds that our little monster friends are the result?"

"I think that it explains a lot," Kaltog said.

"Well, regardless, this information gets us no closer to knowing how to handle the withdrawal from this drug. How does any of this help Stephan?" Kristina asked helplessly.

"I'm afraid it doesn't," Theo replied. They all sat quietly listening to Theo tap his fingers on the table. After a matter of minutes he said, "I think we should see if we can find the descendants of those who were disenfranchised."

"What?" Kristina exclaimed.

Jacoby turned wide eyes on him, "Highly dangerous that seems if not impossible."

"Let's take the dragons east over the ocean to see if we can find anybody or anything," Theo said. There was a measure of excitement in his voice. "If there were survivors, we might learn something from them, or rather from their great great grandchildren. I think it's worth a try."

They all looked at each other waiting for someone else to respond to Theo's proposal. Finally, Kali spoke up, "Let's do it. I'm curious about what happened to those people."

"Maybe they have the information we seek. I guess that is our course," Kristina said.

"Why not?" Kaltog agreed.

Jacoby groaned.

They found their way back to the front steps of the library and waited for the dragons to return for them.

## Plan Deviation

Gabriel left on Skymaster early in the morning. Everybody slept as she quietly left Castle Xandia and met the high dragon mage in the courtyard. It was cold and she wrapped a warm woolen cloak around her to keep the chill away. A warm fire and a good night's sleep would do her wonders, but for now she would have to do her best to persevere despite the rain and the cold. *"Good morning, Skymaster,"* she greeted the silver dragon.

*"Mistress,"* he said simply.

*"Are you ready to go to New Chance this morning?"* she asked.

*"Perhaps."*

*"Did you post another dragon to watch the cave?"* she asked. Skymaster had been serving as sentinel at the cave entrance throughout the night.

"*Yes. Agape is there right now,*" he replied.

"*Good. Are you all right, Skymaster? You are usually not so . . . so conservative with your words,*" Gabriel said as she seated herself after climbing up the ladder. She pulled it up and attached it to the loops that were there for that purpose. Skymaster took in a deep breath causing his sides to expand dramatically.

"*Did you just sigh? Is there something the matter?*" Gabriel asked again.

"*I cannot take you to New Chance. The wisps have found something you must see,*" Skymaster said.

"*What is it?*"

"*A lair. His lair,*" he said. *I'll show you. Hang on.*" Skymaster launched and was gone before Gabriel could digest his words.

# Chapter 10
## EFFECTIVELY INEFFECTIVE

Jacob held onto the handle on the door as they took a corner at a high rate of speed. The man in the black cloak drove like a mad man. It occurred to Jacob that he had no real concept of the rules of the road. He actually wondered if the dark man had any true concept of the rules of gravity or physics. What happens when an unstoppable force encounters an immovable object? "Maybe you should let me drive," Jacob suggested.

"Are you afraid, kid?" Candaz asked with a smirk.

"Not of you. Just of dying in a fiery crash," he said as his hand found the dashboard as the bump in the road they flew over felt more like a launching ramp at the speed they were going. Hoover Dam and Las Vegas had just been a flash as they drove over and through it on the highway. How the police were not all over them, Jacob couldn't even begin to guess. "What's the hurry, dude? You got a hot date?" he asked.

"Just shut up. We'll be there soon." Candaz pulled the stopper on a little crystal bottle with his teeth and took a long swig before restopping it and stuffing it into one of his many hidden pockets.

"You know that drinking and driving is against the law," Jacob observed.

"Shut up, kid," Candaz said.

"Where we goin'? Is Jesse gonna to be there?" Jacob asked, not for the first time.

"You'll see. You'll see," Candaz replied.

"Yeah. So you've said. Where is Jesse?" he persisted.

"Do you ever shut up?" Candaz asked in exasperation. It had been a long drive with Jacob being a constant buzz in his ear.

"So, tell me how you got Jesse's medallion. Obviously, she didn't give it to you willingly," Jacob said, fishing for information.

"You are right about that, boy," Candaz said.

"She isn't hurt, is she?" Jacob asked.

"She might get hurt if you don't do what you're told. Now, shut up, kid," Candaz repeated. He pulled the car over to the side of the road and parked it. "Get out," he ordered as he opened the driver's side door. In the trunk were many items that the dark man tucked into the many pockets of his voluminous cloak. Jacob was sure he saw something marked "C-4". With great strides old, dark and crazy began to walk straight into the desert. Throwing his backpack on his back, Jacob watched for a second longer before following.

"Aren't you hot in that coat?" Jacob asked as he trailed after the man. He wasn't sure what was happening. At the school he seemed to have been spellbound. Those two other men had said they were on Jesse's side. If that were true, and he was beginning to think it was, that meant that the guy he was following was *not* on Jesse's side. He was the enemy; an enemy with explosives in his pockets. Was he really leading him to Jesse? The odds were that she was involved in this somehow. Her medallion hanging around creepy dude's neck was proof of that.

The man wasn't paying any attention to him at the moment. Jacob turned his back on him and surreptitiously checked his cell phone. There was no network. Well, that was inconvenient. He would have to bide his time to see how all of this played out. Right now he knew one thing. This man was not to be trusted and was very very dangerous. He wished he had a gun, or at least a knife, but he didn't have anything he could use as a weapon. His knife was sitting safely on his dresser at home. A lot of good it did him there.

Eventually they came up to a cave camouflaged in the side of a hill. It was cool and dark within the cave, a welcome relief from the heat of the desert. The man was busy observing the strange phenomenon at the back of the cave. An opening in the shape of a lightning bolt framed a fantastic display of a constellation. As he watched the constellation changed from one to another. This occurred twice before the dark man turned to Jacob and said, "Go gather some wood. We will need to wait a little while longer."

"What? Wait here? For how long?" Jacob asked.

"For as long as it takes. Gather wood as I told you to, boy," Candaz said. He took out a book and started studying it with a glowing light from between his fingers. "And, boy, come back soon if you want to see your sister again."

Actually, Jacob *was* thinking about disappearing. Maybe not quite yet. He exited the cave and went in search of fire wood. He managed to find some dry scrub, not particularly firewood, but it would burn. When he returned to the cave Candaz still had his nose buried in the book. The scrub he deposited on the ground at the cave entrance before wandering to the back of the cave to observe the constellations. He noticed that the dark man had done something besides read while he was away. Three bricks of

C-4 were arranged around the lightning shaped opening, complete with wires sticking out of them and connected to some type of digital device. From what Jacob could tell, with what little knowledge he had of such things, the explosives were ready to be detonated.

He looked back at Candaz, who was busy reading. He bent over and removed the wires from one of the bricks of C-4 and stuffed it in his pocket. The second was within easy reach and he quickly did the same. "Boy!" he heard behind him.

Jacob looked back quickly, thinking he had been caught. "Come here, boy!" the man ordered.

He complied, curious, but also more than a little afraid now. "Yeah?" he said with as much attitude as he could muster, trying not to show his fear.

From outside of the cave he heard a small noise, a rustling of brush. Candaz quickly swung around him and held him from behind with a knife to his throat.

An old woman stood before them dressed in leathers for motorcycle riding. She wore a grin that was full of boldness but held no happy greeting. "Candaz, you old dog, finally, we meet again," she said.

*Finally we meet again? Really? Who was this woman?* Jacob thought.

"I thought you were dead, old witch," Candaz spat.

"Obviously you were mistaken. Let the child go. You have no business with him," she ordered.

"Oh, I think not, Shareen. Jacob and I are just becoming friends. Aren't we, boy?" he said as he tightened his hold.

Jacob chose not to answer.

Candaz took his eyes off the woman to look behind him at the lightning bolt. The constellation rotated to another that looked something like a crown.

Through the cave entrance marched the two men he had met at the school. One of them brandished a shimmering sword ablaze in blue electricity. "Let the boy go!" the younger man ordered.

"Let Jacob go, Candaz," the older man said with quiet authority.

"Yes. *Let him go. Let him go.* That seems to be the consensus. But, no. The boy stays with me," he said as he laughed and edged toward the back of the cave slowly, keeping the knife at Jacob's throat the whole time.

"Do not move, Candaz," Jesse said as she walked through the cave entrance followed by her father and two dogs, one white, one gold. Her hands were hanging casually at her side, but they crackled with electricity, both green and blue. She began gathering the energy into an orb with her hands.

"Jesse! Dad!" Jacob said and tried to pull away, but the knife at his neck kept him close to Candaz as the sorcerer continued to back away from them, using him as a shield.

"Jacob," Jesse said, "Do you remember when we used to play Batman and Robin?"

He knew immediately what she was getting at and focused on the position of his feet. With a twist and a lunge, he drove his heal into the top of Candaz's foot and was instantly free from his abductor. As Jacob ducked out of the way, Jesse hurled the free-current energy at Candaz, hitting him squarely in the chest. The impact drove him back to the very edge of the lightning gate where the constellation "The Condor" was visible. He hesitated only a split second to ignite the charges to blow the C-4 before he leapt quickly through the gate and was gone.

Jacob raced toward them when the blast hit and he was suddenly flung through the air. The atmosphere exploded. Time seemed to slow down as a mass of rock and earth crashed to the floor. Dust filled the small space. He landed hard and heavy, knocking Jesse from her feet and back into her father's arms. They all ended up in a pile at the opening of the cave. Rocks and dust enveloped them.

## Search and Rescue

Jesse needed to cough, but the great pressure on her chest was prohibiting her from doing so. She groaned and pushed with her hands against the weight that was upon her. It budged a little and then it groaned as well. Beneath her she could also feel movement; her dad was trying to move underneath her. She pushed against the weight on her chest again and felt the pressure lessen and then subside.

"Jesse," she heard Jacob's strained voice very close to her ear.

"Help me," she said and reached up and grabbed Jacob's arm. He pulled her up and she turned immediately to her dad. He was already pushing himself up to his feet.

"Are you okay?" he asked as he surveyed the destruction.

"Yeah, I think so," Jesse responded. "Jake?"

"I don't know. The blast blew me away from it. I think my backpack took the worst of it," he said as he tried to look over his shoulder, but couldn't. Instead he swung the pack off and gazed in awe at the shredded and scorched material. "My legs are . . . they're hurt." When he turned away from Jesse she saw the back of his legs were bleeding and burned through his tattered jeans.

"Okay, let me take a look," she said. Jesse examined the injuries and with her hands and used the freecurrent energy to facilitate healing. "It's not too bad, Jacob. You'll be okay."

He turned to her and gave her a hug. She held him close and then wiped away her tears, noticing, without being obvious; his own eyes were filled with tears. "I thought I would never say this but I've missed you, Jacob," she said.

"Yeah, you too *little* sister," he said with emphasis as he looked down at her. He had grown a lot over the summer and was now taller than her. Like a magician he flourished his hand in front of her face and let drop her gold medallion. It hung from its chain that was entwined around his fingers.

"No way! How did you get that?" Jesse asked as she took it from his hand.

"I snatched it from 'Mr. dark and dreadful' at the last moment," he said smiling broadly.

"Good job, little brother." She fastened the chain around her neck before giving him a playful slap on the arm.

"Jesse," her dad said, "I hear whining. Shhh. Do you hear it?"

"*Jesse?*" Tempest whispered in her head.

"*Tempest, where are you. Are you all right?*" Jesse asked.

"*Help,*" the dragon said.

"Dad, can you tell where the sound is coming from?" Jesse asked and then listened.

"Over here!" Bill said as he moved quickly to where he was pointing and started removing rubble. Jesse and Jacob joined him and soon they saw white fur poking through.

"*I am right here, Tempest. Are you hurt?*" Jesse asked.

"*I think I am not right. This body is broken,*" Tempest replied weakly.

"*Hang tight, sweetie. We've almost got you,*" Jesse reassured her as she saw one of Tempest's eyes look up at her.

"Dad, move that piece--that one right there. Okay, I think we've got it." Jesse bent down before Tempest on her knees and gently touched the fur between her ears. "*It's okay, sweetie. I'm here.*"

"*I don't think I can move, Jesse,*" Tempest cried.

"Dad, Jacob, we need to get her outside so I can transform her back into a dragon. Can you clear a path so we can get outside of the cave?" she asked.

They began to work moving what they could physically handle, one handful at a time until they could feel the soft desert breeze breath freshness through a small opening. Eventually they were able to expand the hole to make it large enough for a person to fit through. "Jess, do you want me to carry her?" Bill asked.

"No. I'll get her," Jesse said as she carefully slid her hands under Tempest's small body. She let the freecurrent penetrate the little dog's body to immediately heal what could be healed, but the damage was extensive. Her back was broken. Cradling the tiny white dog, Jesse slid through the opening that her dad and Jacob had labored to make. They followed close behind.

*"Tempest, I'm going to change you back to your dragon self. You should be healed in the process. Are you ready?"* Jesse asked as she placed the dog gently on the ground.

*"I am ready to be a dragon again, Jesse. Yes,"* Tempest said.

Jesse's hands were shaking as she placed them on Tempest's body. Her thoughts were not only on the injured dragon before her, but of Nick, Jim, Shareen and Felcore, who were still buried somewhere inside the cave, maybe hurt, maybe dead. If they were seriously hurt, time could be running out for them. She felt an overwhelming sense of urgency and the frustration of not being able to act fast enough. But, first things first. Tempest needed her right now.

The heat from the medallion burned against the skin of her chest as she focused the freecurrent energy and let the healing begin. It burned like lightning through her as she absorbed Tempest's pain into her own body, but it was only temporary and she endured it. She pictured Tempest, the dragon in her mind, seeing the full majesty of the beautiful creature that was her true self. The white scales upon Tempest's body had a fabulous iridescent glow, a prism of colors, changing with every movement and every breath of her robust lungs. She was about the size of a small RV, but streamlined like a Lear jet. Ridges ran the length of her back all the way from where the crowns converged on the top of her head to the very tip of her tail. Her eyes swirled with shiny red orbs. Magnificent she was to behold in her entirety. Never had a dragon possessed beauty so profound.

Tempest rose to her fullest height, spread her wings and launched herself into the desert night sky. She circled overhead, stretching her wings, reveling in her reborn freedom.

"*Tempest, you must come back down. You cannot be seen here,*" Jesse reminded her.

"*I know. Silly place,*" Tempest said.

"*Yes, I know. How do you feel?*" Jesse asked.

"*I feel fabulous!*" Tempest said and then let out a mighty dragon roar.

"*Shhh. Tempest, can you come back down? You can help us dig,*" Jesse suggested.

"*If I must,*" she grumbled.

Felcore, Nicky, Jim and Shareen were buried under there somewhere. They had work to do and they had better get started. As Tempest came to land behind Jesse and the breeze from the mighty dragon's wings swept across her face, she felt a canine nose push into her hand. Felcore stood there with his gold eyes sparkling and tail wagging as if it were Christmas morning. "Felcore! Hi, boy!" Jesse said as she knelt down and hugged her big dog joyously. "Felcore, my boy, you're okay! Thank God! My sweet boy! Do you know where Nicky is?"

Felcore spun in a circle and then went directly to the pile of rocks in front of them. "Rrowff!" he said and started digging.

Before Jesse joined him, she noticed her dad and Jacob watching her friends with utter disbelief, especially the white dragon who began helping the golden retriever, teaming up with him by delicately removing larger rocks with her jaws that the dog encountered.

"Dad, Jacob, you okay?" Jesse asked.

"Wow. That's . . . some . . . wow!" Bill managed to say.

"Yeah. Wow!" Jacob concurred.

"Thanks for clarifying. Let's get to work, boys," Jesse said, trying not to jump out of her skin with the panic she was trying to suppress.

They all began to dig.

## Rock and Roll

By the time the dust settled, Jim could see that they were surrounded by large heavy rocks. Space was tight, but he was able to wiggle his way to a standing position. He looked around and spotted a glimpse of gold in the rubble. With adrenaline fueled energy, Jim started removing the rocks until he uncovered Nicholas's hand which still held his sword. He kept digging until he was able to uncover Nick's head and face.

"Nick," Jim said quietly as he checked to see if he was still breathing.

"Nick," he said louder as he continued to remove debris from around the young man. "Nicholas, answer me," Jim said as he put a hand along-side of Nick's face. "Nicholas."

"What . . . ?" Nick groaned and opened his eyes slowly.

He groaned again and pushed himself up into a sitting position before trying to stand up. "What happened? Where's Jesse?" he asked.

"Take it slow, Nick. Are you hurt?" Jim asked.

"Yes. I think my leg might be broken. I can't seem to put any weight on it and it hurts like hell," he replied.

"Let me look at it," Jim said as he examined Nick's leg. "I'm going to have to splint it. Stay put." He found some twigs and tore some strips of cloth from his shirt. After binding Nick's leg, he helped him to his feet and they began searching for the others.

Jim used the light on his cell phone to see by. "No network" flashed on his screen when he attempted to make a call. "Of course not," he said mostly to himself.

"I have an idea, Jim. Let's change into wolves. That will sharpen our senses considerably," Nicholas suggested.

Jim gave him a long look before he laughed despite the seriousness of their situation. "I'm not laughing at you, Nick. It's just that this is all so incredible to me. Who would have thought that after all these years . . ." he began.

"As incredible as cell phones and automobiles?" Nick asked before he continued. "This is what we need to do, Jim. Changing into a wolf is much the same as changing into an eagle. You have to feel it within your being. Reach deep and find the wolf nature that is an integral part of who you are," Nicholas said.

Nicholas stretched his lean muscular frame before dissolving into a rusty colored wolf. He bounded forward with a slight limp in his hind leg. His nose began working out the various scents around him and right away he isolated a human scent nearby. Immediately he began to dig in the area around the source of the scent. His ears pricked up when he heard the breathing of the woman he knew as Shareen. The leather she wore had a distinctive and somewhat delicious smell, old and imbued with various traces from throughout the years since it was tanned. The lavender soap that she used to bathe with was especially evident as was the mint that flavored her toothpaste. Blood, strong, sharp in the nostrils, was significant. She was clearly injured.

Soon Jim, in his wolf form, joined him in his dig. The big silver and black wolf was energetic, but meticulous as he made his way through the rubble. They reached Shareen after a stretch of time that was much too long for Nick's sense of urgency. She was alive, but gravely hurt. Transforming back into their human form, they administered first aid as best they could without the necessary supplies. She opened her eyes for a brief moment but did not say a word. Nick laid his jacket over her to keep her warm. They had done all they could. Jesse was needed to help her further. She had the ability to heal, a gift from the wisps, but also something more that was a part of her character, inscribed into her being.

With a glance and a nod they became wolves once again and continued with their search. Nick could pick up the scents from everyone who had been in the cave, including Candaz. All were familiar to him, Jacob, Shareen, Jim, Felcore, Tempest, especially Jesse. The only exception was Bill whom he had not met yet. He identified all of these tendrils with his very sensitive sniffer.

From a specifically and precisely pinpointed direction his exceptional hearing was picking up the sound of someone digging. Yes, he could clearly hear noises of frantic activity in progress. But, there was more than that indicating the location of his friends. Dragon musk was also strongly evident. They couldn't be far. He vocalized his findings to Jim in what sounded like a series of growls. They began to dig frantically as well.

## Home Sweet Home

The floor of the cave stung Candaz's hands as he landed hard upon them. He rolled like a much younger man and came back up onto his feet. Taking a moment to let his eyes adjust to the darkness surrounding him, he caught his breath and let a small chuckle escape his lips as he thought of what he had just accomplished. Gone was the girl, her dog, her dragon. Shareen, whom he thought was dead, was dead again. That Skymaster brat would not be bothering him again. Unfortunately, he had at the last moment lost Jesse's pendant. It would have been useful, but not necessary. He could live without it.

Slowly he made his way out of the cave and into the Risen night. The reek of dragon was strong, but there wasn't one of their kind in sight. Cautiously, Candaz worked his way through the forest toward Castle Xandia. He was energized. Things were finally going his way. In his possession were the items he needed to implement his plan, save one, and that was easily obtained.

Pulling the stopper from the crystal decanter with his teeth, he took a swig from the bottle. He noted that there were maybe only two or three doses left before he returned the decanter to his pocket. Soon he would remedy that as well.

He heard a twig snap to his left and froze in his tracks to listen. Someone was approaching slowly and quietly. Staying watchful, he remained where he was and waited.

"Don't move," a man ordered. Stephan stepped almost soundlessly in front of Candaz and brandished his sword.

It took only a moment for Candaz to assess the other man's condition. He looked like he had aged twenty years in the past week. His face was drawn and ashen in color. Eyes that were once bright blue and alive with the joy of life, were now filled with stress and surrounded by shadows. Although the sword remained a real threat, there was a tremor in the hand that held it. The signs all pointed to one thing. He had seen it before long ago. A sorcerer he knew in his youth who had shown him his secret stash was heavily bound by the substance. Candaz cured the man *permanently* and kept the stash hidden away for a time when he would need it. That time had come. Withdrawing the crystal bottle from his cloak pocket, he brought it forth.

"Don't move," Stephan repeated.

"This will help you, son. It has what you need to feel better. Go ahead, take a drink," Candaz offered the bottle to the young man who was watching him with apparent disgust.

"You have nothing that I want. You can come with me back to Castle Xandia or die here. It's your choice," Stephan said, flourishing his sword.

"I know what you need. I can get you more. It's not too far from here. You know you can't live without it. When was your last dose?" Candaz asked.

Stephan's eyes wavered, as did the weapon in his hand and his resolve. "What do you know of it?" he asked.

Candaz reached out and offered the bottle of elixir once again to Stephan. "Take it," he said.

The conflict was apparent in the young man's face. He stood on the edge of a barbed-wire fence. Thoughts raced through his head, but he found it difficult to focus on any single one. The people he loved would not understand--they *could* not understand. He watched as his own hand reached forward and took the crystal decanter from the sorcerer. The lure remained clasped in his hand as he gazed at its liquid contents. Nausea threatened. Stephan swallowed against it. He let his sword drop and with a shaking hand he unstopped the bottle and brought it up to his lips. The taste was sweet compared to the bitterness in his throat as he took a small sip. The effects were not instant, but were not long in coming. The relief the liquid brought was immense, like a warm blanket on a cold winter's night. It wasn't as good as the needle, but would do for now.

"I can get more. Go ahead and finish it," Candaz coaxed. He watched closely.

Stephan worked his mouth soundlessly for a moment before stopping the bottle and handing it back. "I'm good. Thanks."

"I'll save it for you for later." The bottle disappeared into one of the pockets in the voluminous cloak.

"You have more?" Stephan asked. His attitude was defeated, but anxious and seasoned with anger.

"Yes. It is possible to get more. I will need your help, however. The process is not magical by any means," Candaz said.

"How far do we have to go?" Stephan asked.

Candaz watched as Stephan picked up his sword and placed it back in its sheath. He hadn't planned on having this young man accompany him, but considered it another stroke of his good fortune. The boy would be extremely useful. He knew beyond a doubt that before too long he would be willing to do just about anything to get a drop of the elixir. The sky was starting to become the dark cobalt blue of early morning. The sun would be rising shortly. "It's about a day's ride. Do you think you could get us some horses?"

"I can do better than that," Stephan said.

## Rejection

"*Zlato?*" Stephan called.

"*Yes, Stephan?*" Zlato answered immediately.

"*Can you take me and . . . someone else some place?*" Stephan asked, hesitating at disclosing the name of his companion.

"*I will take you, Stephan. I will not take him. Do not ask that of me. Your mind is open to me. I do not like what you do, but I love you and will help you, but I will not take him. No,*" Zlato's refusal was not only verbal, but forceful in emotion as well. Stephan could feel the dragon's sadness at the choice he was making, but he could not change the circumstances or his physical need for the drug.

"*I'm sorry, Zlato. I will have to go without you,*" Stephan said with an aching heart. To Candaz he said, "I can get horses at the castle. Follow me."

Stephan didn't see the victorious grin on Candaz's face as he followed after the defeated man.

# Chapter 11

## ADVERSE HOSPITALITY

Theo shifted uncomfortably in the saddle that was usually relatively comfortable. He leaned forward and then leaned back, stretching his stiff legs and trying to find the best position to alleviate the pain that radiated up and down his injured leg.

A fresh breeze blew gently over the ocean waves, bringing with it a slight salty tang that could be tasted on the tip of the tongue. They did not fly high, but quite low, close to the water; skimming over the surface close enough that B.F. could reach down and touch a cresting wave with his extended talon should he desire to do so.

They flew in a "V" formation. Theo and B.F. were in the lead, with Kaltog on Grand Oro on the left wing and Kali on Sweet Vang on the right wing. Kristina rode on Sweet Vang with Kali. Down below Jacoby, in the form of a dolphin, swam in the waves, only occasionally to be spotted breaking the surface by the rest of the party.

"*My wings are getting a bit tired. Are we almost there?*" B.F. asked in his whiniest tone.

"*I have no idea where we are going. We are searching, remember. What do your dragon senses tell you?*" Theo asked him back.

"*My senses tell me that I'm tired of flying and the babies say that they are very hungry. Will we be there soon?*" B.F. asked again.

"*Again, I have no idea. We'll go back if we don't find a place to land soon. For now, just keep flying.*"

"*Of course, your hiney. . .I mean 'highness',*" B.F. snorted.

"*Did you just snort?*" Theo asked.

"*Hardly. I do not 'snort',*" B.F. replied with indignation.

"*Right. I really thought I heard a snort,*" Theo insisted.

"*You must have heard a seagull. I saw a flock of seagulls fly by just a moment ago,*" B.F. said.

"*Right. Snorting seagulls,*" Theo laughed, enjoying a brief moment of levity in an otherwise stressful day.

They had been flying for many hours and had not seen anything but ocean. Theo wished they *would* see seagulls. That would at least indicate the presence of land. He was beginning to think this was a fool's errand. Their time would have been much better spent looking for his wife. His thoughts of Jessabelle were full of fear and laced with worry. Sleep was creeping up on him although he fought against it. Jessabelle's face came to him in his dreams beseeching him to help her.

He awoke suddenly with a start when B.F. announced, "*Kaltog says he smells land. I concur.*" It was past midnight, but with the brilliance of the stars and the two moons of Risen shining bright, there was a glow to the cold blue night. Dozing in the saddle was not something Theo liked to do. It was dangerous for one thing, especially on dragon back. Falling out of a saddle while on a dragon would be fatal. It wasn't the first time he had lost the battle with his eyelids while in the saddle, however. Sleep had claimed him both while on B.F.'s back and on his horse from time to time before. He shook himself fully awake and took a long drink of water from his canteen.

"*What do your powerful dragon senses tell you?*" he asked.

"*That and more. There is a community of humans on the island. They live somewhat primitively, lacking running water and cooking over a fire. I believe they had chicken for dinner last night, chicken and root vegetables. Blleck!*" B.F. said. He didn't care for chicken or vegetables either.

"*How far?*" Theo asked.

"*Not very. Do you want to make a covert entrance or go in boldly?*" the dragon asked.

"*Let's do some reconnaissance first. Do a sweep of the island from a discrete distance. I want to get an idea of what we are about to encounter,*" Theo said.

"*Sounds like a wise choice. Descending on humans in the middle of the night with three enormous dragons could seem a little threatening to the natives.*" He paused a moment and then said, "*Kaltog and Kali agree.*"

The island was relatively large and mostly forested. A large lake flanked the small village on the north. It sparkled beautifully in the moonlight. There was a campfire in the center of the thatched-roofed dwellings that was presently burned down to glowing coals. All was quiet. The residents seemed to all be sleeping.

They surveyed the entire expanse of the island and spotted a couple of quaint cottages set apart from the rest of the village. There was a set of three small dwellings together on the other side of the island. Here too a campfire smoldered warmly and appeared abandoned for the night.

"*Let's find a place to land where we won't be seen. I don't want to scare these people with our sudden presence,*" Theo said.

"*There is a spot on the south side of the island. I will put down there,*" B.F. remarked as he did a quick spiral and headed in the opposite direction. He took them to a high cliff that overlooked the ocean below.

"Kaltog, can you give me a hand?" Theo asked as his first attempt to dismount B.F. was made impossible by his stiff and sore leg.

"Sure, Theo. Easy now. Sore, huh?" Kaltog asked as he helped Theo down to the ground.

"Yeah. Did you see Jacoby out in the water?" Theo asked. He left B.F.'s equipment in place, but grabbed his pack.

"No. I haven't seen him in a while. Kali?" Kaltog deferred the question to the banderg woman.

"No sign of him yet. He was keeping up with us for most of the night so I assume he'll come across the island if he maintains a straight course." She was watching Theo with concern. "How's the leg?" she asked.

To B.F. he said, "*See if you can find him*". Then he answered Kali, "It's sore but I'll live. Let's leave the dragons here and walk down to the village. Morning should be on the rise soon. Kris, what do we have that we can offer as a gift? Something to show that our intentions are good," Theo said.

"I'm sure I must have something . . . how about this bottle of nectar?" she asked as she pulled a tall blue bottle out of her own pack. Its label had the crest of the Landtamer Vineyard, a sword entwined in a grape vine with the initial "L" in an elegant script.

"That's a start. What else do you have?" Theo asked as he took the bottle from his sister.

She gave him a sharp look, but dug deeper into her bag. In a moment she clasped in her hand a beautiful gem-encrusted dagger in a finely crafted leather sheath. Her eyes went to Theo's and she said quietly, "This was a gift from Link. I hate to lose it, but I'm sure he would understand. Please don't offer it unless it is necessary though." She handed the dagger to her brother reluctantly.

He shoved it in his belt and tucked the bottle of nectar in his pack and said, "Okay, let's go make some new friends."

It was a beautiful open wood with soft pine, birch, oak and poplar. They quickly found a path that led to the village and made easy time. Theo maintained a steady pace, despite the pain he endured and a noticeable limp. Kaltog was a natural woodsman and strolled practically without sound as did Kali, who was also completely at home in the woods as well as an advanced and talented tracker. Kristina, on the other hand, was less than light on her well-pedicured feet. Leaves crunched and twigs snapped as she followed behind Kali.

As the sun rose, light began filtering through the trees in a brilliant display as it touched the green leaves, reflecting on their surfaces and finally finding its way to the soft ground. A cool and gentle breeze stirred their surroundings every so often bringing with it the scent of the ocean. Birds chirped in a sporadically orchestrated sing-song.

They stopped on a hill that overlooked the village and observed the early morning activities down below. The fire was stoked into flaming existence and a large pot of water was hung on a tri-pod over the flames to heat. Two women had set to this task and were soon joined by a man and a younger boy. The man went to a storehouse and brought back some type of meat that the women got to work preparing in a pan over the fire. Apparently the boy's task this morning was to gather eggs from the chicken house and he returned with a basket full.

The smells of cooking wafted up to the observers' noses enticingly. Theo's stomach growled in response and he pushed against it with his hand in an attempt to quiet its disgruntlement.

Slowly more people emerged from their humble dwellings and began the task of preparing the community table for breakfast. Quiet pockets of conversation could be heard as greetings were made and plans for the day were initiated.

Theo turned to his companions and whispered, "Let's walk down there and make our presence known. Follow my lead."

A well-travelled path led down into the village. They hiked casually, but with anxious anticipation. As they entered the village, the first people to spot them stopped in their tracks and stared. A woman screamed and what followed was chaos. Everybody in sight dropped what they were doing and ran to hide in their shelters.

"Wait," Theo said, "we just want to talk to you." The party of travelers stood by the cooking fire and looked around. Everybody had disappeared.

"Well played, brother," Kristina chimed.

Theo sat down on a nearby bench to rest his leg and looked around. "Come out. We mean you no harm. We have travelled far to talk to you."

The boy who had gathered the eggs emerged from one of the small shacks and approached them cautiously. He was probably ten, but quite tall for his age. The clothes he wore were simple and comfortable, made for work and play. His eyes and hair were both light in color. "They won't come out. They are afraid," he said.

"There is nothing to be afraid of. We mean you no harm," Theo said gently.

"It doesn't matter. They have been warned for generations to fear anyone who does not belong to this community. It is a deep-seated fear from long ago." The boy paused to appraise them with special attention to their big friend, Kaltog.

"What is your name?" Kali asked.

"I am called Jared. What is that?" he pointed at Kaltog.

Kaltog's voice sounded deep and gravelly in the quiet of the village as he said, "I am known as Kaltog Vengar of the Torg Nation. Why are you not hiding like the others?"

Jared showed no fear. He looked Kaltog square in the eye for a moment and responded, "I am curious. Why are you here?"

"We have some questions," Theo said, as he stood up and turned the strips of meat that were still cooking over the fire. He snatched a piece and popped it into his mouth. "Do you have a king or a mayor or somebody who might answer some questions for us? We have travelled from the city of New Chance on the main land. Do you know anything about your history?"

"Very little. I know that our ancestors came from the mainland on ships. But, that was a long time ago. The ships are now all at the bottom of the sea. There is nobody really in charge here. We all do what is necessary to survive and live in relative peace. Are you a knight?" Jared asked Theo.

"I'm a warrior." He didn't add that he was the king. "Is there someone who has insight into your past?" Theo persisted.

"We seek knowledge," Kristina said with a charming smile. "Jared, is there possibly written chronicles that we could look at?"

His eyes were bright as he addressed Kristina and his cheeks became infused with rouge. "Everything written down was destroyed in a fire a long time ago, long before I was born."

Theo turned the meat another time before removing it from the fire so it wouldn't burn. He placed the large pan on a flat rock beside the fire. He snatched another piece and after chewing and swallowing it said, "I'm afraid we've come a long way for nothing, then. I sure wish there was someone, anyone who could help us."

Jared looked around and then quietly, so he could not be overheard, said, "There is the old man. They say he is crazy. But, I know him and I don't think he is crazy; just a little odd. He lives on the other side of the island by himself. He is a wizard. His name is Roland. He might be able to answer your questions."

"Thank you, Jared. We will leave you in peace. I hope we didn't frighten anyone too much," Theo said.

"I can take you," Jared said quickly. "Roland knows me. He'll be more likely to talk to you if I introduce you to him."

Kristina looked a little concerned. "Will your parents allow it?"

"I'm on my own," Jared said brightly. "My parents are dead. I have only myself to answer to. I have been alone for three years now."

Maternal instincts kicked in and Kristina felt a tug at her heart. She said loud enough to be heard by any on-lookers or anyone who might be concerned for the boy's welfare, "You may come with us if you wish, Jared. Thank you for your help. Lead the way."

The boy grabbed a couple pieces of meat from the pan before leading them to the same path they had taken into the village. When they crested the hill, Kali turned back and witnessed the residents gathering at the cooking fire, deep in discussion about the excitement of their recent visitors. "Why are they so afraid?" she asked Jared.

"It goes way back. We have been taught to fear anything that is beyond the confines of our small village. Of course, you are the first visitors ever," he replied as he continued down the path. When they came to a "v", he took the right fork without slowing. It was obvious he knew these woods well. They walked without conversation for a time. It wasn't until they reached a small rise that Jared paused and looked back to those who followed him. Theo could tell that he was pleased to be a part of something other than the day-to-day routine. The king smiled at him and Jared returned the smile before turning back to continue the trek.

The beach lay on the other side of the rise. It was a long expanse of sandy beach that had three little cabanas tucked against the side of the hill. Smoke rose lazily from a chimney that extended from the roof of one of the structures.

"Come on," Jared said as he waved his hand and started down the sandy hill with great bounds. The adults followed more slowly. "Come on," Jared said again.

"Greetings, Jared!" a cheerful, booming voice called out. "Who are your friends?"

"Hello, Roland," Jacob responded just as cheerfully. He hesitated when he realized he had not learned the names of his companions except for Kaltog who had introduced himself. "The big guy is Kaltog."

Theo stepped forward and introduced himself, "I am Theo. This is Kristina, my sister. My other friend is Kali. It is a pleasure to meet you."

The old man sniffed Theo's hand that he had extended in greeting. He brought it up to his nose and took a good long sniff. "Ahh. Oh, yes. I thought so. Oh, yes. I knew it!" he exclaimed.

Theo withdrew his hand swiftly, smelled it himself and said, "I beg your pardon?"

"Dragon musk! You flew in on a dragon didn't you? I thought I smelled dragon musk this morning. I thought it was very odd. Where is he? I want to see a dragon," Roland was literally dancing with excitement.

"Well," Theo began, "actually we have three. How do you know the smell of dragon musk? Surely you've never encountered a dragon before."

"Of course I haven't seen . . . a . . . drag . . .Say, why are you here?" Roland asked. His bright blue eyes rested on Theo only for a moment before darting to the closest cabana. His long hair and beard were snow white and moved wildly in the ocean breeze. He was very tan and wore nothing but a pair of shorts on his lean body. His feet were bare.

Kristina spoke, breaking his distraction, "We are here to get some information. My son is in danger and we were hoping you could help us."

He refocused his intelligent eyes on the party, appraising them one by one. When he again met Kristina's gaze, he asked, "What is wrong with your son?"

"He has an addiction," she began.

"An addiction! Oh my. Oh my. You came on dragons? Can I see one?" Roland asked, seeming to have lost track of the conversation.

"If you can help us," Kali said smartly.

"Well, that depends I guess. What is the boy addicted to? I had an addiction once. I couldn't get enough catfish. I had catfish for breakfast, catfish for lunch, catfish for dinner, catfish for a midnight snack. Catfish, catfish, catfish. Morning, noon, and night. I was out of control. Had to quit cold turkey. I am glad I wasn't addicted to cold turkey. Can't stand the stuff," Roland shook his head in disgust.

Kristina and Theo exchanged looks. "It's a drug addiction, an opiate," Theo said.

The old man turned without a word and walked into the nearest cabana.

"Do you think he heard me?" Theo asked, dumbfounded by the old wizard's actions.

"I think he's off his rocker," Kaltog said calmly.

From within the cabana they heard the old man start to sing, but only for a moment. He poked his head out and said, "Come in. Come in."

Theo was followed into the small enclosure by Kristina and Kali. Jared rushed ahead of them all. Kaltog remained outside.

What Theo encountered was unexpected. It seemed to be part laboratory, part library, part kitchen. A small stove was in the middle of the small space. It was stoked and a pot of soup bubbled happily upon it. Shelves lined the entire back of the enclosure and on each shelf were neatly arranged bottles. They started small and gradually ranged up in size. To the side sat a small table and a chair. Leaning against the chair was an intricately carved wooden staff about seven feet in length. On the table books were neatly stacked, largest on the bottom with the smallest on the top.

Roland stirred the pot, took a small sip from the spoon, and then laid it on a small bowl which he used as a spoon rest. "Mmm. Could use some more garlic." He went to the shelf and selected a small clear bottle. He unstopped it, smelled the contents and then poured a tiny measure into the boiling pot. Giving the soup another stir, he replaced the spoon and returned the bottle to its place, turning it once to position it just right.

He seemed briefly surprised when he turned around and realized there were other people with him. Quickly, he returned to the shelf and picked out another bottle. With a grin he removed the cork and took a deep sniff. Handing the bottle to Theo, he continued to grin knowingly.

Theo hesitantly took a whiff. "Dragon musk," he identified the smell and handed it back.

"You betcha! Dragon musk!" Roland inhaled again deeply before returning the bottle precisely to the same spot he had gotten it. "Ha. Ha."

Jared went to Roland and took his hand to get his attention. He said, "They need your help, Roland."

"Right," he said, smiling down at Jared. "Opiate addiction. Nasty. Nasty. Nasty." From the shelf he selected yet another bottle. This one was cut crystal and small in size. He didn't remove the stopper, but held the bottle in his hand and contemplated it for a long time.

Theo cleared his throat.

"It was a long, long time ago. Ships set sail from the mainland from the city of New Chance with people who were no longer welcome there. They were ousted, shunned, sent to find a way to survive on their own or to die trying. It was a long, long time ago. The people on the ships had an addiction. They were addicted to this elixir." Roland turned the bottle over and over in his hand and then placed it gently on the table.

"What happened?" Jared asked before anyone else could.

"It's a product from the poppy plant, an opiate, not pure, but a mix of different ingredients. The opiate is the addictive substance contained within the elixir. The rest of it just makes it more palatable. This particular elixir also has a side effect that makes one more youthful. It is a very odd trait. They had brought an ample supply with them on the ships and what they thought were the ingredients they needed and seeds to plant a new crop when they found land. It was a good plan, except that they didn't find land in time to plant a crop and have enough time to wait for it to grow before their supply was gone. Not only that, but the conditions were not quite right for growing that type of crop once they did find land. They were doomed to fail. A few of them died from the sickness that followed, mostly from dehydration and an utter lack of knowledge on how to treat the symptoms. Those who overcame the need for the drug started over without it. Those who couldn't, who desired to find a way to obtain the drug again, were eventually asked to leave the colony. There was small group that deserted and never did return. Nobody knows what became of them. The elixir was forever banned from the community. They built the little village where Jared lives. We are descendants from the survivors."

"How did they overcome the drug? How did they endure the withdrawals and live without the drug? Can you tell us how?" Kristina asked desperately.

"Well, they ran out. They didn't have any more and had no choice. Easy, peasy, fleasy," Roland flourished his hands in the air and gave Kristina a look that read *"end of story."*

"So, we came all this way for nothing. There is nothing we can do to help Stephan." Kristina started wiping away unwanted tears.

Roland turned from Theo to Kristina and back again and then threw his hands up in the air. "Well, I didn't exactly say that, did I? Please, don't cry," he begged. "I cannot take people, especially beautiful women, crying. There are various methods to alleviate the symptoms of withdrawal. In fact, I have something here that will help." He went back to his shelf of bottles and selected one that had a dark green liquid in it. "This could be very effective I believe, and maybe," he turned and selected another bottle, "this one might help. But, I think," again he selected a bottle from the shelf, "this one, yes, this one would definitely do some good." He smiled and patted Kristina on the hand. "You see, all is not lost, young lady. There is always hope. It is not the end of the world. All is not lost." Without looking up, Roland arranged the bottles he had selected, lining them up according to size in the center of the table.

"I will never give up hope," Kris said as she wiped her tears.

"Good. Hope is important--hope and faith and love," Roland said as he turned from them and stirred his soup. Taking a small sip from the spoon, he said, "Could use some more garlic. Garlic is important. Garlic and hope." Again he went to the shelf and selected a bottle, unstopped it, poured a portion into the pot and returned the bottle to exactly the same position he had gotten it from.

"Now, let's have a look see at that leg, Theo," Roland shot a sharp stare at Theo until he complied by exposing the wound to the old wizard. "Well, well, well. I have something for that. Don't move young man. I'll get you fixed up lickety split." Again Roland returned to his wall of potions and selected one. He coated Theo's wound with the thick liquid and bound it with clean cloth, quickly and skillfully. With that accomplished, he replaced the bottle precisely, selected another much larger bottle and pulled the cork. From somewhere he materialized two goblets and poured the concoction into both. "One for the patient, one for the healer. Down the hatch," he toasted Theo and poured the liquid down his throat. The king quickly followed suit and enjoyed instant relief from the throbbing in his leg that he had been enduring.

"Thanks," he said.

Roland refilled both glasses and then replaced the bottle on the shelf. He grabbed some bowls from somewhere and began dishing soup in generous portions for them all. "Eat up before its cold. Do dragons like soup? There's plenty here."

"I'm sure they have found their own repast. Thanks. This is very tasty. Just the right amount of garlic," Theo commented politely.

"Could use some catfish, though," Roland said with a scowl on his face. "Did you know that catfish are negatively buoyant, which means they sink rather than float."

Theo zoned out to his host's voice as his dragon communicated with him mentally.

"*I have bad news, Theo,*" B.F. said. "*Zlato reports that Stephan is now in the company of the bad man. Candaz, no doubt. Zlato refused to take the bad man where ever it was that Stephan wanted him to go early this morning. He says that he is very sad and misses his Stephan.*"

"*That is very distressing news. Do the others know?*" Theo asked.

"*The other dragons know. I shared this news with you because you deserve to know. You are the king after all,*" the dragon implied with a matter-of-fact tone. "*I don't know if the other dragons have shared this with their humans or not, if that is what you are asking.*"

"*Does Gabriel know?*" Theo asked.

"*She does,*" B.F. responded.

"*Where is she?*"

"*She is with the wisps and Skymaster at a place Skymaster calls the 'lair',*" B.F. replied.

"*What is this 'lair'?*"

"*Apparently it is Candaz's little hidey-hole,*" B.F. said lightly.

"*Has Stephan completely lost his mind? I can't even imagine teaming up with Candaz for any reason. Where is this lair? Do you think the two of them might be heading there?*" Theo asked.

"*Could be,*" B.F. seemed to be losing interest in this subject. His mental tone was becoming bored. "*It's located somewhere between Saberville and the northern forest. Zeth and Terese are following them.*"

"*Hmm. Keep me informed,*" Theo commanded.

"*Yes. Always.*"

From outside came a voice calling, "Theo!"

Kaltog's voice joined in, "Theo, come out here. It's Jacoby."

"Who's Jacoby?" Roland asked.

Theo found his brother-in-law outside of the cabana, flustered and trying to catch his breath. "Jacoby, are you all right?" he asked.

Through his heaving he spit out the name, "Jessa . . .belle."

Immediately Theo had him by the shoulders and pinned him with his eyes, "Jessabelle what? What do you know of Jessabelle?"

"Found her, I have," Jacoby said weakly. He stood taller and looked Theo squarely in the eye for only a second before he looked away again. "Found her, I have, Theo. Alive she is."

"Tell me. Tell me now everything you know," he demanded as he shook Jacoby's shoulders.

"A dolphin she is," he said.

"Why didn't she come with you? Why isn't she here now? Tell me what is going on, Jacoby," Theo pressed.

"Give the boy a minute," Roland said quietly, putting his hand on Theo's shoulder. "He needs to catch his breath."

Theo stepped away from his confrontational stance for a moment, but only for a moment. "Jacoby, where is my wife?" he asked.

"Your wife is a dolphin?" Roland asked, but was ignored.

"With a pod she is. A dolphin she thinks she is. Remember all else she doesn't. Her memory is lost," he said. Jacoby was cringing like he was expecting to be attacked by Theo for delivering this news.

"Go and get her, Jacoby. I want to see her *now*," Theo said.

"Understand she doesn't, Theo. I tried to get her to come with me, but refused she did. Stubborn she has always been," Jacoby said as he shook his head.

Gravity seemed to grab hold of the king and pull him to the sand. He sank into it and stared out at the ocean waves. He mumbled, "That she is. That she is."

Kristina sat down next to him, put a hand on his shoulder and said, "We'll figure this out. At least we know she is safe. Maybe her memory will return to her."

"Yes, at least she is safe," Theo said.

"Memory sometimes does return after the trauma that caused its loss in the first place. Given time your wife, the dolphin, might remember that she is your wife. Sometimes victims of trauma do not recover their memory at all, or in some cases just bits and pieces. There are treatments that might help, but that would be for humans not for dolphins. How did you become married to a dolphin in the first place? I wonder if she knows where there are any catfish. Did you know that a dolphin can drown with a smaller amount of water in its lungs than a human?" Roland asked merrily.

"Jacoby, I want to you go back and find Jessabelle. Try again. See if you can get her to meet me somewhere offshore at the mainland. And . . . tell her I love her," Theo said quietly as he stood up. "Let's get back to the mainland. Roland, give us what you've got and give Kali instructions on how to use it."

"I'm going with you," Roland said. "I'll just get my stuff. Wait here. I'll just get my things. I'll be right back." Without hesitating, Roland disappeared into one of his cabanas.

"Wait. He is going with us?" Kaltog asked. "Theo, I don't think . . ."

"I think it's a good idea," Kristina said. "He seems to have some knowledge and may be able to help us."

"I want to go, too," said Jared.

Everyone stopped and waited for Theo to decide what to do. He looked at Jared for a long moment before saying, "Are you sure? This is your home. We probably will not be coming back."

"Can I please come? Roland is more like family to me than anyone else here. Please let me come with you, Theo," Jared begged.

"Won't the community miss you? They'll think we've stolen you away--the evil strangers," Kali said.

"I am a burden to them. I don't belong. But, I don't want to be a burden to you too. If you don't want me, I'll stay here," Jared said sadly.

Kristina wrapped her arms around the boy and brushed gentle fingers through his hair. "I want you to come with us, Jared, if you are sure that is what you want."

His smile was brighter than the brightest star, "Oh yes. Yes, I want to go. Thank you." He hugged her back enthusiastically.

"B.F., *I need you and the other dragons on the beach immediately*" Theo said.

"*We are leaving?*" B.F. asked.

"*Yes. As soon as possible, please. Also let the other dragons know that we have located Jessabelle. Tell Breezerunner and Skymaster to inform Serek and Gabriel of this development,*" Theo requested of B.F. "Jacoby, get going. I'll meet you on the beach at New Chance tomorrow at dawn. I'll see you then," he said dismissively.

"Whatever I can do I will," Jacoby responded as he changed into an eagle and flew into the sky over the ocean. He immediately went into a nose dive and disappeared behind a wave.

The three dragons landed on the beach with a sandstorm caused by their powerful wings. B.F. was the largest of the three, although not by much. His silver scales reflected the colors of the scenery in a shimmering mirage. He was larger than any of Roland's quaint cabanas and a presence to be respected and admired. Grand Oro and Sweet Vang, although fully grown, still had the energy and playfulness of youth. They nipped at each other and rolled their golden bodies in the sand after splashing in the surf. The glimmering of their gold scales looked like treasure washed ashore as they frolicked on the beach.

Roland came running out of his cabana and dropped several bundles in a heap along with his staff. He ran directly up under B.F.'s mighty head, placed his two hands on the dragon's foreleg and pressed his head against him. Remaining that way for some time, Roland began to hum a happy tune to himself. B.F. tried to free himself of the unwanted pest by picking up his leg, wizard and all, and giving it a good shake. "*Theo, who is this?*" B.F. asked. "*And why is he touching me?*"

"Roland," Theo called. "Roland!"

The old man released his grip on B.F. and turned to Theo. "It's a real live dragon! Can you believe it? He's silver. And, oh my, oh my, look! There are two more. They are so beautiful . . . awesome. They are *sooo* big! Do you smell that? Dragon musk. Wow! This is fantastic! Great good fortune. Three dragons on my beach! Whew hoo!" he sang as he danced with excitement.

"Roland. Roland!" Theo called again.

"What?" Roland asked as he gazed in wonder at the dragons.

"This is my friend, B.F. He prefers *not* to be touched. The golden dragons are Sweet Vang and Grand Oro. They are just babies so they must be treated carefully--in other words, leave them be. No touching! You will ride with me on B.F." With a scowl on his face, he surveyed the five large satchels Roland had left in a pile nearby. On top lay his long wooden staff. "Do you have to bring all of that?" Theo asked.

"Well, yes, of course I do. I could bring more. Do you think I should bring more? Maybe I should . . .well. . . Do you have catfish where you are from?" Roland's inquiry was deliberately ignored by the king.

# Chapter 12

## A WHISPER AND A SCREAM

Serek had taken ten of his best men with him and with thoroughness they had scoured the area north of the forest all that day. No sign could be found or any evidence encountered that indicated that Jessabelle had ever been in the vicinity. With foreboding, he turned his attention to the forest itself. As they rode south the trees thickened as did the darkness. The sounds also thickened, if that is possible, as if from quiet to chaos. The soft tinkling of rustling leaves and chirping song birds was slowly replaced by shrill whistling in the upper canopy and an occasional blood-curdling high-pitched shriek. Night would be upon them soon. It was the same night that Candaz and Stephan met outside of Castle Xandia and the same night that his wife and her companions descend on the island where the outcasts of New Chance are located. That night still lay ahead of Serek and he was heading into a place that was best not traversed in the dark.

The horses grew harder to control as their sensitive instincts pushed against what they were being forced to do. Every inch of their flesh screamed at them to run, to get away, but instead they treaded deeper into the forest with the guidance of their trusted riders.

Serek had not heard from Breezerunner since early this morning. The dragon had nothing new to report except that he had consumed a large ripgar the night before and was feeling full and sleepy. He was probably curled up somewhere warm and isolated snoring loudly.

"Halt," called Tallith, who was the best tracker in Saberville. He jumped nimbly off his horse and examined a pile of leaves on the ground, which to Serek looked like, *well*, a pile of leaves. "There's a drop of blood." He picked up a single leaf and sniffed it. "It's from a deer." He continued to probe around the area, following the blood trail. "Here," he said. "Something feasted on the deer carcass here." There were a few bones strewn about, all of them picked clean.

"Everything is gone except the bones. What kind of creature does that?" The man behind Serek, nicknamed Shorty because of his excessive height, asked as he held the reins of the horse tightly against his stallion's ever increasing anxiety.

"There are stories about this forest," Tallith said in a gravelly voice that seemed to grow deeper as he grew older. "Things live here that live nowhere else. Crazy and murderous are these things. Vicious and cruel. Without a soul some say. Others say they are evil spirits."

The men behind him shifted uncomfortably in their saddles. These men were trained to be men of war. Although none of them had seen actual battle in their lifetime, all of them had trained hard to become the warriors they were. They were not without experience in adverse situations, but this was something different and it made them edgy.

"I've seen these things. They are just animals. Nothing more," Serek said. "Let's do a sweep. If there is any sign that Jessabelle was here, I want it found. Shorty, take the left flank, Stash, you take the right. Tallith, lead the way. Stay sharp, men."

Working in the waning light, they spread out to cover as much ground as possible, but still remain within sight of one another. The horses obediently walked through the forest south toward the path that served as the boundary between the forest and the swamp. The foliage was thick and tough going. As they continued, Serek got the distinct feeling that they were being watched. His nerves were frayed although he would not, *could not*, show his men. Discomfort was his ever-present companion. He was worried, tired, hungry, and his left hip throbbed from an old injury. Shifting in his saddle brought a little relief, if only temporarily.

From overhead came a shrill chattering cry. Another answering almost bark-like vocalization came from further away. This continued for a disquieting period of time before ceasing abruptly, leaving an eerie silence in its wake.

"I found something," Stash shouted from Serek's right. They all joined him and gathered around the small item he held in his hand. "It's a feather from a bald eagle. It must be from the Queen. She is the only one of her kind in the realm. There is blood on it. I'm afraid she must be injured."

"Search the area," Serek ordered.

As they complied with his command, the shrill cries started up again. Despite the noise, they focused on their task. With meticulous care, they circuited the spot where the feather was found but found nothing more. "Serek."

"What is it, Tallith?" Serek asked over the uproar.

"She must have flown away from here. There is no more trace of her," his shout was interrupted by the sudden cessation of the horrible cries. At the same time, darkness enveloped them completely.

"Yes, I believe you must be right," Serek said, as he peered through the impenetrable gloom. "Perhaps we should find a place to make camp for the night." The shrieking cries once again shattered the quiet. "On second thought, let's get out of here. I don't think we'll find anything more."

"I agree, Serek. But navigating through this forest in the dark could be dangerous for the horses. Perhaps we should make camp," Tallith gave his advice based on the practical choice, not on his instinct which told him to flee.

Quiet prevailed once more. Serek waited, knowing the other men would have their own opinions on the matter. After a relatively short discussion, he deferred to his men's wishes. "Okay, let's head back to the north and find a place to make camp until the clouds clear and we have some light to travel by or until morning." Screaming and squawking started once again seeming much louder than before. "I don't think we're going to get any sleep tonight," he shouted.

Serek followed behind his men and tried to adjust his seriously unhappy attitude. Although his body complained painfully and demanded rest, he did not want to spend the night in this forest, not tonight, or any other night but his men had decided and he would comply with their wishes this time. Regardless, he wasn't happy about it.

It wasn't too long before they came across a small clearing and quickly had a large fire blazing in the center of it. They unpacked enough gear to prepare a meager meal and shared a bottle of wine. Although relaxing was impossible, they did take the opportunity to rest their tired muscles. The tethered horses remained jumpy and did not settle down, not even with the gentle coaxing from Stash's expert hand. They stomped their hooves and pulled on their ropes in constant distress as the noises in the forest assaulted their ears once more.

Exhaustion overtook Serek and he began to phase in and out of sleep, with his heavy eyes working their way into a nightmarish dreamland before popping open when awakened suddenly by one sound or another or by the absence of sound, which was just as significant. It became difficult to differentiate between reality and nightmare. His concern over the unrest of the horses became amplified in his nightmare by the animals stampeding through their small camp raining death and destruction. He awoke and gulped down his terror only to fall asleep moments later and in his mind's eye see the monkey-like monsters in the trees descend upon them with long and flashing teeth biting and tearing flesh. In his dreams he saw Kristina being dragged away by the swamp creature once again. A slight cry escaped his lips as he jolted himself awake again. He began to fight to stay awake so as to not fall into the terror of his own mind, but eventually would lose that battle and find some other horror awaiting him.

The screaming in the trees suddenly intensified and crashing could be heard from the canopy as limbs were broken and leaves ripped apart. Something landed hard on the ground in front of him and Serek felt hot breath and spittle in his face. He rolled and reached for his sword. For a time he wasn't sure if this was real or if he was trapped in his dreams. Going with his instincts, he let his muscles work the blade in his hand. The paralysis of sleep did not hinder his motions and he knew he must be awake. When the sharp edge tore into the flesh of the monster creature in front of him and rendered the life forever from it he knew it for sure this was no dream. Not a nightmare, but reality.

His companions were on their feet and fighting off the monkey-like creatures that were coming in mass and from all directions. Blood flew everywhere as the humans with very sharp steel spared nothing within reach of their flying blades. The screaming was deafening. As the carnage around them mounted so did the frenzy of the creatures that attacked with ferocious recklessness. In the midst of the tumult the horses pulled loose and bolted, announcing their own terror with high pitched brays.

Slick with blood, Serek's sword slipped from his grip and fell to the ground. He quickly retrieved the two daggers from his boots and brought them into action, slicing and stabbing at his attackers as they sliced him with their claws and tried to maul him with their long sharp fangs. The skill he displayed in handling his daggers was exemplary and he fended off the beasts with each stroke. By now he was fully alert. With adrenaline driving his body, energy coursed through him. All of the years of training kicked in and his actions became automatic as he fought the unending assault throughout the night.

With dawn came the departure of the monkey-faced monsters. Their retreating cries could be heard withdrawing into the distance as they went.

Wiping his soiled blades on his equally filthy pants, Serek sheathed his weapons one at a time and glanced around at the grim scene. Furry bloody bodies lay in piles all around them. Not just a few, but dozens, maybe hundreds of the monstrosities. The smell was horrendous and Serek felt his stomach roll, but he managed to control the urge to vomit. He did a quick head count of his men. All ten were still standing. A couple of them were tending wounds, but nobody seemed seriously injured.

"Shorty, let's stoke up that fire as high as you can, we need to burn these bodies. Tallith, take Stash and see if you can round up the horses. Don't go too far, though. I'd rather we stick together.

If you don't find them, we'll be hoofin' it. Dylan, let's check to make sure there is no life left in any of these things. Dispatch them quickly if you find any alive. Let's get to work, men. It's been a long night, but we're not through yet," he said. Finding his pack, he retrieved from it a long-necked bottle which he uncorked expertly with his knife. Serek took a long drink of wine before passing it on to the closest man and started his grotesque examination of their slaughtered assailants.

As the day advanced, the task of burning the bodies progressed at a pace that was slow and painful. They were almost finished by the time Tallith and Stash returned with all but two of their horses.

They found a place to clean up and get some much needed nourishment. It had been a long night and a long day. Rest was much needed. Serek hoped it was possible. Odds were good that they would be attacked again that night. After consuming an easy meal and drinking a lot of wine, the men took the time to sleep. Serek sat with Tallith and Stash and ate some dry road rations. "I think we should finish this. Hunt the rest of these things down and finish them once and for all. Breezerunner has informed me that the Queen has been located so that mission is over," Serek told them. "If we are ever going to reestablish a community in New Chance, these creatures must be dealt with sooner or later."

"We could use some reinforcements. It won't be easy," Tallith said.

"I don't want to be here any longer than we need to be. Let's get this finished now," Serek said.

"It's possible. We managed well enough last night. How many do you think there are?" Tallith asked.

"I couldn't tell you. They are driven by pure blood lust. It's merely a matter of tactics overcoming the massive numbers. We can do this with a good plan," Serek replied as he closed his eyes and lay back and let sleep take him.

# *Wisp-erer*

Rew tossed an apple to Lodi who in turn lobbed it to Wes. He took a big bite and licked the juices off of his lips with excessive pleasure as he threw the remains of his first apple away. Rew flung another apple to Lodi and bit eagerly into his own. It was his second and it tasted as good as the first, juicy and sweet. He smiled and asked, "Gabriel, do you want one?" A beautiful apple tree just outside the entrance offered large ripe fruit ready to be picked and enjoyed. The wisps had no trouble taking advantage of the free food.

"Not right now, thanks," she replied as she examined the parchment in front of her.

They were in an underground man-made cavern. The small round door that served as the entrance was locked with runes infused with freecurrent energy. Gabriel spent at least an hour deciphering and circumventing the magic to gain entry. It was a small laboratory with an even smaller library in the back. The walls were sleek white and there was a long shiny table down the center of the narrow space. Vials were neatly arranged in racks around the room and labeled according to their contents. A thin layer of dust covered everything indicating that the lab had not been visited in a long time. It seemed to Gabriel that this must be leftover from when Candaz ruled Saberville or maybe even from his ancestors. All of the notes she had perused were dated many years ago. Exactly what was being researched was unclear but components were used in different combinations and the results recorded.

There were graphs and ledgers and lists along with piles of notes, most of which were illegible. The penmanship would not win any awards for neatness. Gabriel set aside the parchment in front of her. She walked further back into the cluttered library and started shuffling through a stack of papers. For a moment she froze with a single paper in her hand. She stared at it and then gasped.

"Rew!" she called urgently.

When he didn't answer she spun on her heel and looked to see where he was. "Rew!" she called as she walked toward the entrance with her shoes clicking loudly on the floor. "Rew!" She rushed to his side and knelt beside him. He was flat on his back on the floor barely breathing. Close by lay Wes and Lodi in the same condition. Gabriel let some expletives escape her lips. *"Skymaster come quickly!"* she called to him mentally.

*"What is it, Mistress? What has you so distressed?"* Skymaster asked in response.

*"The wisps have been poisoned. I must get them to Elysia immediately,"* she said.

*"I will be there soon. How did they get poisoned?"* Skymaster asked.

Gabriel quickly arranged props under the necks of the three wisps to make sure their airways were clear. She checked pulses, which for a wisp was normally relatively fast. Their pulses were regular for a human, but slow for a wisp. Leaving them where they lay, she went to the parchment she had run across in her exploration of the laboratory. On it was a drawing of an apple tree with equations and a list of chemicals scrawled across every inch of the page. Folding it up, she stuffed it into her belt and answered Skymaster's question, *"There is an apple tree at the entrance of this place. It is a trap . . . a defense against intruders. The apples are poisoned. They probably would have killed a human with the first bite. Candaz must have placed it there to execute any unwanted guests. The wisps are in mortal danger. We must get them home."*

*"I'm almost there,"* Skymaster said.

"Grace and Gold Stone," Gabriel called two other dragons, "I need you to find Terese and Zeth and meet us here immediately."

*"Yes, Mistress Gabriel,"* Grace replied.

*"Yes, Mistress Gabriel,"* Gold Stone also replied. *"We are close by. We will join Master Skymaster after we fetch our humans."*

"*Good. I need your help.*" She could not transport the three unconscious wisps all by herself.

Quickly she checked on the wisps again and found their condition unchanged. Stepping outside of the door, she plucked a couple of the apples from the tree and stuffed them in her pockets. Placing her hands on the trunk, Gabriel focused the freecurrent energy to try and discern the tree's essence. It was complicated and would take time to analyze, time that she did not have, time that the wisps did not have.

"Mother, what's happened?" Zeth appeared quietly behind her. She hadn't even noticed the three dragons that had landed nearby.

Removing her hand from the tree, Gabriel turned to Zeth and said, "This tree is poisonous. The wisps ate of the apples and are in grave danger. We must get them to Elysia."

Zeth approached the tree and ran his fingers over the rough surface of the trunk. He took a moment to do his own examination of the tree's essence. "This is familiar, but different too. There must be an anecdote to this poison. Did you find anything inside?"

"There are many bottles filled with potions. I don't know if there is an anecdote. Take a good look, Zeth," she said. "Maybe you will find something that I missed."

"I will have a look around," he said.

"You must hurry. I don't think the wisps have much time. Their breathing is very shallow," she warned as she stepped inside with her son.

Terese came in behind them and began checking on the wisps. "Dying they are Zeth. We must go. Time there is not," she said. Without waiting for them she lifted Lodi in her arms and headed out the door.

Zeth quickly checked the bottles lining the shelves. Confused, but not completely clueless, he selected three different bottles and stuffed them into the pockets of his tunic. "Let's take these. I'm not sure. If only we had more time. Let's get them to Elysia. That is their best chance at this point." He gathered Wes in his arms and followed Terese out the door.

Gabriel bent over Rew and gently picked him up. "Rew, you must be okay. Please don't die on me," she said as she placed a gentle kiss on his forehead and wiped her tears away with her shoulder. "Hang on, my friend. Hang on."

# Chapter 13

## LOVE BITES

"Dad, are you okay?" Jesse asked as she clapped the dust from her hands and wiped the sweat from her forehead.

"Yeah. I just need a break. I'm not as young as I used to be," he replied as he rose back off the ground. They had been working throughout the night. Dawn was on the horizon. "I'm good," he reassured her. "Are you okay?"

"Just worried," she said.

"Let's get back to work. Your dragon seems to have pinpointed where we need to focus our efforts," he said. "Look at the way she and Felcore are working together." He still could not believe there was a dragon in his midst. He looked upon her with awe.

As Tempest removed another large boulder from the area that Felcore was digging through, the two of them became instantly excited and began working more feverishly.

*"What is it, Tempest?"* Jesse asked.

*"I can smell them--wolves,"* Tempest told her. The dragon pushed her nose through a small opening they had managed to make and then withdrew it, making a much bigger hole.

Out of the opening emerged two huge wolves. Both of them were panting and paused where they stood. One was an unusual rust color and the other was dark gray and black. Simultaneously, they shook the dust off of their shaggy coats and looked about, letting their eyes adjust to the dim morning light.

The rust colored wolf took one look at Jesse and was upon her in a single massive leap. It buried its muzzle into her neck, seemingly to bite into her tender throat and end her life.

Even though Bill and Jacob both acted to intercept the dangerous animal, they could not reach her fast enough. They ran to her side and tried to intercede, but the wolf paid no attention to them.

Jesse wrapped her arms around the wolf's neck and as she rolled him off from her he turned into a man. She lay on top of him and they began to kiss each other happily through their tears. "Nicky, thank God," Jesse said.

His soft warm lips travelled to her chin and then back to her mouth again. "Jesse, you're okay?" he whispered. His gold eyes sparkled as they explored her face.

"Yes. You?" she asked with concern. She could read that something was wrong in the set of his jaw.

"Um. I think I have a broken leg," he told her. "But, Shareen is seriously injured. You must come quickly." They were both on their feet and Nick was pulling Jesse toward the opening from which he had just emerged. The two of them disappeared into it.

Bill's mouth was wide open as he watched this unfold. He turned to Jacob and discovered the same shocked expression on his son's face. "Nicholas I presume?" he asked.

"Jesse's boyfriend is a wolf?" Jacob's face was incredulous.

"Actually, he's a kendrite," Jim said from where he stood petting Felcore. "He's a shape changer." The gold in Jim's eyes flashed as he grinned at them.

Tempest made a strange huffing sound and once again began to dig, enlarging the hole through which Jesse and Nick had just disappeared. Felcore barked once and joined her.

"I guess we have more work to do, folks. Unless you can fit a dragon through the eye of the needle, we need to expand that hole," Jim said before he melted back into a wolf and started digging once again.

Jacob locked eyes with his dad, "It's a strange new world. Let's get back to work."

"Right behind you, son."

## Honor and Respect

Jesse followed Nick to where Shareen lay. She was still breathing but was unresponsive when Jesse pressed her hand to her face and said her name, "Shareen, it's Jesse. Can you hear me?"

She examined the older woman with gentle hands, running them over her body and finding her injuries with an instinct and skill that had been bestowed upon her by the wisps. Tears ran down her face as her fingers found broken bone after broken bone. The damage to Shareen's body was extensive.

Jesse's eyes found Nick's in the darkness. "I don't know if I can help her," she whispered, the words catching in her throat.

"She is dying, then?" he asked, also in a whisper.

"I'll do what I can," she said, "but first . . ." She touched Nicholas's broken leg and let freecurrent flow through the injury, binding bone and healing ripped flesh. As the medallion burned against her chest so did the pain of the injury burn through her as she absorbed it quickly, to dissipate just as quickly, leaving him restored. While she healed him she experienced his nature and knew without question that she could completely trust him, that he was honorable all the way down to the very core of his being. Her love for him deepened. The revelation brought her emotionally to her knees.

Sensing her surrender, he brushed her face ever so tenderly with his fingertips and leaned in to touch his lips to hers just as tenderly. "Jesse," he whispered sending tiny shivers through her body. "Thank you."

She responded by saying, "I love you, Nick." She was crying openly now.

He said, "I love you, Jesse." His voice was throaty with passion and emotion. With his eyes still drinking in hers, he asked, "What can I do to help?"

"Keep your hands on me. Let me feel your energy," she said as she placed her own hands on Shareen. Closing her eyes, Jesse focused completely on the older woman. Although her injuries travelled the expanse of her small frame, she was pleasantly peaceful. Pain was dealt with in the confines of her mind, nullified and dulled for endurance sake. Healing was a process, a slow progression, inch by inch, one touch at a time. Freecurrent flowed through the three of them, no wait, *four* of them. Felcore was with them as well, loaning his own energy to the effort. She hadn't noticed him at first, but now felt his furry body pressed up against her leg. The energy reached into the broken woman and the destruction of flesh and bone was minimized as it was drawn out and restoration infused in its place.

Even though Shareen's own system had shut out the worst of the pain, Jesse experienced it as it shot through her cruelly. Without realizing it, she screamed and cried out with the intensity of it. Nick wrapped his arms around her and held her as she struggled to achieve a miracle. It was beyond her grasp, however. She gave it her all, but it wasn't enough. The damage was too extensive. Shareen was dying and Jesse could not stop that. With the last of her resources, she did her best to make the dying woman comfortable, to increase her sense of peace. When she was finished administering what aid she could, she placed her hands on Shareen's face and bent over to kiss her on the cheek. "I'm sorry, Shareen. I can do no more to help you," she said before she sank back into Nick's arms and cried. Felcore pushed his head against her side, offering comfort and she gently pulled her old friend into her embrace, treasuring his warm softness.

For a moment, Shareen opened her eyes. With more breath than whisper she said, "Take me home."

As Shareen closed her eyes again and sank back into a comfortable sleep, Nicholas responded, "We will, Grandmother. We will take you home."

## Excavation

Jesse fell asleep as well. She awoke some time later comfortably and securely encased in Nicholas's strong arms to a world that was buzzing with activity. Felcore had taken a protective stance alongside Shareen's prostrate form. The golden retriever acknowledged his mistress with the thumping of his tail. She scratched him affectionately. Nicholas stirred and groaned as she moved to get up. "Jess, stay here," he moaned.

"No," she sighed as she swept her lips against his, "I'm going to help dig." She did not want to leave his warm loving arms, but this was not the time to linger in their intimacy. There was work to be done.

While she had slept, Tempest, Jim, her dad and Jacob had been working on clearing the debris that blocked the lightning gate at the very back of the cave. The explosion had deposited boulders and piles of sediment directly in front of the gate entrance. Tempest was as good as a bull dozer and moved the majority of the heavy material on her own. The other three men worked along with her slowly and methodically removing the rest of the debris with determined doggedness.

"Jesse, how's Mistress Shareen?" Jim asked as he paused at her approach.

"She's the same; sleeping quietly for now. You've made good progress. I can see the top of the lightning gate." She pointed over the debris field. "Dad, how are you hanging in there?" she asked as she stopped him from going back for another rock.

"I'm fine, Jesse. Your dragon . . . Tempest, she's really something," he said. "How's the patient?"

"For now she's stable. She wants to go home," Jesse told him.

"Where is home?" he asked.

"That's a good question, Dad. We'll have to figure that out. Why don't you take a break? Can you watch over Shareen while Nicholas and I take over for you? We can rotate, but I don't want her left alone," she said.

"Sure, honey. I think we're almost through. Do you have any more water?" he asked.

"There are a couple of bottles left in my pack. Go ahead and take one," she offered.

"Thanks Jesse," he said and stopped her by grabbing her hand.

"Yes, dad?" she asked.

"I never would have believed this, not in a million years. I'm sorry I doubted your motivations. I should have known your character better after all that we've been through together. I am very proud of you," he diverted his face as his eyes misted over.

"Thanks, Dad," she said and gave him a hug. "That means a lot to me."

They all continued to dig until a narrow path was cleared to the gate. There appeared to be no damage to the lightning gate itself. The constellations rotated at their usual pace.

"Tempest," Jesse said, "Can you fit through there?"

"I am most definitely sure," she replied. "Jesse, I am in need of a bath."

"Yes, sweetie," Jesse laughed. "We all need a bath."

"How are we going to move Shareen?" Jim asked.

Bill's voice came from nearby where he sat with her, "I think we should make a stretcher and carry her. We'll need some long poles and strips of cloth. Any ideas?"

"We can use my shirt for cloth strips," Jacob said.

"And mine," Bill added.

"Where are we going to find poles in the desert?" Jacob asked.

"I have an idea," Jesse said. "Tempest, come with me." To the others she said, "I'll be right back."

She placed her hand on the edge of the lightning gate and rotated the constellations until the shape of a condor came into focus. Without hesitating, she disappeared through the gate.

On the other side of the lightning gate was Risen and past the cave was a vast expanse of forest. She quickly chose two saplings that were the right size. "Tempest, could you do me the favor of uprooting these trees, stripping the branches, and nipping off the ends?"

"Yes, Jesse. Can we go hunting after that?" Tempest asked with her normal narcissistic point of view.

"As soon as we can, sweetie. We need to take care of Shareen first," Jesse answered.

"Oh, all right. I'm hungry, though," Tempest whined.

"As soon as Shareen is at Castle Xandia you can go find yourself a big fat ripgar," Jesse said. "Okay?"

"*Okay.*" Tempest bit the saplings off and cradled them in her mouth. She looked like a very big dog waiting for his owner to play fetch.

"*We'll go back . . .* " Jesse began, but was interrupted.

"*Skymaster is almost here . . . and Grace and Gold Stone. They carry Gabriel, Zeth and Terese, but also Rew, Lodi and Wes. The wisps are injured,*" Tempest told her.

"*Skymaster, what's going on?*" Jesse asked the dragon mage directly.

"*The wisps ate poisonous apples and are presently unconscious and possibly dying. Mistress Gabriel intends to take them to Elysia. How are you sweet human?*" Skymaster asked.

"*I'm good, thanks, Skymaster, but Shareen is injured badly and we need to go back to get her. How far away are you?*" Jesse asked.

"*We just passed Castle Xandia. We will be at the cave shortly,*" Skymaster informed her.

"*I'm going to go get Shareen and the rest of them. I'll be right back,*" Jesse said. *Poisonous apples? Really?* She took the small trees from Tempest and returned to Earth, leaving her dragon behind. It only took her a moment to traverse the worlds.

"Jesse," Nicholas greeted her immediately. "Here, let me get those." He took the trees from her and proceeded to where Jacob and Jim were busy tearing shirts into strips. They began to bind the strips together and around the saplings to form a make-shift stretcher.

When they were finished Jacob climbed onto it and let Bill and Jim hoist him up just to test it to make sure it would hold. "I think we're good," Bill said.

Gently and slowly they moved Shareen onto the device. She groaned, but did not wake up or show any other signs of consciousness. Nicholas took one end and Jacob took the other as they approached the lightning gate. Jesse quickly made the Condor appear and waited for the others to proceed through in front of her. First Jim, who ducked as he went through even though he didn't have to. He was followed closely by Nick and Jacob carrying Shareen. Felcore remained vigilant at Shareen's side. Bill, who was very tired and dirty, stopped and looked into his daughter's face. "You okay, Jess?"

"Some friends of mine are in trouble on Risen. Are you ready for this?" she asked.

"As ready as I'll ever be. Let's go," he said.

Jesse clasped her dad's hand like she used to when she was a little girl and together they walked through the lightning gate to Risen.

The cave on Risen was suddenly crowded. After Gabriel greeted her grandson, Jacob, with a warm embrace she knelt down beside Shareen. She spoke quietly to the unresponsive woman as she held her hand. Nearby Zeth and Terese held Wes and Lodi in their arms and waited anxiously. Jim, who had been handed Rew, was examining the wisp with his eyes as he cradled him.

Gabriel stood up as she saw Bill and Jesse enter. She gave Jesse a quick hug first. "Bill," she approached him and then they embraced. "It's good to see you. I'm so sorry I wasn't there for you after Marguerite died. I couldn't face it. I should have been stronger . . . for you . . . for them." Her eyes shot glances at Jacob and Jesse.

"It's all in the past now, Gabriel. Let's just say you are forgiven and move on. I know Marguerite would have wanted it that way," Bill said sincerely.

"You are a good man Bill Gates. I am proud that you are my son-in-law," she smiled and wiped away a tear or two.

Gabriel addressed Jesse next, "The wisps have been poisoned. I have one of the apples here." She pulled a shiny red apple out of her pouch and handed it to her granddaughter.

Jesse rubbed the tainted fruit with her thumb and then walked over to Rew and placed her hand on his forehead. Freecurrent energy flowed between her fingers as she used it to enable her examination of the wisp. It was as if a fog encompassed his mind. She could not penetrate it or in any way negate the poison that caused it. His heart rate was slow and his breathing was shallow. "Rew," she whispered.

"We need to get them to Elysia," she said as her eyes fell on Shareen where they rested for a full minute before she turned to Gabriel. "She said she wanted to go home, but where is home to her? Grandmother?"

"I don't know if she meant Castle Gentlebreeze, Tower of Ornate, or possibly her latest home. It could be any one of those three," Gabriel replied. She again knelt beside her former mentor and spoke quietly to her. "Shareen. Shareen, can you hear me? Shareen, can you open your eyes?"

The older sorceress fluttered open her eyes for only a moment, "Gabriel," she sighed before lapsing back into unconsciousness.

Jesse joined the two women. She placed one hand on Shareen and the other on Gabriel. Blue fire shot between them as the freecurrent resonated. Focusing on Shareen's mind, she attempted to read her thoughts. It was something like trying to read a novel by reading individual sentences in random order. Flashes of impressions shot through Jesse's own mind. People, places, things, and feelings came and went. "Where is home, Shareen?" Jesse asked.

The reaction was instant. First the image was of Shareen's Sedona home in the desert, but then it changed to images of the Tower of Ornate with her friends Nina and Hugh, but finally her thoughts of home settled on the setting of Castle Gentlebreeze and of her family, some still alive and some long gone. She was sad and happy, regretful and peaceful, all at the same time. All these thoughts occurred in an instant. Jesse found that tears were streaming down her own face as she withdrew her focus. "Gentle-breeze," she said simply.

"Gentlebreeze," Gabriel agreed.

"We will take her to Castle Gentlebreeze," Nicholas said. "Agape is on his way here. I'll see grandmother home, and then I'll seek out Candaz."

"Speaking of Agape," Gabriel said, "where was he when Candaz came through? He was supposed to be guarding the gate."

Nick was silent as he communicated with his dragon and then he said, "He says he was hungry and needed to hunt and that he is sorry."

"Yes, I heard him," Gabriel said. "I guess we'll have to accept it for what it is."

Jesse interrupted, "I'll take Rew and catch up with you later. Zeth, Terese, you ready?" Jesse asked.

"What do you mean?" Zeth asked.

"Do you want to go to Elysia with me? I can't carry all three of them by myself," Jesse said.

"Do you think they'll let us in? The Elysians I mean." Zeth asked with doubt in his voice.

"Let's try, shall we? Terese, you in?" Jesse asked as she approached the gate.

"Yes. In I am," she said as she joined her at the gate.

"RRowwf!" Felcore barked as he jumped up and ran to Jesse.

"Come on, boy. You can come too," Jesse laughed.

"*Tempest, stay here and wait for us to return. You can go hunting, but don't go too far. Keep the babies with you. We'll need you all when we return,*" she told the dragon mentally.

"*Good-bye, Jesse. I'll be here when you get back,*" Tempest responded.

"Nick?" Jesse swallowed the lump of longing in her throat. She suddenly felt a pit of desolation at leaving him, like she was leaving a part of herself behind. "I'll see you soon."

"Jesse. Take care of them. See you soon," Nicholas maintained eye contact with her for an extended moment before pulling his gaze away. "Jacob, Bill, Jim, you are with me and Gabriel," Nicholas said.

They watched as Jesse, Zeth and Terese, carrying the wisps and accompanied by Felcore, disappeared through the gate.

Agape trumpeted at his fellow dragons as he came in for his landing. The other four dragons bellowed their greeting back. The air echoed with their flamboyant voices.

"We're gonna ride a dragon?" Jacob asked excitedly.

"We're going to what?" Bill asked anxiously.

"Yes, Jacob, you and your dad will ride on Agape. Jim and I will fly as eagles along with you. We'll stop at Castle Xandia to rig up something to carry Shareen all the way to Brightening. Gabriel, are you going to be okay from here to there with her?" Nicholas asked.

"We'll somehow manage. Let's get going," she returned.

Jacob and Nicholas lifted the stretcher and carried Shareen out of the cave. It took them awhile to get her positioned on Skymaster's back with Gabriel steadying her, but they did the best they could under the circumstances to safely transport her to Castle Xandia, their first stop.

Bill and Jacob mounted Agape, and together, with a little coaching, they launched into the sky and followed Skymaster closely. Next to them flew Jim and Nick in eagle form.

Castle Xandia was a welcomed sight to all of them and they spent the night there preparing for the flight to Castle Gentlebreeze. Shareen's condition remained the same. Gabriel stayed with her throughout the night accompanied by Stephan's little sister, Kate. The next morning they were ready for the flight ahead. Jacob and

Nick had engineered an ingenious contraption to comfortably and safely convey Shareen on Skymaster, slung under his belly.

The somber group left early in the morning. Kate saw them off. As the dragons and eagles ascended, the sun rose over the horizon in a brilliant display of red, orange and pink. Humidity in the air was thick and sticky, making it uncomfortable, almost intolerable. The breeze off the water was brisk and brought no comfort with it. Waves crashed on the shore in a relentless demonstration of the ocean's power. The clouds were building in the west and painted an ominous picture.

# Chapter 14

## SPIDER'S LAIR

Stephan reached up and grabbed a shiny red apple off the tree and brought it up to his lips.

"I wouldn't do that if I were you," Candaz said as he opened the door and walked inside.

Sniffing the fruit, he gave it a cursory examination and then tossed it aside. With a shrug of his shoulders, he followed the old man into the strange facility. He watched Candaz as he walked through the narrow room between the long clean table and the shelf-lined wall. He seemed to be doing a mental inventory as he pointed his finger one at a time to the bottles that lined the shelves. When he got to the back of the room, he paused to make a notation on a piece of parchment and then proceeded to inventory the other side of the room.

He paused again when he came to Stephan and mumbled the number thirteen. This time Stephan followed him to the back of the room. "Sir, do you have any more of that elixir? I could use a sip."

Candaz let his gaze rest on the young man for what he deemed to be the appropriate length of time to intimidate the boy and said, "Do me a favor first."

"What favor?" Stephan asked grudgingly.

"Get the saddle bag and load the bottles on this shelf, and this shelf only, into it." He pointed to the exact type of crystal decanters that he carried the elixir in. Stephan was eager to do this job. He figured he could easily slip two or three bottles into his pockets in the process of loading them into the saddle bag. Without hesitating, he went and fetched the saddle bag from his horse and returned to load it up. "Oh, and boy, I've counted them. I am very aware how many bottles there are. Don't even think about taking any for yourself," he warned.

Carefully, Stephan began loading the small crystal bottles into the saddle bag and despite Candaz's warning he surreptitiously stuffed one into his pocket. When he was done he asked, "Do you want this returned to the horses?"

"Yes, return the saddle bag to the horses. But, first return the bottle you stole to the saddle bag. You will now have to wait another turn before I give you any more elixir. You will learn not to steal from me, boy," Candaz said as he returned his attention to whatever he was doing in the back of the laboratory. Stephen returned the bottle he had taken to the saddle bag and loaded it onto the horse. He wiped the sweat off the back of his neck with his hand that was beginning to shake. A long drink of water from his container did little to help his upset stomach.

Patting his horse, he contemplated taking the saddle bag and leaving. There was enough elixir to keep him comfortable for a while. At least, he assumed it was elixir. It was the same bottle. He was becoming increasingly anxious and couldn't help checking

# DYNASTY

the door for Candaz. *Where is he? Why doesn't he come out? Maybe I should leave.*

Suddenly the old man was standing there in front of him. "Stephan, we are going to get the last ingredient needed to make more of the elixir. Here," he handed him some small ceramic jars. "Put these in the saddle bag and we'll be on our way."

Candaz mounted his horse and Stephan mounted his own and followed. "Do you think I could have a drink of elixir now?" he asked anxiously.

"Not yet," Candaz replied quickly. He rode quietly without comment for some time before saying, "I am sure you will not steal from me again. Should you ever again consider taking something from me that doesn't belong to you; you will find the consequences less than desirable. Do you understand me?"

Stephan was trembling visibly now and his face was drawn and pale. He apologized, "Yes. I am sorry. Do you think that I could have some now?"

When Candaz handed him the bottle, he swallowed down the liquid and was rewarded with gradual and welcomed relief. He sighed and let the tension dissipate from him in a slow stream. "Thank you," he said as he handed the bottle reluctantly back to his companion.

The laboratory they had just left was located in the foothills east of Castle Xandia. They rode south southeast at a leisurely pace, the steady motion of the horse was pulling Stephan's eyelids closed. He fought against it but was losing the battle. When they arrived at the boundary of the forest Candaz paused and took a long pull off the elixir bottle before handing it to Stephan who drank greedily. "This forest holds many little secrets from a past that are lost. Within it lays the key to my future on Risen, a future where I hold all of the power," Candaz said.

Stephan was having a difficult time focusing on the old man's ramblings. He tried to look attentive, like he was interested, but the man did have a tendency to drone on. Again, he closed his eyes and let his horse do the driving. When he awoke again he found that they were deep in the forest. Darkness prevailed even though it was the middle of the day. A horrendous noise assaulted his ears from all directions. It was a screeching, screaming vocalization that brought the hair up on the back of his neck. "What in the world is that?" he asked.

"That is the cry of the scalawag, a mutant creature that has been driven mad by the constant consumption of poppy excretions. They live in this forest," Candaz told him.

"Why are they so loud? Are they in pain?" Stephan asked, wincing.

"Scalawags are savage animals, savage and insane. Don't worry. They will not bother me," he said calmly.

"They won't bother *you*? They might kill me, but *don't worry*, they won't bother *you*," he said incredulously. "Why not?"

"They have encountered me before. I taught them a lesson that the colony will never forget. Upon their attack, I caused blood to boil inside them until their arteries exploded from their skin and burst from the pressure. Many of them had to die before they learned to leave me alone, but learn they did. As long as you are with me, you should remain safe as well," Candaz said.

"Wonderful. I wish they would shut up. That noise is driving me crazy," as Stephan said this statement, the racket ceased. A thick silence echoed in his ears.

The forest ended as suddenly as the noise. They rode into an open area that was filled with mature poppy plants. Large pods sat atop thin stalks about a foot and a half tall. Once the plants displayed vibrant red flowers, but they weren't ready to be harvested yet at that stage. More time was needed. The alien looking pods were the source of the opium gum that could be harvested and processed into a usable form.

"Ah, here we are," Candaz said brightly. He dismounted and examined some nearby specimens. "They are ready to be harvested. Look here, Stephan. The scalawags have done some of the work for us."

Stephan slid out of his saddle and looked to where Candaz was pointing. The poppy pod had been scored with claws and was leaking a thick milky gum-like substance. All around him, poppies leached out the sticky goo. Candaz took out his knife and scraped the stuff off and examined it critically. "Stephan, give me one of those ceramic jars." When he had the jar in his hand he scraped his knife against the edge depositing the gum. "Grab a jar. Get to work. Collect what you can. If you come across a poppy that hasn't been scored, do three or four cuts across the surface with your knife like this," he demonstrated with his own knife.

All around them screams of hostility erupted from the tree tops and continued relentlessly as the two men went meticulously from poppy to poppy. The work was hot and painstaking. When Candaz shared a nip from his little crystal bottle, it revived Stephan and kept him at task. It was odd how the elixir had a rejuvenating effect that was different than the drug that he had shot into his veins, which made him happy but quite drowsy after a short amount of time, certainly not energetic by any means. Whatever was in this elixir gave him the comfortable feeling from the opiate, but something more that made him feel younger and stronger. It was odd. He became determined to find out the secret as he scraped more gum off another poppy.

He looked at Candaz uneasily as the frenzy in the treetops continued to intensify. Now the creatures were so worked up that they tore through the trees, ripping leaves and breaking branches as they sprang from tree to tree. Their wails were horrific. The noise was tremendous. He felt for his weapon and realized that he had left it strapped to his horse's saddle. The chances that he would be able to make it to his sword should the scalawags attack were pretty negligible. His work had brought him close to the center of the poppy field, some distance away from the horses. Another glance at Candaz showed the old sorcerer bent to his task, oblivious to the fury that was mounting around him. Stephan decided to get his sword just in case and started to work his way quickly in that direction.

Before he could get there, one brave creature crossed the boundary from the forest into the poppy field and sped directly at him, followed closely by several others who were emboldened by the act. Soon a whole band of scalawags both flew and ran toward him. The knife in Stephan's hand seemed small and inadequate, but he held it tightly and prepared for the strike.

The vocalizations of the attacking creatures changed from a high pitched screams to ferocious snarls as they came. They did not hesitate, but hurtled at him at full speed. Stephan defended himself automatically, countering the assault as best he could with the knife in his hand. He let instinct drive his actions as he sliced and stabbed and spun while the creatures drove at him without pause, unrelenting and merciless. Teeth and claws punctured and sliced through his skin. It would not take long for the scalawags to overtake him.

Thoughts of his family ran through his mind as he fought without hope of prevailing. A range of emotions bombarded him as quickly as the teeth and claws were tearing him apart. He had never realized before how much his family meant to him. His mom and dad's love had always been with him, steady and without conditions or parameters. Thinking of how they would grieve for him made his heart break. Trevis and Lauren would mourn him, but they had their families and it would be easier for them. His sister

Kate . . . he couldn't think about what his death would do to her. And Nick . . .

Abruptly the assault stopped. All around him the creatures froze where they stood and screamed as their bodies erupted from within, literally seeming to turn inside out. The wails ended almost as soon as they had started and dead bodies lay everywhere, puddles of flesh and blood. A deadly silence followed.

Stephan slumped to the ground. His energy was spent but he was still alive. From behind him Candaz approached. "Are you injured?" he asked.

When Stephan didn't answer, he asked again, "Are you hurt, boy?"

"Yeah," he groaned. Through his shredded clothing were deep lacerations and puncture wounds where the scalawags had connected with their claws and teeth. He felt pain everywhere.

"Here," Candaz handed him his little crystal decanter. "Drink some of this."

He gulped down the remaining contents of the bottle and managed to get to his feet.

"You'll be all right after you get those wounds cleaned up. Take one of the containers and collect some blood from one of the creatures. I want to study it. I think we have enough poppy gum for now. We'll get back to the laboratory and begin preparations for the next phase of my plan," Candaz said and walked to the horses without further comment.

Stephan wanted to throw his knife at the old man, but instead he gathered himself and used an empty container to collect blood from one of the horrible creature's remains.

When he returned to his horse, he secured the containers in his saddle bag and mounted with considerable difficulty. His wounds were bleeding profusely. He could feel the wetness saturating his feet within his boots. Ripping some of the shreds from his tattered clothing, he tied bandages around the worst of his cuts, somewhat stemming the flow of blood.

Shadows were beginning to lengthen as twilight approached. Gray clouds were building on the western horizon. The air seemed denser than usual. As they entered the threshold of the forest, the scalawags once again began screaming. Looking back, Stephan saw a group of horses entering the poppy field. At the head of the group was his dad's tracker, his old friend, Tallith. His good friends Stash and Shorty were there as well. Right behind them was Serek. Stephan watched them from within the confines of the trees as they slowly surveyed their surroundings. His heart cried out to them, to *his* people, to Serek, *Dad.*

As he followed Candaz deeper into the forest, his emotions were in turmoil. The pull of the drug kept him shadowing the old sorcerer, but the core of his being wanted to turn around and join his father. He almost complied with his heart--almost. As his horse felt his hesitation, it paused and whinnied at the indecision of its rider. Stephan coaxed his mount back into motion with the heels of his boots, trailing Candaz and at the same time betraying his heart.

## Serek's Vengeance

The horses answered the call of their stable mate with their own nickering as they crossed the poppy field from the opposite side. With senses alert, they approached the carnage that remained from Candaz's slaughter. The others held back as Tallith jumped off his horse and examined the area. He took his time and then motioned for the others to join him.

"You're not gonna like this, boss," he said. "This here is Candaz's work. Do you see this print here? That's Stephan's boot. His boot prints are all over the place here. This one here is Candaz.

The edge of his heel is worn down because of the way he walks. I've seen it before. He has a slight limp." As the creatures in the forest made their presence known by loudly shrieking, Tallith had to raise his voice to be heard over the cacophony. "Stephan's print is quite distinctive too. This slice on the right boot is from my own sword when he made contact with it with a well-placed kick during practice a couple of years ago. He's lucky he didn't get his toes lobbed off. They spent the day harvesting whatever this is leaking from these weird-looking pods until they were attacked by these creatures that now lay dead. It appears that Stephan was pretty badly wounded. His blood is all over the place. He walked over here to this animal and then to his horse. The two horses left in that direction a short time ago." Tallith watched Serek as he let the information soak in. The screaming in the trees accelerated.

"Breezerunner informed me that Stephan had joined Candaz's company. But, I really didn't believe that he would help him!" Serek was fuming. His eyes were ablaze with torment and anger. "Let's go after them!" he said and he swung back into the saddle.

Before they could act on Serek's orders, as dusk began to fall, the scalawags attacked.

They came from all directions at once, bellowing their battle cry with blood-curdling decibels. The strong smell they brought with them was like that of rotting fish, fowl and putrid. Rushing without pause or concern, they attacked without thought or plan; a madness infused full speed charge.

"Defensive circle, men. Make your strokes count!" Stash shouted.

"Bring it on!" Serek yelled as his sword sung out its sweet song as he pulled it free of its sheath.

His first swing lobbed off the head of one of the monkey things. Its scream was abruptly cut off. Taking its place was another, and then another, until a pile of bodies hampered Serek's movement in the defensive circle. He expanded the perimeter by advancing to the other side of the corpses, as did his men. The onslaught continued well into the night with the scalawags numbering in the hundreds advancing and being cut down just as fast. The men did not cease nor change tactics. The attackers did not waver in their ferociousness despite their numbers being ravaged.

Although the men suffered some injuries with claws and teeth driving at them constantly, they dominated with their biting swords taking down any creature within reach. It was a blood bath, the suicide of a race as they kept coming in a mad frenzy until every last one of them was annihilated. The second moon of Risen was high in the night sky before the gruesome clash ended.

Serek's anger was exercised, but he felt sick to his stomach as he glanced around at the carnage. *"Breezerunner, I need you here. Bring Zlato or any other dragon within range. We're going to torch this place,"* he said.

*"Sounds fun,"* Breezerunner replied happily in stark contrast to Serek's sour mood.

# Chapter 15

## FIRE DANCE

Theo's party of travelers had arrived on the beach at New Chance late the previous night. Three dragons landed lightly on the sand and waited patiently while their passengers disembarked after the journey over the ocean. Baggage and saddles were removed, relieving the beasts of their burdens and freeing them to frolic for a while in the ocean before finding places to curl up and sleep.

Their human companions built a fire and made themselves comfortable. It was the perfect night for camping on the beach. A warm breeze blew off the ocean. Up above, a beautiful display of stars shone brightly in the sky along with Risen's two moons. Quiet conversation with occasional light laughter added to the warmth of the mood.

Theo gazed out over the waves lost in his own meditations. He was anything but content. Anxiety about Jessabelle was plaguing his every thought. What had happened to her that had caused her to lose her memory? Would she know him when she saw him? Would she be able to transform back into a human after being a dolphin for so long? Would she simply cease to exist if she didn't transform back to her true form? He did not fully understand the kendrite magic that gave them the ability to shape change, but knew there were dangers inherent to the species. All these fears and questions ran through his mind as he sat quietly looking into the fire. He couldn't wait for dawn when their meeting was to take place. He was excited to see her. Their lives were entwined and he could not imagine life without her. She was the love of his life and he would not be whole again until she was back in his arms.

"Theo," B.F. addressed him with a serious tone, "*Your grandmother Shareen has been found alive on Earth. However, she is now seriously injured and is dying. Gabriel and Nicholas, along with Jim McCaw and Jesse's father and brother are taking her to Castle Gentlebreeze.*"

"*How long does she have?*" Theo asked.

"*That is unknown. She has as long as she has. There is more. Rew and the other wisps, Lodi and Wes have been poisoned and are in serious jeopardy. They are dying. Jesse, Zeth and Terese are taking them to Elysia,*" B.F. informed him.

"*And Candaz?*" he asked.

"*He is presently unaccounted for,*" B.F. answered.

"Damn!" he said out loud and then proceeded to tell his companions about the latest developments.

As the night wore on the people around the campfire quieted down and eventually fell asleep. Theo dozed off and on but did not fully find the rest he so desperately needed. The night was long as a result and when the sun finally rose over the edge of the horizon, he was relieved. Theo strolled down the beach away from his party.

He watched the waves, expecting to see two dolphins surface. After the first tense moments of expectation, he sat down and waited with his eyes glued to the water. Standing up, he paced as he watched and waited. The morning ebbed but still there was no sign of Jessabelle or Jacoby. Theo fought the panic that was rising inside of him and continued to watch, continued to wait.

He was dimly aware of the camp stirring. Breakfast was being cooked and the smells reached him where he remained on the beach. Frustration brought him quickly to anger. Where were they? Did Jacoby find her? Was she unwilling to come? If Jacoby couldn't find her, where was *he*? Why didn't they make their scheduled meeting? It was *this* morning, right? Yes, he was sure he had told Jacoby this morning. This morning at dawn, he had told him. Where were they? *"B.F., do you see anything?"* he asked the dragon who was circling overhead.

*"Sorry, Theo, nothing at all,"* B.F. responded promptly.

*"Look again!"* he shouted mentally.

*"I continue to survey the whole area. I am sorry. Gold Oro is flying up and down the beach, but sees nothing either."*

"Theo," Kristina said as she walked toward him carrying a plate of food. "Nothing yet?"

She sat down next to him and handed him the plate which he looked at but did not touch. "Where are they, Kris?" he asked.

She put her hand on his shoulder before saying, "We'll find them, Theo. Nicky will be back soon. *He* will find her."

"Oh, Kris, I love her so much! I could not stand it if something happened to her," he said, sat the plate down and wiped tears from his eyes with his powerful hands.

"We'll find her, brother. Have faith. Eat something. You need to keep up your strength," she prompted, lifting the plate back up and handing it once again to him.

"I'm not hungry," he said.

"That's not the point. Eat it anyway," Kris ordered.

He took a small bite and then another. Without tasting the food he finished it and handed the plate back to Kristina.

She stood up and asked, "Are you coming back to camp? B.F. can keep an eye on things here. Why don't you come back with me, Theo?"

"No," he said with his eyes once again scanning the waves, "I'm staying here. You go ahead. Thanks for the food."

"Yes. You're welcome." She took a few steps and then turned and said, "We will find her, Theo."

"Thanks, Kris," he said, "I know. It's just that . . . well, I can't stand to think that she might need me and I can't help her. It's killing me not to be able to go to her. Right now I wish I was a kendrite."

"I know. Me too," she said before walking away.

During the course of the day Theo was visited individually by his entire party. All of them, except Kaltog, had words of encouragement along with some type of nourishment, whether food or drink or both. B.F. remained vigilant and kept in constant touch with Theo, updating him, even though there was nothing to update him about. Roland brought with him a lotion that was supposed to keep his skin from burning, which after much badgering on the part of the wizard, he agreed to put on. Kaltog just sat with him for a while, silently giving his strength and companionship without unnecessary words.

It wasn't until the sun was setting behind him on the far horizon that Theo left his post on the beach and joined the others. They were just getting dinner together while they waited for him. He looked tired and older than he had looked in a long time. Stoking the fire by poking it with a stick and turning the bird they had roasting on a spit, he remained deep in thought.

After dinner was consumed and cleaned up, they all reclined around the fire. It was another beautiful night on the beach, but the mood was subdued. Kristina was anxious to get going to Castle Gentlebreeze to see Shareen before she died, as was Theo, but he was conflicted about leaving without having made contact with Jessabelle. He needed Nicholas here, but Nicky was on his way to Castle Gentlebreeze with his dying great grandmother. The weather was about to turn for the worst. Storms were inevitable. He could feel it in his bones. As the night deepened, Theo's mind became decisive.

It pained him, but he said, "I think we need to get to Castle Gentlebreeze, Kris. We should be there."

"Yes. I agree," she replied quietly. It was obvious she had her own set of conflicts.

Kali's gentle and confident voice spoke from the other side of the fire, "You both should be at your grandmother's side. I will take Sweet Vang west to see if I can locate Candaz."

"I will stay with Kali," Kaltog said softly without looking up.

"Jared, you and Roland can remain with us," Theo announced.

"No," Roland disagreed. "I, me and Jared, that is, will go with the giant man torg and the banderg girl. You do not need us with you. They need us with them. The boy is with Candaz, is he not?"

"Yes. I suppose you are right," Theo reluctantly agreed. For some reason he felt a strong need to keep an eye on the crazy wizard, but the old man had a point.

They were packing gear in preparation to leave when B.F. said, *"Serek would like us to join him in the northern forest."*

*"Why,"* Theo asked tiredly.

*"He and his men have slaughtered the monkey bat things and they want the dragons to rain fire on the poppy field and the creatures' bodies to cremate them. The babies are too young to make dragon fire and Skymaster is on his way to Brightening, so that leaves just Breezerunner*

*and me. Can we go? It is on the way. Can we Theo?"* B.F. asked with child-like enthusiasm.

To the others Theo said, "Serek wants us to join him in the northern forest. Let's finish packing up the dragons and meet him there. Kris and I will head home afterward."

*"Yes, B.F., we will go,"* Theo told him.

The dragon let out a mighty roar in his excitement.

Once they were completely loaded up, Kaltog spread out the fire so it would naturally extinguish itself and they took to the sky. Although it was night, the light from the stars and both moons illuminated the land with a dull glow.

# Jacoby

As soon as the beach was vacant, from out of the waves walked a man, who watched the dragons fly away before he made himself fully visible on the beach. Jacoby managed to stir the fire back into a flame and warmed himself in front of it. He added some wood before settling into the sand and watching the flames. His thoughts were dark with self-recriminations. He could not face his brother-in-law with his failure. Jacoby did not know what he was going to do so he did nothing.

# Dance Of The Dragons

The dragons were all in a spirited mood and flew with exuberance. It wasn't far past the outskirts of New Chance where the boundary of the northern forest began. Time seemed to flash by and before Theo knew it they were descending into an open field.

The stench that rose to greet them was tremendous. Theo put his hand over his face and noticed that Roland behind him did the same while he grumbled, "Good creator, what is that stink?"

Serek looked up at them and waved a greeting. They landed next to Breezerunner and he helped Kristina off from Sweet Vang and gave her a long hug and kiss. They whispered to each other briefly before he turned and spoke to Theo, "I believe that all of the monkey creatures are dead. You can see even the young ones were in on their attack. They seemed beyond even their normal insanity, driven to a suicidal frenzy. After we are done cleaning up this mess, the men will see if they can find their nests and make sure of it. This poppy field was tended by the creatures to feed their insatiable appetite for the opium gum it produced. They lived for it and died for it. Now they will burn with it."

Theo gave a nod of his head. "Let's get to it then," he said, slapping his riding gloves together in a dusty clap.

The men had been working for hours piling all of the bodies into the middle of the poppy field. Serek gave instructions to Breezerunner to work from the outside in, controlling the burn by first creating a break between the forest and the field. B.F. and Breezerunner began on opposite sides, using dragon fire to flame the perimeter first. They were soon joined by Tempest, who was not going to miss out on any of the fun. Zlato, Grace and Gold Stone arrived with her, but observed from the ground.

It was like watching a choreographed dance the way the dragons moved in formation, weaving, diving and flaming in a beautiful pattern. Although the task was distasteful and gruesome in function, the dragons made it a wonder to behold. After a time, Tempest encouraged the baby dragons to join them and soon they were taking their own part in the dance. Flaming for a dragon was something that came with maturity. The babies were fully grown, but not yet fully mature. Even though they could not yet produce flames, they could take place in the dance and did so with joy. Grand Oro, Sweet Vang, Zlato, Grace and Gold Stone weaved in and out of Tempest, B.F. and Breezerunner.

The humans on the ground watched from a short distance away. The smell of burning hair was sharp in the small amount of smoke that reached them. Dragon fire burned hot, like an acetylene torch, so it left nothing smoldering, but incinerated quickly, leaving nothing but ash. There was very little smoke. The remains of the scalawags were soon returned to dust. The crop was destroyed. For more generations than could be remembered the poppies that had been planted, harvested and replanted would be no more.

In a unified chorus the dragons trumpeted with gusto. The job was done. They landed lightly on the burned-out clearing and were soon joined by their humans who congratulated their success with vigorous ridge scratchings.

Tempest quickly left with Grace and Gold Stone. They were heading back to the woods north of Castle Xandia to await their humans' return from Elysia.

The rest of them set up camp nearby to get some rest for the remainder of the night. Snoring was the newest tune in the forest with Kaltog being the lead singer. Everybody slept, except for Theo. He again found his much needed sleep to be elusive. Frustration at not being able to sleep made it even more difficult to relax and find rest. The humidity in the air made his discomfort more profound. Leaving wasn't an option because he had to wait for his sister, who was cuddled up with her husband at the moment. Anxiety was gnawing at him. Lying wrapped in his blanket, he was itching to get up and do something, but he didn't know what to do. He didn't want to wake everybody up, either, so he lay quietly wrapped in his exasperation.

"*Theopolis?*" B.F.'s voice came into his head.

"*I thought you were asleep. You were snoring,*" Theo replied.

"*I was sleeping. Now I am awake . . . and, I do not snore,*" B.F. said indignantly.

"*Right.*"

*"Would you like me to sing to you? You seem to be having problems sleeping,"* he said.

*"You can sing?"* Theo scoffed.

*"Close your eyes . . . and your telepathic mouth,"* B.F. told him before he started humming in Theo's mind. The melody was soft and beautiful. It wove a fabric that fell over Theo's psyche like a comfortable blanket. Hypnotic was the song that B.F. unfolded for his friend. Within moments Theo was sleeping soundly and added his soft snoring to the chorus.

With morning came thunder and the foreshadow of storms. Theo was even more anxious to get going and get some flight time in before the storm hit. He at least wanted to make it as far south as Skyview if possible. Serek was busy working out details with Stash. Theo wished his brother-in-law would hurry up. *Honestly, tell him what to do and get on with it. The man doesn't need instructions on how to wipe his butt,* he thought. He kept his sarcasm to himself, however.

The plan was for the men to hunt down and destroy any remaining scalawag populations and then take Roland to evaluate the swamp. Kaltog and Kali were going to remain with them to make sure Roland and Jared stayed out of trouble, but more importantly to be with them should they cross paths with Candaz and Stephan. Serek had decided to accompany his wife to Castle Gentlebreeze to pay their respects to Shareen, but he planned on returning to find his son as soon as he could. It was frustrating to have to leave without having encountered Stephan. He wanted to make Candaz pay for inducing his son to make the wrong choices.

"Serek, are you ready?" Theo asked not for the first time. Kristina shot him a scathing look. He shrugged his shoulders at her.

"Serek, let's get going. The weather is threatening," Theo pointed up. He was standing beside B.F., ready to go.

Catching Theo's impatience, Serek raised a finger, indicating he needed another minute. He said a few more words to Tallith, turned to Stash to add his last instructions before striding across the campsite to where the dragons were saddled and waiting. "Sorry. Let's go," he said as he climbed up into the saddle on Breezerunner's back. Kristina followed him up the small ladder, settled herself behind him and wrapped her arms around his waist. He brought up the ladder and secured it in place.

When Serek looked up, Theo was already in the air, hovering overhead, waiting once again.

The thunder rolled with honest intent as the dragons sped south.

## Vituperative Chemist

"Come on, boy, keep up!" Candaz spat at Stephan. "You are as worthless as my son. Your generation is lazy and useless."

They were just outside of the hidden laboratory. Stephan dismounted and tethered his horse next to the other horse without comment. He was tired and emotionally drained. It had been a long day. His body hurt all over and many of his wounds seeped through their bindings.

"There is work to be done. Move it, boy!" Candaz said.

Again Stephan chose not to respond. Slowly he began unloading the horses. He removed each saddle bag and container from the horses and conveyed them to the confines of the small laboratory. He took his time at the task. His more severe wounds needed to be treated and he did the best he could to stem the bleeding and bandage them without earning the wrath of Candaz. Returning to the horses, he took off their saddles, wiped them down and gave them some hay to eat. As he was scratching his horse's nose, he thought of Zlato.

"*Zlato?*" he called.

"*Yes, Stephan?*" his dragon answered instantly.

"*Where are you?*" Stephan asked.

"*Near Castle Xandia. Would you like me to come and get you?*" Zlato asked hopefully.

"*No, not yet,*" he hesitated, wanting to say more, but unsure what to say. "*I miss you, Zlato.*"

"*I miss you too, Stephan,*" Zlato said sadly. "*Let me know when you are ready and I will come and get you.*"

"*Yes, I will,*" Stephan said dejectedly. He wanted to go home, but wasn't quite ready yet. "*How is everybody? Did they find Aunt Jessabelle?*"

"*She has been located. Shareen is being conveyed to Castle Gentlebreeze by Gabriel so she can spend her last days at her old home. Your mom and dad and Uncle Theo are on their way there right now, as well as Nicholas. You should be there, too,*" Zlato said.

"Boy! Get in here," Candaz yelled, interrupting the conversation.

Stephan chose not to answer, but he patted the horses and started inside. "*Don't give up on me, Zlato,*" he said.

"*Never. You are my Stephan and I am your Zlato,*" the dragon replied.

When Stephan entered the laboratory Candaz was organizing materials on the long narrow table that spanned the center of the space. He didn't look up, but said with venom injected in his voice, "You are the laziest piece of ripgar dung that I've ever seen. Where have you been?"

Stephan easily pushed down the anger that was rising to the surface and replied stiffly, "I was tending the horses. Do you need something?"

"I need you to take this gum we harvested today and lay it out on these sheets of metal to dry. Get to work, boy," he ordered.

Quietly, again without comment, Stephan began the meticulous task of spreading out the opium gum onto the sheets as Candaz had told him to do. "Hey, can I have a swig?" he asked.

He felt the other man's icy eyes upon him. "Do you need another dose so soon, boy? You just had some."

Stephan said simply, "Yeah, I need more."

"Get that done and then you can have a sip. Now, get on with it, boy. We have other things to get done today."

"Yes, sir," Stephan continued working. He was curious about how Candaz was going to process the opium to make it into the elixir. Until that curiosity was satisfied he would tolerate the old man's obnoxiousness, but he swore to himself to someday even the score, someday soon. Patience was one of Stephan's virtues.

# Chapter 16

## ON A WING AND A PRAYER

Terese and Zeth followed Jesse through the cave on Elysia and out into the bright sunshine. Rew's breathing seemed to be shallower than it had been before and Jesse had to put her cheek right next to his mouth to feel the subtle breath being exhaled. He was pale and seemed so frail to her. She hugged him close and whispered, "Hang in there, Rew. Let me get to your house and then we'll see what can be done for you. We'll go to Dolli."

Felcore stayed very close to Jesse's leg as they walked past the tree that was still suffering from some type of malady. She could sense the wrongness that consumed it. If she wasn't mistaken the tree filtered wickedness that leaked through to Elysia through the lightning gate. Her spine tingled and the tiny hairs on the back of her neck stood up in warning. It was such an oddity and it was odder yet that she could feel it. Quickening her step, she followed the path that led to the village.

Cottages lined the cobblestone paths that curved gracefully through the village. Lovingly tended gardens displayed a wide array of bright colors and textures. Not only were flowers adorning the gardens on the ground, but hanging baskets decorated the trees and overhangs. It was a beautiful summer day. There was a blue sky with lazy puffy clouds drifting slowly on the light breeze. The temperature of the air was perfect in the mid-seventies.

She passed Lodi and Wes's house first. They lived next door to Dolli and Rew. Originally she had planned on taking them to Rew's house. But she had second thoughts because of all of Rew's children. She didn't want to panic them. Instead she led them up the path to Wes and Lodi's cottage, opened the small wooden door and went inside. Terese and Zeth followed close behind her and lay Wes and Lodi on the hammocks in their sleeping chamber. Jesse found a comfortable cushion in the common room on which to place Rew. "What do we do now, Jesse?" Terese asked.

"Rew's wife lives next door. I'll go get her," Jesse said.

"We'll stay here with them. Hurry, Jesse," Zeth said.

Quickly, she ran next door and knocked on the door. A musical voice from inside said, "Come in."

When she opened the door, Dolli was very surprised to see her. "Jesse. Is everything okay?" she asked.

"Please Dolli, come with me," Jesse said as she grabbed her hand and quickly pulled her outside.

"What's the matter?" Dolli asked.

"Rew, Wes and Lodi have been poisoned. I don't know how to heal them. Come quickly!" she said and led the way to where the three wisps and the two humans were waiting.

Dolli was by Rew's side immediately and had his hand in hers. She kissed him and whispered, "Oh, Rew. Come back to me. I need you." Tears were shining in her eyes when she looked back at Jesse. "Tell me what happened."

Zeth stepped forward and said, "They ate one of these apples." He handed a shiny red apple to Dolli, who examined it closely. "Apparently the apples contain some type of poison. All three of them have been in this state ever since. I have some bottles which may or may not contain the antitoxin." He pulled the bottles out of his pockets and gave those to her as well. "Their breathing seems to be getting slower. Can you do anything for them?" he asked.

For a long moment Dolli examined her husband more closely. She then took the apple and ran a sharp fingernail along the skin, cutting it open. She smelled it and taking the tip of her finger sampled a tiny taste of the juice.

All three of them reacted at the same time to stop her. "Dolli, no don't."

She held up her hand in a stopping motion. "How long have they been like this?"

"A little less than a day it has been," Terese said.

Dolli opened each little bottle individually and smelled the contents. She used her finger to sample the taste of one and then she set them all aside. "I don't know," she said.

"I have this paper that shows the calculations for whatever it is he did to the apple tree. Can you help them?" Zeth asked again.

"I'm afraid this is beyond my abilities," she said as she laid her head on Rew's chest for a moment. "But, I do know of someone who might be able to tell us what to do. Tali is her name. We'll have to take the three of them to her, however. She is about to have a baby and cannot fly."

"How far away is she?" Jesse asked.

"She lives in the village at Mount Galaxia," she said. Dolli looked very pensive for a moment and then added, "You will need wisp wings."

Felcore jumped up and started spinning in circles. "Rrrowff!"

"Yes, boy, you are going to get your wings back," Jesse said as she patted him on the head.

Dolli started with Felcore. She bent down in front of him and put both of her hands on his back. From between her hands four wings began to sprout. They grew and unfolded until they were long enough to support the golden retriever's body. As he flapped them experimentally, they stiffened into shiny iridescent wings. "Rrowff!"

"You are next, Jesse," Dolli said.

"Just a minute, Dolli. I want to change into my bikini top. I'll be right back. Do Zeth first," Jesse said as she grabbed her backpack and left the room.

Zeth stepped forward tentatively and asked, "Do I need to do anything?"

Dolli smiled at him, sensing his nervousness and said, "Just remove your shirt, so your wings can grow properly. I'll never understand why humans wear clothes when the weather is so nice."

He complied by pulling off his shirt revealing his trim, fit figure. Dolli placed her hands on his back and between them fresh new wings sprouted. They grew nice and long. Zeth flapped them while he looked over his shoulder in amazement. "Wow," he said.

Jesse returned with her bathing suit top on and let Dolli give her the gift of wisp wings. "Thanks. They are amazing," she said as she fluttered them to let them dry.

"I guess next I am," Terese said quietly with her eyes wide as she gazed at Zeth's wings.

She had already removed her shirt. With a gentle touch, Dolli placed her hands upon Terese's back and sighed. "You are a kendrite," she said.

"Yes," Terese said.

"You can change into an eagle. Why would you want me to give you wings?" Dolli asked.

"I am unable." She looked down at her feet. "Transform I cannot. Never have I been able to transform."

Dolli walked around Terese so she could look her in the face. "Of course you can, sweetie. You just need a little push out of the nest, so to speak. Now, let's see. . ." She placed her hands on the side of Terese's face and closed her eyes. "You just have a little mental block, sweetie. When we go to see Tali, ask her what she has to say about it. She is very wise."

"Okay," she said. "I will."

"For now, let's give you wisp wings." Within moments of Dolli placing her hands on Terese's back, she sprouted her own set of wisp wings.

Experimentally, she fluttered her new wings. "Always I have wanted to fly. Thank you," she said and gave Dolli a quick hug.

"You are very welcome, sweetie. Now let's get these wisps to Mount Galaxia. We will stop on the way and get Lew. We'll need some coats as well. There's snow up on the mountain."

They gathered what they needed and stuffed what they could into Jesse's backpack. The humans carried Wes, Lodi and Rew cradled in their arms.

Flying takes a little bit of skill and practice. Jesse and Felcore both had experience and helped Terese and Zeth get used to their new wings. Dolli quickly fetched Lew. Several of her children wanted to come as well. Rew and Dolli had seventeen children in all, seven sons and ten daughters. Only five accompanied them; Cori, Tami, Gabi, Kalto, and Mini. They all spent time excitedly greeting each of them, including kisses for their father, Lodi and Wes. The young wisps were extremely energetic and their happy mood, despite the circumstances, was refreshing and contagious.

They flew a direct path to Mount Galaxia which took them over the desert terrain and the lake oasis where Jesse had once spent a week relaxing. From there they could see the snow covered mountain in the distance. Continuing at a very fast speed, they were soon soaring over dark green forests and ice blue lakes until the cold moist air of the mountains touched their exposed skin and made them stop only long enough to pull on warmer gear that was specifically designed to accommodate wisp wings.

The small village in the mountains was quaint with tall alpine style roofs, all of which had chimneys with smoke rising lazily from them. Sparkling snow covered everything in a thick frosting and evoked a feeling of Christmas morning in the snow region.

Dolli led them down to the outskirts of the village to a small cottage that was painted a cheerful pale yellow with intricately carved details on the peeks and corners that were painted deep blue in contrast. They all landed, all fourteen of them, and Dolli knocked on the door. There was no immediate answer and they waited in an impatient silence. Finally, the door slid open.

The wisp that answered was as wide as she was tall. She wobbled as she walked from the load she carried in her belly. Her face was young and smooth with bright blue eyes that danced with happiness. "Dolli? Is everything . . .? Come in. Come in," she said as her eyes took in the crowd that stood behind Dolli looking back at her.

They piled into the house one by one. "Please take off your coats. Make yourselves comfortable. Kids, take our guests' coats." From different rooms around the main room several young wisps appeared and relieved them of their coats. They zipped around the little house quickly and were full of curiosity about their visitors, especially the human ones. Felcore also drew much attention, which he enjoyed thoroughly as the wisps touched and patted and petted him. "Okay, kids, thank you," Tali dismissed them and they disappeared as quickly as they had appeared.

"How did this happen?" she asked as she examined Rew, Wes and Lodi.

"They ate poisonous apples," Jesse said, handing her the apple and Candaz's notes.

She smelled the fruit and then set it aside. "Take them to the pool inside the Galaxia Gallaria. Bath them in the water until the poison is extracted from their bodies. Jesse, you should be able to facilitate their healing once this is done."

Once again there was a lot of activity as Tali's children returned with everybody's coats and said goodbye to Felcore with more excessive attention.

Terese shyly approached Tali, who smiled sweetly and took the girl's hand in her own. Terese said, "Kendrite I am, but am unable to transform. Dolli said that you might help me."

After Tali spent a moment peering intently into Terese's eyes, she said, "Well, I cannot help you, but you can help yourself. Take this container and fill it with water from the pool. There is a tree outside the lightning gate cave that I'm sure you've seen. Look inside yourself and find what is behind the fear that holds you back. Dig a small hole at the base of the tree and picture that fear as a seed and bury it. Then drink your portion of the water and pour the rest on the ground at the base of the tree. Once you facilitate the healing for the tree, you will find yourself healed as well." She patted Terese's hand. "Sometimes the hardest part is finding what's been inside you the whole time. Trust me. You can do this. You are meant to do this."

"Thank you. Try I will," Terese said.

"I know you will. Dolli, let me know how things go. I would go with you, but . . ." She cradled her belly. "I'm about to burst." She smiled brightly.

"Thanks, Tali," Dolli said and gave her a hug.

It wasn't a very long flight to the largest building in the village. They entered through the huge double wooden doors into a massive foyer. Jesse had been there before. To the right was what the wisps called the "App-endix", which turned out to be an index to the instruction manual to the gate, which was now in Candaz's possession. Upstairs was a beautiful display, a mosaic of the different worlds that the lightning gate went to.

They followed Dolli to the back of the foyer to a staircase that led down. It was a wide staircase made of beautifully polished wood that glowed in the soft lighting. They started down and Jesse was surprised when the stairs continued on and on. Down and down they went for an endless amount of time into the very heart of the mountain.

Finally the stairs ended. They entered an enormous domed cavern. A sparkling canopy of lights in a natural stone umbrella served as the ceiling to the room. The water of the pool that filled the center of the space was still and the glassy surface reflected back the lights from the ceiling like a mirror. Black sand made a beach that led up to the water's edge.

They were quiet, even reverent, as they traversed the sand. At the water they paused to strip off their clothes. Slowly they entered the water together and continued to wade in until they were waist deep. It was cold but not too cold. Terese filled the container that Tali had given her and placed it on the beach by their clothes and then rejoined them.

Forming a circle, they had Rew, Wes and Lodi floating on the water between them. Taking turns, they scooped up the water and bathed their faces and the rest of their bodies as they drifted. After a while Rew's eyes opened. He looked surprised and confused and began to panic a little in the water. "Easy, Rew," Dolli said and brushed his face with her hand. "How do you feel?"

"Woozy," he said with a slight slur.

Jesse went to him. "Hi," she said.

"Hi, Jesse," he said.

"Let me see if I can help you feel better," she said as she placed her hands on his temples. She could sense the remnants of the poison lingering around the edges of his systems. On her chest her medallion began to burn as the freecurrent went to work cleaning the rest of the poison from him. It was much stronger than she expected. A human consuming it would not have survived its effects. The remnants quickly ran through her and dissipated into the water to be nullified by its healing properties.

"How do you feel, son?" Lew asked.

"Great," he said as his children mobbed him joyfully.

Lodi roused next. She opened her eyes and looked around in confusion. Rew spoke to her calmly, "It will be okay, Lodi. Let the water take away the fog. Jesse," he said, calling her over to do her thing.

She repeated the process with Lodi, who smiled up at her the whole time and ended her healing with a grateful hug.

Wes remained in a state of unconsciousness, however. Try as they might, they could not get him to come out of it. Jesse could not break through the fog with the freecurrent energy yet and it worried her deeply. His breathing was very shallow. Lodi spoke to him softly, "Wes, wake up. I need you. I love you. Wake up, please."

Eventually they brought Wes to the sandy beach and lay him down. By now Lodi was crying as she continued to whisper to him. Without any drama he simply quit breathing. "No, Wes, no!" Lodi cried.

Jesse and Dolli held her as she wept. They didn't see Felcore approach and start licking Wes's face. They didn't see Wes as he turned his face away from the invading tongue. They did not see until Wes pushed the dog away with his hands and sat up. "Is there something wrong?" he asked.

"Wes!" Lodi cried and hugged him and kissed him excitedly. "Oh, Wes, you're alive!"

"Of course I'm alive. How did we get here?" he asked as he started to half-heartedly fend off his wife's affection.

"It is a long story," Jesse said. "Welcome back, Wes."

"Thanks. I'm hungry," he said. "We didn't miss dinner, did we?"

They all laughed. With joyous energy the party dove back into the water and played, dunking and leaping into the air before diving back in again. Rew's children attacked him with a frisky onslaught and he returned their attention in kind. Lew watched it all with a proud and happy smile on his face.

Jesse retired to the beach and watched them all play until she fell asleep. She was awakened some time later by Terese, "Jesse, back to Risen we must go now."

She felt completely refreshed and wondered how long she had slept. It was quiet in the cavern and the pool had gone back to being a glossy mirror surface. All of the wisps had gone. Zeth was sleeping quietly nearby. Terese gently woke him also.

"Where did they all go?" he asked.

"To the village they went. Hungry they all were," Terese said.

"Okay, let's go find them and start back. I feel great. That was the most refreshing swim I've ever had," Jesse said.

"Rrowff!" Apparently Felcore agreed.

They found their companions in the village common room fully enjoying the extravagant meal that was set before them. "Come, join us," Lew invited.

"Glad to," Zeth said as he took a seat beside Rew.

Jesse looked at Terese and shrugged her shoulders. "When in Rome," she said as she sat down and began to fill her plate.

Terese let the confused expression fall from her face, shrugged her shoulders and sat down next to Zeth.

After they were done eating, which included a sampling of many decadent desserts; they said their goodbyes and expressed their gratitude.

Swiftly they flew back to the village where Dolli, Rew, Lodi and Wes lived. It was another round of goodbyes, although this time many happy tears were shed. Rew was going back to Risen with them. The wisps were amazing the way they hugged and kissed and cried in their goodbyes, displaying their love with exuberance that seemed exhausting. Their enthusiasm for life was inspiring.

Lodi and Dolli removed all of their wings by simply plucking them off. It was no more painful than plucking an eyebrow. Jesse changed quickly back into her last clean shirt and they were on their way back to the lightning gate cave.

They walked the path single file lost in their own thoughts. Terese was digging deep into her memory trying to discover the cause of her block. She had never been able to change like the other kendrites. Typically it wasn't until past puberty when a kendrite gained the ability to transform. That age had come and gone for Terese without the long awaited gift of shape-shifting. What held her back? That was the question. She examined the feelings associated with her inability to transform. Mostly she was ashamed. She had been made to feel more than inadequate being a kendrite in Colordale who could not shape change, but that was not the root of the problem. She remembered when she came of age the fear that assaulted her at the thought of transforming. Fear had dominated her feelings back then, but she really wasn't aware of it at the time.

So fear was what blocked her. Where did the fear come from? Her childhood had been fairly uneventful. After her inability became known her parents had distanced themselves from her, but it was unintentional on their part. They did not mean to hurt her. And, again, that was after the fact. Her parents, her family had always been loving, nurturing at least in her early years. There was a time when they were so happy. Her brother and she used to play together, pretending that they were on great adventures. Her brother . . .

Terese suddenly fell down to her knees in mid-stride. Jesse and Zeth turned to her, "Terese, are you okay," Zeth asked.

"Terese," Jesse said. She bent down beside her and grasped her hands. "Terese, what is the matter? What's wrong?"

"I remember," she cried. "I remember my brother Brody." She was crying so hard it was difficult to understand her words.

"It will be okay, Terese. You can remember now. You can deal with the pain," Rew said calmly.

Zeth wrapped his arms around her and held her close. "Tell us, Terese. Tell us what happened," he coaxed.

She wiped her face on her shirt and took a deep breath, letting her grief be felt. "I loved him. Five years older than me he was. I idolized him. It was just after he went through the change. At the beach we were, just the two of us playing in the surf. Brody became a dolphin and it was fun. Great everything was. But, then something happened and he couldn't hold his shape. In and out of different forms he phased. I watched him. Terrified he was. I could not help him. I could not save him. Before my eyes he drowned. I could not save him," she cried.

"Oh, Terese, how horrible for you. I'm so sorry," Jesse said.

"It was so unbearable I blocked it out. The memory was wiped from my mind until just now. I remember now. I remember my brother Brody and it is okay," she said.

"That must be your block, Terese. The reason you cannot transform," Zeth said.

"We're almost to the cave. Do what Tali told you to do. I think you will find healing," Rew told her.

The path led them to the cave. When they came across the tree that stood as sentinel before the opening they all paused. Sickness permeated the stoic tree. The branches wilted as if they had given up the fight to stay upright. Once vibrant green leaves were brownish in color and sparse instead of lush. It seemed to radiate foulness. Jesse was revolted by it and shied away from it, as did Felcore.

Terese did as Tali had instructed her. She knelt beside the ailing tree and dug a small hole. In it she placed a tiny pebble. "Brody," she said as she buried the small pebble beside the tree. Taking out the container of water she had collected from the heart of Mount Galaxia, she took a long drink. The rest of the water she poured out at the base of the tree.

Nothing happened for a moment. Terese stood up and Zeth joined her and grasped her hand. The tree suddenly seemed to quiver and shake. Leaves that were on the branches dropped to the ground. The branches appeared to find renewed strength to lift toward the sky. Upon the branches tiny buds began to sprout, fresh and green. The sickness receded. The vileness was vanquished.

"Creator be thanked," Terese said brightly.

"Thank God it is healed," Jesse said, just as brightly, feeling a lifting in her own spirit.

"It is as it should be," Zeth said. "Let's get back to Risen and track down my father. He needs to be stopped from spreading any more poison."

"Just one more thing," Terese said. Before their eyes, her image shimmered and before them stood a beautiful black wolf.

# Chapter 17

## HOME SWEET HOME

The village surrounding Castle Gentlebreeze was the population center of Brightening. For the last twenty years its bustling marketplace has offered wares from every corner of Risen. Theo and Jessabelle were working closely with the other races to enhance the trade experience for everyone. They had made incredible progress, especially with Saberville and Skyview. Farreach and Jessabelle's home village of Colordale on the far coast still needed to come up to speed, but they were working on it.

The castle itself was architecturally dominant with its six stories of stone dressed with expansive windows that ran the entire height of the building. Four large towers with smaller turrets sat looming on each corner of the castle. Although a massive rampart surrounded the entire castle and grounds, the gates on all four sides stood wide open to welcome the outside world.

Overhead thunder boomed a warning making Natina Wing-master's eyes look up from her shopping. A new shipment of cloth had just arrived from Farreach and she was bargaining with the vendor for a beautiful green weave that would look marvelous with her eye color. In her position as princess she could afford the most expensive wares in the marketplace and she was willing to pay all of the vendors generously for their goods, but haggling was expected so she played the game and played it skillfully.

With another look at the sky, she wrapped up the deal asking that the cloth be delivered to the local dress maker promptly. She smiled and thanked the woman before starting back toward the castle. Many of the vendors were packing up early with the threat of inclement weather and she nodded greetings as she made her way to the main walkway.

A dragon trumpeted as it swooped in to land on the castle grounds. She hurried her footsteps, anxious to get back now. Since her father and mother had left several days ago, she had not gotten any news from them and she was beginning to worry. Perhaps it was B.F. She hoped it was. Before she got back to the castle, another dragon made his presence known with a different, less throaty, trumpet. It was one of the golds from the sound of it. She wished with a pang of regret that she had ridden down to the marketplace today. Pushing herself, her steps quickened even more.

# Homecoming

Nicholas followed Agape to the field on the far side of the castle where the dragons typically landed. As Agape circled around he could see Jacob's expression of excitement. Bill, on the other hand, who was in the saddle behind his son, looked somewhat terrified.

Jim, who flew next to Nicholas, trilled his own excitement as they landed beside Skymaster and Agape. The two eagles transformed instantly and began helping the passengers off the two dragons.

The sling under Skymaster's belly had worked wonderfully and Shareen slept peacefully as they lowered her to the ground.

Within moments horsemen approached from the castle to greet them. "Your highness, welcome home!" the lead man said to Nicholas. He turned to the man behind him and ordered him to fetch an ambulance wagon for Shareen. That man rode off at a gallop.

"Bill, Jacob you can take one of the horses. Jim and I will hoof it. Have you ridden before?" Nicholas asked.

"Well, it's been awhile," Bill said.

"Just keep a firm grip on the reins. The horses will follow the leader anyway. You good?" he asked.

"We'll manage," Bill said.

They arrived with the wagon and the attendants quickly had Shareen settled for the ride to the castle. It was a short trip from where the dragons landed to the back entrance. They handed off their reins to the waiting stable boys and entered into the family's living quarters without having to go through the more public area of Castle Gentlebreeze.

Nicholas gave instructions to the staff to take Jim, Bill and Jacob to the guest rooms and to have Shareen set up in her old apartment, which was used occasionally these days as a guest room when they had visitors. Gabriel retired to a room that she always used when she stayed there.

With his guests taken care of, Nicholas started toward his own room to get cleaned up. His sister Natina intercepted him. "Nicholas, you're home finally. Have you heard from mom and dad?" She gave him a brief hug and waited for him to answer.

"Nati, dad is on his way home. Mom is in her dolphin form off the east coast of New Chance. She had an injury apparently that has caused memory loss. Uncle Jacoby was supposed to bring her to meet with dad a couple of days ago, but they didn't show. I plan on going to find her as soon as I can. We had to bring Great Grandmother Shareen home. She was living on Earth, but now she is dying from injuries she sustained from a blast at the lightning gate. Jesse has taken Rew and two other wisps to Elysia because they were poisoned. Let's see. I think that's about it," he said.

"We really need better communication when the dragons aren't around to keep us up to speed. I had no idea what was happening outside of Brightening. It's very frustrating. Did they find Stephan? How is he doing?" she asked.

"He's with Candaz. He's become a traitor," he said with bitterness.

"I can't believe that. Not Stephan. He would never put in with Candaz," Natina said.

"Well, he has. I can't believe it either. Look, Nati, I really need a shower and a change of clothes. Can we talk later? Oh, and Nati, Jesse's brother and father are here. I sent them to the guest rooms. Can you make sure they are provided with whatever they need? That includes my friend Jim. Make sure he has everything he needs as well."

"Jesse? Gabriel's granddaughter? Why is her family here?" she asked.

"I promise to fill you in later," he said and then turned and climbed the winding staircase, taking them two at a time.

His apartment was at the top of the stairs on the sixth floor. It had apparently been cleaned while he was gone and his bed was neatly made. He paused briefly at his wardrobe to get a fresh set of clothes before going to his wash room to take a much needed shower. Stripping off his dirty garments, he let them lay discarded on the floor without much thought.

Shaving off the scruff on his face was his first action, but when he looked in the mirror, he was surprised by what he saw. The man who looked back at him was not the boy he had left behind when this journey began not so long ago. Maturity had somehow caught up with him. Nicholas had been struggling with the prospect of having to grow up. He was fighting the responsibility his father was trying to thrust upon him he felt all too soon. It seemed so long ago now, even though it had been only a month. So much had happened to change him. Agape had bonded with him. He never dreamed he would bond with a dragon of his own. He had travelled to another world and discovered all kinds of wonders. The biggest change of all was that he had fallen in love, and fallen hard. His future now belonged to an amazing girl named Jesse and he would never again be complete without her. No longer did he want to delay the future. His expectation of what lay ahead for he and Jesse was sweet to imagine and he couldn't wait for their life together. If that meant taking on the responsibilities of being a man, he was more than willing to embrace them.

After his shower, he made his way down to the guest rooms to check on their guests and was told that they were sleeping. He had wanted to talk to Jesse's dad, but it would have to wait. Instead he went back up to the fourth floor to Shareen's apartment. The door stood open and staff members were active setting up to care for her. He greeted their doctor, Barnaby, who had just finished examining Shareen. "She's stable and comfortable," he said. His bright blue eyes quickly assessed Nicholas, whom he had watched over since he was a baby. "You look good Nick," he commented with a smile.

Nick chose to ignore the comment and asked, "How long does she have?"

Doctor Barnaby took his time before giving an answer. After a moment he looked back at Shareen and said, "It's hard to tell. Without taking in any food or water her body will begin to shut down. It could be hours or it could be days. Death is very individual."

Gabriel walked in accompanied by Natina and Nedra. They got a quick update from Barnaby and then went to Shareen's bedside and spoke to each other quietly. Gabriel got up and came to Nicholas's side. "What are your thoughts, Nick?" she asked.

"My first thought is to go after mother. What do you think?"

"Yes, I can see where that might be your priority. But, I would like you to wait until your father gets here before you go," she said.

Outside of the big window lightning lit up the sky followed by a heavy roll of thunder. Rain finally began to fall, pelting the window with an impending ratta tat tat. It was going to come down heavy. The wind began to blow with greater intensity as the storm came upon them.

"*Agape, where is B.F.?*" Nicholas asked.

"*They are just north of Skyview. The storm is hitting them as well. They are going to take shelter until is passes,*" Agape replied.

"Okay, good," Nicholas said. "I will wait until the storm passes," he said to Gabriel who nodded to him in response.

He walked over to the window and gazed out at the storm. His worries were many this evening and he felt suddenly much older than his years. It was frustrating to have to just sit and wait. He didn't like feeling helpless and being unable to take action made him feel powerless.

Sighing, he turned and went to Shareen's bedside. Touching her frail hand, he thought of what she had been through in her life. She had been the Queen of Brightening, married to his great grandfather. When her son Cleo took the throne she became their sorceress and served in that capacity for many years. Arthritis had plagued her during her last years of service and she had suffered in pain as her joints slowly became warped. At least she had some relief in Sedona. She was able to finally retire from public service and have some years to herself. He stood up and kissed her gently on the forehead.

The storm surged against the castle with ferocity. Lightning strikes were frequent, causing a strobe-like effect on Shareen's apartment walls. Wind was gusting at tremendous speeds just outside of their haven. They all sat with the dying woman and watched the storm without conversation. They would be there all night.

## Skyview

The rain was soaking their faces as the dragons dove toward the path that led to Skyview. Trees whipped in the wind around them as they were assaulted by the storm. Even though the weather was dangerous the dragons refused to take their passengers any closer to Skyview. They would have to walk the last two miles to the entrance gate.

Along the path near the entrance gate grew the weed dragon bane which was extremely repulsive to dragons. They could not stand the scent of it, although to humans it smelled like fresh ground coffee.

*"This is very inconvenient, B.F. I would think you could suffer a little to help a friend in need, especially considering that I am dealing with a leg injury,"* Theo said.

*"This has nothing to do with you,"* B.F. said as he flew away.

*"It has to do with the stubbornness of a dragon,"* Theo said.

*"Yes. I am stubborn, but that is beside the point. Dragon bane is horrible. If the bandergs want dragons to visit them, they should kill that stinky weed,"* B.F. said.

*"The dragons make deliveries to Skyview all the time,"* Theo said.

*"Deliveries are made outside of the perimeter where the dragon bane grows and transported from there by wagon,"* B.F. reminded his friend.

"*I'll talk to Link. That seems rather impractical. What kills dragon bane?*" he asked.

"*I don't know. Dragon fire maybe. If we could torch it, maybe it would be gone for good. Do you want me to try?*" B.F. asked.

"*In this wind you would burn down the whole forest, even with the rain. I'll check with Link and find out what he thinks. They'll probably have to form a committee to study the problem. It could take a while for this question to make its way through the banderg bureaucracy. There is a lot to be said for aristocracy when it comes to getting things done without forming a commission. The only person I have to answer to is my wife. Well, and of course, all of the people I rule,*" Theo said.

"*And your dragon,*" B.F. said.

"*Right. Find some shelter, B.F. I'll see you on the other side when the storm passes,*" Theo said.

"*Tell Link I'd be happy to take care of that dragon bane problem for him,*" B.F. said.

"*I'll tell him.*"

They were almost to the northern gate when the weather turned severe. The wind was gusting hard enough trees could be heard snapping all around them. Lightning flashed one right after another and the booming thunder continued on without ceasing. "Let's get inside!" Theo yelled over the noise.

"Come on!" Serek's voice was drowned out by the storm. He grabbed Kristina's hand and they ran the rest of the way to the entrance of Skyview.

Theo waited inside the tunnel for his sister and brother-in-law. He wiped the water from his eyes and shook it out of his hair. A tremendous crash followed directly on their heels. Behind them an enormous tree fell, blocking the southern entrance and destroying the gate. It just barely missed them.

"Oh my!" Kristina cried out as she buried her face in Serek's shoulder.

"That was close," Theo said. "Let's get moving. Are you okay, sis?"

"Yes. I'm good. Just a little scared," she said.

"We're safe now. Let's go find Link," Serek said. He took Kristina by the hand and led her down the tunnel.

They ended up locating Link at home. He was enjoying a rare night off from his very busy job as head chef. He and Berry welcomed them warmly. They were offered warm, dry clothes, food and drink. The evening was spent in relaxed conversation in spite of the anxious situations that all three of them were in.

Where they were deep underground they could not hear the storm. Natural light filtered in through ingenious skylights that ran from the surface on the mountain all the way down to the depths of Skyview, so the lightning was visible, but there was no other indication that a storm raged outside.

When morning came, they ate a lavish breakfast before Link told them the bad news. The southern tunnel was flooded and would not be accessible until they pumped it out. That could take several days. Their exit was blocked.

"How about the northern gate?" Theo asked in agitation. "How long before that exit is cleared?"

"The storm dropped a mighty large tree on the gate. They are working on it now, but it will take time to clear it out of the way," Link said while he pulled on his beard, feeling anxious about having to give the king, *both kings,* the bad news.

"I could send B.F. to clear the way," he suggested.

"The crew is very troubled by the amount of damage that was done to the gate already. They just finished rebuilding it. Dragon fire would completely destroy it. That is out of the question, Theo," Link said.

"Isn't there some other way in and out of here?" Serek asked.

"There is the cargo access, but that too is blocked with debris from the storm. I think we had some straight-line winds last night. It's been reported that trees were snapping like toothpicks. I've heard that they are down all over the place. I'm afraid you will have to wait," Link said while his beard got a good work out.

"What can we do to help?" Theo asked.

"I can get you assigned to a clean-up detail. Do you want north or south?" Link asked.

"I'll take north," Serek said.

"Then I'll take south," Theo said.

# Chapter 18

## SIDEWAYS

Processing the opium was a tedious, lengthy process. Stephan worked hard for his irritable boss, doing the dirty and the heavy labor-intensive jobs that needed to be done. They boiled the raw opium in large pots and then filtered the product using a rough cloth. Once this was accomplished Candaz used different chemicals in his vast laboratory to step-by-step reach the final product.

With that accomplished he began mixing the ingredients to make the elixir. He consulted a sheet of paper as he added this and that until he was satisfied with the batch. Some of the product went into the little crystal bottles that Candaz had collected from New Chance many years earlier. Using a small funnel, he filled the bottles and then sealed them with wax and a stopper. The majority of the potent liquid was poured into jugs and corked and loaded onto their horses.

Once they had everything packed, Candaz sealed the laboratory door and they began the trip back to Castle Xandia. They rode in silence. It was a beautiful day. The severe storm that had driven through the area had left its mark on the landscape. There were trees down everywhere. They had to weave their horses around the downed trees many times as they continued on their route.

Castle Xandia was a day's ride away, but with the storm damage it took them much longer than normal. They arrived late in the evening. Stephan had intended on going to the castle itself, but Candaz wanted to bypass it. They made camp on the outskirts of the village in a secluded valley.

As Stephan unpacked the horses and gave them food and water, Candaz started a fire and began cooking some meat and potatoes for dinner. Stephan grabbed one of the crystal bottles from the supplies and with a sweep of his hand he showed it to Candaz. "Do you mind?" he asked casually.

Candaz looked up from stirring the contents of the pan and grinned. The expression lacked warmth and did not relate friendship by any means. On his face it just looked creepy. "You are getting bold, little man. Give me the bottle. It is mine," he said with his smile turning into a sneer.

Hesitating slightly, Stephan slowly walked over and held out the bottle. "Just a sip?" he suggested.

"After you collect some more firewood, boy. Get to work you lazy thief. You are less than worthless," he said.

"Yeah, worthless," Stephan said as he turned and walked away. "Firewood," he said to himself as he started to scan the ground. When he was far enough away from the fire, he pulled another small bottle from his pocket and took a long swig.

He returned with his arms full of wood. He felt good, comfortable in both body and mind. Depositing the wood next to the fire, he sat down and let the warmth of the flames soak into his skin.

Candaz handed him the bottle of elixir and said, "Just a small sip, boy."

"Sure," Stephan said as he tipped it up and drank. Comfort like a soft blanket, comfort like a warm bath, comfort like a loving hug enveloped every inch of his body. Sweet comfort. He knew it wouldn't last. When the drug started to wear off, he would get itchy, anxious, and restless. It gave him pleasure to know that he had his own stash he could partake of without Candaz's permission. He felt he deserved it for all the work he had done and didn't really consider it stealing. Of course, he knew Candaz would, but it was doubtful he would even know one of the bottles was missing.

"Boy, do you want some food?" Candaz asked as he handed Stephan a bowl and spoon.

"Thank you," Stephan said and began to eat even though he wasn't really hungry.

"*Stephan, where are you?*" Zlato asked in his head.

"*I am in Saberville. Where are you, Zlato?*" he asked.

"*I am south of you hunting. Would you like to join me?*" Zlato asked hopefully.

"*I cannot, Zlato,*" Stephan responded, feeling suddenly sad and lonely.

"*But, I miss you, Stephan. When are you going to go hunting with me?*" Zlato asked.

"*Soon, Zlato,*" Stephan said, although he wasn't sure that he meant it. His warm fuzzy feeling was suddenly gone. He felt awash in sadness. Setting aside his dinner that was only partially eaten, he touched the bottle through his clothes, wishing he could take another drink. Standing up, he started toward the wooded area nearby.

"Where are you going, boy? Clean up dinner," Candaz said.

"Yeah, I will. I just have to take a leak," Stephan said.

"Take a leak? What does that mean?" he asked.

"I have to pee. I guess I picked up the slang in Vegas," Stephan said. He quickly walked into the woods and found a private place to imbibe in another dose of the elixir. His bottle was getting close to empty sooner that he expected. He figured he could probably get away with taking another bottle without Candaz's notice. When he went to where their gear was to clean up the dishes he could snatch away another bottle. He could actually put water in the one he had and then replace it without Candaz being the wiser. Quickly, he finished off what remained in his bottle and walked back to the fire.

"Are you done eating?" he asked Candaz, who shot him an irritated glare before handing him his empty bowl.

"I'll just get these cleaned up," he said. He went over by the horses and used the water sack to clean the dishes and fill his little crystal bottle back up. Quickly he switched bottles, leaving the one with water with the rest of them in the saddle bag. Stuffing the other one in his pocket, he returned to the fire where Candaz was pushing the embers around with a stick.

"Pack the horses. We're leaving," Candaz said.

"What? I just got firewood. I thought we were spending the night," Stephan protested.

"You thought wrong. Get moving, boy. We've got work to do," Candaz said as he continued to scatter the burning coals.

"Have you lost your mind? It is the middle of the night. I need to sleep. I'm not going anywhere," Stephan said defiantly.

Candaz stopped stirring the remains of the fire and stared at Stephan with death in his eyes. With a calm and icy voice he said, "Pack up the horses." From his voluminous robes he withdrew the small crystal bottle, opened the top and drank deeply from it. Pushing the stopper back in, he waved it in front of Stephan. The intended bribe was sickeningly obvious, but it worked.

Deciding quickly that it was not the right time to challenge his supplier, Stephan went to the horses and began saddling them and strapping on all of their baggage and things. Candaz was watching him with a sharp eye without pause. He worked at a constant, steady, but slow pace. When he was done, Candaz shared a sip of elixir with him, his token reward for obedience.

Without much guidance his horse followed Candaz's horse toward Castle Xandia. The people of the land were asleep after a hard day's work. Everything was peaceful and quiet. Stephan was beginning to dose off in the saddle as the motion of the horse rocked him to sleep.

He awoke when they came to a complete stop. Candaz dismounted in front of him and made his way to the edge of the reservoir. The smooth water glistened as it reflected back the stars shining in the night sky.

The reservoir served the entire population of Saberville as their fresh water source. Underground pipes ran to the castle and the village providing drinking water as well as water for washing and bathing. The vineyard and winery also drew water from the reservoir for its many industrial needs.

"Boy, bring me the jug marked with an 'x'," Candaz ordered.

Stephan slid off his horse. The question in his eyes remained unspoken as he went to Candaz's horse and started looking through the jugs that were tied to the saddle. He found the one that was marked, but left it in place.

In his mind he was trying to work through the situation. The drugs in his system made nailing down his thoughts difficult. Focus was illusive. But he sorted through them the best he could. Putting two and two together, his assumption was that Candaz was planning on dumping the elixir into the drinking water of his people. He really didn't think they had enough of the product to effectively have an impact. Surely it would be deluded in that vast body of water as to be virtually undetectable. So why waste it!

"What are you planning?" he asked Candaz as he stalled.

The sharp glare of the sorcerer pinned Stephan where he stood. Then surprisingly he laughed. "You want to know what I'm planning, boy?"

Stephan stood still and did not respond, except for the slight nod of his head.

"I'm going to provide an incentive for the people of Saberville to come to me for their needs. Once this water is treated with the elixir and it is distributed throughout this land and it is consumed by the masses, they will need and desire more to maintain their happiness. For that they will have to come to me. It is very simple. Do you understand, boy?" he asked.

"Yes," Stephan said, "but won't it be deluded? There is not enough here to make a difference in such a large body of water."

"You forget, boy," Candaz said with disdain, "I am a sorcerer. With just a small amount of the elixir, I can enhance the effects with just a nudge of magic. It will be effective and it will be immediate and complete in ensnaring the people. Now, get me the jug as I asked, boy."

Hesitating again, Stephan stepped away from the horses and drew his sword. "No, I can't let you do this."

Candaz was surprised by Stephan's betrayal, but only for a moment. He laughed once again. "Do you really think you can impede me? Foolish, boy! I am powerful. You cannot stop me!"

Stephan attacked. He was skilled with a sword and did not hesitate to take the advantage. His blade met Candaz's flesh several times, slicing through his voluminous cloak and into his skin before the sorcerer could respond. He felt out of practice and sluggish in his motions, but he did not let his condition deter him.

Candaz drew on the freecurrent energy and hurled a sizzling bolt at Stephan, striking him squarely in the chest. Although it slowed Stephan's assault, it did not completely end it. He shook off the pain with great effort and continued fighting. Using the butt of his sword, he rammed Candaz in the face. Blood spewed forth from the impact. Twisting, he sliced through the sorcerer's shoulder, causing a serious injury.

Grabbing his shoulder, Candaz went down to the ground. Stephan raised his sword to finish him off, but as he stroked down for the final blow, a bolt of energy hit him again directly in the heart. The pain was tremendous. He dropped his sword and fell immediately to the ground, curling up into a fetal position as he clutched his chest and groaned.

Candaz made his way to the horses and with tremendous effort pulled himself up into the saddle. Seizing the reins of Stephan's horse, he turned and galloped away.

Gasping for breath, Stephan rolled over in agony, and felt the little crystal bottle in his pocket break. The liquid soaked into his pants, but the sensation was almost imperceptible. His heart felt like it was exploding within his chest. He cried out in pain.

"*Stephan?*" Zlato called to him. "*You tried to stop him and he hurt you. I felt it. I know.*"

He found it hard to speak even mentally. "*Zlato,*" he managed to say.

"*I'm coming, Stephan. Don't die,*" Zlato cried.

"*Zlato,*" Stephan thought as he began to slip away.

"*Hang on, Stephan. I'm coming,*" Zlato cried again.

"*Tell them I'm sorry. I didn't mean to . . .I'm sorry, Zlato,*" Stephan said finally as his last breath left his lips and he thought no more.

"*Stephan!*" Zlato screamed, but no one heard.

A short while later the golden dragon landed beside the peaceful reservoir. He nudged Stephan's body with his snout and let his tears fall freely around him. After a time, Zlato lifted his head and let out a long, mournful cry that could be heard for indefinite miles around. The sadness that filled the cry was heartbreaking. All over the land of Risen other dragons answered their fellow's cry with sorrowful utterances of their own.

Zlato gently picked up Stephan's body in his mouth and launched into the night sky. He was returning him to Castle Xandia. His heart was shattered and as he flew the wind whipped the tears from his eyes. He did not know what he was going to do. His Stephan was dead. Despair overtook him.

# Escape

Favoring his injured shoulder, Candaz slid off his horse. He had stopped under a thick canopy of trees and took a long drink of elixir. It eased his pain and he took another drink before stuffing it back in his pocket.

His fingers brushed against the remains of the hand he carried in his left pocket and he recoiled involuntarily. Lately images of Molly's face had been haunting him day and night. He kept seeing her eyes looking up at him as she fell. She had been alive. He had thrown her over the cliff while she was still alive! She stared at him accusingly. "You killed me," she screamed as she fell. Consciously Candaz avoided the bulge in his left pocket as he tried to bind his injured shoulder. He was suddenly horrified by the lump of flesh that he had carried with him for many years. The comfort he had always gotten from the remnant was gone replaced by repulsion. Now he was terrified to touch it. He couldn't even force himself to remove it from his pocket to dispose of it. Instead the hand remained where it was in his left pocket and the aversion was constant and consuming.

Refocusing on what he needed to do, quickly he went through the saddle bags until he found what he was looking for. The instruction manual to the gate was large and heavy and as he opened it he again felt the pain shoot through his shoulder.

He knew what he was looking for. The time he had taken to study the manual was about to pay off. This was the back-up plan of back-up plans. Turning to the specific page he sought, he took a moment to study the constellation depicted graphically on the page. It looked to him like an arrow. The one before it looked like a flower and the one before that looked like a circle. He quickly returned the book to the saddle bag.

"Soon the Tromeck will serve me," he said to himself.

He mounted his horse once again and headed directly to the lightning gate.

.

# Chapter 19

## HAZARDOUS SHMAZARDOUS

Jesse, along with Zeth and Terese dismounted their dragons in the courtyard at Castle Xandia. Before they had walked half way to the doorway, all three dragons crooned a sweet, but sorrowful song into the stillness of the night. Felcore joined them with a low mournful howl.

"Stephan is dead," Rew said.

"Oh no!" Jesse said, stopping in her tracks. She listened as Tempest filled her in on the details of what had happened. "Zlato says he died a hero," Jesse said.

"Zlato will be here soon. He brings Stephan back home," Rew said.

Zeth came up beside Jesse and said quietly to her, "I'm so sorry about Stephan."

"Candaz killed him, Zeth. He was so young," Jesse said.

"I am truly sorry," Zeth said as he looked at the ground.

Zlato circled overhead and landed lightly beside them. With the greatest care he placed Stephan's body on the ground before them.

Gazing at his face, Jesse felt a pit in her stomach. She knelt down beside him and brushed the hair from his face with a sweep of her hand. He seemed so thin. "Oh, Stephan," she said as she started to cry. "I'm so sorry." Terese and Rew wrapped their arms around her and let her sob. "Nick is going to be so devastated," she said as she stood back up.

From out of the castle ran a girl about the same age as Jesse. She was in a nightgown and her long dark hair streamed behind her as she ran. Her bright blue eyes flashed at them quickly before they came to rest on Stephan's still form. "Oh, no," she cried. "No. No. No. Not Stephan." Her knees seemed to buckle underneath her and she slid to the ground beside him. "Open your eyes," she said. "Please, open your eyes. Stephan!" Sobs wracked her body as she laid her head on his chest and cried his name over and over again, "Stephan. Oh, Stephan."

Rew drew her into his arms and comforted her. He whispered, "I'm so sorry, Kate. I loved him, too. We all loved him."

Zlato began making horribly doleful noises in his throat. He lay with his nose pointing toward Stephan. His head was perched on his front legs much the way a dog lays when he is relaxed but watchful. Tears were streaming down his face and making small puddles on the lawn. Jesse walked over to him and lay across his big nose. *"I'm sorry, Zlato,"* she said.

*"My Stephan. My Stephan. My Stephan,"* he repeated over and over again.

"Jesse," Terese touched her gently on the back. "The men are here to help move Stephan's body. There is a chapel down in the old part of the castle where they will take him until after the funeral."

Zeth said quietly to Jesse, "We need to prepare his body to pre-serve it for the interim until his family can be here for his burial."

Visibly shaken, Jesse stared at him before answering, "I don't know how to do that."

"I do," he said. "We'll use freecurrent to keep him in stasis until the burial can take place."

"Oh my God. I can't believe this is happening. I feel so bad for his family. I remember losing my mother--how hard it was. I just can't imagine losing a child," Jesse said. She patted Zlato on the nose and gave him a quick kiss. *"Tempest, take care of him,"* she said.

*"Of course,"* the she-dragon replied. *"All of the dragons mourn with Zlato. To lose your human is the most horrible thing that can happen to a dragon."*

As a couple of men gently loaded Stephan's body onto a stretcher to take him to the chapel, the noise in Zlato's throat grew more intense. Tempest, Grace and Gold Stone began hum-ming a mournful song, joining Zlato in his sorrow. It was so sad and beautiful.

Jesse accompanied the rest of them, following the stretcher as it bore Stephan's body to the chapel. It was a long march. She spoke to Kate as they walked along and they shared their grief.

They placed Stephan on a stone pallet before Kate and one of her staff washed his body and dressed him in clothing that re-flected his royal rank. After he was dressed properly they arranged him into a dignified position. Jesse let Zeth take the lead as they performed the procedure that would preserve him. She could not contain her tears as they worked. When they were done, they all stood side-by-side with arms around each other's waists and looked at the still form of Stephan, remembering him when he was alive and feeling desperately sad that he was gone. It was so hard to believe that he was dead. They kept expecting him to sit up and say something witty.

Eventually they made their way back to the living area of Castle Xandia. After Kate expressed her discomfort at leaving Stephan alone, they arranged for one or two persons to spend time in the chapel watching over him. They had many volunteers as Stephan was well loved and the staff of Castle Xandia wanted to honor him.

Terese, Zeth and Jesse immediately got back on their dragons to see if they could locate Candaz. The sun had risen while they were down in the chapel. Although they spent the morning sweeping the area between Castle Xandia and the lightning gate cave, they found nothing. Rew later reported to them that Candaz had used the gate and had gone into another world. Unfortunately, without the instruction manual, they were unable to follow him. They could only wait for him to return to avenge Stephan.

They regrouped at the castle. Jesse instantly made the decision to travel to Castle Gentlebreeze to be with Nicholas. He relayed through Agape his deep torment over the loss of his cousin. He wanted to be there in Saberville, but Shareen lingered on, although it would not be long now.

Nick wanted Jesse with him. He *needed* her with him and she wanted nothing more than to be there.

Gabriel told her through Skymaster that the family would attend to Shareen's funeral first before travelling back to Castle Xandia for Stephan's funeral. It was going to be a difficult week for everyone.

Zeth was going to go after Serek's men, who were in the northern forest, to give them the news about Stephan and send them back home. They would want to honor their prince and their friend. Since Kali and Kaltog had left after the storm to help out at Skyview the message could not be relayed through the dragons so Zeth volunteered to make the trip.

Terese decided to stay behind at Castle Xandia to help Kate with arrangements. When the time came, the two women planned on taking Gold Stone to Castle Gentlebreeze to attend Shareen's memorial.

By the time Jesse and Tempest said their goodbyes and packed to make the trip to Brightening, Stephan's older brother and his family had arrived. Jesse paused to greet Trevis and his wife Jules and pay her condolences to them. Their three children, all boys, were quite young still and full of energy. Jesse liked them all immediately. Trevis resembled his father in many more ways than Stephan had. He was tall and slim and had dark features that gave him an air of mystery, but he was open and honest and demonstrated a gentle patience with his rambunctious children. Stephan's other sister, Laurel, along with her family, was set to arrive the following day. The two of Serek and Kristina's oldest children and their families were going to stay in Saberville and forego Shareen's funeral.

Before Jesse climbed onto Tempest she went to see Zlato, who hadn't moved. The moaning deep in his throat resonated throughout his body. She put her cheek against his nose. Instead of speaking to him, she felt compelled to hum along with him. Feeling his grief was too much for her, but she could endure a portion of his pain and her compassion was exposed to him fully by the time she kissed him on the nose and departed.

"Jesse," Rew said as he flew over and sat on Tempest's nose, "I'm going to Castle Gentlebreeze to say goodbye to Shareen. Can I fly with you?"

"Well, of course, Rew. I would be happy to have your company." She hesitated and a smile brightened her face. She said, "Maybe you should ask Tempest, though."

Of course she couldn't hear what Rew said to Tempest, but the dragon's reaction said everything. She wiggled and wagged like an excited puppy dog. "*Let's go, Jesse. Hurry up,*" Tempest said.

"*A race with Rew?*" Jesse asked.

"*Yes. Yes. A race. Get on. Let's go.*"

*"Okay,"* Jesse said, laughing as she helped Felcore up, positioned herself in the saddle and hung on tight.

## You Can't Keep A Good Monster Down

Zeth instructed Grace to keep a sharp eye out for the group of men they were seeking down below. They had left earlier in the day and Zeth had thoroughly enjoyed the exhilaration of soaring over the land on the back of his dragon. He was free in more ways than one. Mercy and forgiveness had given him a second chance and healing had made him emotionally capable of becoming a new man. The veil of darkness had been lifted from him. It was an amazing gift. The bitterness and anger that plagued him for most of his life were gone and it left him with feelings that were enjoyable to experience, that made him feel good for the first time in his life. Even the painful grief that came with Stephan's death was somehow sweet, filled with an extreme sense of love from those who were closest to Stephan. The emotions were vibrant in their intensity. Through his bond with Grace, he knew something of the pain of loss that Zlato was adrift in, but even that great loss was rooted in love.

His relationship with Terese was something new to him as well. He was in love with her, but it wasn't the obsessive type of love that he had experienced in the past and he liked it that way. Their friendship was growing, expanding with experience and time together. She was an amazing person with a great capacity to see the best in others and it seemed an endless amount of compassion. Best of all she was real, straight forward, without the disposition to deceive or manipulate. After his up-bringing by Candaz, who manipulated him constantly, she was exactly what he needed and wanted. He could easily see spending the rest of his life with her as his partner. If she would have him, he intended to marry her.

The acrid stench of char reached his nose from down below. He could see where the clearing had been obliterated with dragon fire. There was nothing left but a large black blank spot where the poppies had once thrived. There would be no more crops cultivated there. Eventually the forest would take the land back over and what once was grown there would be forgotten, as would be the monkey-like creatures, the scalawags, who propagated the crop and existed because of it.

A little while after they passed the burned out clearing, Grace began to descend. *"I think I've spotted them,"* the dragon said. They circled around and Grace trumpeted to the men below declaring their presence.

The horses Serek's men were mounted on were used to being in the presence of dragons, so they did not panic, but whinnied a greeting to the incoming dragon.

Zeth had met Stash only once in passing, but did not know any of the other riders. The looks on their faces revealed curiosity but also caution and weariness. Standing out from the warriors was a man who sat upon Serek's horse. His white hair and beard framed a face that was animated with delight as Grace landed. He laughed as he dismounted and walked forward boldly. "What an amazing looking dragon. He looks just like Grand Oro and Sweet Vang only green. They are made of gold, you know. Is he made of emeralds? What's his name?" he asked.

Zeth was amused by the strange man and smiled in return before saying, "She is a she and she is called Grace. I am Zeth."

"Grace. Ahha," he said.

"Jared, look at this dragon. She's made of emeralds just like Grand Oro and Sweet Vang are made of gold," he declared.

"Actually . . ." Zeth began.

A young man peaked around the older man from the back of the horse and nodded to Zeth. "Your dragon is very beautiful, sir," he said politely.

"*Tell him, thank-you,*" Grace said to Zeth.

"She says 'thank-you'," Zeth said.

One of Serek's men rode forward and said, "I am Tallith. You are Candaz's son?"

"I am," Zeth said. "My name is Zeth. Candaz is my father. Gabriel is my mother. I no longer serve my father, but work now to serve the people of Risen. I bring bad news, Tallith. Your prince, Stephan Landtamer, has been killed by my father. He died protecting his people."

Stash swung down from his horse and drew his sword as he approached. "How can we trust you? Stephan cannot be dead! You are a liar," he said.

Zeth climbed down from Grace's back and confronted the angry man with his hands outstretched. "The news I bring is true. Stephan was killed defending Saberville from Candaz's plan to poison its water supply. He now lies in the chapel at Castle Xandia awaiting burial with his ancestors. I am deeply sorry."

For a long moment Stash held his position and evaluated the man who brought news of his friend. His sword went back in his sheath and he turned abruptly and went to this horse. He started adjusting straps on the saddle fiercely before giving up and hanging his head against it.

Tallith dismounted also and said to Zeth, "This news is very distressing. Stephan was a good man, a good warrior, a friend. He will be sorely missed. What is the plan for his funeral?"

"The king and queen are still in Brightening. They await the death of the previous Queen of Brightening, the lady Shareen. She is not expected to make it through the week. They intend to remain in attendance before returning to Saberville to bury their son," Zeth said.

"So we have some time before we need to return to Castle Xandia," Tallith said. He seemed lost in thought before making a decision. "We will continue on our mission before returning to Castle Xandia to honor our prince. Stash, let's finish this."

"As you wish," he said and he swung back into the saddle and spurred his horse forward, leading them south without further word.

Zeth and Grace decided to tag along. They were almost to the path that led from the Skyview region to New Chance. Surveying from the sky, Grace looked for any sign of life down below. She found nothing. The monkey creatures were gone.

Since Serek had left, the men had encountered only three small nests of scalawags. The vicious animals had attacked without hesitation and the men returned the violence with death dealt out as quickly as possible. They had swept the entire forest and Tallith was fairly confident that they had found and annihilated any and all of the creatures that remained. The difference was palpable in the forest with birds chirping happily and smaller animals like squirrels and rabbits scurrying around in a natural manner. A feeling prevailed that was lighter with the oppression lifted.

A pathway divided the forest from the swamp. Although it had hardly been traversed in recent decades, it remained fairly open and clear of vegetation. Zeth landed there and waited for the men on the horses to join him. He let his gaze fall on the swamp that emanated an eerie glow.

It triggered a memory. He had been there before. It was a long time ago with his father. He must have been ten or twelve, something like that. He couldn't remember for sure. However, the *fear* he remembered clearly. He had been terrified. The scalawags attacked them from the forest, but Candaz scattered them with freecurrent shot from his fingertips. The screaming was horrible and endless. It sounded like the creatures were in constant and excruciating pain. For him it was the first time he experienced the adrenaline rush exhilaration from the pain of something tortured, from the fear that was like a tonic. The feeling was something he would pursue thereafter into a cruelty that chipped away at his humanity.

But, his father hadn't travelled to the forest path for the scalawags. He had come to this place to collect a sample of the water from the swamp. Despite Zeth's terror, Candaz had forced him to approach the glowing water and fill his little jugs until the old man thought he had enough for whatever reason he intended. A tentacle had found his leg and wound itself around it, slowly, as if it had no real reason to rush. Zeth had screamed for help as he dropped the jug he was filling. Candaz casually came to his aid, it seemed as slowly as the tentacle moved, but he did come. He fired freecurrent energy at the constricting tentacle until it released Zeth's leg, scorching his skin in the process. He still had the scar. Candaz then punished Zeth for dropping the jug by making him drink from it. The taste was something that he couldn't even categorize, something foul and rancid, but it was beyond putrid and he was sick to his stomach for days afterward.

They had used the sampled water for various experiments throughout the years. It had unique properties. Zeth had even used some in a potion he had tested on Tempest.

Although that wasn't so long ago, he was a different man now. He had hurt the she-dragon in many ways that he now very much regretted. She had given him the gift of forgiveness for his crimes against her. All of the dragons had forgiven him. They were amazing, generous creatures and he was very, very grateful. Even as the memories came to mind, Grace comforted him with feelings of forgiveness.

From the forest a team of horses and riders appeared on the path. Roland's blue eyes were large with wonder as he gazed at the swamp. "Wow! Look at that. It glows like a lightning bug--only green and kind of eerie. Why does it glow?" he asked.

Zeth said, "It's easy really. Chemiluminescence is a chemical reaction that results in the emission of light. The reactants collide which in turn eventually results in an electron excited state, which gives off light. Bioluminescence is a form of chemiluminescence. Many deep-sea animals produce light with most marine animals having a blue or green illumination. In addition to the creatures that inhabit these waters, the water itself contains bacteria which is bioluminescent and causes a glow effect."

Roland stared at him for a moment and then said with just as much excitement, "Did you know that catfish breathe through their skin?"

Zeth smiled, "Well, sure, but can they glow?"

"None that I know of have developed bioluminescence, but I have never been to the ocean's deep. Perhaps Theo's wife, the dolphin would know," Roland said as the others dismounted and began chatting quietly with each other.

"Jared!" Roland cried, looking around, trying to find the boy who was right behind him on the horse. "Oh, there you are. Get my staff for me, will you, son? I'm going for a little walk."

"You can't walk safely around here. There are monsters in the water," Zeth told him as he climbed down from his dragon's back.

"Yes, I want to see them," Roland replied brightly. He smiled at Jared as the boy handed him his staff. "Thank you."

He started walking briskly toward the water's edge. Zeth sighed in exasperation and followed after him. Jared also followed close behind.

When they reached the water Roland knelt down, closed his eyes and let his fingers dangle under the surface for the longest time. Zeth watched him closely. He wasn't sure if the man was genius or crazy. Maybe he was both.

He was startled when Roland's eyes popped open and he began to laugh.

Jared exchanged a look of confusion with Zeth.

"What is a monster? Jared? Zeth?" Roland pinned them both in turn with his bright blue eyes and asked, "Are we monsters? What about when you stomp on a spider, Jared? Do you think the spider sees you as a monster? Maybe. Maybe."

He started whistling and twirling his staff like a baton in his hands, very nonchalantly, like he had forgotten where they were or what he was talking about a moment before.

"Are you all right?" Zeth asked him tentatively.

"Roland, what are you thinking?" Jared asked as he tried to get the old man's eyes to focus back on him.

From out of the water inched a probing tentacle. It was getting quite close to Roland's bare foot when Zeth drew his sword. "Watch out!" Zeth cried as he began to swing the blade.

Faster than a flash, Roland spun around and planted his staff on the tip of the tentacle. It wiggled and writhed, trying to get free. "Perspective can be very peculiar," he said. He planted both hands firmly on his staff. The carved wood began to glow down at the base by the pinned tentacle. Slowly, inch by inch, the tentacle began to shrink as the glow moved up the wooden staff. A tiny creature was the result and as Roland lifted the pressure from it, the miniature cephalopod climbed up the staff and clung to it.

This occurred over and over again until Roland's entire staff was studded with the tiny creatures. He smiled happily and said, "Now, to clean up this mess." He quickly rummaged through his myriad of bottles until he found the one he sought. Wading into the swamp up to his knees, Roland submerged the end of his staff in the water and dumped out the bottle, pouring the sparkling liquid into the murk. The staff acted like a beacon to the luminescent matter in the water. From as far as the eye could see the glow in the swamp found its way to the staff and was absorbed into it until it smoldered bright green. All along it the tiny creatures that clung to it radiated bright neon green as well.

"This swamp is uncontaminated," Roland declared as he gazed in wonder at his staff. "Look at this, Jared. They are very happy little monsters."

"It is amazing," Jared replied, reaching out to touch the staff. His fingertip glowed at the touch and he quickly pulled it back and wiped it on his shirt.

Zeth reached out to touch the staff as well. He drew back his glowing finger and gazed at it in astonishment. "What? . . . How?" he stammered.

"The swamp was polluted. Long ago the *good* people of New Chance decided to dump the remaining elixir in the swamp to rid their town of its scourge. They created a mutation. Aren't they cute?" Roland twirled his staff, giving them a light show.

"Yeah, cute," Stash said sarcastically from behind them. "I'd say we've accomplished what we came here for and then some. We're going to make camp for the night and then head back to Saberville." His face was awash in grief as he turned back around and walked away.

# Chapter 20

## TRIBUTE

Jesse's belly was dancing not only from the accelerated rate of speed that she travelled at atop her racing dragon, but also because they were nearing their destination and she would soon be in Nicky's arms once again. The closer they got, the more she couldn't stand to be away from him.

Mostly the ride had been a blur as Tempest and Rew raced each other across first Saberville, then Skyview and finally Brightening. They flew without a break. She didn't know how fast they were going; she just hung on, closed her eyes, and prayed that she wouldn't fall off.

Suddenly they were diving and she felt her stomach become uncomfortably weightless within as it seemed to push into her throat. A slight scream escaped her lips.

*"We're here,"* Tempest declared joyfully. *"Rew is dust!"* She landed her bulk on the grass of the courtyard outside of the castle.

*"Congratulations Tempest,"* Jesse said with a sarcastic undertone.

The beautiful white dragon did not take it as such, however. *"Thank you. I am fast, don't you think?"*

*"You are faster than a speeding bullet, sweetheart. Just let me know if you develop x-ray vision,"* she joked as she climbed down and tried to find her balance. Felcore seemed quite happy to be grounded once again as he ran around wagging his tail.

*"I have dragon vision. Is that like x-ray vision?"* Tempest asked seriously.

*"Maybe,"* Jesse answered, but she was distracted from her conversation with Tempest.

Across the courtyard galloped Nicholas on a majestic black horse. He was a vision of masculine elegance as he easily controlled the speeding horse with his muscular thighs and a strong hand on the reins. He had shaved the scruff off his face. His unruly blond hair streamed behind him and his golden eyes flashed with excitement. When he got to them he swung, in one fluid motion, off his mount and ran to her.

She felt her feet leave the ground as Nicholas swept her up into his arms. His scent was heavenly. When her lips found his there was a gentle urgency behind the kiss that left her wanting more when they finally parted. As she brushed a lock of hair off his forehead, his charming wily grin, although genuine, did not mask the pain behind his eyes.

"I'm so sorry, Nick. I keep wondering what I could have done differently. 'If onlys' keep running through my head." Jesse buried her face in his neck.

"I know," he said. "I really think I failed Stephan. There is so much I could have, *should have* done differently." He sighed and laughed. "I'm so glad you're here, Jesse. I've missed you." He placed her back on her feet and put his hand on the back of her neck while he gazed at her, drinking in every feature of her face.

She was lost in his golden eyes and found her desire for him compelling her actions as she reached up on her tip toes and melted into another kiss. The flame of their passion was being fanned into a roaring blaze. Jesse groaned as Nick's hand slid to the small of her back and pressed her body closer to his.

"Umm. Hmm.," Rew said from the perch he had taken on Tempest's nose. "Excuse me. Sorry to interrupt. Really. I'm so sorry. I could watch this all day, but I think maybe . . ."

Jesse reluctantly separated herself from Nicholas. When she glanced over Nick's shoulder she realized that there were three men on horses trying to look otherwise occupied as they waited for Nicholas and Jesse to join them. They were there to escort the prince and his lady back to the castle. She felt her cheeks flush with added heat as she found Rew and Nicholas wearing the same silly grin, finding amusement in her discomfort. "Really, Nick. You should have said something," she admonished.

"I'm sorry. I really didn't think about it. I'm used to having people around me all the time, I guess. When we are married, Jess, you'll have to get used to it too. Castle Gentlebreeze may seem large, but when you get all those people living under one roof, sometimes it seems pretty small and at times confining." He laughed and wrapped an arm around her waist as he guided her to the horses. "Don't worry about it, Jesse. We won't always be under scrutiny."

She laughed as well and said, "You haven't asked me yet, you know."

"Asked you what?" Nick asked.

"You know," she hinted, feeling suddenly shy. Felcore pressed up again her leg and she reached down to pet him.

"Oh, *that*," he said smiling as the blank look left his face. "I didn't know I had to ask. I just assumed . . . "

"Nicholas," Rew said, interrupting intentionally as he flew in front of them, "how are your aunt and uncle doing?"

"They are still stuck at Skyview. Apparently the storm damage there was extensive. I have a crew on their way to help with the cleanup. But, as of today the entryways remain impassable. According to the dragons Uncle Serek and Aunt Kristina are devastated. It's hard to believe that Stephan is really dead," Nicholas said wistfully.

"I know. But it is very real," Jesse said.

Nick swung back into the saddle and held out a hand to Jesse. He pulled her up to sit behind him and she wrapped her arms around his waist. Much too soon they arrived at the door to the castle.

In the foyer Gabriel was there to greet them. Bill and Jacob soon joined them. Felcore was quick to go to each person in turn and demand attention. They sat in the library and caught up on the latest news until Natina rushed into the room, flushed and out of breath. "She's awake. She's asking for you Gabriel. Hurry!" The two women swept out of the room quickly. The rest of them followed at a more reserved pace.

Rew was already with Shareen and had been with her since he had arrived. Jim was there too, sitting in a chair nearby. Rew held Shareen's hand gently resting on the blue blanket that covered the frail woman in the bed. They spoke quietly. Sweetly, Rew drew Shareen's hand up to his lips and kissed it gently. He looked up at them with tears overflowing his eyes. "She doesn't have long now," he said as he stood up and let Gabriel take his place in the seat beside the bed.

"Hi Shareen," Gabriel said as she took her cold hand, thinking as she did of all of the power that it once wielded. She smiled and asked, "Can I get you anything? Do you want a drink of water?"

"No," Shareen barely whispered. "Gabriel, listen." Her breathing came in raspy uneven cycles. "The book . . . must get it back." She wheezed the last few words. Laboring to relay her message, she gulped for more air. "You must . . . get . . . to Rew. Dangerous . . ." Shareen's last breath left her. Gabriel gently closed her mentor's eyes and then bowed her head and closed her own. Felcore pushed his head onto her lap.

From behind Jesse placed her hand on her grandmother's shoulder. Her eyes rested on Shareen's passive face, all signs of life now gone. Her spirit had left her tired old and injured body and gone on to be with her creator. All that was left on the bed was an empty shell. They would honor the woman they had known and bury the body, but the person that was Shareen, her essence, her soul was beginning a new adventure someplace beyond their reach. Jesse believed that absolutely. Jim touched her hand and said softly, "She's moved on."

She had not known Shareen long, but she felt a strong connection to her. It was strange, but with her death came a sense of peace and a measure of relief unlike Stephan's untimely death that was compounded with heavy grief and feelings of regret. Jesse had lost her mother to a car accident when she was younger and with that loss came a gut-wrenching emptiness. With both Stephan and her mother the pain felt like her heart was being twisted. Shareen's death was acceptable, tolerable somehow.

From above them came the resonant bellow of a dragon. Skymaster was circling the castle vocalizing the loss of his mistress and honoring her with his wailing refrain. The other dragons around Castle Gentlebreeze joined their dragon mage in his chorus. It was beautiful as well as heart breaking to listen to the soulful song and it touched Jesse's heart deeply.

She felt Nicholas behind her. He wrapped his arms around her waist as she turned to him. They held each other only briefly before

Bill touched her on the arm. "Jesse," he said. He pulled her into his own arms for only a moment and asked, "Do you know what she was talking about? She said something about a book. What book?"

"I could only guess, dad. She said to get it back and give it to Rew. She must have meant the instruction manual to the gate. Candaz has it. He stole it from the Tower of Ornate," she told him.

"This gives him access to the lightning gate?" he asked.

"It gives him information on how the gate works and where it goes," she answered.

"I have to agree with Shareen. That could be very dangerous, not only for Risen, but also for Earth. How many different societies are there? How many different worlds could be affected?" Bill asked.

"Hundreds. Thousands," Jesse said.

"I'll bet not all of them are peaceful domains either. Could you imagine someone like Hitler having that kind of knowledge? If someone with a sick need to dominate the world or maybe all of the worlds and the ability to do it along with access to that book it could be exceedingly perilous," Bill commented.

"Like Candaz?" Jacob asked sardonically.

He held his eyes on Jacob for a long moment. "What can I do to help get it back?" he asked finally.

"We're going to go after him, find him, and stop him. I'm tired of chasing this man. He always seems to be able to slip away. I think we need to come at him from all sides, rally as many allies as we can to coral him so he has nowhere to escape to. Unfortunately, we have not only one, but *two* funerals to attend first. We also have some VIPs trapped and another VIP who is MIA. Again, Candaz is given the time he needs to escape our grasp," Jesse said in exasperation.

"I don't think we ever really had him in our grasp," Gabriel said. "There always seems to be one distraction or another that stops us from putting an end to his plans. We have no choice now but to regroup. Stephan is gone. Shareen is gone. It is time to honor our dead and then we can and will move on."

Jesse suddenly gasped and held her hands up to the sides of her head. The dragons were all rampaging inside of her head with voices that shouted warnings. It was a cacophony of chaos, but she eventually made out the images that they conveyed and it was horrendous. Huge beings resembling muddy green praying mantis only much larger were swarming all over Risen. The creatures were the size of giraffes and had multi-faceted bulbous eyes and massive mouths with lethal pinchers that extended to sharp points. They invaded on foot and in the air, flying low to the ground on wings that extended the length of their bodies.

Any animal in their path was devoured immediately, quickly and without mercy. They used their long front appendages like hands to grasp and hold onto their victims as they ate the animal head first, one bite at a time.

Villages were being invaded as well. Small houses gave no sanctuary to the human or banderg inhabitants as the beings attacked without ceasing until structures were destroyed and the terrified people killed and eaten. The same was taking place in the Torg nation of Farreach, with the giant torgs living in the outskirts of the mountain village succumbing to the advancing horde as the bugs quickly outnumbered the defenders. Ten or more of the bug-like beings could take down one torg and have the body gone in minutes.

"Oh my God!" Jesse cried out loud.

"We've got to act quickly," Nicholas started shouting orders as he ran. "Get the doors to the castle open. Let's get as many people inside as we can. Hurry! Ring the warning bell! We're under attack. I want every able-bodied man downstairs as soon as possible. Let's go people! Move!"

Jesse, Jim and Natina ran down to the front doors of the castle and started ushering frightened villagers inside as the bell tolled the warning high up in the tower. Gabriel and Rew edged their way out into the main courtyard to help organize the massive undertaking. It was loud. People were shouting and crying as they sought refuge from the invading bugs.

The dragons, led by Skymaster, were attacking from the air, devouring the devourers and raining dragon fire on the invaders down below. When the bugs burned, they popped and crackled like ants isolated by a magnifying glass under the rays of the sun. Skymaster led Tempest and Agape in a defensive circle around the villagers, giving them time to run for their lives. Many were saved, but some were not and were cruelly consumed with screams cut off as their heads were snapped off by the bugs piercing pinchers. The dragons were greatly outnumbered and could only curtail the flow.

Agape could not yet produce dragon flame, but was a lethal weapon with quick reflexes and very sharp teeth. Bodies of the creatures fell to the ground as he killed one after another. The bugs it seemed had only one weakness, which was a slow reaction time. Their eyes could see in all directions without even moving their heads, but their large stick-like bodies moved stiffly like machines.

From the castle emerged men in armor mounted on horses also clad in armor, the king's troops with weapons in hand and ready. They were trained in battle techniques and tactics and had practiced for years in the art of combat, but none of them had ever been in a real battle. There was never the need. In the lead was their prince, young and inexperienced, but brutally passionate about defending his people.

He sat tall upon a silky black horse clad in black armor that matched his own. A lightning bolt blazed across the black field on his helmet and his shield. The insignia was his father's idea. Nick had preferred something more like a dragon or an eagle, even an eagle's wing representing his kendrite heritage as well as the name "Wingmaster", but at the time he had conceded the matter. It had lacked importance to him. But, now the lightning bolt did have significance. The gate had brought Jesse to him. He would fight for her, for them, for their future together. He would die for her if need be. The lightning bolt was the perfect insignia for him and he wore it with pride.

He wielded the king's sword, enchanted by the Lady Shareen to seek out and destroy evil, a gift to her husband King Theodore Wingmaster II on their wedding day. Nicholas's great great grand-father had used the sword in battle, as had his grandfather King Cleotus Wingmaster, even though the blade had been cursed by the evil sorcerer Ban. Nick's father had taken the sword to Gabriel and had the curse lifted from it. Shareen's original intent was re-stored and the weapon would glow with brilliant blue freecurrent energy when evil was detected.

Although the blade shimmered and the gold filigree radiated sparkle, it did not burn with blue light. Nicholas handled it with ease. It had been many weeks since his father had offered it to him. Carrying it for that period of time had given him a chance to become familiar with it. At first it had felt heavy and cumbersome, but now he was used to the feel of it. His muscles had adapted to handle the weight. The heft of the weapon and the balance was perfect. He held it now with a strong arm and hand, but knew by the end of this day his muscles would protest the heavy work. Nevertheless, for now he was fresh, strong and had a job to do.

"Men, today we fight for our homes, our families, and our lives. Find the fire in your bellies that has remained unkindled until now. Break the binds of fair play for there is nothing fair about this in-trusion. Show no mercy for I guarantee you will be shown none. These creatures will not have our home! I ask the creator of all things to protect our souls as we may not all live to see another day.

For Risen!" Nicholas lifted his sword high in the air and galloped forward to engage the enemy.

A roar rose up from the men behind him. "For Risen!" they shouted. They spread out as they galloped forward, brandishing their weapons. The bugs continued their advancement without hesitating at the onslaught. For every one creature that went down another quickly took its place.

Swords were swinging fast and loose as the men attacked. Limbs were lobbed off in all directions, leaving the bugs unbalanced and flailing madly. With more swinging strokes the first beasts were beheaded and fell lifeless to the ground.

Nicholas drove forward like a mad man, hacking and slicing as he went. He used his mental link with Agape to work together as a team. The dragon kept the bugs busy as he darted in and out of their midst, picking off one at a time. Without leisure, Nick was relentless as he dismembered all within reach of his biting sword. His horse huffed and puffed as he stomped over the bodies of the fallen and obeyed the commands of his rider given with a squeeze of the thighs or a slight lean in the saddle. Subtle was the body language between rider and horse, but well received and quickly responded to.

Nearby his friend Michael was about to be overcome. Nick spurred his mount forward and bowled directly into the stick legs of the creature, driving it sideways into a tumble. With quick action he swung and severed the triangular head and it thudded audibly as it hit the dirt. The two men exchanged looks that spoke of gratitude and relief. Together they continued slaying the monsters that were unrelenting in their advance. Michael took left and Nick took right, Agape worked around them both, biting and snapping efficiently. Jim was in eagle form and struck from above with his lethal talons over and over again, lending his skills as a kendrite to the fight.

As Nicholas watched with a scream of warning on his lips, one of his father's men was a second too slow with his sword and had his head bitten off at the neck and eaten. The poor man's body stayed upright in the saddle for what seemed like a frozen moment before toppling off onto the trodden ground, joining the carcasses of the bugs that were piling up by the minute. Burning rage drove Nicholas forward and he severed the offender's own head before it had swallowed the warrior's helmet. The armor fell from its open maw as the pinchers released their hold and crashed onto the dead man's chest.

Time inched forward. The ground below Nick's horse's hooves was thick with dead bugs and slick with their greasy blood. He paused to take a long pull of water out of his canteen. Over his shoulder he heard a scream that was suddenly cut short. When he turned to look he saw one of his men go down without his head. Another soldier charged and hacked with gusto at the bug until it was in pieces. The winded man gazed down at his fallen comrade for a long moment before giving him a silent salute. Nicholas re-alized that the men were Alexander and Lan, good friends of his father. They had been buddies for more than thirty years. At first he couldn't tell who was who. They were both so covered in blood that the red dragon on Alexander's helmet was barely visible. Lan was the one who was dead. As Alexander turned to Nick, his eyes were wild with rage and pain.

Nick gave the sign to fall back. It was passed on from man to man until all received the order. *"Agape, can you and the other dragons give us a defensive perimeter? We need to regroup,"* he said. "Fall back," he yelled over the din.

The dragons swept the area behind them with dragon fire keeping the bugs at bay while they retreated to behind the castle ramparts. People rushed out of the castle to tend to injuries and provide food, water and comfort to the warriors. There were many tears shed for those who had not returned, but the threat was far from over. The possibility existed that none of them would live to see another day.

Jesse found Nicholas in the mass of chaos finally. She had been busy using her skills as a healer to help those who were injured. He was talking with several of his men trying to come up with the best plan for stopping these things. Jim spoke with him urgently about the possibility of bringing in help. Nick was telling him he didn't think it was possible. "Nick, are you hurt?" Jesse asked as she rushed to him.

"No, I'm fine, Jesse. Are you getting everybody patched up?" he tried to sound light, but she could detect the distress in his voice.

"Yes. There have been a lot of puncture wounds. I am doing everything I can to keep up with the injuries." She swallowed, remembering the agony. "Did you get something to eat?" she asked as she handed him a fresh flask of water.

"Yeah, I had some of that energy bread that the cooks make. It's full of good stuff to keep a warrior strong. Awesome stuff. Here, take some. You need to keep up your strength as well. Where's Gabriel?" he asked handing Jesse a hunk of thick bread.

She could tell he was working hard to sound positive and up in spirit. "She's just over there," she said as she pointed. "Grandmother," Jesse called as Felcore came up next to them and pushed his nose into Nick's hand.

Looking up from the man she was talking with, Gabriel held up one finger and turned back to him. She was disheveled with tufts of brunette hair poking out of the usually neat bun at the back of her neck. Her blue dress was stained and tattered and her face was drawn into a scowl that accentuated the wrinkles that had gently touched her over the years. When she turned, she smiled slightly as she approached them. Felcore wagged his tail as he greeted her.

"Nicholas, how is it going out there?" she asked.

"Endless. We need to approach this differently. The men cannot keep this pace up for long and those monsters keep coming. I'm thinking of dividing us into two shifts, so half of the troops can rest and then we can rotate. I think it will help to keep us fresher," Nick said.

"Skymaster is bringing in more dragons to help. They should be here soon. With the added dragons, I think your idea is a good one," Gabriel said.

"Grandmother, I've been thinking," Jesse began. "Do you remember when you played the harp for the warwolves and they went berserk and killed each other?"

"It is something I will never forget. Are you thinking what I think you're thinking?" she asked.

"Where is the harp?" Jesse asked.

"It is stored in the armory at Farreach," she replied.

"I'm going to go get it. As soon as the other dragons arrive, I'm taking Tempest to Farreach," Jesse declared.

"Jesse, I would like you to take Rew with you. I'd feel . . . " Nick started to say.

"Rew's gone," Gabriel informed him.

"What? Where did he go?" Nick asked.

"He said he needed to get back to Elysia to find out where these bugs are from and possibly stop their ingress into Risen through the gate. I have never seen a wisp so angry before," Gabriel said.

"Is this Candaz's doing?" Nicholas asked.

"I'm not sure, but it is the likeliest explanation," she replied.

"How could he have orchestrated a full invasion so quickly? He was just in Saberville a little less than a week ago," he commented in disbelief.

Jesse remembered Shareen's warning and the fact that Candaz was in possession of the instruction manual to the gate. She had advised them of the danger. "Time is subjective, Nick," Jesse said. "It depends on the rotation of a planet around its sun and its own rotation around its axis. Earth and Risen are quite similar as far as time. One day on Earth is one day on Risen. But, all of the locations through the gate are not the same. Candaz could have left here a few days ago, but in actuality he's been where ever it is he's gone for years. It all depends."

"I wish I would have killed him when I had the chance," Nicholas fumed. "That bastard killed Stephan. How many more people are going to die because I failed to kill him?"

"We've all missed opportunities to put an end to his life. We must deal with the reality we are in right now. There is no going back and such regrets help no one," Gabriel said. "Jesse, go get the harp. I think your idea is definitely worth a try."

"Nicholas," Bill called as he made his way through the crowd of people. Jacob was right behind him. When he finally got through to them, he was winded, but said, "I want to help. What can I do? Where can I be of help?"

"Can I fight?" Jacob asked with excitement in his eyes.

"No, Jacob," Jesse protested adamantly.

Nicholas quickly took charge. "Bill, I need you and Jacob to help Natina coordinate things behind the lines. Make sure there is fresh food and water available to the troops. Keep the grooms rotating the horses regularly. Be sure everyone stays on task and is doing their job. Jacob, you have a time keeper, I see. I want to rotate troops every other turn. Can you keep track for me?"

"How long is that?" Jacob asked, looking at his watch.

"A turn is an hour, Jake, so every two hours," Gabriel said.

"So," Nick said, "every two hours ring the bell in the tower twice. Someone will show you where it is. Make sure all of the staff is ready to serve the spent troops. Make sure the men standing by are ready to go when their time is at hand. Can you coordinate all of that?"

"Sure, but I really want to fight," Jacob said.

"Experienced men are dying, Jacob. You don't have the skills needed to fight. It would be suicide and I can't have that. I promise to train you when all this is over, but for now I need you here, behind the lines," Nicholas said as he extended his hand and sealed the deal with a handshake.

"The other dragons are here," Jesse said as she watched them begin attacking the bug creatures immediately. Seven more dragons had arrived, four adults and three baby goldens.

The bugs seemed unaffected by the arrival of the extra dragons. They maintained a steady advance as they consumed everything living and dead thing in their path. "Look at those things. They are eating each other's corpses. They're cannibals," Jacob said, fascinated by the brutality.

"I never imagined anything like this," Nick said, shaking his head before turning his focus back to Jesse. "Be careful." He handed his helmet to Jacob, wrapped his arms around her and gazed into her eyes.

"You be careful, Nick. I love you," she said as she leaned in to kiss him. It was warm and sweet despite the salty sweat that shimmered on his skin and she didn't want it to end. What if she never saw him again?

"I love you," he said before he let her go. A groom brought him a fresh horse and he swung up into the saddle and drew his sword.

"I'll be back soon," Jesse said as Felcore pressed close to her leg offering her comfort.

"I will see you then," With effort, he pulled his eyes from her and put on his helmet. Nicholas spurred his horse and galloped back out into the field of battle, followed by half of his troops. The other half remained behind awaiting their turn.

# Chapter 21

## SUSPENDED PAIN

B ringing down the axe, Serek absorbed the impact with muscles that were used to wielding a sword. He wiped the sweat from his brow and glanced up to see Link coming toward him up the tunnel. The other bandergs did not pause in their labors. They were very close to having a path cleared to the outside. Wood was stacked everywhere and the smell of fresh cut lumber permeated the air.

They knew what awaited them on the other side of the barrier. B.F. and Breezerunner kept them well informed of the current events in their storm-induced imprisonment. There had been a very long and drawn out debate among the banderg council concerning continuing the efforts to clear the way to the outside world. Most members on the council felt that they were better off staying trapped in Skyview for the interim. After all, they were safe and sound, had plenty of food and water and could live a long time without having to leave their haven. Theo, Serek and Kristina all took turns advocating that they could not let the rest of Risen succumb to the bug creatures while they did nothing.

At first they only had two members of the banderg council on their side, including Link, but after an inflamed and passionate petition by Theo, they were down to just one. Serek tapped into his business man side and pointed out that the financial losses they were sure to suffer should trade be suspended for a long period of time could be substantial. When that didn't work he tapped into his more natural angry man side and raged about their cowardice and stupidity. It wasn't until Kristina made her plea and appealed to their strong family connections and shared a measure of her grief that they finally decided after much discussion and tears to allow the clean-up crews to continue. They would join the fight for Risen.

"Link, do you have news?" Serek asked as he caught his breath while he leaned on the hilt of his axe.

"How long do you think?" Link asked anxiously as he tugged vigorously on his beard.

"We're almost ready to remove the last of it. Are the warriors ready?" Serek asked.

"They are. Theo is going to lead the southern defensive force. He is awaiting your signal to go," Link told him.

Serek could tell that there was something more Link was hesitant to say. "What is it Link?" he asked.

After a long moment he finally looked Serek square in the eye and said, "Kristina. There I said it."

"Kristina what?" Serek growled.

"She ah, ah, ah. She insisted," he hedged.

"Insisted on what? Link I don't have time for this. What is it? Spit it out," he bellowed.

"She's in the northern defensive force. She wants to fight," he finished as he tried to read Serek's face, trying to determine whether to stay put or run.

Unexpectedly Serek started to laugh. "I'm not surprised. Does she have armor?" he asked.

"Well, actually, she and Berry have been putting together something for her all morning. Let's just say that she is well equipped," he chuckled and then thought better of it and shut his mouth with a snap.

Serek gave him a scathing look and then said, "Breezerunner and B.F. are working the sky. They've been joined by two other adult dragons and two of the baby golds. As you know, they won't get close to the gates because of the dragon bane, an unfortunate inconvenience at the moment. But, they continue to kill those things by the hundreds around the perimeter of Skyview. Kali on Sweet Vang and Kaltog on Grand Oro are defending Anna's property. According to Breezerunner, they have their hands full."

The resounding hollow clap of horses' hooves was heading their way. Along with it the jingle-jangle of armor followed with a repetitive rhythm of its own. Serek wiped the sweat from his face and chest with a dirty towel and threw it aside. "Where's my shirt?" he asked no one in particular before he spotted it and retrieved it from where it hung nearby.

From down the corridor came Kristina leading another horse for her husband. An army of banderg warriors walked behind her. She was a statuesque figure in the saddle, both tall and beautiful with an aura that demanded attention. Her armor was polished silver from the helm on her head to the sabaton on her feet. Underneath her armor were white leathers that made her look every bit the queen.

Blond flowing hair fell free as she removed her helmet and observed Serek who was staring at her with his mouth open. Although stunning, grief had drained her face of its color and her normally sparkling green eyes were red and puffy from crying.

All of the hard labor Serek had been doing to dull the pain of his own grief came ebbing back through the cracks of his facade as he looked into his wife's eyes. His heart twisted and all he wanted to do was take Kristina in his arms and sob. Their boy was dead. All of their hopes and dreams for him were forever vanquished. The moment was poignant. He could not talk. He could barely breathe.

He walked up beside her horse and took her hand in his. Their eyes locked and he could tell she was having as much trouble keeping it together as he was. Still he couldn't speak. Instead he gently squeezed her hand. She whispered so quietly he almost didn't hear her, "Serek, I'm so sorry."

The dam he had so carefully put in place was starting to crumble under the emotional flood. He pressed his face against her hand and gulped down the lump of sadness in his throat. Now wasn't the time to deal with this! A flash of anger ran through him. He grasped a hold of that emotion, isolating it from all of the others. Anger was something he could work with. With gentleness he kissed Kristina's hand and let it go.

He allowed the bandergs to help him on with his armor. Strapping on the belt that held his scabbard and sword, he reached for the rage that burned inside him and strapped that onto his heart. He would feed off from it for the battle ahead. Once in the saddle he signaled the banderg general that he was ready.

*"Breezerunner, inform B.F. we're under way,"* Serek told his dragon mentally.

The bandergs he had been working with finished clearing the fallen tree that blocked the passageway. Slowly, the warriors began moving through the gate into the afternoon light.

Immediately they were engaged by large creatures that resembled praying mantis. Serek roared a battle cry and drew his sword. He hacked viciously as he drove forward, keeping Kristina always to his left. She was as effective with her weapon as he was and together they made a lethal team.

Behind them the banderg warriors took down the creatures one at a time by first cutting their legs out from under them and then tearing them apart. Link fought with his fellow bandergs. He was a surprisingly good fighter considering that he was more at home in the kitchen. His skills with a knife were amazing, like the blade was an extension of his hand.

From well-chosen positions, the archers rained arrows down upon their foes very effectively, exacting a heavy toll on the bugs that did not cease in their death march.

The bandergs' tactic of ganging up on each creature individually was working well. They were able to defend each other while picking apart the much larger bug, like ants taking down a wasp. Their losses were minimal but the task was huge. Endurance was a legendary characteristic of the banderg race. With steady persistence, they took on one foe and then another and then another, never ceasing, never even stopping to rest.

Kristina swung her blade, hacking apart the bugs with a heart filled with sorrow. Her vengeance was for Candaz, who had brought all of this upon them and had killed her son. She let her emotions drive her long after her muscles cried out for relief. Nothing mattered except the destruction of the terror that Candaz had brought. Her skill with a sword was brilliant and she fought with brutal finesse.

On the south side of Skyview the mud that remained from the flooding was hampering the effort. Footing was slick and treacherous. After Theo's horse balked several times, he gave up fighting on horseback and joined the bandergs on the ground.

As king of Brightening his interest was not only for the bandergs he fought alongside, but for his people. Concern over Lakeside and Vinnia, both virtually defenseless villages, motivated him to strike with vigor. He was determined to finish defending Skyview and get to Brightening as soon as possible. But, things did not look good. Accomplishing that goal meant eradicating all of the long legged creatures, but there seemed to be no end to their numbers. They just kept coming in a relentless swarm.

The things seemed thoughtless, driven primarily by the instinct to feed. Where they came from he did not know--through the gate perhaps. Most likely this was Candaz's doing. Not for the first time he wished he had taken the extra step to end that man's life back when he had the chance. Another regret to add to his growing list of regrets. It's funny how age gave a man the opportunity to look back at all the things he had done wrong. Of course, he had done a lot right too. But, at the moment the wrong choices seemed to be coming to fruition.

He swung his sword and lobbed off the head of one of the bugs. Slimy blood spewed out of the wound covering him in it. Quickly, he wiped his eyes clear so he could see. Sinister pinchers came down toward him at lightning fast speed. Before Theo could act, the bandergs with him took the creature's legs out. Losing its balance, the thing missed taking his head off by only inches. The chatter of the bug's pinchers as they clapped together empty rang in his ear. With a chopping motion the head that had nearly been the end of Theo Wingmaster rolled to his feet. The dead eyes stared up at him. With disdain, he kicked it out of his way.

"*Theo,*" B.F. called.

"B.F.?"

"*That was a close one. I suggest you pay attention to what you are doing,*" he reprimanded.

"*You saw that?*" Theo asked.

"*Yes, I am far overhead. If you looked up you could see my shadow. But, don't look up! Behind you!*" B.F. warned.

With a smooth move, he turned his head and struck with his sword in one fluid motion. The blade pierced the bug between its bulging eyes. As it fell he said, "*Thanks.*"

"*You are welcome. I have bad news. Lan is dead,*" B.F. told him.

"*Lan?*" It took a moment for the news to sink in. Lan was one of Theo's oldest and dearest friends. He stumbled, "Oh no."

The bandergs that surrounded him kept him safe while he recovered. "*What happened, B.F.?*" he asked.

"*Alexander was with him when the bug killed him. He did not suffer. I am sorry about your friend, Theo,*" B.F. said.

"Yeah, me too. He has a wife and young children. How many of these things are there, B.F.? Tell me what to expect." An archer took out a bug that was about to set upon him. It fell with a crash.

"*They cover the land. Out of the lightning gate they have marched as a forefront to the main assault,*" he said.

"*Main assault? Talk to me, B.F.*" Theo ordered.

"*They are called 'Tromeck'. Warriors they are--conquerors. Power is what they seek--dominance over all. Even though their numbers are few, they are formidable. Their race has killed each other off until all that remains are the strongest of the strong. That is why so few remain. Risen provides them with another chance to conquer and obtain new subordinates to oppress. They are humanoid, but less than human in the spiritual sense. Monster lizards with poisonous spikes on their tails and razor sharp teeth they ride upon. Candaz has them under his control somehow. For now, however, we have bugs to squash. Stay focused, Theo. Above you!*" B.F. said.

When Theo looked up there was a sharp pair of pinchers coming down upon him. He lifted up his sword and impaled it, again getting drenched in goo when he ripped his weapon loose. "*Oooowh. I've had enough of these things.*"

"Steady man. You have many more to go," B.F. said.

"How do you know all of this? Where are the Tromeck? Where is Candaz?" he asked.

"Rew told me. They have just come through the gate. Candaz rides with them. Saberville will be the first on their path," B.F. told him. "Watch out!"

Theo spun and countered the grasping claw that came at him with the swipe of his blade, severing it cleanly. He finished the thing off with two strokes. Another was quickly upon him and he dispatched it in a similar manner. "At least Jessabelle is safe where she is under the water," he said.

"Yes. That is one good thing. Theo! You have got to pay attention to what you are doing at this moment in time. That one almost got you! I'm going to quit talking to you and go exterminate some of these bugs. They taste terrible, by the way. Mind what you are doing, your highness," B.F. said.

"Tell Agape to tell Nicholas that . . . well . . . that I'm proud of him and that I love him," Theo said.

"You are wasting time. He knows that," B.F. said.

"Just tell him," he ordered.

"Done. He says to tell you he is sorry about Lan. Oh, and, he loves you too," B.F. said with a mental sigh. "Humans. They are so sentimental."

As the sun set in the east they continued to maintain a state of steady preservation. It was going to be a long night.

## Into The Darkness

"Go, Terese. See if you can find Jessabelle," Kate said.

They had been fighting off the bug-like creatures for days now and their defenses were wearing thin. Trevis was doing the best he could to lead what remained of their depleted forces, but the men were exhausted.

Without the dragons' help they would already have succumbed to their invaders. Skymaster had incorporated the help of his fellows and they had arrived yesterday to help Zlato and Gold Stone, who were still babies and could not produce flame. Four adults came to their aid and lent their abilities to the defense of the castle and the surrounding village of Saberville.

It was a losing battle, however. They could not maintain the constant onslaught of the creatures for much longer. People were dying where their defenses did not reach. Trevis needed more help or all would be lost.

"Find her I will," Terese assured her new friend. Although she was going to fly, it wasn't going to be on her dragon. She was going to leave Gold Stone there to help with the bugs. "Kate, if the castle succumbs to them, then on either Gold Stone or Zlato I want you to leave. Go to Castle Gentlebreeze. You and Lauren and the kids can all ride to safety on one of the dragons. Promise me you will escape. Promise me."

Kate did not answer right away, but eventually she said, "I promise you Terese that I will do what needs to be done to protect the children. Be careful." She gave her a hug before Terese stepped back away from her.

Through Gold Stone Zeth had communicated to her that their company was on their way back to Castle Xandia. They should arrive by tomorrow at the latest--everybody but Zeth, anyway. He informed her that he had something he needed to take care of first. What that something was he would not disclose to her. Grace would not break the trust and tell Gold Stone what they were up to. Regardless, Kate and Terese were desperate to get help to defend the castle.

Being a kendrite, Terese proposed help from Colordale. The kendrites would be the best choice in that they would be free to move about despite the invaders numbers. The problem was that to convince the kendrites to come to their aid might prove to be difficult if not impossible. Kate suggested that Jessabelle would be the best person to make the proposal to the kendrites. She was the daughter of King Shane and perhaps he would listen to her appeal. Jessabelle, however, was lost. Terese intended to find her.

They were on the upper floor and could see out over the battle that was taking place below. Terese began to shimmer and transformed into an eagle. Her sharp eyes gave one last look at Kate before she went to the window sill and launched into the sky. Immediately she was attacked by a flying bug, but she fought him off and sped away.

# Warrior Kate

Behind her Kate watched her fight off the bug and then turned and ran quickly down to the armory. Sorting through the multitudes of armor remnants, she finally found pieces that might fit her and put them on. It felt cumbersome to her, so she removed some of the more bulky pieces until she felt comfortable and could move freely. Selecting a sword, she tested it and decided it suited her well. She did not intend to sit idly by while her people were dying. Hours upon hours she had spent training with her brother and cousin and she was as good as either of them. Terese said she was too young to fight and had kept her safely protected in the castle. Her brother Trevis would not allow it either. But, Terese was gone now and she knew she could get past Trevis. Exiting the castle, she made her way to the stable and selected a spirited mount. Once in the saddle, she joined the battle.

Trevis gave her orders without recognition and she fought partnered with Stephan's long-time friend, Landon. It didn't take long for him to figure out with whom he fought alongside. He knew she was good, having seen her train with Stephan and Nicholas for years. Landon welcomed her, accepting her for her bravery and skill with a sword. Together they worked well. Kate was graceful as well as lethal and she was driven by retribution for her brother's death.

## In Flight

Terese would have been angry with Kate for putting herself so close in harm's way, but she also would understood her need to fight. She hoped Kate would choose her own fate. Although she had protected the girl while she was there, she could do so no more and she had a feeling the Kate would do as she pleased regardless.

As she flew, she gained enough height to fly above the bugs. Looking down at them was like looking at ants crawling over the landscape below. It felt so good to experience the freedom of flight. With her wings spread she could cruise on the wind currents. Her spirit soared as she felt the air ruffle through her feathers. She loved being an eagle.

A dragon came into view. She dove toward it and immediately recognized Grace with Zeth riding on her back. Angling her wings, she soared down and landed behind him, shimmering as she turned back into a human and gently wrapping her arms around his waist.

He looked over his shoulder at her and smiled, "Terese." Leaning back he was able to touch her lips with a kiss. "Terese," he breathed. "Will you marry me?"

She was a little startled by the question and did not respond immediately. Instead she asked, "Where are you going, Zeth? Grace would not tell Gold Stone."

"I'm going to find my father. I can't let him continue this," he said with bitterness in his voice.

"Going alone are you? You could be killed," she said.

"I do what I feel must be done, Terese. I know you understand why I must do this," he told her as he again sought her mouth for another kiss. "Will you marry me when all of this is over? Will you be my wife?" he asked.

"Yes, marry you I will, Zeth. Now I must go. Please come back to me," she brushed the back of his neck with her lips.

"I love you, Terese. Be careful," he said.

"I will," she replied and immediately returned to eagle form and flew away.

It wasn't too long before she spotted a group of riders far below--Serek's men. They fought as they rode along, riding fast and leaving carcasses in their wake. There was freecurrent energy being used evident by the bright flashes of green and blue light. They had a magic wielder in their midst.

She banked until she found a good current that blew in the direction she wanted to go. It was amazing everything she could see down below. Her eyes were so precise in their vision that she could pick out individual leaves on trees, even down to the small detail of the veins on the leaves. It was remarkable.

New Chance came into view and she marveled at how large the city was. Now mostly in ruins, in its time it must have been a magnificent place. Set on a gentle rise on the ocean shore, it faced the rising sun. The wide boulevards were paved with stone. Houses had small courtyards in the front and patios with yards in the back. Lining the ocean shoreline were the remains of once elegant mansions.

Surprised to see a small campfire burning on the beach, she circled once around before coming in to land next to it. Someone had been there recently, but no one was in sight. Footprints went out to the ocean and then disappeared. She transformed into human form and looked around. A make-shift shelter was built close by, just a basic lean-to, not very well constructed. A brisk wind would easily take it down.

Before she could investigate further, a man walked out of the water and spotted her immediately. He looked a little embarrassed, hesitated and then approached her. She knew him from Colordale. It was Prince Jacoby.

"Hello, your highness. Terese is my name," she said, smiling pleasantly.

"Why are you here?" he asked inhospitably.

"Unaware you are of the invasion?" she asked in return.

"Aware I am. Here the creatures do not come," he said. "Why are you here?" he asked again.

"In trouble is Saberville. Hoping I was . . . well, your sister Jessabelle I came seeking," Terese replied.

"It is not possible. Gone she is. Gone she is," he said. He sat down in front of the fire and gazed into it despondently.

"Show me your highness. See her I must," Terese insisted.

"No," he refused.

"You must. She is needed," she pleaded.

"No," he said more forcefully.

"You must understand your highness. About to fall is Saber-ville," Terese said, moving to stand between him and the fire. She wanted him to look at her. "You must help."

"Must I? Answer to you I do not! Be gone!" he shouted and stood as his anger rose.

"Without her I will not leave. Why do you not try? Why do you just sit and do nothing?!" She could get angry too. She had watched people die while this coward lay on the beach.

"Listen to me she will not. I have tried. Lost she is," he said.

"No. I will not give up. Take me to her," Terese said.

"No. Be gone!"

"Your highness, listen. Important this is. This could be the last chance for Saberville. If you will not help me find your sister, could you at least fly to Colordale and petition King Shane to send help north. We are desperate. I beg you," she looked up at him through her eyelashes, setting aside her anger and trying a humble approach.

"No!" he spat and sat back down and stared into the fire.

She could not believe this man. "Fine! I will find Jessabelle myself!" Terese said angrily as she turned and walked into the ocean.

"Wait," Jacoby said. "Wait."

"What?" Terese asked as she turned back around.

"Help you I will. It's only that . . ." he looked down and didn't look back up or finish what he was going to say.

She didn't know what to make of him. First he refused and now this. "You changed your mind. Why?"

"Determined you are to find her. I cannot allow that to happen without me," he said with obvious discomfort.

Terese didn't know what his problem was. But, right now she didn't care as long as he could get her to the queen. "Come on then your highness," she said and waded knee deep in the water waiting for him. Without further discussion, they transformed into dolphins and joined the water world.

## Dolphin Queen

Her belly was wonderfully full. The pod had been fishing all morning and everybody was satisfied with their catch. They used a method where they surrounded a group of fish and kept them contained until the pod had fed. It was more than just fishing, it was fun.

She let her sleek body take her up to maximum speed and then jumped and dove in succession playfully. The other dolphins in her pod followed her lead and frolicked in the waves along with her. There were six other cows and three bulls along with seven calves, four of which were fairly young. She vocalized in what sounded like clicks and whistles to the younger children, encouraging them to keep up.

One of the bulls came up beside her and challenged her for the lead. They had violent encounters in the past. His disposition could be brutal at times. He brushed against her, but she broke away quickly changing directions. There had been moments when he had pushed himself too far with her. He had wanted her to mate with him, but she had refused. She would not mate with any of the bulls. It wasn't from the lack of desire, for her body was willing, but something in her mind kept her apart.

Changing directions again, she swam nearer to shore. Lately, she had been pulled to get closer to land. Something inside her was curious, but it was more than that. Instinct told her that there was something out there that she was missing. At odd moments, often in her dreams, she saw a face, a man's face. That face with its green eyes haunted her. She felt an empty hole in the pit of her stomach that was like hunger, but all the fish in the ocean could not satisfy it. She didn't understand it but she felt strongly drawn to him.

There were also times when she was with the calves, playing or teaching, that she felt a grounded sense of motherhood. Being a mother was a part of who she was, but she did not know her children. They were not a part of the pod and that confused her. She would not be apart from her children for any reason that she could think of.

Her dreams were not dolphin dreams. She dreamed of being with the man with the green eyes. They were bonded by love and her body responded with desire for him. She did not understand that either. He was a man and she was a dolphin.

There were two dolphins heading their way. One, the male, was calling to her. She had met him before. He was her brother he had told her. But, her brother was human . . . no, that could not be right. She swam toward him and his companion, curiosity getting the best of her. Her whole pod followed, although some of the mothers voiced their apprehension at venturing so close to strangers because of their little ones. She reassured them that it would be okay.

Curiosity drove her forward and she vocalized to the pair that she was coming. For a reason she couldn't identify she felt anxious and excited at the same time. She spotted them just under the surface of the waves and when they saw her they sped her way.

The male seemed to hold back, but the female approached her boldly and touched her nose to nose. In clicks and whistles the cow told her that she came from the land and that she needed her to come back with them. She called her 'Jessabelle.' *"Remember"* she said. The cow told her she was a "kendrite" and that she wasn't just a dolphin, but also a wolf and an eagle and a human. *"Remember Theo,"* she said. *"Your husband."*

Could Theo be the man with the green eyes, she wondered? But, she was a dolphin. How could she be anything else?

She swam to the bull dolphin and touched him on the nose. He was familiar to her. *"Kendrite you are?"* she asked him in dolphin.

He vocalized, *"My sister you are. Kendrite I am."*

She was confused.

From behind swam the bull dolphin from her pod. Violently, he rammed into the one who called himself 'brother'. He opened his mouth aggressively to take a bite out of her brother, but Jessabelle interceded and received the bite instead. It was a minor injury and would heal with time, but it was still unacceptable. She drove her body into his and chased him until he gave up and left them alone. She had had enough of him.

When she returned to the pair, the cow again touched her nose to nose and then shimmered and transformed into a human for only a brief moment, long enough for her to see the dark-haired woman. She was as she claimed then, not dolphin, but kendrite. The human's gold eyes brought back a memory. It was the memory of a boy--her child. Nicholas was his name. Her son.

Memories and the emotions that they evoked came flooding back to her and she remembered her life. She was Jessabelle the White. She was the wife of Theo Wingmaster and the queen of Brightening. Her children were Nedra, Natina and Nicholas. She had two beautiful grandchildren, Bryce and Kyle. Bryce, her grand-daughter had gold eyes like her own. Her husband, Theo, was the man with the green eyes and he was the best man she had ever known, gentle and handsome and good. She missed him with all of her being. *Theo, my love, to you I will return soon.*

She dashed around in excitement and jumped and dove with joy. The female joined her in her happy play. When Jessabelle finally settled down, she paid her respects to her dolphin family and said goodbye, paying special attention to the young ones and giving them her affection and promise to return to see them soon.

Returning to shore with her brother and the female, she transformed and felt her feet in the sand with fascination. She wiggled her toes and enjoyed the feeling as if for the first time in her life. Smiling, she strolled to the campfire and turned to wait upon her rescuers. The heat warmed her skin in a delightful kind of way. The sensation of being human again was marvelous. Her skin was so wonderfully sensitive not only to touch but to temperature and the soft breeze that brushed against it. She was desperate to return to Theo, but she knew that the two kendrites who had come for her had other intentions.

"Jacoby tell me," she ordered.

Her brother's eyes found the ground as if he was ashamed to look her in the eye. "Sorry I am. I did try," he said defensively.

The woman stepped forward and introduced herself. She had very dark hair, almost black and her caramel colored gold eyes stood out in stark contrast. Rich and fierce was her beauty. Jessabelle recognized her from Colordale. She had worked in the manor for a short time, but they had never been introduced. Her voice fit her look. She said, "Terese I am. From Castle Xandia I have come. Invaded by monsters is the whole of Risen. Danger has come to us all. Help from Colordale is needed. I beg you for your help, lady Jessabelle."

Jessabelle's flashing golden eyes fell on her brother's back. Her red hair blew wildly around her face in the ocean breeze. "Why Jacoby? Why have you done nothing to help Risen? This fear you live with, when will you be done with it?" she asked. "The Prince of Colordale you are. Where is your pride? Where is your courage?" Her eyes flared with passion. "To Colordale we go immediately. Let us fly faster than we have ever flown."

# Chapter 22
## GO WEST

Tempest flew faster than she had ever flown before. The land below zipped by in a streak of colors, all running together like paints on an artist's pallet. Jesse held on to Felcore and Tempest at the same time and prayed for her loved ones who were in such terrible danger. With all the humility she could find within herself she asked God for his protection over them.

Farreach was a day's flight if a tail wind prevailed, but they made it in record time. Rew would have been proud of Tempest's speed. They landed directly in the square at Farreach. It was clear of bugs with an army of torgs defending their home on all sides. Tempest was very pleased with herself as she trumpeted loudly, announcing their arrival.

*"Great job Tempest. Why don't you do some fishing and then take a nap. We'll head back as soon as we can,"* Jesse said as she and Felcore's feet touched the ground.

"*Yes. I need to refuel,*" Tempest said with gusto and was quickly gone.

Felcore barked as a female torg came out to investigate. Jesse recognized her immediately. It was Lindi. She looked very tired, but she smiled when she recognized Jesse. "Hello, child. Why have you come to Farreach in these unlikely times?" she asked.

"Lindi, I have come for the harp. Do you know the one I speak of?" Jesse asked.

"Oh, yes, the harp that freed us from enslavement. I remember it well. Why don't we go inside? Come." Lindi led the way through the square to the door that led directly into the kitchen. Wonderful aromas permeated the air as she followed the torg woman through the busy kitchen. The Farreach kitchen was better than granny's house on Thanksgiving Day. The torgs loved food and good things were always cooking. Felcore quickly found some willing handouts as he wagged his tail and presented his best puppy dog eyes to the kitchen staff.

"Let me make you a plate," Lindi said. Without waiting for a response, she grabbed a plate and started with a roll, some chicken and glazed carrots. She headed into the massive dining room with it and set it on the table. "Sit down, Jesse. I'll get you some ale," Lindi said as she went to the beverage bar.

"Thank you, Lindi, but I'd prefer water," Jesse told her. She was hungrier than she thought and sat quietly and ate everything on her plate before she looked up. "Thank you. That was great."

"You're welcome. Can I get you some dessert?" she asked.

"No. Thank you. How are things going here?" Jesse asked.

"We are holding our own. The fighters have developed a method to take the bugs out one at a time, but it is long work. They are mindless creatures and have no real strategy other than to eat everything in sight. But, there are so many and they never stop coming," Lindi said and then took a long sip of her ale.

"Do you know where the harp is, Lindi?" Jesse asked.

"It is in the armory in the king's suite. What is your intention with it, Jesse?" Lindi asked.

"Did Gabriel ever tell you about the first time she used the harp?" Jesse asked.

"She said it could be dangerous if played with the wrong mind-set. Why? What happened?" Lindi stood up and refilled Jesse's water glass and topped off her own ale before she sat back down.

Even though Jesse felt a huge sense of urgency, she tried to not rush, but to go at torg pace. Taking a deep breath, she told Lindi the story about Gabriel and the warwolves. She finished by saying, "I believe that I can perpetuate the same response in the bugs."

"Well, let's see. The king is out fighting, but I believe it is something he would agree to readily enough." Lindi excused herself and returned a short time later carrying a small silver harp. It was beautiful and polished to perfection. She inserted it into a soft leather pouch. The torg woman handled the harp carefully, like it was a stick of dynamite. She seemed glad to hand it over to Jesse. "Be careful with it," she warned.

"I will. Thank you for dinner," Jesse said before she made her way back through the kitchen and out the door. Felcore followed after her with a full belly as well. She called to Tempest.

The dragon swooped down out of the night sky, a pearl of light in the darkness.

"Take me to Rocnor Vengar, Tempest. Take me to the fight," Jesse said as she and her dog climbed on the dragon's back.

The air felt cold on her face and she shivered as she held onto Felcore, feeling his warmth through the softness of his fur, taking what comfort she could from her loyal best friend. She was scared. Could she use the harp and make it work the way she wanted it to? Gabriel had written about it in her diary. Her grandmother's diary was in her backpack and that was at Castle Gentlebreeze. She tried to remember how the harp worked and what Gabriel had done wrong to set the warwolves into their killing frenzy. Freecurrent caused the harp to play, emotions chose the tune. What was Gabriel feeling at the time in the tree with the warwolves all around her? She knew one of the emotions was fear. Pity was something Gabriel had felt for the creatures and anger toward Candaz.

Fear and anger she knew she could summon, pity not so much. She had no pity for these treacherous mindless murderers. She never had liked bugs. A large can of Raid would be useful, but instead she had a harp. Fear--done. Anger--easy. Pity, pity, pity. How did she dig up pity? She thought of all of those abused animal commercials on television with those sad little puppy dogs. They evoked pity . . . which turns to anger at the s.o.b.s who did that to them. Was there pity without anger? Maybe she could feel both at the same time, but anger was certainly easier to get to.

Tempest began her descent, flaming bugs as she went. At least the dragon flame brought her some warmth. She was shivering uncontrollably. Her nerves were staging a revolt against her.

There were torches lit all around the hill where they landed. It was the staging area for the warriors. After she dismounted Tempest, she laid her head on the dragon's nose, gaining strength from the close proximity to her large friend. "*I am afraid, Tempest. My fear is getting the best of me.*"

"*Do you want me to sing to you?*" she asked.

"*I don't see how that will help,*" Jesse retorted, a little harshly.

Tempest did not pay attention to her, but began to hum inside her head. It was a beautiful song and wove a pattern intricate and magnificent. It calmed her. Her shivering lessened and then released her altogether.

"*Thank you sweetheart,*" she said and kissed Tempest on the nose.

The torgs fought with axes and spears and huge hammers. Most of them were farmers, some were lumberjacks. Very few of them were warriors, but they were all good fighters. Like the bandergs, they found the most effective method against the bugs was to gang up on them one at a time, while at the same time protecting each other's backs.

Jesse stopped someone and asked about the king's whereabouts. Another torg was sent to fetch the king from the battle. She and Felcore set about tending the wounded until Rocnor arrived.

"Bring me ale!" Rocnor ordered as he arrived. Someone did his bidding and handed him a large mug that spilled over with froth. He drank it down and handed it back. "Bring me ale," he said again.

Jesse had met the king before, but she was not familiar with him. She approached him slowly and humbly. "Your highness, may I speak with you?" she asked.

"Please, call me Rocnor. You are Gabriel's granddaughter, Lessa?" he asked.

"Jesse, sir."

"Jesse, of course. Would you like some ale?" he asked.

"Actually, yes, I think I would," she accepted a mug of beer from the man who was serving the king. She drank it slowly and it began to warm her from the inside out. "I have a proposal for you Rocnor," she said.

"Yes, what is it, girl?" he asked handing his mug back for another refilling.

"I have the silver harp. I wish to play it to entice the creatures to turn on each other. Gabriel did this once with the warwolves. Do I have your permission to try?" she asked the king.

"Let me call my warriors back. When they return here, you may play," he said.

"That seems wise," Jesse said.

"Blow the horn!" he yelled. "Call everyone back!"

A low mournful note resonated across the battlefield. The torgs arrived back at the staging area and ale was passed around freely to the weary warriors. When everyone was accounted for Rocnor turned to Jesse and gave her a nod.

Felcore pushed against Jesse's leg as she moved to the very edge of the torch lit area. She closed her eyes and brought the harp up to rest on one hip. Freecurrent sizzled on her fingertips as she touched them to the strings. Uneasiness came over her in a wave of nausea and she nearly dropped the harp. In her head she heard Tempest say quite plainly, *"Don't do it, Jesse,"* before she passed out.

When she came to, Felcore was licking her face. "Okay, boy, okay," she said, pushing him from her. The harp was still in her hands, but the freecurrent had ebbed away. *"What the hell's going on, Tempest?"*

*"We need to take the harp to Gabriel. She must play it,"* Tempest replied.

*"How do you know?"* Jesse asked.

*"I don't know how I know. I just do,"* Tempest replied indicating with her tone that the knowledge should be obvious.

*"Okay then. We go to Brightening, I guess,"* Jesse said feeling a little discouraged, but somewhat relieved as well.

She made her apologies to Rocnor, who did not seem at all inconvenienced by the revelation. He wished her luck and they were soon flying back east toward Castle Gentlebreeze.

## Colordale By Moonlight

Three eagles crossed in front of the moon, making similar shadows skim across the land. The bugs did not look up, or in any way respond. Anything worth devouring had been consumed and they were on the march, moving on to find food elsewhere. As the creatures left the area, small pockets of activity became evident as kendrites returned from where they had been hiding, either in the sky, in the ocean or deep in the woods.

Colordale was a natural setting. The homes were little wooden cottages scattered among the trees, camouflaged by design and intent. A stroll through Colordale was like a stroll through the woods. Tucked into a copse of birch trees was the manor that housed King Shane and his family and served as the center of government. It was a log building that was built in a way that only showed a small portion of a much larger expanse.

The three kendrites circled around and then landed on the railing of the front porch. Once transformed back into human form, they entered using Jacoby's key. The foyer had a wonderfully rustic smell of wood and oil with the faint traces of wood smoke. All three of them were quite at home in the building. Jessabelle had grown up there. Terese had worked there in service to the king for a couple of years before moving on. Of course, Jacoby still lived there and would someday inherit the residence as his own.

They immediately made their way to the east side of the building where King Shane's rooms were. There was nobody around. Only their footsteps could be heard echoing down the hall as they drew closer to the king's chambers.

Jacoby knocked on the closed door and they waited for King Shane to bellow his usual "What do you want?" However, there was no response, bellowed or otherwise. Jacoby knocked again, louder and longer. "Father," he said.

When again there was no answer Jacoby turned the door knob and they went inside. "Oh my," Terese said, bringing her hand up to her nose. Jessabelle and Jacoby did as well.

Lying on the bed was King Shane. He obviously had been dead for some time. Jessabelle went to his side and gazed down upon him for an extended moment. She was experiencing an onslaught of mixed emotions, but none of them were evident on her face. Slowly she reached down and picked up his left hand and placed a kiss on it. Carefully she removed the heavy gold ring that was on his middle finger. Using the blanket that was folded at the base of the bed, she covered his body and his face.

Tears were shining in her eyes as she turned to Jacoby and took his hand. Getting down on her knees she put the ring on the middle finger of his left hand and kissed it softly. "Your highness," she said.

He lifted her to her feet with his hands. "For this day I have been groomed all of my life. Ready I am not now that the day has come."

Terese could see the color in Jessabelle's cheeks rise. She was angry but she spoke with restraint, "No choice have you now brother. The King of Colordale you are."

Terese also humbled herself respectfully before the new king. "Your highness, now it is up to you to send help to Castle Xandia. I beg you to do as I bid," she said as she knelt before him.

When he didn't answer, Terese got to her feet and grabbed his arm. "Saberville needs the kendrites. We are their last hope," she said as she looked him in the eye. He turned and walked away.

They exited into the hallway and closed the door behind them. Jacoby started to stride down the hall and then turned back to the women. "What to do, I don't know," he said.

Jessabelle grabbed him roughly by the upper arm and said, "Jacoby, Saberville needs the kendrite's help. An opportunity you have to change things now that you are king. Isolation was what father chose for this community. Change that you can."

"Yes, if I choose to," Jacoby said as he started to walk toward the foyer again.

Jessabelle and Terese exchanged worried looks and then followed after the new king.

There was a pull rope in the foyer that connected to the bell in the tower. Jacoby took hold of the rope and pulled it three times and the bell rang throughout Colordale calling all within earshot to gather at the manor.

At that moment King Shane's personal assistant, Dillon, walked through the door and immediately asked what business they had ringing the bell. Before they could answer his eyes came to rest on the ring on Jacoby's finger and his face fell. "Dead he is?" he asked.

"Yes," Jacoby said. "Where have you been? Attending to the king, obviously you have not been. Your duty it is."

"Gone he was with the rest of the staff when the bugs came. I left too. He is dead? You are sure?" he asked in disbelief. Dillon was a good man and was loyal to the king.

"Dead he is," Jessabelle confirmed. "Jacoby is now King of Colordale."

Dillon's eyes darted to Jacoby and slowly he inclined his head. "Your highness," he said.

"Dillon, King Shane's body will need to be prepared for his funeral. Take care of that you must. I am sorry. He was more than your king, a friend he was to you," Jacoby said, putting his hand on the man's shoulder.

Jessabelle watched this encounter with a critical eye. She approved of Jacoby showing this man compassion, she just hoped it was sincere.

"It will be done," Dillon said. He again bowed his head to Jacoby and quickly left to do his bidding.

A group was gathering just outside the front door. Jacoby grabbed a cloak from a nearby hook and combed his fingers through his hair. With a quick look in the mirror, he opened the door to his people.

He waited for them to quiet and then addressed them, "Greetings friends and neighbors. Serious news is brought to you this night. Dead is your king." Jacoby paused as gasps and whispers passed through the crowd. "Mourning we all are this night. The time of Shane is over. Ever shall we embrace him in our hearts. His funeral is for another time, however. Immediate is our situation with the creatures that ravage the land. Although Colordale has been spared by the invaders of Risen, others remain in peril. To their aid we will fly. As eagles we go to our neighbors in need to fight until the fight is done. Do I have your support? Do I have your allegiance?"

A cheer greeted their ears confirming the kendrites' endorsement. Terese breathed a sigh of relief. Her heart was pounding with excitement. In spite of her doubts, Jacoby had come through.

"This night we fly for Saberville!" Jacoby shimmered and took to the sky. His people along with Terese and Jessabelle followed.

# Chapter 23
## HARMONIOUS DISHARMONY

Tempest was refreshed at Farreach with food and a long nap so their return trip was once again a sprint as they sped through the night. Jesse was still cold, but had quit shivering uncontrollably due to Tempest's intervention. She held onto Felcore, enjoying the comfort of his soft warm coat. He slept quietly in her arms. Before they arrived it started to rain.

Some distance away from Castle Gentlebreeze the sight of the dragons firing on the bugs was visible. As they drew closer the castle lights glowed brightly even though the village below was dark due to the inhabitants having evacuated to the safety of the castle grounds.

Banking hard, Tempest came in at an angle where Jesse could see the troops as they fought the bugs. Jim was overhead and she waved to him in greeting. She tried to spot Nicholas. As she flew by, one of the warriors saluted her with his sword raised and she knew that it was him.

They landed in the area that was usually the village market, but at the time served as the staging area for the warriors, a place apart where they could eat and rest and get medical aid if needed. Jacob was there. He was dirty and bloody and very busy giving orders and making sure any of the warriors' needs were attended to. When she greeted him, he gave her a big smile and came to her right away. "Jesse, you're back. How did it go?" he asked.

"I need to see Gabriel. Do you know where she is?" Jesse asked as she looked around.

Jacob poured some water in a cup and gave it to his sister. She drank it down thankfully. He refilled it and offered the same to Felcore. The dog also lapped it up happily. He answered her at the same time, "She's out on the battlefield using freecurrent to fight the bugs. Jesse, you're not gonna believe this! One of the dragons, Gold Nugget, bonded with me. He landed to get a drink of water and said, 'My name is Nugget, you are my Jacob.' He said that to me! We talk telepathically. It's frickin' better than a cell phone. I just told him to tell Skymaster that you are looking for Gabriel."

"That's great Jake. Thanks. Has Nick been out in the field all this time? And where's Dad?" she asked.

"For your first question, pretty much he has. I've been trying to get him to sit out for a round, but he hasn't yet. He's a bit stubborn. Maybe you'll have better luck. Here he comes now. Second question, Dad's working with the horses at the stable. He's like the horse whisperer I guess. I've gotta go. Let me know if you want anything, Jess. I can get you anything you need. Nugget says Gabriel will return immediately," he informed her before going back to work.

Jesse was awestruck. Her brother had always been a natural leader, but she never thought he could organize. His bedroom was always a mess. But, as she observed the behind the lines efficiency with Jacob in charge of the whole show, she couldn't help but be impressed. To hear that he had bonded with a dragon was wonderful news. It meant that he would want to stay on Risen with her and Nick. It meant this was going to be their new home and that they would be together as a family. Sure Jacob was her pesky little brother, who at times could irritate the hell out of her, but she loved him. Her heart was lifted.

She turned and watched Nicholas ride through the defensive perimeter on his spirited black horse. His armor was covered from head to foot with dirt and grime, blood and goo from the bugs. He dismounted and removed his helmet, shaking the sweat out his hair after he did so. He spotted her out of the corner of his eye as she ran to him and wrapped her arms around his neck, not caring that he was a mess. She kissed his face until he responded by kissing her back. When she pulled away, he appraised her with his honest gaze. He looked tired and the serious expression he wore aged him. He had watched people die in front of him. A boy he would never be again.

"How are things at Farreach, Jess?" he asked as he was handed a tall glass of water.

"They are holding their own. The torgs are well equipped to deal with these creepy crawlies now that the surprise factor is over. They have suffered minimal losses. Rocnor Vengar is a great king," she said.

"I agree with you there. He is a great man, or a great torg more appropriately. Did you get the harp?" he asked.

"Yes. Did Tempest not tell Agape about it?" she asked, surprised the grapevine had not supplied him with this information already.

"You know dragons. They disclose information at their discretion or only if you ask specifically for it," he said.

"Yeah, I guess you're right about that. I'll have to remember that in the future. I couldn't use it, Nick. Tempest told me it was for Gabriel to play. I don't know why, but it made me physically ill when I tried. Here she comes now," she said and greeted her grandmother with a hug.

"This is for you," Jesse said and handed Gabriel the silver harp.

Gabriel hesitated and then took the instrument. "Your highness, call back the men. Let's give this a try," she said.

"Jacob," Nicholas shouted, "Ring the bell. Let's get everyone back behind the perimeter."

"Yes, sir," Jacob answered and then yelled, "Ring the bell!"

The bell rang out three times and the thunder of hooves followed as the warriors returned. Jesse and Felcore began making the rounds and tending the wounded as Jacob made sure everyone was served with food and drink.

Gabriel called Skymaster to her. She had the harp tucked firmly under her arm as she mounted the dragon mage. Her face was set with a stern seriousness that reflected the gravity of the situation. As Skymaster began his flight, Gabriel nodded to Jesse before they returned to the battlefield.

Jim in eagle form flew alongside Gabriel and Skymaster, guarding her from any aerial attack and keeping a close eye on her in case she ran into some type of trouble.

Jesse was surprised that she could feel the freecurrent flow so strongly as Gabriel gathered the energy to her. The medallion burned hot against her chest as she looked up from what she was doing and went to the edge of the barrier to observe. The air was charged with electricity. From atop Skymaster's back Gabriel began to play.

Music streamed from the harp in a mournfully sad melody that ripped at the heart. Jesse was frozen in place, paralyzed by the emotion that the notes evoked. Felcore began to howl as he responded to the harp's voice, but Jesse did not comfort him. She could not. Her feet were frozen in place. She was mesmerized in the horror of the moment.

The bugs stopped gorging on the carcasses of their dead and turned on each other and began to kill the living. As the music played a ballet of carnage took place before their eyes. One bug took out another and then another, on and on until only two remained standing. Without hesitation the two came together with lethal results. Skymaster quickly finished the survivor off with dragon fire. As far as the eye could see the land was covered with dead bugs.

When Gabriel returned she was sobbing. "Grandmother," Jesse whispered to her as she wrapped her arms around the distraught woman. "It's all right. It's all right."

Gabriel held on to Jesse and let herself have a good cry before she stepped back and said, "I'm okay. It's just a lot of intense emotion to deal with. Skymaster and I will continue on to Vinnia, Lakeside, Skyview and then Saberville and Farreach until we've covered Risen from shore to shore. Theo says there is another wave in this assault that we haven't encountered yet. Candaz is not done yet. All of the leaders need to come up with a plan for the next round."

Jim landed beside her and became human. He put a strong arm around Gabriel's shoulder and pulled her against him. "You won't be going alone, Gabriel. I will stay with you," he said.

Gabriel smiled and blushed, "Okay, Jim. You are welcome to come with us."

"Be careful," Jesse said with a smile. "I'll see you soon."

"I'll be in touch, Jesse." She quickly climbed back onto Skymaster and waited for Jim to transform. Soon they were gone.

Jesse turned to Nicholas and he gathered her in his arms where she wished she could remain, safe and secure from the bad things of the world, comforted from the pain of loss, hidden away from the responsibilities that came with her gift. But, all too soon he was called away to deal with his own responsibilities and she had to let him go.

## Like Father Like Son

It took time for Zeth to find his father in the woods north of Castle Xandia. Grace took him into the midst of the invading army where they found a secluded place to land. The beasts moved slowly and paused for long periods of rest. Although the beings were humanoid, they seemed to lack human nature. They were ferocious, driven by base instincts without conscience or reserve. If they were hungry, they hunted and ate. If they were tired, they slept. They fought amongst themselves constantly. The distraction allowed Zeth to penetrate their forces without being noticed.

In the middle of a dense group of pines, he found a place to hide where he could observe. He didn't have to wait long before his father strolled into the midst of the chaos. His voluminous robes billowed behind him as he walked with an arrogant authority. Zeth would know him anywhere. He knew his posture and his gait. Although his limp from a prior injury, an injury that Theo had inflicted years earlier, wasn't evident, it was still subtly noticeable.

From out of one of his many pockets Candaz withdrew a small crystal bottle. He held it up where all of the Tromeck could see it. The fighting slowly subsided and the Tromeck settled down until all was quiet. Their attention was focused on Candaz and what he held in his hand.

"Gentlemen," he said, "the northern region of Saberville will be ours before the sun sets tomorrow. I have one of these for each of you when Castle Xandia is mine. The bugs have decimated the region and it is ours to take."

A roar rose up from the Tromeck. They climbed on their mounts, large lizards with spiked tails that made horrendous noises. The sound the lizards made was close to that of a steaming tea pot. The high whistling was enough to frighten and set the nerves on sudden edge.

As the lumbering creatures moved off to the south, Candaz hesitated. When the Tromeck were out of sight he took the top off the crystal bottle and drank down the contents. Zeth did not miss the opportunity to get him alone. He stepped out of his hiding place with his dagger in his hand.

"Father," he said. "It is time for this to end."

Candaz turned quickly and a slow smile distorted his face. "Well, if it isn't my traitor son. What is it, boy? What are you going to do, boy?" he asked.

Zeth did not hesitate but charged forward, aiming for the heart with his dagger.

Candaz gracefully side-stepped the charge; he spun, chopped Zeth's neck with his hand and placed a kick harshly in his stomach.

Zeth went down with a cry of pain, but quickly recovered and came at his father again. He brought the sharp knife across Candaz's face, drawing a line of blood.

When Candaz brought his hand up to the cut and discovered the bloody wound, his smile faded and he encouraged Zeth to try again, taunting him, challenging him.

His son took the challenge and charged, slashing at his stomach in an attempt to inflict the most damage.

Candaz punched him in the face and knocked him again to the ground. He did not wait for Zeth to recover. He kicked and punched and grabbed a large stick and began to beat him with it. A buried rage took over and Candaz's brutality was revealed tenfold. The thrashing continued until Zeth passed out and beyond to the point where the young man was very close to death. With one last kick, Candaz threw the bloody stick down and left his son for dead. Before walking away, he removed his cloak and emptied his pockets, save one. Molly's wilted hand he left bound inside the pocket where he had kept it tucked away for most of his life. It had tortured him for some time now, but he was hesitant to be rid of it. The hold it had over him was nothing short of insane. He decided in some illogical demented way that to use it as a shroud would be the proper way to be free of it. In his mind he watched as Molly fell from the cliff and screamed at him with her distorted face, "Why did you kill me?" Carefully he draped the cloak over Zeth's still form and quickly left.

After catching up with the Tromeck, Candaz led the warriors to a small clearing where the emerald green dragon, Grace, waited for her human. She was sleeping quietly when they came upon her and did not wake until she felt the first blow to her face. They beat her without mercy until she lost consciousness. Candaz stood over her feeling sickeningly gratified as he landed one last kick to her nose. The dragons would learn that he was to be feared.

## Stepping Up

With the bugs dead, Nicholas wanted to head out and check on the outlying villages in Brightening and then on to Skyview. After a quick shower and a bite to eat, he left instructions with Natina to manage the cleanup at the castle and surrounding area. There was a lot to be done. Bill was going to stay there and help. He was very good at managing people and Natina was happy to have his assistance. He seemed just as happy to be needed.

Nick's first priority was to get help to those who needed it. He called Agape to come and get him immediately. Jacob and Jesse were going to accompany him on dragon back. Two crews were heading out on horseback--one to the south toward Vinnia and another north toward Lakeside.

"Jesse, are you ready to go yet?" Nicholas asked as he waited beside Agape.

"I'm coming, Nick," she called as she crossed the courtyard. "I had to say goodbye to dad. Sorry if I took too long."

"You are worth the wait," he said as he gave her a quick kiss.

Jacob was already on Nugget waiting for them both. He rolled his eyes, and said, "Can we go?"

Felcore barked in agreement.

The dragon riders flew south first to the small village of Vinnia. Dead bugs lay everywhere and people were starting to emerge from whatever safe havens they had found. A search had already begun for the missing. Families who had lost loved ones to the bugs gathered together to provide comfort to each other.

Jesse and Felcore did the rounds helping the injured while Jacob and Nicholas helped with search and rescue. When they could do no more they got back on their dragons and flew north to Lakeside.

Gabriel was still there, in fact had just finished playing the harp. The bugs lay dead, some of them still twitching from their nerve impulses, some of them just a dusty pile where Skymaster's dragon fire had engulfed them.

They landed by the dock beside the lake toward the center of the village. As with Vinnia, survivors were beginning to come out from their hiding places and assess the damage and the losses. Again Nicholas and Jacob worked together to help out where they could. Jim joined them and lended his great ability to instill calm in the midst of chaos.

Jesse tended to her grandmother, who was weak and exhausted from the ordeal of playing the harp, which leached off from the player's emotions. It had left Gabriel drained. She found a small pub that was still standing and was able to get some food and drink for her and then requested that Gabriel lay down and get some sleep before moving on. Although she resisted, her condition required a rest and finally she succumbed to its needs. Jesse gently placed her hands on her grandmother and used her skills with healing to renew Gabriel's strength before she left her slumbering quietly in a small room above the bar.

By the time Jesse rejoined them, Nick and Jacob were ready to move on to Skyview. They had done all that they could in Lakeside. Rebuilding lives and structures would come with time. Now was the season to mourn. Jim promised Jesse he would take good care of Gabriel before they left.

They flew to Anna's cabin with plans to walk to Skyview from there. Morning was well established by the time they landed beside Grand Oro and Sweet Vang. The dragons were keeping the bugs at bay while Kaltog, Kali and Anna took a much needed rest from the fight. They were back by the kennels and Felcore quickly found Tica among the other dogs and they pounced and played happily together. "It must be nice to be a dog," Kali said. "All of this death and destruction doesn't seem to affect them in the least." She laughed, but the sharp edge in her tone made it sound a little maniacal.

"That's why dogs are so nice to have around," Anna said. "They are incurable optimists."

"It looks like you have weathered the storm well. I'm going to leave the dragons here and work my way to Skyview," Nicholas said. "Jacob and Jesse can stay here as well. Kaltog, will you come with me?" he asked.

"Yes, I'll go," Kaltog said, picking up his predator battle axe.

Jesse started to protest. "I'm going with you," she said.

"No Jesse. Stay here," Nicholas said using his authoritative tone, which immediately rankled her.

"I can fight, too. I'm going with you," she said again.

"I'm asking you to stay here with Kali and Anna. Please, Jesse. I don't want you on the battlefield. It isn't necessary. I'm only going to connect with dad. We're almost through with this," Nicholas said.

Her pride was chafed with that comment. She wanted to go with him. She wanted to fight. The argument was on her lips, but when she saw the look in Nicholas's eyes, she shut her mouth. It was obvious he was tired and stretched emotionally thin. He wanted to know she was safe and she guessed she could understand that. As he wished, she would stay here at Anna's. She could fight here too after all and Nick wouldn't have to worry about her. Instead of arguing with him, she wrapped her arms around his neck, reached up and brushed her lips against his before she murmured, "Okay. I love you, Nick. Please be careful."

His strong arms wrapped gently around her waist and he whispered, "I love you more than anything, Jess." He brought his face to hers and let his lips explore hers thoroughly.

When they parted, Jacob made his case known. "Let me go with you, Nicholas. I can fight. Just give me a sword. Let me prove myself," he said. *I wish I had a gun but I guess a sword will have to do,* he thought.

Jesse shook her head no, but Nicholas took a moment to consider it. "If you can use a sword, Jacob, I can use you. You've earned a chance to fight. Kali, what do you have that this boy can put on?"

"I've got plenty," she said. "Come on Jacob, I'll get you set up with armor. I have the perfect sword for you. It's been hanging on the wall in the kennel for some time collecting dust. Such a waste. The weapon was crafted by the best sword maker in Skyview many years ago. I think you can handle it."

"Wicked," Jacob said and went with her.

After he had left, Jesse confronted Nick. "Really, Nick. You're letting him go and not me! Haven't I earned the chance to fight too?"

"Jesse, listen," he began.

"No. You listen, Nicholas Wingmaster," Jesse fumed. "I will not be treated like a delicate piece of china to be put on the shelf and never used because it's too fragile. I am very capable of fighting. Do not expect me to give up my freedom to be who I am. I will fight for what I believe in when and where I want to. I love you, Nick, but don't try to control me or oppress me or suppress me."

"I did not mean to insult you or demean you in any way, Jesse. I just want to keep you safe. You can understand that can't you?" Nick said.

"No," Jesse said. "It is not up to you to keep me 'safe'. I can take care of myself."

"Jesse," he began.

Jacob and Kali returned just then. He was armed and ready and unaware of the dissention in the air.

"I'm ready," Jacob said. "Nicholas?"

"Yeah. I'm ready. Let's go. I'm sorry Jesse. I really didn't mean to offend you," he said as he gazed at her with tired eyes.

"I'm sorry too Nick. Maybe I over reacted," she said, although she was still upset and the apology was less than sincere. "Be careful," she said, meaning it.

Jesse watched with her heart in her throat as Jacob, Nicholas and Kaltog fought their way to the path that led to Skyview. They worked well together, like they had been a fighting team for years. Jacob showed a natural skill with a sword in his hand. Soon they were gone from view.

# Chapter 24
## CORNERED

The eagles of Colordale, numbering over one hundred descended on Saberville with their lethal talons extended. They attacked quickly and effectively with a speed that the bugs could not counter. Below the warriors who fought on horseback raised their swords in solute and began fighting with renewed gusto.

Gold Stone found Terese in the flock and nudged her mentally to climb on her back. As Terese transformed in a human, she asked, *"What is it, Gold Stone?"*

*"Grace is missing,"* her dragon said.

*"Zeth, where is he?"* Terese asked.

*"I don't know. He is missing as well,"* Gold Stone said.

*"Their last known position, do you know?"* Terese asked.

*"I will take you,"* she said and headed north over the woods.

They quickly came to a clearing where Grace was last heard from by Gold Stone. Circling, they found nothing immediately. *"Let us split up. Cover more ground, we can,"* Terese said before she changed back into an eagle.

It wasn't long before she spotted the shimmer of green down below. *"I have found Grace,"* she told Gold Stone. She landed next to the still dragon and transformed immediately back to human. Her belly expanded with every breath. She was out cold, but still alive. "Grace," Terese called quietly.

Gold Stone landed beside her sister and nudged her motionless body with her nose. *"What is wrong with her?"* she asked.

*"I do not know . . . "* Terese gasped as she walked around to the front of her nose. Grace was bleeding from her nostrils and she appeared to have been beaten savagely around her head. *"Zeth we have got to find,"* she said in a panic.

They both took to the air once again and not too far away Terese spied something down below. She was on the ground in no time and transformed instantly. She quickly removed the black cloak and knelt beside Zeth, touching his tattered face gently with her fingers. He still breathed, but it was by no means strong or steady. His body was broken in many places and he lay in an unnatural position with one leg pinned under the other. Both hands covered his face. "No," Terese cried. "Zeth. Zeth, it's Terese. I will get help. All right you will be." She wiped her face with her sleeve as her tears continued to stream. "Oh Zeth. All right you must be," she cried.

*"Gold Stone, tell Tempest I need Jesse here now,"* she said. "Hang in there, Zeth. On the way is help. Hang in there my love."

# Flight For Life

"Jesse, Terese needs us in the woods north of Castle Xandia. Zeth is badly injured. Grace is also in serious condition. We must go now," Tempest said as she swooped down, blowing dust into the air and landing directly in front of her.

"Felcore," Jesse called and he was immediately there. "Let's go. Kali, Anna, we have to go north. Zeth and Grace are hurt." She mounted Tempest quickly and they left without further word.

She flew directly over Skyview and could see the battle taking place below. "Where is Gabriel? Is she still sleeping?"

"No, Mistress Gabriel and Jim are on their way to Anna's cabin. We just missed them," Tempest said. "Hang on, Jesse. I'm going to fly faster than I ever have before. The situation is dire."

Jesse closed her eyes and buried her face in Felcore's fur as they sped through the air. The flight usually took hours. Zeth might not survive if they didn't get there soon.

"Tempest, can I enhance your amazing abilities with freecurrent energy?" Jesse asked.

"You are going to make me go faster?" Tempest asked in response.

"If this works, yes," Jesse said.

"Yes. Yes. Yes. I want to go faster," the dragon said excitedly.

"Okay." Jesse gathered the freecurrent and channeled it into Tempest. Green and blue electricity sizzled around them as the freecurrent was released. They streaked across the sky like a fighter jet. Jesse dug her fingers into Felcore and Tempest and prayed she wouldn't fall off.

When they arrived at the site where Zeth lay, Tempest landed next to him and Terese ran to Jesse. "Help him. Please help him, Jesse," she begged. She grabbed her hand and pulled her over to Zeth.

Jesse ran her fingers over his tattered form. He had so many injuries. How could someone do this to another person? "Zeth, I am going to use freecurrent to heal your injuries," she told him gently. She began to collect freecurrent energy from her surroundings, focusing it for use in the healing. Placing her hands on Zeth's torso, she concentrated on letting the healing transpire. As always, her gold lightning bolt medallion sizzled on her chest. Jesse knew through their connection that it was Candaz who had done this. He had nearly killed his own son. In the course of the healing, she reached down and straightened out his leg. She felt the pain run through her body as it left Zeth's. She endured it, letting it run its course through her and then dissipate into the ground. "Zeth?" she asked quietly.

"Terese," he whispered.

"She's right here," Jesse said.

Terese touched his face, "Zeth, here I am. Who did this to you?"

He managed to sit up. "My father. He did this. Where did they go?"

"They?" Jesse asked.

"He has a small militia with him. You didn't see them?" Zeth asked.

"No," Jesse replied.

She walked over to where the cloak lay discarded nearby. Jesse picked it up and inspected it slowly, checking the pockets one by one. Out of one of the pockets she removed a small package wrapped in silk cloth. "Look at this," she said and she threw the cloak aside and began to unwrap the unusual bundle. Terese and Zeth joined her and watched with interest. As she unfolded the last corner, she gasped. "Oh my God! It's a hand!" Jesse said as she examined the gruesome artifact with morbid interest. There was a gold ring upon one of the mummified fingers that sparkled when the light hit it. "What is this, Zeth?" she asked as she wrapped the hand back up.

"I don't know. This is the first time I've seen it," he said. "I can't imagine why he would have such a thing."

"Creepy," Jesse said.

"Maybe we should bury it," Terese commented quietly.

"First we need to get to Grace," Zeth said suddenly. "She is hurt. We need to find her quickly."

"I know where she is. Far it isn't. Is she talking to you, Zeth?" Terese asked.

"She's not making a lot of sense. I just know she's hurt. Can you heal her, Jesse?" he asked.

"I don't know. Let's get there and find out," she said. Without knowing what else to do with the strange hand, Jesse returned it to the pocket of the cloak which they left where it lay on the ground. There it would remain.

They traveled on dragon back the short distance to where Grace lay unconscious. Zeth leaped off from Gold Stone's back and ran to the dragon. "Oh, no. Oh, why, why, why? Poor baby. Why would they hurt you?"

Felcore ran around the dragon in pure agitation until Jesse called him to her side. "Let's see what we can do," she said as she placed her hands on the big green dragon's nose. Felcore pushed up against her side. Zeth placed his hand over hers and gave her a meaningful look. "Okay, we do it together," she said.

The freecurrent energy collected to them like metal to a magnet. Jesse used Felcore and Zeth to help facilitate the energy transfer from herself to Grace and then back again. The healing was a reflex and she let it happen with the medallion focusing the energy to its best efficiency. The dragon's pain was profound and it burned through her bones excruciatingly slow before ebbing and then leaving all together.

Grace lifted her head and crooned. Her injuries were gone. *"How do you feel?"* Jesse asked.

*"I am whole again. Thank you, Jesse,"* she said and crooned again.

She sat back and allowed herself to feel the overwhelming anger that she had been keeping at bay. The cruelty displayed here was extreme. In the past, her encounters with Candaz were wrought with hesitation on her part. But, he had killed Stephan and Shareen. He had almost succeeded in killing Zeth and Grace. He had tried to kill them all. With the recent events, she knew she would not hesitate again.

Her thoughts were interrupted by the steady hum of wings. From overhead descended six wisps, all of them buzzing around the area like curious humming birds. Rew landed on Tempest's nose and began taunting her. He refused to believe that she had just crossed Risen in less than a turn. *"Tell him Jesse,"* Tempest said.

"I am afraid it is true, Rew. She was faster than lightning," Jesse said.

"We have a serious situation," Lew said, interrupting them.

"It is very serious," Wes agreed.

"The Tromeck are serious warriors," Lodi said.

"They are serious trouble," Dolli contributed.

"They made a serious mistake coming through the gate," Tali said.

"Seriously?" Jesse couldn't resist.

"They were heading for Castle Xandia," Zeth said.

"To Xandia then," Tali said and she smiled at Jesse.

"Tali, you had your baby!" Jesse said.

"Yes, a boy. We named him Tes, after Terese," Tali said, smiling at Terese who had her arms wrapped around Zeth's waist.

"Honored I am," Terese said.

"The honor is all mine," Tali said. "You healed the tree. You are a legend in Elysia."

She smiled shyly and buried her face in Zeth's shoulder. "Wow," she said.

"We have work to do," Rew said. "Let's get going before the Tromeck do any more damage."

Light rain began as they mounted dragons and flew south. Night was just upon them and the lightning far out over the ocean was an ominous sign of a storm to come. Felcore growled low in his throat as they approached Castle Xandia. The lights burned bright in the windows in a welcoming manner. But, signs that the Tromeck were there were evident. Outside in the courtyard large lizard creatures milled about. Every now and then a dark shadow passed in front of a window. They were searching the castle.

Jesse's first thought was of Kate, Lauren, and Jules and their children. She wondered what had happened to them. Had they been captured or killed? Did they find a way to escape?

They landed the dragons close to where Trevis and his men were busy fighting the bugs. With the eagles' help they were driving them back away from the castle. How the Tromeck had snuck through their line of defense, Jesse did not know.

Jessabelle swooped in and joined them. She transformed into her human form and was greeted excitedly by Rew and Jesse.

Trevis paused to greet them as well. "The kendrites have made all the difference," he said. "We were almost overcome when they arrived and turned the tide of the battle."

"We have a far greater problem than the bugs," Rew told him. "The castle has been taken by a group called the Tromeck. Candaz is with them."

"My family is in the castle," Trevis said. "We've got to get in there."

"I agree," said Rew.

"To save your family, we will do what we can, Trevis. Though, don't think that they are without resources. Very clever are your sisters and your wife," Jessabelle said as she gave her nephew a brief hug and shot a meaningful look at a certain warrior nearby.

"Here's the plan," Lew said. "We'll leave the kendrites to fight the bugs. Trevis, you take your men and take care of the lizards in the courtyard. Jesse, Terese and Zeth, take the dragons to the top of the castle and go in through the roof trap door. Your job is to find Candaz. We will take care of the Tromeck. The dragons can help out with the bugs and the lizards."

"The wisps are going to fight the Tromeck? I thought they were mighty warriors," Jesse said.

"They are, but, we have our ways," Tali said. "They have violated the gate. It is our job to stop them."

"Why didn't you stop them before they came here? My family is in danger because you let them through the gate. Stephan is dead because of you," Trevis said angrily.

"Trevis! The wisps you cannot blame for your brother's death. His own fate he made," Jessabelle reprimanded him.

Rew defended the wisps. "We couldn't stop them," Rew said. "We didn't know where Candaz went when he left through the gate. We had to wait until he returned to act and we had to get this back." Rew pulled out a large book that he carried in a leather pouch. It was the instruction manual to the gate.

"How did you get it from him?" Jesse asked.

"I stole it from him while he was . . .well, let me just say he was otherwise occupied with personal necessities," he said. The devilish grin on Rew's face was charming. Jesse smiled back and gave him a high five.

Trevis sighed and wiped the sweat from his eyes. He had waited long enough. "Let's get to it, then," he declared. He and his men mounted their horses and rode at a gallop toward Castle Xandia.

The rest of them took immediately to flight.

# Down Under

When Stash saw that the castle had been compromised, he turned around and led the way back to a hilly area about two miles away where he knew there was an entrance to the underground cata-combs. Tallith and Shorty were with him along with Roland and Jared. They had lost one man to the bugs and the other six he sent to rendezvous with Trevis.

The rain was starting to sprinkle down on them as they crossed the threshold of the hidden entrance. Cool air touched their faces and the wet scent of mustiness permeated the stale atmosphere. Tallith led the way down into the darkness of the catacombs. The tunnels were old, older than Castle Xandia. "I hate this," he said. He preferred to be above ground, being much more at home in the outdoors.

"Hate is an over-used word," Roland said. "Probably what you meant to say is 'I don't like this' or 'This makes me uncomfort-able'." 'Hate' is a very strong emotion. It is completely out of place in this situation. I used to hate catfish, but now I don't anymore." He started whistling and twirling his staff, which glowed brightly with the luminescence of the creatures that embraced it.

Tallith ignored Roland's rambling. It was becoming very famil-iar to him and although at times he wished the man would shut his mouth, well he *always* wished the man would shut his mouth; he was usually able to disregard it. Roland had proven himself to be a very powerful wizard and a great asset. With his staff the old man had slaughtered multitudes of bugs as they marched back to Saberville. Tallith wasn't sure of the man's sanity, but he did not question his skill or his loyalty.

They were able to traverse through the catacombs by the light given off by Roland's staff. Jared walked directly behind the old man. He was fascinated by the markings on the tombs that lined the way. There were shields of various styles and descriptions. Some of the tombs were marked only with a letter or a symbol. It was creepy but not spooky and Jared was enthralled. Stash had to nudge him every once in a while to keep him moving.

Roland started singing a happy little tune as they went along. The men exchanged glances and then Shorty tapped him on the shoulder and said, "Shhh."

"Oh, okay. I'll be quiet then. No more singing. Gotcha. How about humming? Is humming okay?" Roland asked before he started humming.

"Hush," Tallith said.

"Hush? All the way hush or just hush, no humming hush?" Roland asked.

Tallith stepped in front of him quickly and put his finger to his lips. Suddenly he whipped off his cloak and threw it to Roland. "Cover that up," he whispered, indicating the staff.

They all stood perfectly still and held their breath.

Footsteps could be heard coming toward them through the tunnel. "Do you know where you are going?" a woman's voice asked anxiously from that direction.

Another woman's voice answered back, "Yes, this way." A lantern light could be seen up ahead.

Stash said, "It's Lauren." Louder he said "Lauren, it's Stash."

"Jules, it's Stash," Lauren said as they approached each other in the tunnel.

Lauren gave all three of her dad's men a big hug. "They've taken the castle. We escaped through the chapel."

Jules also greeted the men with hugs. There were three staff members with them, two women and one man. They also welcomed Serek's men warmly. The children ventured out from behind their mothers, taking particular interest in Roland and his staff. There were four boys and two girls ranging in age from four to nine. The oldest boy resembled his father Trevis and his grand-father, Serek.

Roland twirled his staff for the children and talked to them about the tiny creatures that had made the staff their home. Jared added to the commentary, clarifying the story to make it more un-derstandable to the young audience. Although the children were relatively shy about meeting Jared, they soon warmed up to him and eventually began chatting eagerly to him. They were both scared and excited and once they began talking, they didn't want to stop. Their mothers quieted them when they started getting too animated.

Stash gathered information from the escapees about their invaders. The Tromeck, it seemed, were mostly interested in sat-isfying their fleshly needs. The bar and the kitchen were being ravaged by the group of warriors. There were fourteen of them plus Candaz.

Shorty said to Stash, "If we're lucky the scum had too much to drink. That will make our job easier."

"Yeah. Hopefully they will be fat and happy and drunk," Stash agreed.

Roland took the lead again with Tallith by his side, guiding him through the catacombs. The tunnels continued with crypts lining them, ending with the oldest. The Landtamer crypt would soon get a new addition. The thought was hard to stomach for Stephan's friends. A staircase went up, widening as it went. A beautiful mosaic done in tiles decorated the stairs. It showed a nat-ural scene of a sunset over the ocean breakers. Puffy clouds were colored orange, pink and purple from the setting sun.

Stash asked for complete silence by putting his hand up before opening the door to the chapel.

# Chapter 25

## A STORM TO REMEMBER

When the signal came to pull back into the tunnels, Nicholas pushed on Jacob saying, "Go on, Jacob. You've got to take cover before she plays the harp."

"I'm not leaving you," Jacob said as he pushed his hand against the wound in Nick's side. It was bleeding badly. He pressed harder and turned to look for help. He spied Kaltog across the battle field and called to him.

Kaltog made his way over to them, hacking bugs with his battle axe as he came. "What happened?" he asked as he knelt beside them.

"One of the bugs pierced his side with its fore claw. It just happened, but it looks bad. I can't stop the bleeding," Jacob told him.

"You've got to retreat with the bandergs," Nicholas insisted. "When Gabriel starts playing the harp, those things are going to go nuts."

"Let's get him up," Kaltog started to lift Nicholas, but the prince groaned horribly and blood gushed from his wound. "Okay, maybe not," he said lying Nick back down.

"I'll get Theo through the dragons." He paused a moment while he communicated with Grand Oro. "B.F. agreed to pick up Theo and Nick despite the dragon bane. They will be here in a minute. You'll be okay, Nicholas." He tore some strips of cloth from his clothing and used them to bind the wound tightly.

B.F. landed next to them and Theo dismounted the dragon quickly and came to his son's side. "How are you?" he asked.

"I'm not dead yet," Nicholas told him.

"Let's get you out of here," Theo said. "Help me get him onto B.F. I'll take him back to Castle Gentlebreeze. Be careful," he said as they lifted him up. Once they were settled in place on the dragon's back, Theo shouted down to Kaltog and Jacob, "Get to safety. Gabriel is about to start playing."

"*Let's go B.F. Let's get Nicky home,*" Theo said.

"*Home, where there is no dragon bane,*" B.F. said with a snarl.

As B.F. lifted into the air with Theo holding Nicholas in his arms, Gabriel arrived on Skymaster. Jim was there along with them in his eagle form keeping watch. He trilled at them in greeting. They circled the area, giving those down below the chance to make their retreat and get to the safety in the tunnels of Skyview. When Skymaster gave the "all clear" Gabriel put her fingers to the harp for the fifth time and played. The reaction of the bugs was nearly instant and they turned against each other in a manic feeding frenzy until only one remained. Skymaster finished the job engulfing the sole survivor with dragon fire. It was all over in minutes.

"*On to Castle Xandia,*" Gabriel said, nodding to Jim.

"*To Castle Xandia!*" Skymaster repeated as they turned and flew northwest.

# Home Bound To Heartache

From the ruined gate, Serek watched the bugs devour each other with a sense of satisfaction. A fine mist had been falling all evening and the ground was starting to get slick. He wrapped his arm around Kristina's waist and said, "We must go home now, Kris. Home to Stephan."

"Yes, we must face the unimaginable. I dread going home. But, we are not done with this yet," she said as she pulled away from his arms and made herself busy tending to her horse while she dried her eyes.

"Breezerunner has told me that the situation at Castle Xandia is serious. Candaz and his followers are ransacking our home. Kate, Lauren, Jules and the children are unaccounted for. Jesse, Zeth, Terese and the wisps are planning to try and take the castle back by themselves. Trevis and his men are taking on the monsters the Tromeck arrived on while Jessabelle and the kendrites' are going to hold off the bugs. We aren't out of this mess yet," Serek said.

"Let's go now, Serek. I will not lose any more children to that man's ambition," Kristina let her maternal instinct drive her forward despite her exhaustion. She jumped on her horse and guided the other mount to her husband.

He looked up at her, but said nothing. The rain was starting to come down harder. Mounting his own horse, they both headed north where they would rendezvous with Breezerunner and fly home.

# Higher Ground

Jesse and Felcore dismounted Tempest after she landed on the roof of Castle Xandia with a gentle touch. Grace and Gold Stone arrived with Zeth and Terese and then quickly left again. The dragons' part of the plan was swiftly finished, leaving them to help in the assault against the lizards.

The wisps joined the humans and they padded across the wet roof until they reached the trap door that led to attic and then down to the upper level rooms. Stealthily they disappeared inside.

Rew was the most familiar with the castle so he became the leader by default. He slid the door to the hallway open a little at a time and then motioned for them to follow him through. They tip-toed down the hall until Rew held up his hand and stopped them. He peeked into one of the rooms and waited before proceeding past it.

When they got to the staircase he paused again and waited, watched and listened.

There was much noise with men being raucous and loud, furniture and glass were being thrown and broken with complete disregard. Fighting seemed to be a natural state for the Tromeck and they did so constantly amongst themselves.

Rew told them with hand language to stay and he snuck down the stairs. He returned a moment later and held up eight fingers. To Lodi, Tali and Lew he pointed and motioned for them to come with him. Together, the four wisps again descended the stairs.

## Lower Ground

Sconces glowed on the walls illuminating the chapel with a soft glow. Stash stopped by the slab of marble where Stephan lay in repose and gazed upon his friend's passive face with anguish on his own. Tallith and Shorty paid their respects as well as they passed by their deceased prince. Tallith bowed, passed his hands hastily over his eyes, abruptly rose and drew his sword. "I will avenge your death, my friend," he said.

Shorty whispered to Jared, "Take everyone back to the cata-combs and wait for us there. Protect them with your life if it comes to that. Don't come out until somebody comes for you." He handed Jared his dagger and joined Tallith and Stash by the door.

Roland joined them as well, his bare feet padding quietly on the stone floor as he walked. The staff glowed brightly in the dim firelight. Every now and then one of the tiny live creatures that clung to the staff would slowly reposition itself. The movement was unsettling, but Roland was unaffected, and in fact, seemed charmed by it.

They opened the door and walked down a long hallway that was lined with closed doors and ended with another closed door. Beyond it was a staircase that led up. Quietly, with the utmost cau-tion, Stash led them up the stairs to yet another door. He stopped and put his ear up to the wood before opening it. Again they tra-versed an empty room with a door at the other end.

This time, Stash knew there was someone on the other side. The noise was loud and destructive in nature. He inched the door open and peered out. Slowly he closed it and turned to his com-panions. "Ready?" he whispered. "There are six of them in the next room eating and drinking. Ready, Roland?"

Roland nodded. He wore a serious expression and held his staff in front of him.

Stash threw open the door and the four of them confronted the Tromeck who were surprised, but quick to act. The table was dumped over as the Tromeck jumped up from their seats, pulling their swords at the same time.

Tallith engaged the first to react and they struck each other's steel with clanging intensity. At first Tallith was overwhelmed with the force of the attack, but he quickly adjusted and gave as well as he got.

Roland's staff began to glow brighter than ever. With a quick flick of his wrist he shot a barrage of energy at the nearest Tromeck, whose heart immediately stopped. The large warrior fell to the floor with a heavy thud.

## A Tail To Tell

Felcore left Jesse's side and started running down the hall. All that she could do was follow so she did so quickly and quietly.

Tempest chose that precise moment to give Jesse some news, *"Nicholas is injured, Jesse. Theo has taken him back to Castle Gentlebreeze. It looks serious. I'm sorry."*

She stopped and backed up against the wall, feeling like she had just been punched in the gut. "Nick."

*"If we leave now we might get there in time,"* Tempest said.

*In time?* Jesse was torn. She hesitated with the wall holding her up.

Agape spoke to her, *"Nicholas says to finish what you're doing here, that he'll be all right. He instructed me to tell you that he loves you. My opinion is that you should come as soon as possible and take care of my Nicholas."*

"Tell Nick I love him and that I'll be there as soon as I can," Jesse told Agape.

"Tempest, where are you?" she asked.

*"Eating lizards. Do you want to go?"* Tempest asked.

"Soon sweetie. Soon," Jesse replied.

Felcore was standing in the hallway waiting for her. His head was held high as he sniffed the air. When she caught his eye, he turned and continued quickly into the next room. She followed.

With her heart beating in her throat, she entered the room after Felcore. It was expansive in size and furnished with large ornamental furniture, a bed, a desk, a wardrobe and a throne. The throne was back in the corner and had clothes slung casually over it. Standing by the window, looking out over the courtyard was Candaz.

Zeth and Terese followed Jesse, but stopped just short of the door, out of sight.

Candaz didn't turn to look at her, but continued gazing out the window. "Well, little girl, we meet again," he said. His tall slim figure was clothed all in black. When he finally did turn toward her, she saw that there was red silk detailing the lapels of his jacket. The look suited him. He smiled. His eyes however threw daggers of hate.

She did not hesitate, but took a running start and launched a kick at him, hitting his body squarely in the torso. The small crystal bottle he held went flying from his hand and smashed into the window, shattering into tiny pieces on impact. He doubled over but quickly recovered. There wasn't enough time for him to gather the freecurrent before Jesse swung around with another kick to the chin and a hard punch to the back of his head.

Undeterred, lightning quick Candaz reached for his sword and held it before him. As he swung at Jesse, she moved smoothly back and he only managed to nick her skin, drawing blood from a cut on her rib cage. She backed away slightly and said, "You killed Stephan."

He held his sword ready and replied, "He defied me and he deserved to die."

Feeding off from her grief and anger, Jesse attacked again. Her next kick landed sharply on the hand that held the sword and it fell from Candaz's grasp and clattered to the floor. Driving the palm of her hand into his nose she immediately swung with her other hand to land a punch. He countered with a heavy backhand across her face, taking her down to the floor. A black boot kicked her in the side of the head and she rolled away from him with a groan.

"You cannot defeat me, little girl. I am powerful beyond your wildest dreams. My dynasty is just beginning. Your future ends today," he said. Blue and green light started glowing from his hands as he began gathering freecurrent to him.

Stepping in front of Jesse, Felcore crouched like a tiger with a growl coming from his throat. His lips were pulled back in a snarl showing his sharp and deadly teeth. Fur on the back of his neck stood up, making him look bigger and more ferocious than ever before.

"Play dead," Candaz said. He flung his fingers, now ablaze with freecurrent at Felcore. The charge hit him directly between the eyes and he collapsed instantly lifeless on the floor.

"No!" Jesse cried as she ran forward and knelt beside him.

"Felcore, wake up," she said.

Candaz laughed. "Felcore, wake up," he mocked and started pacing with his hands clasped at his sides. Jesse laid her head on Felcore's chest and tried to revive him with freecurrent.

Terese and Zeth entered. Before Zeth could stop her, Terese ran at Candaz and vaulted. In midair she transformed into an eagle and targeted Candaz's face with her lethal talons. Her large wings swept the air with wind. The predator's daggers sank into Candaz's eyes, ripping flesh from his face and rendering the sorcerer instantly blind. He screamed in pain. Despite that he managed to grab on to one of her wings and fling her against the window. The glass cracked with a popping sound and Terese fell to the floor with the window giving way and smashing down on top of her. She became human again and lay there gasping for breath.

"Terese!" Jesse cried at the same time as Zeth. He lunged for his father's sword and came up with it in his hand. Candaz immediately hit him with a charge of freecurrent energy sending him reeling back.

But Zeth had been ready for the assault. He recovered quickly and sent the energy hurling back at his father. It sizzled around Candaz and he screamed again.

"You will all pay for this. You are all going to die," Candaz said. Again he began collecting freecurrent energy between his hands. Although his face was bleeding and mangled, he ignored the injury.

Terese began to recuperate and sat up. Her nose was bleeding but otherwise she seemed unharmed. Zeth approached Candaz at the same time. "You tried to kill me," he said.

"Apparently I failed. I won't fail again," Candaz spat back. He again launched the energy at Zeth who returned it with even more force. The freecurrent hit Candaz in the chest and he went down, but as he gasped for breath he hurtled another volley of freecurrent at Zeth and knocked him to the floor.

"I knew you were corrupt, but to kill your own son?" Zeth said with a groan. He once again picked up the sword and climbed back to his feet.

"You betrayed me. You deserve to die," Candaz proclaimed with bravado, but he was clutching his chest and trying to inhale. He was bleeding profusely and gore dripped down his face and dropped off his chin in tiny droplets.

"Jesse healed me. I am free from all of the pain you inflicted on me. I've even fallen in love," Zeth told him as he hesitated, holding the sword in front of him.

"Love will just result in pain. I was in love once and it ended with her dying and destroying me in the process. Love just causes pain," Candaz said as he spat blood onto the floor. He tried to get up but his legs couldn't support him and he remained slumped where he was. "I didn't kill you, Molly!" he screamed. "No. No. No," he cried. His breathing was getting heavier and more labored.

"Look at all of the pain you have caused. People all over Risen have been killed in the past week because of you. Families have lost their loved ones. Lives have been destroyed. You killed Stephan. There is no excuse for that. How could you be so cruel?" Zeth asked passionately.

"Pain precipitates pain. I was made what I am and I have taken what I could take. Being born does not entitle anyone to happiness. It doesn't entitle anyone to anything except anguish and heartache," Candaz said as he spat blood again. He seemed to be speaking to someone else, someone they couldn't see as he shouted, "No! It's not possible!"

Zeth continued to approach him slowly with the sword raised.

"That's a pathetic excuse for doing what you have done. Sure, it isn't easy. But, there are things worth living for, like friends and family and love. Even if sometimes those things cause sorrow and grief, they are worth the effort. You have let your pain corrupt you," Zeth said.

"You have no idea what I have lived through. Who are you to judge me? You have no right to accuse me!" Candaz said.

"It seems you have judged yourself, father," Zeth said.

"Perhaps. But, there is no coming back from where I have gone. There is no redemption for me. Molly is dead. I killed her," he said.

There was silence in the room. Felcore had started breathing again and stood up and walked over to Candaz. He pushed against the sorcerer's hand with his nose.

"Don't touch me," he said, shoving the dog away.

"Felcore, come!" Jesse ordered.

"Rrowf!" the dog barked and once again pushed against Candaz's hand.

"Get away from me," Candaz said.

Jesse swallowed the bitterness in her throat and said, "He wants to help you." Her appetite for vengeance was still ravenous. Although she knew what Felcore was up to, she did not want to heal Candaz. She wanted to kill him.

"Jesse can heal you the way she healed me," Zeth said suddenly. "You don't have to live in corruption."

*What!?* Jesse wanted to smack him. *What are you thinking?* "Shut up, Zeth," she said. If she could just find a sliver of compassion for Candaz, she might be willing to try, but she couldn't even come up with that much. He had killed Stephan.

Felcore again pushed against Candaz's hand and instead of pulling away this time he touched the top of the dog's head. "He's soft," he said quietly with a tremor in his voice. His face suddenly changed as he stroked Felcore's fur. He groaned deeply and painfully. "I was so wrong. I am so sorry. Can you help me? Will you help me?" he cried unexpectedly. "Please," he begged.

Inside Jesse groaned. There it was. She felt a small sliver of compassion. *No frickin way!* She couldn't believe the words that came out of her mouth next, "You want to be healed?" Her insides were in turmoil. He deserved to die. *But hadn't he said the same about Stephan and Zeth? Did she have the right to implement that death sentence?*

"How?" he asked as he remained harmless on the floor with Felcore by his side.

"*No. No. No,*" a voice that was her own screamed inside her head. "*Oh God!*"

"Zeth?" Jesse held out her hand to him. He took it and they cautiously approached Candaz. She was shaking visibly as she held onto Zeth and reached out to take Candaz's hand. It was warm and soft to the touch. For some reason it made her think of the small mummified hand wrapped in silk that they had found in Candaz's cloak. She shivered.

Continuing in spite of her revulsion, she closed her eyes and let the freecurrent energy gather to her, feeling the medallion grow increasingly warm until it was burning hot. It was like plunging into a pit of terror. The depth of Candaz's corruption was beyond what she expected. She began the healing process, drawing off the corruption like drawing infection off from a wound. Zeth continued to hold her hand and she could feel his energy contributing to the effort as she proceeded deeper into Candaz's being. The hate was overwhelming and the pain that it masked was insignificant by comparison. Bitterness, hatred, and a lust for power permeated the very core of his nature. As she started expelling the horror from Candaz she began to drown in the depths of his immorality. It was crushing her and she began to struggle to keep from being overcome. She was drowning in corruption.

Jesse tried to release his hand, but he had her in an iron grip and would not let go. Horrible, cruel laughter rang in her ears. Panic was added to the terror that was enveloping her and she knew at that moment she was going to die.

Freecurrent energy was arching all around them, building in intensity as they were fixed in place.

Candaz continued to laugh, loud and malicious, dreadful in its meaning. Jesse struggled against him, pulling on her hand, pushing with the other, trying to get him to release her from his insanity.

The freecurrent energy vibrated the atmosphere around them. All of the windows in the room shattered and the glass tinkled musically as it cascaded down. She could feel that the medallion on her chest was about to explode from the pressure as it continued to grow ever hotter. She heard herself scream as Felcore jumped up on Candaz and sunk his teeth into the sorcerer's arm, causing him to finally let go of Jesse's hand. Zeth shoved her to the floor and rolled on top of her as an explosion ripped through the air around them.

It wasn't her medallion that had detonated; she could still feel it between her chest and Zeth's as it lost the freecurrent energy and was instantly cool. Zeth rolled off from her and groaned.

She sat up and knew immediately what had happened. The gold tag on Felcore's collar had exploded, obliterating both Candaz and her dog. There was nothing left of either of them. Candaz was dead. Her best friend was dead too.

Thunder rolled like a musician rolling his sticks over the surface of a drum. Lightning flashed illuminating Jesse's horrified face.

From far off she heard a dragon wail in mourning. *Tempest.*

"Zeth?" she moaned.

"I'm okay. Is he dead?" Zeth asked as he looked around. A dark circle on his chest was smoking slightly where Jesse's medallion had branded his skin. She had a matching brand on her own chest.

"Yes. He is dead. He is finally dead. You're sure you're okay?" she asked again as she started to get up.

"I will be. Felcore saved our lives," he said.

"He did," she said, choking back her tears. *Her boy was gone.*

Terese gave her a gentle hug and whispered, "I am so sorry, Jesse."

"He was my best friend," Jesse said.

Zeth joined them and they all held each other for a moment longer, letting their tears fall.

"I'm afraid I have got to go. Nick is injured and I need to get back to Brightening," Jesse said.

*"Tempest, pick me up on the roof,"* she said, turning to go. The storm outside was raging and she felt like crying, but she needed to go to Nick before it was too late.

## Wisp Justice

Four wisps descended the stairs into the room that served as Serek and Kristina's living room. The once pristine showplace was destroyed. There were food scraps tossed aside on the floor, things like chicken bones and cheese wrappings. From the bar, bottles of wine had been opened and drank and then tossed aside. Nectar, which was a brandy-wine concoction, was discarded, the bottles smashed against walls and furniture. The Tromeck didn't care for the taste. Kristina's white furniture was stained with food, wine, nectar, blood and dirt. It would never be white again.

There were eight Tromeck in the room. All of them were still involved in eating and drinking. They were combative and would fight for pieces that they wanted or for a bottle of something even when there was another one to be had. Both primitive and foul, they lacked any motivation other than selfish gratification. Thunder and lightning rattled through the room, but they paid it no mind.

They didn't see the wisps coming and had no time to react once they did. Wisps fly fast, faster than the fastest hummingbird. The four wisps attacked. Before an eye could blink they had taken swords, tweaked noses, stomped on feet, pulled on ears, poked stomachs, drank wine, pulled hair, drank more wine, plucked mustaches, pinched skin, punched noses, drank more wine and then they stopped and waited. It was only fair to give the Tromeck a chance to react.

The warriors did reach for their swords and found them gone. Angry, they came at the wisps with their bare hands. A couple of them remembered that they had daggers in their belts and brandished their knives. From above, the two remaining wisps, Wes and Dolli, quickly relieved the Tromeck of their knives too before they even knew what was happening.

Rew, Lodi, Lew and Tali started their rounds again, tweaking, poking, prodding and stomping. Oh, and drinking. The Tromeck were getting progressively aggressive in their anger and frustration. When Rew had them worked up into a frenzy, the four wisps returned their swords and removed themselves from the room.

As planned, the Tromeck directed their anger at each other and quickly eight became seven, seven became six and so on until only two remained. The two Tromeck faced each other with their swords coming into lethal play, but they had lost the spontaneity of the moment.

Rew decided they needed another dose of wisp medicine. Dolli and Wes joined the other four and the two Tromeck did not have a chance. They had so many slaps, pokes and pulls at the same time that they were spinning in circles trying to keep up.

The wisps retreated.

Outside the thunder rolled and lightning flashed brightly in the sky. The rain began in earnest, hitting the windows in a tapping rhythm.

At that moment Serek strolled through the door and drew his sword. Although the Tromeck were seasoned, hardened warriors, they were spent and Serek had the advantage. A few strokes and the first one lay dead. He squared off with the second warrior, who had strength, but no finesse. Serek was not only strong, but he was quick on his feet and knew how to make a blade sing and more importantly he had vengeance in his heart. It only took one fatal stroke to finish the invading warrior's life.

When Kristina walked in and saw her living room, the Tromeck were lucky they were dead.

## Wacky Wizard

The staff in Roland's hand was alive with energy and the old wizard danced and spun on his bare feet as he blazed another blast of lethal fire at one more Tromeck. He was having fun. The mighty warrior went down in a pile of uselessness.

Stash and Shorty teamed up and were engaging in sword play with a meaty looking fellow. He was nasty and snorted and spat in their faces. Just when Stash thought they were winning the Tromeck would make an unexpected move and reset the match. Faster than they would have thought possible the Tromeck spun deftly, swirled his sword and brought it within inches of Shorty's throat.

From across the room, Roland swung his staff and fired a laser-like beam from the tip of it, severing the Tromeck's head instantly before he could follow through on the deadly stroke he intended. The wound smoked as the head rolled to the floor and the sword clattered harmlessly beside the grotesque visage. "Did you see that? I did that!" Roland said to no one imparticular. "Smokin'!"

Shorty brought his hand up to his throat and rubbed it where the blade would have gone. "Thanks, Roland," he said.

"Woo! Hoo! Any time. Any time, Tiny," Roland replied.

The final Tromeck was engaged with Tallith, who was a skilled swordsman. They went back and forth with one of them gaining the advantage, just to lose it a moment later to the other. Finally the balance swung. Striking with effectiveness, Tallith inflicted damage to the larger warrior over and over again. As a last push the Tromeck swung his weapon and hit Tallith's blade hard and fast. It went flying out of his hand and the Tromeck aggressively attacked. He was taking the fatal stroke aimed at Tallith's head when Roland brandished his staff, shooting lethal energy from it and stopping him literally dead in his tracks. The massive warrior went down hard, never to rise again. Roland twirled his staff in victory as Tallith pumped him on the shoulder. "Thanks, old man."

"Any time. Can we get something to eat? I'm starving," Roland said.

Tallith looked around at the carnage and felt like he would never be hungry again, but he said, "Sure Roland. You've earned it. Let's check the rest of the house first. There may be more of these guys."

"Oh, yeah. We are ready for them. Aren't we little guys?" he said to his staff.

They entered the living room where Serek and Kristina were surveying the damage. The wisps flew down to them and chatted excitedly. Finally, Rew confirmed that Candaz was dead along with all of the Tromeck. Trevis, Jessabelle and the rest of the warriors soon joined them. Kate, once her identity was revealed, was honored by her brother and her fighting partner, Landon. She had earned their respect.

The lizards had been killed and eaten by the dragons. For some reason, the dragons enjoyed the lizards considerably and ate them until they were all gone, unlike the bugs which they preferred not to even taste as they killed them.

Just then over the noise of the storm they heard the harp in the distance and they knew that Gabriel was taking care of the rest of the bugs.

Trevis and Kate were embraced by their parents. Their mood was bitter-sweet. Stephan remained dead. Although they celebrated their victory over Candaz, they mourned their beloved Stephan. Serek said to his oldest son, "I am so proud of you Trevis. You are a great leader." And to Kate, "I've heard you are a skilled warrior. Nice job."

That earned him a hug from his armor-clad daughter.

"Thanks, Dad," Trevis said over his sister's shoulder. "I appreciate it. Where are Lauren, Jules and the children?" he asked.

"I don't know. Stash?" Serek deferred the question to him.

"They are down in the catacombs, just past the chapel," he said.

"And Stephan?" the words stuck in Kristina's throat, but she managed to get them out.

Stash's eyes found his boots as he answered, "His body is in the chapel."

"Serek, will you come with me?" she asked.

"Yes," he said, taking her hand. "Let's go get the rest of our family and we'll be able to see Stephan as well."

Serek did not let go of Kristina's hand as they made their way to the chapel. He was afraid his heart was going to burst inside his chest from grief. When they arrived where Stephan lay, Kristina let go of Serek's hand and touched her son's face, brushing his hair with her fingertips. "Oh, Stephan, my son. You were not supposed to go before me," she said and began to weep.

Serek put his arm around her waist as he gazed at his dead son. Sorrow gripped his soul with icy fingers and he cried out in anguish, "Stephan!" Tears were streaming down his cheeks when Kristina turned to him and they held each other and sobbed.

They heard a whisper behind them, coming from behind the door to the catacombs, "It's mom and dad." The door opened and their daughter, along with their daughter-in-law and six grandchildren came into the room. Three staff members came in last and quickly and discreetly exited, giving the family their privacy. Jared followed them out; anxious to find Roland to make sure he was safe. There were many hugs and tears shed. They lingered in the chapel with Stephan and were soon joined by Trevis, who embraced his family joyfully. Lauren's husband, Dennis, joined them a few minutes later, sweeping his wife into his arms and then wrapping his arms around his children. Kate came in last and went directly to Stephan to pay her respects. She laid her sword at his side and kissed him on the cheek to honor him.

It did Serek and Kristina good to have their grandchildren there, alive and healthy, and unable to keep their voices quiet or reserved. Their hearts were so heavy with grief, but in spite of that, there was joy to be had in the love that remained. They would never get over missing Stephan, but the grief would eventually fade and love would prevail. The root of their grief was the profound love they had for their son and that love was an awesome thing, something that made them who they were and the core of their family.

# Chapter 26

## EVER AFTER

With freecurrent energy collected from around her; the storm was an amazing source and she tapped into its strength easily; Jesse laid her hands on the sides of Tempest's neck and infused the dragon with the freecurrent causing her to speed like lightning through the air. As fast as they were moving, it wasn't fast enough for Jesse. Nevertheless, she closed her eyes and tried not to let her anxiety get the best of her. The tears that fell for Felcore were washed away by the rain that drenched her thoroughly.

Tempest hummed to her mentally, providing comfort and commiseration, as she too mourned her little dog friend. Upon Felcore's death, Tempest had trumpeting her mournful lament for all to hear. The other dragons joined in the song for the fallen dog, who would forever be known as a hero. His legend would be seared into the wall at the dragon Temple of Neeg on the Island of Zedra, an honor given only to a select few. To Jesse none of that really mattered. Her heart was aching from the loss of her best friend. She missed him so badly.

"*We will be at Castle Gentlebreeze soon, Jesse,*" Tempest said. "*I like flying this fast. Can we do it this way the next time I race Rew?*"

"*I don't know if that would be very fair, sweetie,*" Jesse replied.

"*Is that important?*" Tempest asked innocently.

"*I think it is. Is a victory a victory if you cheat?*" Jesse asked.

"*Yes?*" Tempest said tentatively.

"*No. Think of it this way, Tempest. What if Rew had some type of power that gave him a huge advantage over you? Do you think that would be fair?*" Jesse asked.

"*Maybe. What if we both had the same power that made us both equally fast? That would be fair, wouldn't it?*" the dragon asked.

"*I guess so,*" Jesse said. She was feeling way too tired to have this conversation.

"*Can we do that then?*" Tempest asked excitedly.

"*We'll see, Tempest.*" They were directly over Castle Gentle-breeze. "*Can you set down right by the door, Tempest?*" Jesse asked.

"*Okay Jesse. Are you going to make Nicholas better?*" she asked.

"*I hope so, sweetie,*" Jesse said, suddenly fearing that she might be too late.

"*Are you going to marry him?*" Tempest asked.

"*I don't know. I hope so,*" Jesse said.

"*Do you love him more than you love me?*" Tempest asked childishly.

"*I love you both very much, Tempest. Don't worry. I have enough love to go around. Why don't you go take a good long nap after we land? I'm sure you could use one,*" Jesse suggested.

"*After hunting. I'm hungry,*" Tempest said.

"*Didn't you just eat a herd of lizards?*" Jesse asked.

"*They were an appetizer,*" the dragon said.

*"An appetizer! Okay,"* Jesse said.

They set down right outside the back door. Jesse climbed down and patted Tempest affectionately on the nose and kissed her goodbye. *"Happy hunting, sweetie."*

When Jesse walked through the door, a woman, one of the staff spotted her first. "Oh, my goodness. Look at you. You are all wet. Come with me dear," she said. She led the way up the stairs and into a bedroom where Jesse was asked to wait.

"But, I must see . . ." Jesse protested as the woman walked out the door.

She came back just as Jesse was about to venture out on her own and find her way to Nicholas. Dry towels were in her arms and a set of clothes. "Dry off, honey. Put these on and then I'll take you to Nicholas. Be quick now," she said.

Jesse went into the attached bathroom and quickly dried and dressed in the dress she was given. She took a moment to look at herself in the mirror and thought how strange she looked in a dress, but the pretty blue color did look good with her copper colored eyes, even if they were puffy from crying. Running her fingers through her hair, she thought briefly, *"I've changed. I'll never be the same again."*

"Will you take me to Nicholas now?" she asked the woman who looked at her critically.

"Yes. Come with me," she said.

Down the hall and to the right they entered a large room that was lit dimly with candlelight. There was a fire burning in the fireplace, adding to the warm glow. On a raised platform was a huge four poster bed with a canopy that covered it. Theo sat in a chair next to the bed. He seemed to be asleep, but he rose to his feet when she walked in.

"Jesse, thank the Creator you are here. He is very weak," he said as he greeted her with a fatherly hug.

She smiled tentatively at Theo and then went directly to Nicholas's bed and looked down on his sleeping form. He was so pale. Reaching out with her hand, she brushed a lock of hair off from his forehead. She leaned over and placed a kiss on his cheek. He skin was cool to the touch. "Nick," she whispered.

"Where is the wound?" she asked Theo without looking away from Nick's face.

He walked up behind her and pulled the covers down revealing a seeping wound in his side, just under the rib cage. The bandages were fresh, but already soaked through. His blood loss must have been substantial.

She sat down on the bed beside him and put her hands on the wound. With her heart in her throat, she let the healing flow through her and into Nick. She extruded the pain and any infection, feeling it run through her and then out again. The medallion heated against her skin painfully because of her burn, but she was so thankful for it and for the gift the wisps had given her. Tears streamed down her face as the wound in Nicholas's side began to close and heal. She was soon sobbing and she let her head fall on Nick's chest. His arms came up and enfolded her in them. "Jesse," he breathed.

"Nick, you're okay," she said through her tears.

"The way you are crying, you would think I was dead," he said teasingly.

"Hey son. How are you feeling?" Theo asked, grasping Nick's hand tightly in his own.

"Great. Ready to rumble," Nick said, again jokingly.

"Maybe tomorrow," Theo said.

"Is the war over? What's happened?" he asked.

"It's over. Candaz is dead. Felcore died with him. The rest of the story can wait until tomorrow," Jesse told him.

"Oh, Jesse. I'm so sorry," Nicholas said.

Theo brushed his hand over Jesse's cheek, wiping her tears away. "Rest now. I'll stay here. You two rest," Theo said as he went back to his chair and closed his eyes. Thunder rumbled off in the distance as the storm moved to the east. It was nearly spent and would dissipate completely before reaching the far shore.

Jesse let herself collapse into bed beside Nicholas and they held each other until they fell asleep wrapped in each other's arms.

## After The Storm

Nicholas held Jesse's hand as they walked down the beach on a warm summer night. Philos, frolicked in the waves, running in and out of the surf as they played fetch with a piece of driftwood. Tica had given birth to Philos several years earlier along with his seven brothers and four sisters. Felcore was his sire and Philos resembled him in many ways. Pausing, Jesse reached up and kissed Nick's cheek a little shyly and said, "I have something to tell you."

Seven years had passed since the bugs had invaded Risen. Clean-up had been a messy affair, but with the dragons' help, the bodies of the bugs were piled up and incinerated quickly enough. Funerals were attended and families mourned their dead, but eventually things started getting back to their "new" normal.

Theo and Jessabelle's reunion was a bright spot in an otherwise difficult time. They had a love that transcended everything including tragedy. When Theo saw her for the first time, flying on eagles' wings back to Castle Gentlebreeze, he couldn't contain his elation. He jumped on B.F.'s back and met her midair. She landed in front of him and they were in each other's arms once again. Jessabelle had a hard time adjusting back into castle life, however. More and more she started deferring her responsibilities to her daughter Natina. Theo gave her the freedom she needed even though it meant spending more time apart. She became wilder as she spent more time in her predatory forms and she would disappear for extended periods of time to hunt or to visit her dolphin family in the ocean off the coast of New Chance, but she always came back to her Theo and they never stopped loving each other.

Another joyous occasion was the wedding of Zeth and Terese. They were married under the stars in the courtyard at Castle Xandia a short time after the clean-up had taken place. Kristina and Kate were especially excited to host the wedding which in turn helped them to start the healing process after losing Stephan. Gabriel was also very involved in the planning and execution of the celebration. It had taken her weeks to recover from her ordeal of playing the silver harp. Considering the emotional energy needed to pull it off, she bounced back rather quickly. Gabriel incorporated the help of the wisps who had the courtyard looking like a magical nighttime garden sparkling everywhere with fairy lights. It was a beautiful wedding with Serek officiating. The dragons honored the couple by doing one of their amazing choreographed flights and with dragon fire blazed the initials "Z" and "T" over head in the night sky.

Bill and Jim both had loose ends to tie up back home before they moved to Risen permanently. Jim, with much difficulty, persuaded his daughter and son-in-law to come with him. Jim's son-in-law and Bill were both architects and that would prove to be a huge asset in rebuilding New Chance. Jim and Gabriel had started a romance that developed quickly into a serious relationship. They were married in a small quiet ceremony on the beach at New Chance. They settled at Tower of Ornate and enjoyed their remaining years together, which were long and rewarding. Knowledge and wisdom made them the "go to" couple for advice and they enjoyed their roles as master and matriarch of Risen.

Jacob stayed with Gabriel and finished his education. He also trained with Nicholas, as Nick had promised, to be a warrior. He flew all over Risen on Nugget and became very popular, especially with the women, at both Castle Xandia and Castle Gentlebreeze, not to mention Lakeside and Vinnia. He was known for his good nature and the great stories he told all over the land. He was also a familiar face at Farreach and Skyview. Jacoby and Jacob became unlikely friends, although their relationship was a combative one and they seldom agreed on anything. Eventually he became the top ambassador throughout the nations of Risen.

Kaltog and Kali's story wasn't as happy. They had spent much time together and had fallen in love with each other, but because of their distinct differences marriage was not a possibility. They treasured their friendship, however, and would see one another from time to time. Eventually both of them married different people and had families of their own. Kali and her family lived with Anna and inherited the cabin and the kennel when Anna died many years later. Kaltog became the king at Farreach after his father Rocnor relinquished the throne to retire.

In Skyview, Link grew to a ripe old age and never gave up his kitchen. He and Berry had many grandchildren and great grandchildren and eventually great great grandchildren.

Soon after Zeth and Terese's wedding, Nicholas and Jesse also tied the knot. They were married on a perfect summer day at Castle Gentlebreeze. It was a small affair for a royal wedding with all of their family and friends in attendance, including dragons and dogs. They were married by King Lew and afterward the wisps took them to Elysia for their honeymoon, where they were spoiled and pampered shamelessly. It wasn't long before they both decided to go back to Earth to attend school. It was an interesting time for Nick, who learned more than just academics, being entrenched in American culture for the first time, but Jesse kept him grounded. They visited Risen often. Their dragons wouldn't have had it any other way. Demanding creatures! But, the college experience was beneficial for both of them and they studied subjects that they would find helpful in their future like business and management and Nicholas took a particular interest in engineering.

After they graduated, Nick and Jesse took on the task of reestablishing the city of New Chance. It was an on-going project. Many of their family and friends relocated to New Chance to be with them and to help with the reconstruction. They adopted one of Felcore's sons, a handsome dog they named Philos, meaning "friend". Philos helped to heal the emotional wound Jesse had over losing Felcore. He couldn't take Felcore's place, but he helped fill the hole.

Roland and Jared lived in a little cottage on the beach, which suited them perfectly. Roland was able to fish whenever he wanted and he wanted to often. However, when he was needed he used his skills as a chemist and a wizard to help others and would travel far and wide with his living staff to accomplish this end.

Jared spent most of his free time with Nicholas and Jesse, who educated and trained him. As an adult he became the mayor of New Chance and he was loved and respected by the people who lived there. Zeth and Terese also established a residence on the outskirts of New Chance and played an important role in the economic growth of the region. Serek had put Zeth in charge of establishing the vineyards and the apple orchards to produce fruit for the winery. Things were coming along just fine.

Nicholas turned to Jesse and wrapped his arms around her. He looked down into her beautiful copper brown eyes and leaned in to kiss her mouth. She let him take his time with the kiss and then pulled away and smiled. With excitement, she said, "We're going to have a baby, Nick. You are going to be a father."

After he let the news sink in, Nick kissed his wife again.

# THE END

Made in the USA
Middletown, DE
27 September 2015